White Rose Witches

This Dark Path

by

Georgie St-Claire

Many thanks to my husband and teens again, for their unending support, to my youngest teen who is my absolute biggest cheerleader (you are valued more than you know, baby girl), and to my readers on Threads whose relentless enthusiasm pushed me forward on this.

Chapter 1

Once upon a time she had run away from England wearing a black jersey skirt and a knotted band T-shirt in dark red, arms adorned with bracelets, multiple earrings in each ear, carrying just one suitcase and a red laptop bag. Her dark brown hair had flown wild and free, tumbling in untamed curls down her back, on the verge of frizz. She hadn't been completely oblivious to the stares from men, but her head had been full of old warnings about being exceptional and she focused on keeping her presence small when she moved through the airport. She tried not to heed those warnings anymore.

Gia pulled a face that reflected back at herself in the train window as the English countryside, with its muted greens, autumnal trees, and bare fields of brown, flew past outside. It stared back at her as a separate entity, a hint of a wickedly sensual smile and sparkling eyes before it changed to her six-year-old tear-streaked, rage-filled face. She could still feel that six-year-old inside, always ready to be unleashed. Gia kept her tightly locked away. The reflection in the window changed again, this time to resemble the adult she hid from the world's eyes, the crazy glint in the eyes, the temper she tried to tone down, her ambivalence to consequences and the need to hurt the world. She was full of emotions she had never been allowed to feel.

Gia wondered if she was kidding herself that she had grown in ten years. The forthcoming reunion was the last hurdle, the test of whether she could stand by her new self, turn into the wild thing her grandmother feared, or retreat subconsciously back into being the good granddaughter she had tried to be when in England. Conversations with her grandmother had dwindled over the years. The fault for the lack of phone calls was all hers. Rosa had tried, first at the same time every day, then the same time every second day. It had worked, for a year or so, then Gia had begun to feel stifled, when in truth she had been trying to avoid homesickness by throwing herself into searching out people and stories until the feeling faded, sometime between her second and third year, but avoiding those phone calls had helped.

Rosa still wielded an unfair degree of influence over her. Her grandmother had a way of talking that could make her feel very much like a ten-year-old girl again whose life had to be checked, and whose upbringing needed protecting. The controlling approach her grandmother had taken in raising her during her tween and teenage years, in direct contrast to the way Rosa had raised her son, had only increased Gia's resistance to the good-girl label Rosa wanted to pin on her.

She was determined to remain the Gia she knew herself to be; slightly wild, free, bohemian, mystical, the ultimate unsettled nomad, a somewhat controlled version of the wildness she really was. Rosa would want Gia to shrink herself and conform. Rosa moved in conservative circles. Big minds full of leftist ideals, certainly, but academic minds in academic settings, hence Gia called it a conservative circle, because when it came to Gia, half were lovely and supportive, the other half thought she *could do better* in all areas. She picked up her hot chocolate and took a sip of the rich velvety drink. London greys had soon turned into countryside greens, they passed through more blue-grey cities and more muted shades of late autumnal countryside until it became a blur of greys then greens with some shades of brown and yellows in between, all underneath a bright blue sky.

Gia had a table seat, and her notepad, newly bought at the airport, lay open in front of her as she wrote ideas and thoughts about her new novel in the English countryside. She had already made a note of the difference that a few extra pounds on her ticket made. Complimentary drinks, a quieter carriage, comfy seats and a window view. After hours on a flight in economy on the first available ticket out of America, she appreciated some luxury on the last leg of a long journey. If her character was going to be living in England, she deserved some good in her life. It was Gia's problem as the author to work out how the parentless foster child came to live in luxury in England as an adult, as her notepad, already a quarter full of scribbled notes and ideas with rough outlines of how the story would flow, demonstrated.

The last novel in her *American Magic* series was due. She was playing around with introducing the start of a new series set in England by doing what her fans had asked and bringing her first ever character, the car-crash reckless chaotic witch Valentina back, ten years later, ten years older, having moved from New Orleans to Harrogate, married and mature. Her heart wasn't in the plan, it was to appease her readers. It was why she found outlining the novel so difficult, why she wanted to go back to where it had all started. Valentina's character had been written by a lost young woman searching for her place in the world, and the travel had never ceased.

Gia started to recognise the names of the stations around Nottinghamshire, even after ten years away. A little pool of nerves and excitement flooded her stomach, growing larger as she neared Yorkshire. She had told everyone she was coming back next year, but she hadn't been able to wait that long. Once the thought of returning home had suddenly entered her head last month, she had been unable to settle down anywhere to write another, final novel in America. Roused from her thoughts by the trains overly loud announcement that they were approaching her station, Gia tidied her book and pens away. She picked up her burgundy leather jacket from her knee and shrugged it on over her black outfit, straightening out the red jersey hood attached to the jacket in a fluid movement, and checking her hair in the window. A messy low bun was now her everyday look, the long skirts were still her thing but packed away in a suitcase. She had swapped the band T-shirts for plain expensive tailored tops, and the big name trainers for subtle shoes and boots that only those with the most elite shoe game would be able to discern. The long braking stop heralded a few concerning ear-splitting screeches that made her grateful she was disembarking.

A group of young giggly teenagers rose from seats in the opposite carriage and crowded the door. They held paper shopping bags emblazoned with clothing store labels she didn't recognise. When she reached them, her eyes read each brightly coloured name printed onto the brown bags fast, absorbing the high street shop names that had changed in her absence. She let them pile out first, pulling off her two suitcases, a cabin bag, plus her laptop bag off the train in one experienced move. The teens rushed off, passing a café which raised Gia's hopes of a caffeine fix, only to have them dashed when she saw the closed sign in the window.

Alone on the platform, the late afternoon sun shone brightly but glaringly low in turquoise blue skies. The sunlight caught the tops of the trees around her, highlighting the yellowing leaves on the branches and leaving the rest of the trees in the shade. It created living two-tone sculptural structures. She noticed the huge bunches of red berries on scattered mountain ash trees, hints of the forthcoming colours of December. Her heart burst out and a smile emerged. Golden rudbeckia decorated the large concrete planters at the exit of the railway station. With a slowness caused by looking around in pure appreciation of sights she hadn't seen for ten years, she pulled her suitcases along, her laptop bag on her shoulder and her cabin bag sitting on the top of one suitcase. She hadn't realised how much she had missed it all until her heart started unfurl. The wondrous excitement of travel had expired now, but a relaxed familiarity of knowing the territory and the people took its place inside her. When she thought of her waiting grandmother, Gia was nervous. She had no reason to be, but she was.

Beneath her feet small tremors reverberated all around. Unseen, unfelt, unheard by most. A few in the village wobbled and covered their ears. A new scent filled the air, the crisp winter sharpness of early morning frosts, a hint of ripe blackberries, the warm richness of the woods in late autumn. A chitter stirred up distorted shadows around the village all at once, that reached, jumped and arched until they found the source of the disturbance. Like the majority of people, Gia didn't notice.

The route to her grandmother's cottage, the place where she had grown up, was a simple walk. Straight out of the local train station she would turn left and take a short walk down a residential street of pretty stone built terraced cottages with tiny square yards. Gia walked slowly and took a delighted interest in each garden. Some had small cottage gardens, a few had roses. A lot had been paved over and held a small patio table and two chairs. That one had trees in pots, this one had a freestanding greenhouse with a plastic cover instead of glass, where ripening tomatoes still tried to change from green to red, despite the lateness of the year. Gia found that she struggled down the street, thwarted by the uneven flagstones on the pavement which made her suitcases rock and threaten to fall.

At the end of the street, Gia needed to cross the main road through the village, stroll along the exquisitely pretty village high street, turn a corner and she was just a few paces from an alleyway that would take her to the street where her grandmother's cottage stood in the middle of the village. The idea of walking home, something she had looked forward to when she had rolled her suitcases easily along the smooth floor of the airport, was now a more difficult trial than she had assumed it would be. Her plan was flawed. She was already second guessing whether she had the patience to carry on.

Gia eyed the traffic for a taxi as she stood at the pelican crossing on the main road through the village. The traffic lights stayed on green and the little red man stared at her from his elevated beacon. A car beeped its horn at her and pulled over into a space just after the crossing. It took her a couple of seconds to recognise the man who jumped out. She took in his height, the muscled frame clearly visible in his long-sleeved T-shirt that had just a gilet thrown over it despite it being October and chilly. His golden-brown hair sprinkled though with lighter streaks was tied up in a bun. He had a beard, and his weather tanned skin indicated he spent a lot of time outdoors. He walked around the back of the large four by four vehicle, 'Gia?'

If she didn't recognise him, she would know that deep, melted chocolate over smooth whisky voice anywhere.

Chapter 2

It conjured up images of Irish coffee in the dark rooms of his farmhouse when windows pattered with heavy rain. Even if the long hair in a bun surprised her, and that his eyes weren't as grey as she remembered but held flecks of fire like the sun setting on his fields in winter. His nose was exactly as she remembered, the broken bump on the ridge from too many rugby tackles. He'd grown a beard. Evie had never said her brother had a beard these days. Atlas had grown into a man in the last ten years.

Gia eyed him up and down slowly, she liked what she saw, and she let out a small smile, curving one half of her mouth appreciatively. Her flirtatious nature wasn't shy about letting people know she liked the look of them, not anymore. She had passed through too many cities and towns to care about the afterwards, the aftermath. It was easy to pack up and move on without a goodbye, easier still to block a number; the problem with men was that they always wanted more commitment than she was willing to give them.

'Atlas?' she checked. He responded with a nod, and simply opened the boot of his mud-splattered shiny car that looked new to Gia who had been driving the same camper van for ten years. He strode up to where she stood at the crossing. Annoyingly it chose that moment to turn itself green and beeped at her to cross. Shadows wrapped themselves around the pole. Gia ignored the message to cross the road and allowed Atlas to take the cases from her fingers with relief.

'You're going to your grandmother's, Gia?'

'Yes. I was planning on getting her some wine first.'

No doubt Rosa would be cooking something, it was a big part of their Italian heritage, providing hospitality and cooking food for family and friends, Gia had figured that she could at least take some wine back to the cottage. It would help ease the awkwardness of having to ask her grandmother to put her up for a while, only until she decided whether she was staying, locally, or just in England, or applying for a visa to live somewhere else. She hadn't quite decided on her next move, and she refused to worry about it. Her thoughts were on catching up with the one friend who still lived here and just taking some time to write her final book in the place where it had all started.

'Evie said you weren't coming back until the spring.' He closed the boot door with her suitcases and bags inside. Gia shrugged the question off, she rolled her eyes lightly, and smiled at him, and noted how he watched her movements with a slight smile.

'Why wait around when you've made a decision? I came back. I kept thinking about this place and I couldn't get it out my head. It was part homesickness and part nostalgia. America had me pigeonholed anyway.'

'Jump in, we'll get you some wine and I'll run you back.'

'Don't you have somewhere to be? It's Saturday night.' Her flirtatious throwback question was met with wry laughter and a shake of his head, even though it wasn't quite night yet, he knew what she had insinuated.

'My Saturday nights are hot chocolate with the kids, and a game of chess these days.'

His Saturday nights had used to consist of drinking with his rugby teammates and ending up in a fight, or with a blonde woman his own age. Her imagination instantly gave her a picture of him smiling at the type of sporty, clean-cut girl with wholesome eyes that he used to go for at school. She would have to hold back on the flirting if he was taken. That would be a disappointment. She was already in the mood for fun.

'You have kids?' she asked.

He looked horrified, 'No. My niece and nephew.'

Relief flooded through her when she realised that he was talking about hot chocolate with family. Her friend Evie had been pregnant when Gia had left for America. Sometimes she forgot that Evie's babies had grown into actual little people.

Gia climbed into his oversized car. It seemed strange that America was full of these big cars and yet here, it looked wrong on the smaller narrower roads next to old stone buildings. Her memories of Atlas jarred against the luxury inside the new car. Her black leather seat was soft and warm. The console looked incredibly modern and expensive. It was far cry from the old rusty basic Land Rover Atlas used to drive when she left England. She glanced quickly at the two grey booster seats in the back and the lowered middle armrest with sculptured dips for cup holders. In contrast, the floor was covered in patches of dried mud that had fallen from boots alongside tattered old leaves. It smelled amazing to her, the type of car that had frequent professional deep cleans, unlike her camper van which she had cleaned herself, and had aired out daily.

In comparison, the professional version always smelt better.

Atlas restarted the car and asked, 'Is Rosa expecting you?'

'Yes.'

'That's a pity, I'm about to get takeaway for one. Do you still like pizza?' There was a hint of a grin on his face as he openly looked her up and down from the corner of his eye.

'Who doesn't?' It was the strangest question.

'Quite a few people.'

It was his expression that told her who *a few people* might be. She smiled to herself and watched as he negotiated the narrow roads with ease and confidence. He had always oozed confidence. Atlas drove up to the farm and into a full car park.

'Does this pizza place have a decent strong coffee?' She stretched her legs and arms out with a yawn. She heard Atlas chuckle.

'I can get you a decent strong coffee. What do you drink?' He reversed easily into a space, one arm behind her head on the headrest, his head turned to look out the back window.

'Cortado or expresso. If I make it for myself it's a black pour over. You're telling me that you sell wine here?' Her voice carried the confusion that she was feeling.

Gia's eyes moved over the new sleek charred-wood and glass buildings that combined modern sophistication with a European plaza atmosphere. The fabricated naturalised landscaping around it all invited her to walk into a fairy tale. She dipped her head to look up through the windscreen, she could just about make out where the old farmhouse used to sit at the top of the hill behind the beginning of new buildings. Everything had changed on the farm. Intuitively, Gia felt that this had Evie's touch all over it, the perfect fairytale landscaping, red apples hanging from branches, trees of different colours, blackberry hedges lining the car park, flowers that still looked summer perfect at the end of October.

Atlas turned off the engine and opened his door, 'Yes. I'll show you around the quadrant. This is all Evie's doing.'

'Wasn't this the stables?' Gia tried to place their location. She followed his movements and got out of the car, not taking her eyes off the changes in front of her. It made sense that her friend had planned this, Evie loved fairy tales, and it was clear that the time spent studying plant sciences had done wonders for her friend's talent.

Gia knew they were at the farm. She was certain that in front of them used to be a muddy path she had crossed numerous times on her way to see Evie, past the rundown unused stables and up the hill to the farmhouse. In bad weather she had taken the longer route up the narrow country lane. A stream had been put in, she assumed to sort out the permanent mud that had always been there, with a wide level bridge over it. A couple of ducks had taken residence on the stream. Wildflowers and alpines had been planted on the slopes. Once over the bridge, daisy-like flowers, Mexican fleabane, welcomed people from huge milk churns. Atlas confirmed it had been the old stables that she remembered, and added that Evie had wanted to add a touch of rustic European charm rather than rely too heavily on English nostalgia.

'Where is Evie?' Gia asked after her friend, his sister.

'She's taken the kids to the theatre in the city to see a

musical.'

Atlas took her into the café, jumped the queues and ordered a couple of takeaway coffees. A woman tried to confront him, then her friend shushed her, Gia heard the reverent mutter of, 'That's the owner'. He would have taken her straight to the wine shop, but her eye caught the window of the first shop they passed. With an easy patience he showed her around the shop, flirting openly with her. Gia loved nothing more than a flirt and quick witty conversations.

Whenever she turned around with a new product in her hand, she caught his eyes as they wandered over her. She winked at him once to acknowledge it. He simply smiled and upped the silent game he was playing. Gia could flirt. She met his magnetism and played poker with it. She raised the stakes with her own tempting, silent looks, winks and arched eyebrows, a playfulness that hadn't surfaced inside her for a while rose up, temptation ran through her veins and it always got the better of her, whether it was a coffee, a cake, a new destination, or men. Their open appraisal of each other showed in the bold confidence they held, their attraction burst from a spark into a flame, she could feel the heat, as real as if they had their own fire burning in the small gap between their bodies. They silently shouted a language that had bystanders looking at them, a smile, whilst their eyes said innuendos, a tilt of the head, lingering looks on each other's lips and bodies, she really couldn't look away from those new gold flecks in his eyes. If she hadn't been expected by her grandmother, she wouldn't have made it home. It didn't occur to her that he was her friend's brother, he was just a man and she liked him.

As though Yorkshire wanted to make her even more at home after delivering her a sunny evening and a man, darkness surrounded them when they emerged from the shops. In the new surroundings she temporarily lost her bearings for a second and took a look around. Lighting was minimal here, low level brightness over the signage of the shops, string lights along the paths and over the bridge. It was pretty on another level, again she was reminded of the fairy tales her friend loved. Gia wanted to wrap the day up in a bow. Dark evenings and nights had always been her favourite part of the day.

'You OK?' Atlas had noticed her hesitation.

Gia gave a nod and a lively, cheeky smile, 'I love the dark. Not necessarily the cold that comes with it, but it's beautiful, a silky cushion that dishes up indulgence and hedonism with a glass of wine.'

He raised his eyebrows in surprise at her answer, 'That's why you're a writer and I'm a farmer. It's a pain when the nights start to draw in, there's always more jobs to do than there is daylight to do them. But I like how you think.' Again, his eyes conveyed the real message to her, even his expression was playful, and his smile broad.

Atlas drove slower than he had previously to her grandmother's cottage, and parked in the middle of the lane. He appeared oblivious to the extreme narrowness of the country road, or the politeness of moving to the side. Gia opened the car door slowly, her eyes fixated on the waist high cottage garden gate she remembered, its green paint pale and new. It had been red when she left England. It was her second indication that life here in the village had moved on, despite it standing still in her mind.

The narrow path of concrete slabs up to the door was

lined by seasonal red rosehips. The two holly bushes in green containers by the front door were new, their bright glossy distinctive-shaped leaves protecting the cottage. Her heart beat faster, racing, excitement drummed its own tune in her stomach, but she still hesitated. She had overlooked part of her childhood. It raced back to her now.

Forgotten fear and trepidation took over the excitement at returning, bouncing in to quash the flirtatious fun she had been having with Atlas. Things had lurked in the darkness in the cottage, things that were not childish fears. Things that had fractured her damaged soul further.

Atlas jumped out without noticing her fear. He had her two suitcases halfway up the path when the cottage door opened, as though Rosa had been waiting and watching. She stood in the doorway, as tall and as proud as Gia remembered her. Her salt and pepper hair loose to her shoulders. Her black and white tailored outfit with matching cardigan and pearls was a direct contrast to Gia's more relaxed, casual clothing. Gia picked up her laptop bag and hurried to the door, reaching Rosa at the same time as Atlas.

'I was driving past when I saw Gia. I couldn't let her walk back with her luggage. Shall I carry these upstairs for you?' Atlas offered. Gia could imagine him eyeing up the old staircase to his left, made for smaller people than him. She bit back a smirk at how a simple act of outrageous flirting made her life easier.

'It's the door on your left when you get to the top of the stairs, the one overlooking the back garden.' Rosa smiled with warmth at Atlas. Gia knew she was looking at the pair through narrowed eyes when Rosa shot her the warning look, an expression perfected by years of teaching, first as an unqualified language teacher, then a qualified teacher, before moving onto postgraduates and lecturing. Gia's own surprise lay in her memories, memories that clashed with the welcoming reception Atlas was receiving. There hadn't been any coldness on Rosa's part towards the siblings, more of a professional detachment mixed with a small dose of disapproval.

Rosa greeted Gia with a hug. The welcoming scent of her perfume rose as Gia returned the hug, the perfume Rosa refused to change because she had been wearing it the day she met her husband, it had notes of orange blossom and raspberry. Gia welcomed the warm thin arms enclosing her. From inside the cottage came the sounds of a radio. Rosa had never been a fan of the TV. Her grandmother's love of music had been a huge part of Gia's upbringing. Even now, it was part of the creative process Gia used when writing, creating playlists whose moods and rhythms matched her scenes. Gia could hear the old stairs creaking as Atlas ascended with her suitcases.

'Welcome home, Gianna. Look at you. You look so much like your mother. You have her face, figure, her curves. How was the flight?'

The comment threw her off balance, and out of character, back to the tween girl growing up desperate to know more about her parents than her grandmother could tell her. The girl inside her responded, 'I planned out my next book. I have research points to do over the next few weeks. It smells great here. Are you cooking? Can I smell garlic? Like proper garlic?'

'Enough Americanisms already. I'm cooking garlic bread, lasagne, there's grapes and cheese if you need to nibble right now.'

'It's a good job Atlas and I brought a few bottles of wine then,' she smiled.

Gia gave her laptop bag to Rosa and dashed back to the car to get her cabin bag and the cardboard box of treats from the farm shops. She hadn't even turned around before she felt the warmth of Atlas's body behind her. He placed a hand on the small of her back and reached around to get the box from her. From that simple touch, a gesture of thoughtful consideration, her back burned with the warmth of lava entering a snowstorm. Gia flashed him a small smile and let him take the box. She stood up straight, her precious laptop bag in her hand, closed the boot with a soft thud and followed him inside.

'The cottage smells good, Rosa. There's a red in there that will go well with it,' Atlas said. He inclined his head to the box in his hands and carried the thick cardboard box across the room to place it on the empty breakfast bar.

'You could stay for dinner, Atlas, if no one is expecting you. There's at least eight portions of lasagne,' Rosa offered. Atlas glanced over at Gia, she put her cabin bag down on the big square step on the stairs, the one before the staircase curved.

'I don't want to intrude.' He held her eyes, the devilish gleam that had been in his eyes in the shops was now replaced with genuine concern.

She shook her head and gave him an impish smile, 'No intrusion. Nonna's lasagne has got to be better than that pizza for one you were talking about. Which wine do you think would go well?' She couldn't stop flirting if her life depended on it, the last question had slipped out without a thought. She knew any of the reds would be fine, but he had surprised her in the shop with his knowledge. He seemed to have a genuine affinity with the sommelier running the wine shop.

She watched his eyebrow rise and fall a fraction, a smile appeared on his face. Instead of responding he looked over at Rosa, 'Do I have fifteen minutes to take the car home and walk back down?'

'You'd better. Someone will have something to say about that thing blocking the lane,' Rosa scolded. Her tone was light and she shook her head once as she spoke, it was less about Atlas's car and more that Rosa liked to avoid antagonising her neighbours.

He looked at Gia when he said, 'It's the bottle with the wolf on. I'll be right back.'

Once Atlas had left, Gia took a few moments to look around. She was oddly out of place and not at all inside the cottage she had thought she was returning to. The front door of her childhood home led straight into a sitting room she barely recognised, despite it still having all the ancient nooks and crannies, wonky walls, and the same old fireplace. A real fire created a cosy heat that filled the space in spite of the still mild temperatures outside, it warded off the damp in the air well and was the only thing that looked familiar.

Rosa had a new green velvet corner settee filled with extra cushions. Each cushion was embroidered with flowers or woodland animals. The sitting room walls were painted a vintage green, that was new too. The kitchen had been knocked through to meet this room, the entire downstairs was open plan, a small breakfast bar was all that remained of the wall that had separated the old large kitchen from the sitting room.

It was… opposite. It was the only word Gia could come up with. The oven used to be on the other side of the kitchen, their missing country table had always sat in the middle of the kitchen. The old stainless-steel sink had been where the new back door currently sat, but the sink was now a white butler vintage sink under a new window. It was smaller too. Definitely smaller.

Rosa pulled out a bottle of wine and held it up, 'This one?'

'Why is the kitchen smaller?' Gia tried to match the old cosy wooden kitchen she remembered with the newer, cute but modernised cottage space. She shifted her weight onto one foot and fought the urge to chew on the inside of her cheek. It was uncomfortable being somewhere she thought she knew to find it completely different. The cottage looked more zoom meeting ready, internet post picture perfect than how she remembered. Even if she had expected Rosa to change it, this was not her grandmother's light academia style.

'I made a few changes.'

A smaller dining table was pushed up against the stair wall between the smaller sitting room area and the kitchen. It was cosy, three of the four chairs neatly tucked under, a tablecloth over it, a vase of deep red roses in the middle. Before, when she had lived here, that particular space had been filled with freestanding bookcases up to her waist, their tops covered with photographs, candles, and the ornaments she had bought Rosa over the years. The bar stools were a short distance away from the dining table and gave a choice of places to sit.

Once, oversized overstuffed coloured settees had mismatched, and a TV had stood on a unit awkwardly taking up space in a corner near the window. There was no TV now. That didn't surprise her. She did spot a Wi-Fi router though, that didn't surprise her either.

Rosa opened a door at the other side of the kitchen and briefly showed Gia a decent sized full bathroom, with a bath sitting under a window that allowed views out to the garden. It was a big enough room to now host a washing machine and tumble dryer. Gia could appreciate a smaller kitchen for a bathroom like that. They had endured a tiny electric shower and one downstairs toilet when she had grown up in the cottage. There hadn't been enough room to raise their arms to put shampoo on their heads in the old shower.

Rosa pointed to a shoe cabinet by the back door and told Gia that muddy shoes went in there, not upstairs on the new carpet or trailed through the house. Gia gave a nod to indicate that she understood and turned to appreciate the new kitchen. The country style lower cabinets and floor tiles were pale green, and the new range oven was built into the old brick fireplace. The walls were white, as were the upper cabinets and the worktop.

Gia remembered a wooden country kitchen, winter fires in the old fireplace, a cold stone floor and their country dining table. She remembered pulling a chair closer to the fire in winter, and sitting with a book whilst Rosa studied. The reality created a disconnect in her brain. She wished Rosa had told her about the changes, she thought that the cottage would have stood still with time.

'When was all this changed?'

'Three, maybe four years ago now.'

Rosa told Gia that she had changed upstairs too, taking space from each bedroom for an upstairs bathroom.

Gia had longed for an upstairs bathroom growing up. They'd only had the tiny cramped downstairs bathroom which had been installed as an afterthought by someone previously. She had hated having to come downstairs alone to use it in the dark.

'Could I go and have a quick clean up?' Gia asked. Rosa let out a broad smile and gave a nod.

Gia picked up her cabin bag and ran upstairs. She looked down and took a quick note of the red antique style carpet on the stairs with green vines and deliberately faded white roses. Rosa didn't do neutrals. Flower paintings lined the wall of the staircase. Instead of the two doors she remembered, there were three. Her room had always been the left door, overlooking the back garden, her grand-mother's room on the right overlooking the front garden. She opened the middle door and looked inside. A simple white bathroom had been installed, but the floor held the real charm. Patterned tiles exuded a pretty vintage charm. Gia bent down to investigate further. Each square tile was broken up into four triangles; two white, two green, where the white part of the tile met the next white tile a vintage red rose surrounded by greenery emerged at the join. It elevated the standard bathroom into something that fitted the age of the cottage, something that her grandmother seemed to be able to do with ease. Rosa had turned the whole cottage into a home that endorsed her name. Gia, named after her father and grandfather, both Gio, wouldn't be able to turn a name into a personality. Valentina, her middle name, had been her mother's choice for her. Musing on a life that might have been, a girl called Valentina with a mother still alive, she turned the shower on and left it running to get warm.

Curiously she opened her bedroom door. Her eyes were drawn to the new wooden four-poster double bed that took up most of the room, already made for her. Her treasured writer's bureau was still there, shifted into a corner adjacent to the cottage window. Gia had spent more hours of her life at that bureau than she could remember, doing homework, studying, or writing stories, and she had loved it. The drop-front desk had been pulled down and a pen lay on a piece of paper. Her old notes and papers had been put away inside the space. She walked past the same wooden wardrobe that had been hers since childhood to look at the pen left on the desk. It seemed so random compared to the tidiness and neatness. There was a number on the old paper, and a name on top *Atlas*. She pulled out her phone and tapped the number into it with short glossy red nails. The pen amused her, it was brown with High Lēah Farm on it in gold. It was heavy, she appreciated that, she had a penchant for weighted pens that wrote well.

Gia remembered leaving behind a cheerful yellow and white country bedroom. A room that had held old second-hand furniture and a metal single bed, a room that was loved because it was hers, but hated at the same time because nothing matched. The new four-poster bed was wooden and solid, fitting in with the same wooden furniture that furnished the room. The walls had been painted a bare winter white now, instead of the happy yellow that they had been. Her bed had been made with white bedding. The almost too short yellow curtains that had skimmed the windowsill and raised outwards in a breeze had been replaced with floor sweeping ivory ones. A vintage red glass vase stood on the deep windowsill, filled with a simple bouquet of colourful flowers. There was less room to move around, but she was grateful to be able to have an upstairs bathroom and a double bed. It was more than she had been expecting. Her fireplace was set up and ready to be lit. Rosa had done that. The new black radiators on the walls hadn't escaped her notice, Rosa had installed central heating.

Gia crouched down and opened a case. Her toiletries, a change of clothes and make-up sat underneath a towel at the top of a suitcase, all prepared for a quick wash and change. She lifted them out and carried them into the bathroom.

Gia was downstairs with Rosa in less than fifteen minutes. Life in a van had taught her to wash quickly. It was the dry shampoo that took the most time to get out of her hair. Her conditioner was left in, a bonus of her Italian wavy/curly hair which she rarely bothered to style properly. It would only be up in a bun the following day. Her sleeveless jumpsuit was casual and comfy enough to curl up and write in, but smart enough to be a piece of clothing and not pyjamas. She had considered travelling in it, but she didn't have any trainers to wear, she always wore black stiletto heels with the outfit, the ones she had on now. She wore a hand-knitted cardigan over it, a deep wine red coloured old style cardigan, picked up from a house sale. She had been driving past on the street when the activity in the yard caught her eye, and her eyes had spotted the cardigan on a clothes rail from the road. Impulsively she had parked up and enquired about it.

'That's a nice cardigan,' Rosa said when Gia came downstairs.

Gia smiled and thanked her. The explanation of how

she found the cardigan tended to end any conversations around it with lingering awkwardness. Yet Gia had no awkwardness about death, for her, it was the living that wanted to sanitise and organise the chaos that came with being alive, as though structure and order would prevent death from arriving at their doorstep. Dying didn't worry her, it was just the next stage in a soul journey. Without religion, she saw life and death as overlapping circles that made up a new pattern, much like the spirograph toy she had as a little girl.

Her hands were pushing the stopper into the bottle after she had poured three glasses of wine when someone knocked on the door. Gia's stomach gave a nervous flutter, immediately assuming it was Atlas. The act of being nervous about a man caught her by surprise, the fluttering and excitement had vanished years ago. She looked at the door with frozen feet rather than move to answer it.

Rosa, busy setting another place at the table, missed Gia's reaction and walked to the door. It gave Gia time to compose herself, to dampen down the excited rush of adrenaline that followed the nerves. Atlas stepped inside the cottage, immediately filling the space with his presence. He greeted Rosa and extended his thanks for the invitation again, then he walked forwards to Gia, his eyes simmered over her wet hair, almost bare face except for mascara and a red lipstick, with a small smile, his pupils dilated. Gia read his thoughts and winked. She handed him a glass of red wine, 'One day, if you're lucky,' she teased. Inside, the woman she was rolled her eyes. One day insinuated a game, a chase and neither of them played on that beginner level anymore.

'How did you know what I was thinking?' he

challenged, failing in his attempt to hide a smirk.

Her sensual curve of a smile reappeared in response to his playful nature. 'I've just come out of the shower. It's written all over your face.'

Rosa had set out bowls of warm garlic bread while Gia was in the shower. Atlas put down the extra bottle of red he had carried back and took a piece of bread with his glass of wine. Gia picked up a full glass from the counter for herself.

'What time do you need to be back?' she asked him. She remembered that he had said his Saturday nights involved his niece and nephew.

'I don't. My sister is still annoyed at me about a conversation we had earlier today. We'll be OK. Sometimes we don't see eye to eye. I'll give her some space.'

'Does it have anything to do with her new man?' Rosa spoke up from the dining table where she had sat down. Gia carried a glass over to her.

'I might have to apologise for something I said to her.'

'Don't wait too long, Atlas, we lose those we love in seconds. Words not said are always our biggest regrets. Gia darling, would you do the lasagne? It feels so good to sit down.'

Chapter 3

The four-poster bed combined with the thick walls of the cottage had given her a surprisingly good quiet sleep. It had disturbed her at first, that she couldn't hear everything happening outside, then she had drifted off to sleep by telling herself that the quietness was less to do with the house and more about the village itself. Nothing happened in the village, despite that it was swamped with lore and rumours, daily life ticked by in a predictable routine for its inhabitants. Unused to the quiet, she kept waking up, comfortable, cosy and refreshed, convinced that it must finally be morning, this time, just like all the other times she had woken, Gia stretched, opened her eyes enough to see that it was still dark and rolled over onto her side, pulling the brushed cotton quilt around her body tightly when it let in the cold air. Unbidden, her brain served her a picture of Atlas, naked and getting out of bed.

He was broader that she had thought, more muscled, more tattooed, she glimpsed light brown chest hair, he put his hair in a bun, then reached over to the drawers in his caravan and pulled out warm clothes, his clean storm-blue farm overalls hung on the back of the door. She opened her eyes, the dream persisted playing out. Atlas turned and looked directly at her, hard, as though he could see through the distance between them, down the hill to the farm shops and café, across the grey car park, down the lane, through Rosa's garden and cottage walls and into the rear bedroom. Those eyes told her he knew she was looking, there was a hint of confusion, of bewilderment, as if he didn't really believe it. It was a flash of a second and she was gone from his caravan.

Gia's heart thumped in panic at the new experience. As much as she was open about witchcraft, this unexpected event was beyond her control. She didn't like someone else being in control. She had not created or willed that situation. Still, the feeling that he had really seen her persisted. Shock forced her to become wide awake and alert at the thought. Gia closed her eyes with a stern reminder to be rational, and failed again to convince herself that it was simply a vivid dream. She rolled over. Late nights and late mornings were her style, not early nights and early mornings. Yet still, the situation plagued her and ran through her mind. She hadn't created that situation, as far as she knew, Atlas wasn't able to, it hadn't felt as though anyone else was involved. If she thought about other people being involved, it would make more sense for whatever magic it was not to happen. She knew his reputation as a womaniser, he had been the local bad boy. As far as she knew, he still was, her experience with him had only taught her how addictive Atlas could be when he turned his attention on a woman. Rational thoughts entered her conscious brain, she told herself it was just a dream, a consequence of liking the man.

After daylight had broken across the sky and her room was no longer dark, Gia stared at her open suitcase. It provided her with a limited choice of clothes in hues specifically designed to go together for a capsule wardrobe; rich reds and burgundies, cream and ivory-coloured clothes, a lot of different black and the occasional caramel pieces. She picked a pair of wide leg, high waisted burgundy tweed trousers, a vintage purchase she'd seen as an investment against the rise of cheaply made fast fashion, much like her leather jacket which was also second-hand. Back in America she had paid a tailor to cut the hood from her favourite red sweatshirt, her school leaver's hoody, and sew it onto the jacket. The sleeves on the red hoody had long since developed frayed edges and holes, yet she had hung onto it as a remembrance of her friends until it had past cutely frayed and moved towards homeless vibes.

She slowly descended the cottage stairs towards the old window. On the deep windowsill a Christmas cactus sat with buds almost in flower. Even on the stairs Gia could taste the coffee her grandmother had made through its strong scent permeating the cottage. She turned at the bottom of the stairs to enter the sitting room and saw Rosa at the breakfast bar, an espresso next to her, her laptop open and lit up. She was already dressed in an elegant outfit; a white shirt, the embroidered collar spilling over her red cable knit jumper. Her posture was stiff, her back straight, as if she was tense and deep in work. The glasses were a new addition. Gia saw a screen of words in front of her grandmother.

'Don't universities have reading weeks anymore?' Gia asked as she walked into the kitchen and started to make herself a coffee.

'They do. I have papers to mark, research to do and church to attend. Are you coming with me?' The last was an insinuation, not a request, that Gia should be attending the church.

As in slow motion, Gia turned to face her grandmother, realised she was serious, and suppressed a shiver that trailed ice along her spine at the thought of sitting in the cold draughty stone church for a couple of hours with nothing to do. The few times Rosa had taken her to services such as Easter, Mass, or Midnight Mass she had amused herself by translating the Latin on display around her, then by making up stories about the people in the images in the stained glass. She had taken the image of Saint George and turned him into Lancelot looking for Guinevere, then into an unnamed knight on a secret quest but he fell in love and the pair fell through a portal into the modern world where they tried to make sense of it all. It had amused her enough to drown out the words she should have been listening to.

'Absolutely not. I'll probably burn up on the threshold.' It was said as a joke.

Rosa's stern glowering expression told Gia that her grandmother thought otherwise. She remembered that Rosa hadn't attended church once either, it had built up so slowly. Ten years of phone calls and it seemed that Rosa had gone from rarely attending to a regular attender. Gia wondered if she had caused that, if her absence had created a loneliness that Rosa had sought to fill through attending church. She hadn't given her grandmother a thought when she had run off to America to explore its streets and cultures.

'Sometimes a group of us go for a coffee after.' Rosa's voice held notes of doubt, as though Gia would both miss her returning immediately and perhaps want to join the group for coffee.

'I was planning to take a walk anyway. I could use some fresh air after travelling yesterday.'

'I had a key cut for you. It's on the little hanger there,' Rosa gestured towards a hook stuck onto a wall under a cabinet.

'Thank you. I don't suppose you'd want to miss church and go for a coffee with me on the farm? It looked busy yesterday even though it was closing time when Atlas took me. I was planning on people watching and just checking it out.' People watching had been their thing for a few years when they had arrived in England, first London, then across Yorkshire. Rosa had sought out the most middle-class cafés she could afford to take them to and the pair would while away two or even three hours observing the hidden mannerisms of the culture they had moved to.

She secretly hoped her grandmother would say no, just as she was also secretly hoping Evie would wander in at some point and she could surprise her friend. Evie had mentioned in her texts that she often took the children to the café for breakfast on a Sunday.

'No thank you. Although there's a tearoom on the high street you should take a wander to for your books. It's called Harriet's. Her lemon curd cake is extremely good, as is her coffee. You'd like the décor.'

'Maybe we could go together later in the week?'

'I'll get back to you. That machine is a bit tricky. Let me show you.' Rosa stood up from her laptop, as oblivious to the fact that Gia had worked as a barista for extra income as Gia had been to the cottage's renovation.

Gia watched a blackbird through the kitchen window as she drank her coffee. His yellow beak pulled hawthorn berries from the gnarled twisted shrub which surrounded the cottage. A wren joined him, hiding in the hedge, then a couple of sparrows, the more she watched the more life she saw in the dying autumnal plants around the cottage. It reminded her somehow of Evie, her passion for the English countryside, and then Gia remembered how much they had both liked to sit and read books in the sun.

Rosa left before Gia had finished the coffee, picking up a smart jacket that matched her trousers and reminding Gia to lock up when she left. Two ladies of a similar age waited at the gate for her. One in typical English tweed, the other in jeans and a cropped jumper, her silver haired Mohican a surprise to Gia, and a relief, that there might still be people in Rosa's circle who had their feet in the current world.

When she eventually emerged mid-morning to walk to the farm café, it was colder outside than she had anticipated. She had forgotten how the Yorkshire breeze could add a depth of coldness to an otherwise mild day and pulled up the jersey hood on her jacket. As she sauntered along, she mused on the twisted and knotted branches in the hedges along the path, forced into contorted boundary shrubs that formed one side of the lane up to the farm. On the other side, stone walls outlined the gardens of cottages. Gia walked past the last streetlight and moved aside for a continually steady stream of cars flowing into the designated car park at the farm. Behind her she heard a family walking, children talking about a play area, a child urged to hurry up who cried and asked to be carried. She pushed her hands into her pockets, picked up her pace and kept ahead, not looking back, not encouraging conversation, unwilling to exchange even a smile on a Sunday morning that she had allocated as hers.

Gia spotted her friend Evie immediately in the café, sat at a table for four people, but only occupied by two adults. She joined the queue unobtrusively and watched from her hiding spot. Evie was in grey, brightening up her outfit with a few touches of green. Neither of those were her happy colours. The expression on her friend's face as she listened to the man beside her spoke volumes. Evie had retreated. Whatever he had done, Gia didn't think there was any redemption. Atlas had said he'd fallen out with his sister over her new boyfriend. She wondered what had happened. The pair looked like a couple, they looked good together. Their bodies mirrored each other, when one moved, the other did. Gia turned her head as a waitress moved past with a tray of neatly stacked clean plates and cups, clearly looking at her watching Evie. She didn't want a staff member to whisper to Evie that a woman was staking her out from the queue.

Once she had her coffee, she carried it over to the table where her friend sat, Gia held back a little whilst Robbie leaned over and gave Evie a kiss, his hands cupped Evie's face with an easy familiarity. She watched Evie reciprocate the kiss, the way her friend's body relaxed, how she leaned into him, and concluded that there may be some redemption.

Drawing closer she heard him say, 'I know what I saw. I know your home's reputation. I don't blame you for hiding.'

'Hi, stranger, can I interrupt?' Gia breezed in with a purposeful light tone, placing her coffee and sunglasses on the table.

Chapter 4

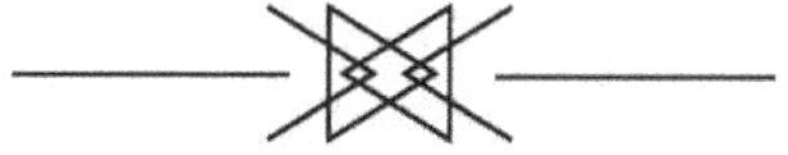

She was curious now. Robbie had clearly seen something, combined with the reputation of the witch farm made Gia want to dive straight into questions. But Evie looked up and jumped out of her seat, clearly happy to see her and glad for a distraction, encasing her in a warm hug.

Still standing they talked faster than normal in a quick succession of questions from Evie about Gia's early return. It surprised her that Atlas hadn't said anything to his sister yet. When Evie went to sit back down, Gia took off her leather jacket and laid it over her knees as she sat, ready to jump up and move if one of Evie's children turned up.

At a slight pause in the conversation when they both took a drink, Robbie stood up, 'I can go, give you time to catch up.' Gia and Evie both looked up at him. Evie's hand moved to catch Robbie's, an expression of yearning clear as day on her face.

'Please stay, don't let me push you away,' Gia protested when she noticed her friend's reaction.

Robbie seemed to understand Evie without words. Gia doubted either of them had heard her speak. He bent down and held Evie's jaw softly, he gave her a quick, light kiss, leaving to get them more coffees. Gia watched her friend melt, then smiled at Evie, 'He looks as good in real life as he does in those pictures of the pair of you on the internet. I love your hair. When did you change it?' Her friend looked better with brighter honey-hued hair.

Evie touched her hair self-consciously and answered, 'Last week. I think it was last week. Things have been a bit hectic lately. You've still not said why you're back early.'

Gia rolled her eyes at the wall behind Evie, then looked at Evie as she admitted, 'My book got cancelled. There's a small release in the East but the Midwest evangelists combined with the rise of the far right have scared the publishers and they're not willing to risk a huge promotion on a book centred around dark witchcraft. I've done the New Orleans promotion, Seattle, New York and the East Coast. I was homesick for English weather, English gardens, the cuteness of the village so I booked an earlier flight.' She didn't tell Evie that people had written to her publishers about her *ungodly* work, the threats and their issues with her apparent promotion of paganism. It had scared her that religious zealots could hold so much sway. It pushed her image of the world from teetering on the brink of dystopia to much further along the line, in freefall and en route to collapsing.

'I know you.' Evie put her head to one side when she looked at her friend.

Gia grinned at her as she admitted, 'I may have a few ideas. I'm researching the history of magic in the isles and the waves of migration and invasion to see how they've changed the magical landscape and incorporated themselves into folklore by looking at the predominate nationalities that would have followed the ice thaws before England became settled, and then after, when we know who came and their cultures. Where better to be than our very own village with its own special deity?' Her tone was light and teasing again.

'Is there such a thing as black magic?'

The question came out of the blue, sparking Gia's curiosity again that Evie had something to hide. She tried to reassure her friend, 'No. Magic is magic. Essentially, it's just another energy in the universe that's harnessed in different ways by different cultures. Honestly, I've met so many people and learnt their cultures and sub-cultures around magic that I don't believe in black, white, or even grey anymore. There's intent, and that's a human trait.' Gia answered her with serious eyes and a shrug. Warnings rose up inside her along with a tremor of excitement that ran through her veins with a tingle, there was a glimmer of a story emerging, the reputation of the farm combined with questions about a topic that Evie had never once talked about hinted at undercurrents of buried tales.

'There's people out there that you believe can use magic?' Her friend was guarded, hesitant, looking at her from lowered lashes, already ready for the rejection.

Instead, Gia nodded to reassure her, 'Of course. I've seen it.'

'Seen what? They'll bring our coffees over. I got Max and Rey more juice,' Robbie set the small glass bottles on the table and sat down. As soon as he had sat down his hand absentmindedly found its way to Evie's neck, his arm resting over the back of her chair. Gia held a smile back at how comfortable they were with each other, and how well they fitted together. Evie needed someone who would give her that type of silent attention even when he was talking to someone else. Her parents' neglect cost her dearly.

Gia didn't need an introduction to one of her favourite topics and continued to talk about magic. She recounted the amazing people she had met in America who could truly use magic, and those that only thought they could. She described the poverty-stricken shamans practising handed-down knowledge, witches, the commercialisation of witchcraft, voodoo and her experiences working with a young priest tracking down demons for the catholic church. She kept her own experiences out of it until she could judge their reactions.

'They honestly believe in demons?' Robbie asked, referring to the people and the church.

Gia took a sip of her coffee and her eyes took in the people in the café, as if reminding herself that she was in public. Then she continued, 'I've seen them. I was sceptical about the whole possession thing. I worked with a priest off and on for the last four years. I'm more curious about how other people and indigenous cultures treat them. He let me tag along after seeing that I was genuinely curious as to their origins and not a dark tourist. I find the more religious people are, the more they believe in demons. Which begs the question, how do native cultures view such entities? What happened before organised religion?'

Coffee quickly turned to a light lunch in the café where Gia and Evie failed to notice the passing of time, what had felt like thirty minutes had been hours according to their watches. Surprise shot through her when she realised that they had relaxed and talked for so long. In America everyone was on schedules, which meant coffee with a friend was an hour at the most. She had gotten used to that, and being labelled the free so-called bohemian one because of her lack of a schedule. Whilst she and Evie still had nearly full lunch plates from talking so much, Robbie and the children's meals were long finished. When Robbie's phone went off and he stepped outside to take the call, Evie's eyes followed him, but their conversation didn't change.

Robbie brought the crisp air inside with him when he returned, the freshness was quickly overpowered by the coffee and blackcurrant juice that permeated everywhere in the café. He explained that he had made plans for the afternoon, and he wanted them to join him in the pub with his family. Evie was overly hesitant. Gia listened as he patiently coaxed her friend round with gentle words and promises of keeping people away from her. When he looked at Gia to support his efforts with Evie, Gia nodded her agreement to go. She rarely turned down the opportunity to meet more people and have fun.

On their walk into the village Evie mentioned that she hadn't been in the pub after she had turned eighteen. Gia burst into laughter. They reminisced about all the nights they had spent in the pub underage, especially the extremely popular Friday karaoke and barbeque nights. The owners hadn't bothered asking for ID in a small country pub where everyone knew who everyone else was.

'They don't do those nights anymore. They haven't for years. It wasn't the same under the new owners, it died.'

'But, how? Literally the whole village would go in, and more. You and V.V would be on the tables dancing when they did musicals last thing before closing.'

'They stopped doing the barbeque first. Then people from further afield started to turn up, it became a night to get drunk and fight, villagers against townies, some staff got hurt and everything was shut down for a bit.' Evie shrugged.

'I can't believe those Friday nights finished. Remember that time they left the barbeque unattended for a few minutes at closing time and we all helped our-selves to burgers before running off.' It had been one of her favourite moments, a wild Evie and reckless Gia leading the way in grabbing burgers and dishing them out amongst their friends before getting their own and running off. Evie's had been piled high with fried onions, Liberty had asked for a double burger with cheese.

'Poor kid had only gone inside to take a few empty glasses,' Evie chuckled.

Gia fell silent momentarily as the pub came into view. The building itself was odd. She'd tried to describe it to American friends and always ended up drawing it on a napkin. One half of the roof was noticeably lower that the other although both were two-storey buildings. Originally separate, a house and a pub, the taller house had a two-storey triangular addition. The low boundary wall, only shin high, was a blessing and a curse, easily jumped over to get in or out, also easily walked into in the dark after too many drinks. The sign was new. The forest green paint on the windows and doors looked new and shiny. The newest name of the pub, proudly proclaimed by the sign, was The Plough, but to locals it was, inexplicably, the brew, no capitals. When outsiders first tried to refer to it as the brew, they always paused, thereby adding capitals to the name as they spoke it. Rumours were that at some point in the building's old history it probably was the village brewery.

Evie's smile was thin and forced as they entered the pub. She exchanged greetings and nods with a few people. Gia's body tensed only because her friend did. When they walked through the pub she didn't recognise anyone, until she saw Evie's children run off towards their friends and realised that these were school parents. A few looked at her next to Evie, Gia didn't assume that they knew who she was, although she did see a couple of people's eyes widen in surprise and give her eye contact and a nod. Robbie let go of Evie's hand to put his arm around her waist and pull her closer, a clear message to anyone who tried to approach her. Gia flanked the other side of Evie and gave her a wink. Evie returned the wink with a genuine smile and visibly relaxed.

Robbie's family had managed to find a large table by a window towards the far end of the pub, a number of empty glasses stood in the centre, a sign that they had already had a couple of drinks. Gia could have picked his parents out without being introduced, but was surprised at the number of siblings around the table, all various shades of blond with bright blue eyes and friendly smiles. Her shy friend's reluctance to face the entire family head-on in public made much more sense now.

To compensate for Evie's quietness, Gia joined in the chat and banter with the whole family with the confidence and naturalness born from constant travel. She treated them as though she had known them all a long time before that afternoon, forever outgoing, cheerful and sociable on the outside. Below the surface, her instincts were telling her to run, her hand tightened around her glass occasionally when she forgot to relax it. There was an underlying darkness to the family that curdled her blood. Out of protectiveness she didn't want to leave her friend alone. Her curiosity, which was always her downfall, told her to wait to see what could happen in a busy pub on a Sunday afternoon, then she wondered if they had the same feeling about her. She wanted to broach the subject, to find out why, to ask incessant questions until she was satisfied, but held back. There was nothing to indicate that the family were experiencing the same pull to escape, they presented a relaxed ease. Yet the tug inside her veins was almost all consuming, urging her to leave, it felt as though her blood was splitting inside her.

Chapter 5

On an impulse Gia connected her phone to the pub's Wi-Fi and called her grandmother to join them on the premise that Rosa loved company. She readily agreed to join Gia and the family for a chat and intelligent conversation about current affairs. Gia also thought Rosa could use something real, away from whatever influence her church friends were exhibiting. Despite working with the calm, quiet, unassuming priest who held serious intellectual conversations with her into the early hours over whisky or bourbon, she had also come up against the violent, loud, aggressive personalities of American religion and she did not wish another round with them wherever she was in the world. She was a confident person but even then they had rattled her and made her shrink a little, it was their overbearing self-righteousness, their loudness, their insistence on talking over people. In hindsight, it was clearly bullying tactics, yet it worked effectively. If she argued back, they were right and she had the devil inside her, if she stayed silent it was because they were right, if she did anything else it became about her body and her lifestyle and her influence over *their women*. She forced the unpleasant thoughts away.

Her drink slid down easily as the conversation flowed and the background noise steadily built up around them. She was still uneasy around the family. Their conversation and laughter remained normal, nothing unusual was mentioned. Her stomach still screamed at her to run from the pub and the family. There was a saying, curiosity killed the cat, and she might very well be the cat by the way her brain overrode her instincts. It wouldn't be the first time she had ignored her instincts and come close death.

Gia decided that more alcohol could be the answer. Another empty glass later she joined Robbie at the bar. His eyes followed Evie as she disappeared with his mum, then to the windows to check on Evie's children playing outside with friends. Inwardly Gia smiled, her friend deserved someone who looked at her like Robbie did. Alone with Robbie, the swirl inside her dulled. It explained why she hadn't felt it in the café. She stood straight and waited until Evie and Phoebe were out of hearing, 'You love her, don't you?' she said.

Robbie looked at her, and a little smile came out, 'I, yeah.' He gave a small nod.

It was the expression on his face that caused her next comment, she recognised the quiet frustration of issues left unaddressed, conversations never had. 'Evie is highly strung.'

'Already figured that out.' He sighed when he said it, his eyes flickering to the bar staff who were busy.

'What happened on Friday?'

'How did—? You've seen the internet pictures?'

'What internet pictures? I was travelling for fifteen hours with no internet access. My American network doesn't exist here. I have to use Wi-Fi for everything. What did I miss?'

'Nothing, someone set a fire on the farm. Atlas and Evie put it out, but someone took a photo and set it up to make it look as though Evie had created it.'

'The witch hunt is still going on?' Gia sighed, her head dropping and shoulders sloping. She shook her head once, 'After all these years?'

'Apparently. I can't mention it,' Robbie raised a hand in a small gesture of frustration.

Gia understood, 'She just shuts it down. They both do.' She didn't tell him that it was always Atlas that shut down any conversations in the beginning, then eventually Evie started to as well, as though ignoring it all would make the rumours and accusations go away. It hadn't, the rumours of witches on the farm persisted.

'Let me get yours, what are you having?'

'Same as Evie, rum and coke please.'

'Is there a story behind rum and coke?'

'Just a Caribbean holiday. The local rum was part of the all-inclusive package.'

'Nothing else?'

'No. We'd get a couple of drinks each after the evening show, take them to the beach, sit and chat. It only took a night or two and the staff recognised us and knew our routine and had our drinks ready. We swam, we chatted, we sunbathed, we read books, we did a few organised trips. No boys, no talk of university, just the seven of us cocooned on a resort.'

'It does sound right up Evie's street. Now I know her, I've no idea why she let the press think she was such a party girl.'

'She was eighteen. Even introvert eighteen-year-olds sometimes party to escape themselves. I know I still find it intense living in my head, even if I can make a living out of it.'

'Could I get the details from you? The hotel, the location and stuff? Don't tell Evie.'

'I'll see if I kept any of the details.'

A couple of hours later Gia let out a burst of loud laughter alongside Evie's softer laugh at the fun banter between Robbie and his brother. Liam clearly got a kick out of winding his brother up. For the most part, Robbie had refused to rise to the obvious baits thrown at him. When Liam retorted, Robbie maintained eye contact with his brother, but Gia saw his hand leave Evie's leg under the table to grasp her hand, put it on his own leg and covered her hand with his, all without breaking eye contact with his brother. Evie squeezed his leg lightly, as if she had needed that. She caught Gia's eye, and motioned to the ladies. Gia gave a nod.

'How do you do it?' Evie asked, when the door closed behind them, pulling out a lipstick. Gia brought out her lipstick to touch her own red up in the mirror.

'How do I do what?' she asked, not having a clue what her friend was referring to. With Evie, experience told her there was a strong chance her friend could be referring to anything. Her ability to swap and change subjects was part of what made her a great television presenter, despite her shyness in real life.

'Be such an extrovert. Fit in. It's like they've always known you and you never left.'

'I like people.' Gia shrugged, not wanting to mention the way Robbie's family made her uneasy. It wasn't the right moment. She wanted the closeness with her friend back first. It might appear that she had warmed immediately to Robbie's family, but the surface pretence belied the muddled mess it was making of her insides. She was cornered and couldn't run away without outing herself.

'You've always been good with people,' Evie sighed.

'You're doing great. I can stay as long as you need support.' Gia hadn't planned to write until that evening, Evie wasn't keeping her from anything important. The family was a riddle she was craving to solve, to unpick why they made her feel like running away the same way she would unpick a seam, stitch by stitch, unravelling it a little bit at a time. There was a thrill in flirting close to the edge and seeing the other side come apart.

'I would have stayed at the farm if you hadn't come.'

'I know. Are you OK?'

'Yes.'

On their way out Evie's phone pierced through any comment she was going to make, 'It's Atlas.' Evie walked out responding to her brother's text.

A few minutes later her own phone vibrated softly in her pocket. Gia took it out to look at it. She angled her phone away from sight as she suppressed a smile at the message from Atlas, the inference that she might want to soak all the alcohol up with some food, and to give him a text when she was done day drinking so they could go and get pizza. Gia wondered if she was reading too much into the offer, then her grandmother's hand landed on her shoulder before she could respond, and her phone was put away, with the intention of replying later, when she was alone and could form a thought beyond typing *Yes* back, yes she did want to see him again. She absorbed herself in the talk and the laughter so Evie didn't have to.

Back home inside the cosy cottage Rosa talked about a light supper for them both. Gia declined the offer of food.

She liked it when the alcohol hit her head and she opened her laptop to let out a viral spew of words and situations. It always needed cleaning up and polishing the following day, a good place to start tonight was the way Robbie's family made her feel torn apart on the inside. If she could get her character into that situation it would lead into a surprising revelation for her readers, especially those who thought they knew Valentina and who she was.

Gia emptied the last of the second bottle of wine they had opened the previous night and took the glass upstairs with her, ignoring her grandmother's disapproval with a flighty remark that drunken ramblings and sober editing had sold more books throughout history than her ten alone. The disapproval ran off her without a care, she wasn't cut from the same cloth as Rosa, she didn't have the refined personality traits that made Rosa regal and capable of moderation.

Settled on her bed, her legs under the quilt for warmth, thoughts that she never knew she had appeared on the screen in front of her, her fingers flew with a pianist's grace over the keys for a couple of hours, finding solace in the normal dark world of nightmares that nestled unseen inside her heart. Her fingers paused, mid word, when her phone lit up, the screen bright in her room. Gia had completely forgotten to reply to the text from Atlas. A smile raised itself on her face when she read the message, and responded instantly with the truth, that she had opened her laptop and forgotten about the world once she started writing in the darkness of her room. His reply told her that he was getting into the car, she couldn't turn down pizza. With a sudden rumbling stomach Gia agreed to meet him. She asked him to wait outside rather than interrupt

Rosa's activities.

Downstairs was in darkness. The fire was out and coldness had crept into the room. There were no strange shadows. The sage green curtains were drawn which was the clearest indication that Rosa had either gone out or gone to bed. Gia realised that she had been so absorbed in her screen that she didn't know which one it was. Her grandmother had not partied all night since they had arrived in England. Rosa mourned her son, but she did so privately, it was tucked away in a place Gia had seen daily but couldn't reach.

It struck her that Evie's anxiety was similar. Gia recalled the way she had watched her children with worry clear across her face. Still musing on that thought, Gia opened the cottage door and locked it behind her. The night was cold and damp, the sort of night that sank into her bones and let her know that winter was biting on the heels of autumn. She walked straight down the narrow path, not noticing the shadows that trailed at her side, fast and light, dancing away to hide in the rosehips, not even realising that she was looking forward to seeing Atlas again until her hand touched the cold handle of the door and nerves flooded her stomach. At the last second a smile threatening to take over her entire face. She pushed them back and dialled down the smile. Nerves didn't dictate her life. She was Gia – flirty, reckless and hedonistic. People entertained her, gave her their stories, she played with them much like a child with a toy. Stomach flutters over someone, a man, hadn't happened to her in a long time.

She closed the car door as quietly as she could, as though the neighbours might hear and rush to tell Rosa. Atlas had a smile on his face. She didn't notice the wool jumper or jeans, just his genuine wide smile. She met it with her own this time.

'Hello, beautiful.' She liked how he said that, how it was deep and genuine, and incredibly intoxicating. It made her head light and her heart melt into her boots. Some inward cynicism surfaced and laughed sarcastically inside. She had finally met a man who was as good and practised at this game as she was, and she was falling for all the standard lines and moves.

'So where do we get a good pizza from at this time?' she asked, at least cool and together on the outside.

'There's a wood fired pizza place in the city. It's freshly made in front of you, if you fancy a drive?' He winked when he said *drive*.

Gia tilted her chin and looked into his eyes a second before she responded, 'I love a drive. Especially at night. Watching the world fall away until it's just you and the road and nothing else is heaven.' She liked a drive, the destination never really mattered.

'You drove at night? Isn't that a bit American horror story stuff?' He started the car and set off.

'Not really. Some of the nicest people were around at night, and they definitely had stories worth hearing.'

'Is pizza OK? The takeaways nearby really haven't improved in the last ten years. I would not recommend them.'

'I think you have ill-conceived ideas about how I've been eating. America is on its own level when it comes to elevating unhealthy fast food and even street food. But good food is incredibly expensive. Convenience and profits are key, way down at the bottom of the list is taste and healthiness.'

'Then you deserve good food. Let's go to the city. What's your favourite topping?'

'Honestly, if it's really decent and freshly made with good ingredients, a classic margherita should stand alone above all others. What's yours?'

'From this place? Their everything pizza. Chicken, beef, olives, onions, peppers, jalapenos, extra cheese, I think there might be other bits I've not tasted.'

That comment was so Atlas that she laughed. The Atlas she remembered had always been hungry and ready for a meal. From what she had seen so far, he hadn't changed either.

His next comment surprised her though, 'I liked those biscuits you used to make on a Sunday and give to Evie to bring up to the farm. The hazelnut ones were my favourites. You used to bring us strudels, and stollen at Christmas. We'd wake up every Christmas morning looking forward to the stollen. Evie used to keep it in a secret hiding spot otherwise I might have eaten it before Christmas day.'

'I like making biscuits. Sometimes bread. I'm not so good at cakes. I keep saying I'll practise more, but the will-power to start always dissolves. It's easier to walk to a café and get a cake than it is to find all the equipment and ingredients I need.'

'What equipment do you need? One of those mixer things?'

'Yes. And then ingredients. Different cakes need different sized tins, and I just didn't have room in a camper van for all that. I missed bread. I made that for myself. I couldn't get used to American bread. I had one loaf tin and the rest of the time everything else was freehand, I would do focaccia in a square casserole dish.'

'You lived in a van? Was that safe?'

'I didn't think about it too much.' Gia shrugged. There were times when it had been and times when it hadn't. She had learnt to protect the van and herself. Explaining it all would ruin her mood, she was fiercely independent and protective of her decisions.

They were out of the village now and headed along the country roads towards the city. It was interesting that Atlas hadn't chosen the motorway. The world outside the car fell away until there was only the dark road made darker by patches of arching trees, and the two of them in the car. Gia loved the night. She felt her mind quieten and start to settle, all her characters and ideas packed up for the night, her body relaxed. After the way she had felt torn apart around Robbie's family, she was glad that Atlas could make her safe and grounded just by being himself.

'You should have.' His voice was quiet, not accusatory.

'Why? I could be killed crossing a road.'

'You always treated life lightly, as though you didn't care if you lived or not. Your characters have that same attitude, they mess with bigger, stronger, more knowledgeable enemies not caring that their lives are about to end.'

'You've read my books?' That amazed her.

'Yes. But why?'

'Why?'

'Why don't you care about yourself?'

'I never had any control over my life, at least not until I secretly submitted that first book to an agent, took my advance and ran away to America. If Nonna had known that I was writing a book she would have critiqued it, and she would have chosen my genre for me. I wrote it because I had this burning desire to find my own voice and my own identity away from her.'

'Why would she disapprove of what you write?' Atlas shot her a puzzled glance before he looked back at the road.

Gia chewed on whether to be honest or blasé about her answer. She chose honest, 'She would ask me to write literary literature. Nonna has a whole back story that we don't tell people about. Life was messy in Italy and what she did, what my parents did, made the community look down on us but they were also scared of us. There's a whole load of subcultures that mainstream people ignore, that's what I like to play with in my writing. We came to England to get away from our reputation, and she controlled my life out of a desperation that I didn't follow the same route as my parents. She changed from a fifteen-year-old mum and then a thirty plus grandma who was fun, sun loving, free, and spirited to a blossoming academic all serious with no party instincts at all once we got here. I still can't believe you read my books.'

'Loved Valentina. Absolutely. The whole New Orleans atmosphere and being a witch there, I loved every minute of that.'

It was her most insecure book, her first, the one where she had relied on other people's descriptions of New Orleans for. The book where she had stared at pictures of the city's streets and shops to accurately depict from her cottage bedroom whilst she attended the university where her grandmother taught. The book she had written in coffee shops in the city to avoid the quiet stillness of the village that suffocated Valentina's voice in her head, because Valentina was used to living in chaos and noise. Gia had memorised a street map of New Orleans that hung on her bedroom wall so well that when she actually flew there, she could find her way around like a local.

'You really have read them.' It surprised her, especially that Valentina was his favourite character. The fragile dark-haired witch with immense unpractised abilities, and a thousand vulnerabilities that always threatened to topple the scales in her opponents' favour had been a marmite character, yet it remained her best-selling book, consistently selling more copies each time she brought a new book out.

'Yeah. I always thought if I had a daughter, she would be called Valentina. I like the name,' Atlas said.

Gia bit her tongue about it being her middle name, that Valentina had been a badly disguised character based on herself. She had learnt a lot of lessons from her first novel, and had grown since, she changed the topic, 'I like the hair and the beard. When did that happen?' She brushed the subject of his future children with some blonde off quickly, trying to resist the urge to reach out and touch his beard. It was too familiar a gesture for her to do that.

'The hair? Gradually. I got caught up in farming. I used to go for a trim at the barbers but they changed hands and stopped opening Sundays. I tried the Turkish place until I forgot to go for a few weeks during lambing. That turned into a summer, by autumn I could tie it back, and that was six or seven years ago now. It gets a trim every now and then. The beard is still new.'

'I like it. Both suit you,' she said. Atlas beamed. He turned to glance at her, gave her a wink, then turned back to look at the headlight lit road, 'Thanks.'

Chapter 6

Atlas led her from the car park through the old part of town where some of the first older buildings still stood, and into the old corn exchange, straight to a takeaway stand. The venue was littered with tables in the centre and surrounded on all sides by vastly different drink and food stalls. The energy and noise in the hall matched what she expected to find in a club. Winter outfits contrasted against glittery miniscule club clothes, worn work boots against delicate heels, tired and weary people in uniforms coming off late shifts were queueing for takeaway food on their way home next to people dressed to party; it seemed that everyone was welcome. The seating area was packed out and people were standing with drinks in hand, filling the place. The stall took their order and gave them bulky black objects that they promised would buzz when their pizzas were ready. Atlas caught her hand, they weaved their way through the crowds and ended up at a drinks stall, 'What's your favourite drink?'

Gia squeezed his hand as she laughed, 'Rum and coke,' like he should already know the answer.

'Aside from rum and coke. I know you all have a soft spot for that.' His expression softened in a way she had never seen before, almost wistful.

'Whisky? Irish coffee? Um, probably a nice red, but not many places that I frequent do really nice reds. I'd rather have a cheap rum than drink vinegar. The red you recommended last night was good.'

'Forgive me for saying, but Rosa seemed concerned about you coming home over dinner.'

'She thinks I should have stayed in America where I've created a market and a brand. She's just worried about my finances crashing.'

'Are you?' He arched an eyebrow at the emphasis he put on the last word.

Gia paused before she answered with honesty, 'I wasn't until she mentioned it. I had loads of ideas about magic and witches in England. I mean, it's one of the first melting pots of immigrants and cultures, it had wave after wave of nomadic migrations during the ice ages, then it became an island when the ice sheets melted and was subject to invasions and attacks. Some communication must have taken place, an exchange of cultural ideas, with the nomads and tribes coming and going, then a few remaining here and settling in the beginning whilst others came and went. I refuse to believe it was all rape and murder.'

'That's interesting,' something flickered across Atlas's face that she couldn't place. If pushed Gia would describe it as apprehensive fear but it wasn't only that, it was something personal behind his eyes. He spoke again but was quieter, 'And you think that magic is in England? That there's witches?'

The air around them changed at his question, he directed the change. Gia could feel the charge in the air, the tingle of long-buried secrets on the edge of his tongue, whatever flirtatious exchange had been happening was gone. Atlas was serious now.

Gia paused before she answered. She allowed her thoughts time to click the obvious clues into place. Evie had avoided the subject earlier and when she had talked about it, evaded joining the conversation in the café after Robbie had joined them. She answered Atlas with carefully chosen words, 'I think certain people grow up with an awareness that's different from the normality of our world. They view nature differently. Maybe things happen to them or they can do things that can't be considered within the realm of normal to others. Sometimes it's not just fairy tales. I am sorry for everything you and Evie had to go through given the nickname for the farm.' She had chosen to take on the reputation of a witch and writer. Atlas and Evie hadn't had a choice. Living on the witch farm as children had been enough to label them.

'How did you find out the information that you used in your books? Did you just make it up?'

'If I made up the *American Magic* series, I could have done that in England. I went over there to find it. I found people, I asked questions, I went to parties and listened to drunken stories and noted names, then I went in search of the names for the real version.'

'You sought out the information? From actual magical practitioners?'

'There's people that claim to be witches, then there's people that actually are, and they're not always the same. There was one woman, my age, mum of four, lived the most amazing life, and she had created every aspect of that life just through her own magic. She didn't even know what she was doing really. She willed what she wanted without any fuss. She wanted a specific house, a huge mansion, that needed a lot of work. There was serious competition for it and she was outbid. I remember her saying what a pity it would be if all the higher bids amounted to nothing for the old lady, and whilst I was stood next to her the realtor called to say all the higher offers had fallen through. She renovated the place with her husband, and it was a beautiful old New Orleans mansion within months. Everything fell into place for her, the renovators, the interior, it was all smooth and perfect. I could see her abilities, but she didn't acknowledge them. The garden looked perfect after she had spent just a day in it. She was a witch, and she didn't even know. The best thing about being with her was how happy she was in her life and her community, she adored New Orleans with all her heart. I hope I can find somewhere here where I feel the same about my home and garden.'

A flash of a thought broke across Atlas's face. It was a look that she understood. He was going to chase after whatever it was that was on his mind. Gia pushed aside the need for a drink, she tilted her head to look him in the eye and asked, 'Do you want me to come with you?'

'No. This person, they're expecting me alone.'

'That's not always a good sign, Atlas,' she tried to warn him.

'I'm me. I'll be fine.' He indicated himself: tall, broad, strong, muscled.

Gia shook her head with a small sigh, 'It's not about brute strength, it's about knowledge. If someone is expecting you alone—,' at his raised eyebrow in silent reference towards his own comments about her safety in the car, Gia offered, 'No one relies on me. You have the farm and Evie.'

'Hey, don't worry. I might know more than you think.'

The sudden flash of a smile changed his demeanour and the worry vanished, his hands were heavy on her shoulders as he pushed them down in a way which released the stress that had built up from writing, and he changed the topic between them with a renewed offer of a drink.

Doubt lingered in her mind, 'Is this related to the stuff Evie was avoiding asking me about directly? I'd be more help if you were both less of an enigma and more straightforward.'

He changed again, and took his hands from her shoulders. 'Do you… you know… practice any of the stuff in your novels?'

Nervous Atlas was cute. Gia noted how one hand went into his pocket and the other rubbed his neck. Despite his size he seemed more the teenage boy she had known and less the imposing farmer he had turned into.

'My skill is words, symbols, sigils, stuff that is labelled demonic, demonology or satanic. The rest of it, I probably need to work on more. Readers want the frightening and dramatic side of being a witch, not the happy woman I told you about who simply created the life she wanted. Sometimes, in practice, I take it too far, but that's how Valentina's story got written.'

Gia didn't get a response. The pizza buzzers let them know that their orders were ready. She offered to get their drinks since Atlas hadn't let her pay for the pizza, he shook his head and sent her off to collect their pizza while he marched to a drinks stall.

Returning to Atlas amidst the buzz of the food hall which hummed with a thousand conversations, Gia found him holding a lemonade and a cocktail. He was stood deep in conversation, facing a tall thin leggy blonde with hair loose down her back. Silver earrings dangled from her ears and sparkled the same way her shoes did. She smiled and flicked her hair back flirtatiously. Gia saw a slip of a tiny pale grey silk dress that she could never wear with her curves, covered by an oversized faux fur coat in the same shade of grey. Gia hesitated. Her steps slowed. She didn't know whether to take her time or walk straight up to the pair. Remnants of her teenage brain whispered that the blonde was much more his normal type. She pushed that insecure kid back into the box, brought out her adult confidence, straightened her back, pushed her shoulders back, and swung her hips as she manoeuvred through the crowd to approach them.

A man appeared at the side of the woman, equally thin, his cheekbones prominent, his almond eyes slightly too large and a little too far apart for his face. Those dark cold glass eyes seemed to sense her, he stared directly into her as she approached. Shock passed across his face in a fraction of a second. Then it was gone. Her instincts, normally spot on, pulled her towards him chest first, as though she had a chain around her which was being tightened. It was the opposite of how she had reacted to Robbie's family in the pub. This man was calling her home. His eyes glittered with danger, a hint of a maliciously mischievous smile played on his face. Gia recognised the unhinged emotions because she experienced them too, when shit was about to hit the fan and it became playtime. Normal people didn't see other people's emotions as a playground of powder colours to stamp in.

Atlas smiled at her when he saw her and turned away from the blonde even though she was mid-sentence. He gave a nod to something on their far right. Gia glanced to see people vacating a table. In an instant the pair were over at the table, slipping into the seats before anyone else had a chance. With her back to the man it was easier to ignore him and escape the hold he seemed to have over her. Empty glasses were pushed to the side to make way for their pizza boxes and drinks. The delicious scent of freshly made pizza rose up from the opened box and her stomach rumbled, making her realise that she was hungrier than she thought. Gia burnt the roof of her mouth on the first bite. Despite that, she carried on eating.

Her silence seemed to push Atlas to say, 'That was Louise. I didn't know she was back. Last I heard she was in London. We were over a long time ago, she wanted city lights,' Atlas offered.

Gia raised her eyes to look at his face, and shrugged to show she didn't care. She assumed that he was talking about the blonde who had been flirting with him. 'You always did have a reputation for going for the wholesome look, the princesses. You were the wolf of Oak Hall blondes.' She would lay bets that Louise in the daytime wore crisply starched shirts with a jumper over them, smart trousers and tied her hair back into the perfect bouncy ponytail.

'I didn't—' he started protesting.

Gia smiled, 'You did. After you had sex with them you didn't want them anymore and moved onto the next challenge. Every girl in your year thought they could change the bad boy if you gave them a chance. Didn't you notice how many brunettes went blonde when you were at sixth form?'

'That's not true!' His brow furrowed in protest.

Gia raised her eyebrows at him, 'It's not?'

'I finished things with my girlfriends the moment I realised that they were pretending to like Evie and they tried to stop her being around us. I was all she had. I wasn't going to invite people around who made her life harder or isolated her further.'

That hit Gia hard, a slap in the face. His consideration of his sister was more than she had ever given to anyone, except perhaps, on occasions, her friends. She looked back through all their reasonings about the end of his relationships and realised that none of them had ever put Evie as the third in the relationship. They had formed wild theories, speculated, the one that she had quoted to Atlas was the popular version, 'That puts a different perspective on things.'

It endeared him even more, that even in the midst of teenage hormones he had the sweet nature to consider his sister's feelings and look after her. She changed the subject to the farm, it had grown dramatically since she left the village, hearing about the countryside from a farmer's perspective might help one of her budding plotlines. Gia freely shared the plot details that she had with Atlas. He promised her help with her farming knowledge whenever she needed it, with a wink and a smile. Gia quizzed him on a couple of points. The change of direction in conversation suited Atlas, he happily ate his pizza and talked about the farm. In the noise of the food hall, sat in the midst of a bustling city, talking about the farm in October seemed at odds with the vitality around them.

When they left, the door closed behind them leaving the warmth, noise and exuberance of the food hall behind. The cold hit her gradually, Gia wrapped her arms around herself to keep warm. The night was cloudy, she looked around for the moon. Atlas put an arm around her and pulled her tight against him. She leaned into him for warmth on the short walk to the car. The way was well lit in an older part of the city where pubs had taken over empty churches and shops, and it seemed that there was nothing in the locality except bars and takeaway food shops.

'You know what we need?'

'What?'

'A night market. We don't have those in the UK.'

'It'd be a disaster with our drinking habits.' He laughed.

If she had expected Atlas to let her go when they reached his car, he didn't. He unlocked the car with his fob but stood between her and the door leaving no room to open it.

There was a hesitation, Gia broke the silence, 'That was a good pizza. In case I forget to say later, I enjoyed it. Thank you.'

'Look, am I? if I'm…' He reached up to rub his neck again, but at the same time he took another tiny step to enclose her between the car and his body. Gia was aware of his size more than ever as he loomed over her, she raised her hand and put it on his chest. He put his own hand over hers, his fingers twisted round her own and filled her cold hand with warmth. Atlas leaned closer, he rested his other forearm against the car, still holding the car fob in a fist. For a time there was darkness and silence, her heartbeat filled her body, aided by the warmth and proximity of his. She met his grey eyes that held sparks of shimmering gold and made a note to bring it up sometime. She thought that there was a moment, a second when he would have kissed her, he lowered his head, then he turned away and left her open to the cold. He shook his head and muttered that it didn't matter, it was impossible. He pulled the car door open for her.

Slightly bewildered, Gia climbed into the car and waited until Atlas was pulling out of the car park before she spoke. She turned towards him. He looked ahead with a focused intensity, seemingly trying hard not to say whatever it had been that he wanted to say. Gia prompted him instead, 'What's impossible?' She watched the struggle move across his face, the way his jaw clenched as he fought to hold back what he wanted to say, his eyes narrowed at the inner corner. She reached over and touched his arm, 'Saying it might be easier than bottling it up.'

He glanced at her hand on his arm. Gia swiftly moved it back into her space, noticing that Atlas tightened his grip on the steering wheel as they took the road that would lead them to the motorway. Gia steeled herself for a silent trip. The flirty texts had been fun, but clearly Atlas had changed his mind. Perhaps his ex-girlfriend had reminded him of the women he liked. He had a type. There was a reason he had been known as the wolf of Oak Hall blondes in his final few years.

'It's going to sound crazy, but there was a moment this morning, I could have sworn that your bed was in my caravan, you were there, just beautiful. Your hair was down and fluffy and mussed up, and you were looking at me with those big soft brown eyes of yours, it's impossible, I must have still been half asleep.'

Gia stared in front of her through the windscreen. It took her a long few seconds before she admitted, 'Not so impossible.'

Chapter 7

Atlas was taut. The whole atmosphere in the car was strained. Gia turned away from him and described the morning, what he had pulled from his drawer, his caravan room, and what he had worn. She finished with, 'I was asleep, I thought it was just a dream. I'm sorry you got tangled in my mess.'

'You did that?'

'I don't know, I need to work out why it happened. I said I use words, spells, I've never done anything like that. There was no spell, it wasn't intentional.' She lifted a hand and waved it around, she used her hands more than she needed to when she talked, she was doing it now.

'It's never happened before?' he asked. His brow was furrowed and he looked concerned.

'No.' She shook her head to emphasise her point.

Atlas relaxed and smiled at that. 'Does that mean we have something?' His tone was much lighter, was teasing her. She smiled back, her stress lifted at seeing his worry dissipate.

'Possibly.'

The strained tension left the car with the city, and their return journey filled the car with the same warm conversation and laughter as before.

Atlas pulled up outside Rosa's cottage. Gia unfastened her car seatbelt and picked up her bag. Atlas turned to face her and placed gentle fingers on her arm, 'I'm an idiot. I should have just kissed you at the car. When that thing happened this morning, honestly all I wanted was to get into bed with you, whisper good morning and take the sleepiness out of your eyes in the best way possible. I'm going to go and sort my shit out and then I'll be free to help you figure out what happened this morning.'

The assumption immediately riled her. Unwanted anger threatened to spill from her mouth. Gia had never needed help or assistance with her magic before. It was the one thing that truly belonged to her alone, and wasn't imposed onto, or conditioned into her. She replied before she even thought about her words, 'If I want help, I have a voice of my own to ask for it, Atlas. Just like you have. If you want my help and experience, come and ask me, I'll be there for you. I haven't been the one denying who I am for years.'

Gia heard the car engine remain still behind her as she unlocked the door to the cottage. She refused to turn her head and look back. The door closed on her urge to run back to Atlas and kiss him. Her head told her that he wasn't in the right place for her. Not yet. It would be a mess. Not a fun mess like she made for herself with lovers in America but a disastrous mess, like Italy. Italy had been messy, with friends and gangs, *family* dinners that stretched into a long night filled with music and wine. Sometimes she thought she remembered glimpses, feelings of those hot nights, music played by neighbours, laughter fuelled by alcohol, the swirl of dresses as people danced.

Alcohol and dancing had led to shouting. The shouting frequently turned into fights. Sometimes she thought she remembered the sound of guns firing, but that could be confusion after spending so long in America. When she had reached England with her grandmother, it had been the two of them, and life became so much quieter and smaller. Neighbours didn't shout hello. The people in the shops didn't know who she was. Rosa had repackaged the pair of them into a simple, clean, neat, low-key grandmother and grandchild, forever working towards the next goal.

Rosa had left their messy life behind. Gia had loved the chaos of that early life, she loved dancing with the grown-ups, watching the fights kick off with butterflies in her stomach and anticipating who the winner would be. The splatter of blood fascinated her. She knew who punched the hardest from the pattern of the splatters. Her dad got angry and punched anyone who touched her mum the way he did. He punched well. Gia closed her eyes and tucked the gleeful six-year-old back inside the part of her she had escaped from. She could not let the chaos that simmered beneath the composed surface out until she left the village.

Whilst she was here, she had to be the granddaughter that they all believed she was, just the slightly rebellious woman in the red leather jacket that wrote books. Nothing more. With the hard coldness of the door against her back, her thoughts jumping over whether she could risk a one-night stand with her friend's older brother without it affecting a long-standing friendship, Gia didn't turn on any lights. The comfort of the shadows that she could relax in changed in an instant. A familiar terror gripped her, tightening around her body, her muscles involuntary tensing as much as possible. This was a thing that you couldn't see, only sense. She never quite knew where it was, only that it was looking at her and she shouldn't be downstairs.

It didn't seem to matter how many times she encountered entities, human fear always kicked in. It was an instinctive reaction that even now, many years later, she still had to force herself to remain still and breathe steadily through those first terrifying moments, knowing that to roll with the fear meant that it subsided a little quicker now than ten years ago. A faint smokiness, familiar to late autumn nights hit her. She wondered if Rosa had left something on in the kitchen by accident, then her brain reasoned that it was probably her own clothes after the food hall.

Gia weighed up her options, she could face whatever it was, challenge it, or go to bed. Her inner self was too near the surface to stay under control, and her grandmother was asleep upstairs. The combination did not bode well for a quiet confrontation. She heard scraping by the table. Gia switched the stair light on and flooded part of the downstairs with light, before she made her way up. She left whatever it was downstairs in the dark. She turned her bedroom light on, then the bedside lamps, and left them on whilst she used the bathroom, turning off the lights behind her. Gia dropped her clothes on the floor in a rush and jumped into bed. She bundled the covers up over her head and closed her eyes. Her phone pinged but she didn't move, she left it where it was, inside her bag on the bedroom floor. She kept her eyes closed and counted her breaths, the slow deep breaths of someone asleep. A presence loomed over her. The downstairs one was territorial. It rarely ventured upstairs, although that wasn't to say it never had.

Gia counted three breaths. Without giving herself

time to reconsider, she sat bolt upright, wrapped the quilt around her and stared directly into the spot where the blackness concentrated the most to become impenetrable to human eyes.

'What?' she demanded.

'Your familiarity with the darkness is enchanting.' It gripped her face with its clawed fingers.

'Again, what?' Her lack of decorum and refusal to dance to the rituals prescribed by some old scholar of a bygone age annoyed this one, it liked to feel in control through the rituals. 'Leave.'

The entity was gone, the intense blackness lightened into normal darkness. Sleep was a long way off after that exchange. Gia retrieved her phone. The last message was from Atlas, *I'm sorry. I'm a presumptive idiot. How can I make it up to you?*

Gia let out a half smile and relaxed her body. Her mood lifted as a playful, light-hearted reply came to her instantly, *I'm pretty shallow. Good food and wine works well for apologies. You're going to have some work beating that pizza though.* She pulled her pillow down the bed and curled up in the centre. Her hands slid underneath the crisp, cotton pillowcase and she rested her head over them on the top of the pillow, it was her comfort position. Gia closed her eyes.

When she woke, the cottage held all the quietness and coldness of her being its only occupant. Gia couldn't suppress a few undesired shivers. She was dressed and her hair was in its customary low bun within minutes. She wore her thick wavy hair the same way with some variation, worn slightly messy for casual days, neat for academic days, and slicked back, decorated with a jewelled comb on formal occasions. Her make-up was as easy and as practised as her hair, black cat eye in liquid liner, fawn eye-shadow to give a hint that she cared but pale enough to not look as though she had tried too hard, and a red lipstick.

Her signature style had become a habit. Most of the time it meant she didn't have to think at all about how she looked. That was part of the reason she had purposefully curated a distinctive signature style, but occasionally she wished she had a more expansive wardrobe and different looks, like Evie did. Evie switched up styles daily. Then she reminded herself that Evie had a whole host of hair and make-up advice on hand from studio experts, whilst Gia had chosen to write in solitude as a career. The contrast was amusing. Shy, sweet, slightly feral Evie in a career more fitting to extroverts, whilst Gia, a people loving thrill seeker, worked alone in any place that could fit a notepad or laptop.

As she made her way downstairs Gia made a mental note to get a thick winter loungewear set and some slippers for walking around the house, alongside warmer clothing. In the kitchen she mused over her grandmother's coffee machine for a few minutes, looking intently at the settings and selections, before expertly making herself the perfect morning coffee. Her past barista experience showcased itself as she worked with the machine. She wondered, as she often did, how many readers had unknowingly had a coffee made by her before she'd hit the bestseller lists several times over and her name had become well known. She had worked in low key coffee places, cash in hand, terrified that any day she'd have to call Rosa and tell the truth about blowing her advance and student loan on a camper van.

Her next few days fell into a quiet routine. Gia entered the familiar self-enclosed obsessional wrap of a writing spurt, frequently forgetting to eat and existing on coffee until Rosa came home. She woke up excited and full of ideas, and then went to bed in the early hours with tired, barely legible scribbled notes in her notebook, crossing out old ideas that hadn't worked and updating them with fresh developmental twists that might contribute to the complexity of the plot. The fire spat and crackled warm orange flames every time Gia sat down with her coffee and laptop on the settee. She answered work emails, ignored the fan emails that had somehow appeared more and more frequently into her new inbox, stared at the religious zealots who had found her email and seemed to make it their life purpose to harass her, then opened her current work and started writing.

Mornings gave way to afternoons, clear autumn skies to wispy white clouds that grew greyer, unnoticed by Gia. The heavy clouds drew a premature veil over the sky that only encouraged the night darkness to arrive before its time, all of which she didn't see. Gia was lost to the characters forming in her head in the quietness of the cottage, their voices their own, the narration hers, the action playing out like a film inside her mind, occasionally returning to reality to top up the fire with another dry brown log, and make a drink before she wrapped herself back up in a rose-patterned knitted blanket and continued to type away at the screen in front of her, her eyes rarely leaving it.

Rosa came home late in the evenings. The sudden soft noise of the door opening always caused Gia to look up and over her shoulder. Rosa would take her raincoat off, then she would always lift her laptop from her bag and place it onto the stairs before she sat down on a stair to take off her boots. Gia always blinked as the world intruded into her head, fighting for space that only seconds before had been filled with characters and scenes more real than the one she was in. Today she jumped up, untangling herself from the cosy blanket she had been wrapped up in.

'What have you been doing all day?' was always Rosa's first question.

Gia had been giving her vague answers the last few days, uncertain as to the direction of her new work. She didn't want to talk until her book had a definitive outline formed by a three-quarters drafted novel that she could commit to. Now, Gia pushed a strand of hair that had strayed from her bun back behind her shoulder before she answered, 'Writing mostly. The bridge between *American Magic* and a new series. A few emails to my agent.'

'You're working again?'

'I never stopped.' Her face crinkled in confusion at the statement from her grandmother, and the assumption that her writing career was over.

'I thought you said you'd come back to England for something new.'

'A new book. *American Magic* is done for now. I wrote the first one when I was nineteen, Nonna, it was published when I was twenty. I'm thirty-one now. I'm working on a book series set elsewhere, this one is in England.'

'That's eleven years of writing and you've been living in a van. Maybe it's time to finish your degree and find a more viable career?'

'Did you have a bad day today? I'll make dinner. Go

and have a nice shower. Get warm, put on comfy clothes, I'll bring you a glass of wine in your room in a minute.' Gia hastened to the kitchen, certain that they had some wine left. Her grandmother was much like herself, crabby and sassy when hungry. For a moment Rosa looked almost grateful. She gave a nod and went upstairs carrying her boots.

A glance in the half-filled cupboards showed Gia enough for her to make a quick decision about dinner. She poured two glasses of wine and carried one upstairs to her grandmother as promised, then started on a simple dinner, pasta with tomato, onion and herb sauce, spinach as a side, and a salad starter. She juggled cooking alongside baking some very simple biscuits for later in the evening with their cup of tea or coffee, from one of the first recipes she had ever learnt for biscuits, a simple, rustic mix of flour, butter and sugar, plus whatever else she wanted to add for flavour. One batch she mixed with grated lemon zest and another batch had chopped hazelnuts scattered over the top. Dinner was ready and on the set table just as Rosa reached the bottom of the stairs. Gia took Rosa's empty wine glass from her hand and refilled it. Rosa glanced at the biscuits cooling on the side. She didn't say anything, but she gave a minute nod of approval and sat down.

Gia stayed up late that night, typing all her ideas into an outline and breaking it down into chapter plans to send to her agent in the hope that she wasn't entirely misguided and that she did indeed have something worth pursuing. It would be an unexpected development for her character, to have moved continents. She had enough of a draft outline to know Valentina's new story.

The first light scratches she missed, unaware. The

second registered but didn't disturb her, it was part of the cottage and its symphony, a tune that she had grown up with. Awareness hit when the darkness changed, it loomed over her, filling the space. A primal bubbling inside her stomach made her look up, recognition inside her body that she wasn't alone any longer. She stood up and drew herself to her full height, 'Don't. Even. Start.'

An anger rose up in her that caused her to speak out of turn. Used to being left alone in the camper van to work, interruptions had been rare, and they were always unappreciated. This thing might be territorial but she wasn't about to let it interfere with her writing. She had done nothing to offend it. Shadows lengthened and twisted around in the room. It appeared to shrink back, immediately Gia wondered if that reaction was her imagination. It reached out. Expecting the normal claws to grip her face or her arm Gia wrapped her hand around what she perceived to be an arm before it could get her, her movement instinctive. Beneath her closed hand it was bony, covered in short rough hairs, her fingers easily fitted around it.

If she didn't concentrate so hard on the central patch of darkness but looked at the peripheral edges, she could see it too. It stooped over, taller than the ceiling, thin, out of proportion and grotesque, its rectangular shaped face held two seed-shaped holes for nostrils, its eyes were enormous and yellow-orange, its mouth was almost a keyhole shape. What passed as a chest curved inwards, Gia had seen the same starved effect on homeless drug addicts in the summer sun when they wandered around shirtless in the States. Bony legs resembling hare or rabbit hind legs were crouched and bent to accommodate its height.

It was stronger than she was, despite the skeletal appearance. When it shook her off, she flew upwards and banged her head hard on the ceiling. She didn't fall downwards, the shadows moved and wrapped themselves around her. She felt nothing from them, they were neither cold nor warm, they didn't hold her tight or loose. The thing pushed its face into hers. Rotten breath gassed her, as though meat decomposed in its dirty teeth.

She glimpsed pointed sharp fangs as it hissed, 'The shadows will come for you, defiant one.'

The last breath it fanned over her was too much. Gia's eyes rolled back, her stomach heaved, the world went black.

Chapter 8

Her head pounded, she was on the hard surface of the floor when her eyes opened again. Tentatively she touched the back of her head and found dried blood. With a deep breath she pushed herself up and saw her laptop was exactly where she had left it, plugged in and charging. Her phone lay face down on the floor, the red case had leftover stickers on it from her last book launch, plus some that she had been gifted in PR boxes for a pre-publication endorsement that her publishers could put on the release cover.

When she shook those thoughts out of her head, pain shot through her skull and neck. She picked up her phone. A piece of glass edged into her finger before she had even turned it over. A tiny pool of red blood gathered. Gia turned over the phone gently and looked at the damage, the screen was shattered completely. She couldn't scroll or take a call without having a shard of glass wedge itself in her. Gia put it next to her laptop. A new one had been on her to do list, the list that she had compiled in her camper van full of excitement and hope, between packing her clothes into suitcases, and advertising the van with all its existing contents for sale. She had been left with no choice now, a new phone was needed. There were jobs that she did on her phone that she didn't like to do on her laptop. Her laptop was her career and she tried to keep internet connections on it minimal, her phone was for emails, social media and research.

Gia checked the time on her laptop. It was still early. She had time to tidy up, put her things away, shower and dress before her grandmother started asking questions. Gia could already imagine the disapproval about her falling asleep downstairs and not going to bed. Since learning to understand societal conventions and structures at university, Rosa had instilled social contexts and the subtlety of cultural narratives into Gia, until even at a young age Gia had understood that perceptions of her were as important as her actual behaviour, because the perception was internalised by her teachers and the villagers, and it would remain the same even if there was evidence otherwise. As Rosa had said years ago, 'Atlas and Evie only get away with their wildness because the villagers fear the reputation of the farm, and the teachers see all their work completed to a high standard so their disruption in class is dismissed as intelligence and boredom.'

Gia took herself upstairs for a shower. She turned the shower on and started to undress as steam filled the room. The first application of shampoo caused her to wince as she washed her hair under the hot water. That job done, she closed her eyes and let the water run over her. In her mind she could still see the thing, the hideous monster that had plagued her childhood in the cottage. Intuitively she under-stood, deep down in a primal part of her understanding that didn't require words or reasoning, that this was a being from the times before humans built cities. Another race, a link to the so-called demons she was searching for answers to, the things that brought fear in the dark.

Out of the shower Gia used her body oil, temporarily smelling of neroli and musk until it dried into her skin. She chose a scoop neck red maxi dress that was hanging in her wardrobe. One of the things she had been thankful for in an Italian grandmother was that Rosa imparted a harsh critique of her clothing choices growing up, but had been generous with praise when she got it right, explaining why the cut suited her. Thus, she wore a scooped neck long length dress made from a thick soft jersey material. Gia loved the long sleeves on it. She had taken off the thin, fabric belt that it came with on the first wear. Today she chose a patterned belt, one that had a sand background bearing a black, white and red tartan pattern, pairing it with black tights, and the black lace-up boots she had worn to fly home.

She turned her attention to make-up. Whilst her brain wanted to do something different, her hands went through their routine motions with a will of their own, deftly applying her signature look. When she was finished, she looked in the mirror at her reflection trying to work out a new look for her features, utterly fed up with the Gia Roselli signature style. It had become dull and predictable now, where she used to be excited to jump out of bed to look like herself, now she wished that she hadn't spent ten years curating one look, one palette of colour. In hindsight, she'd taken the idea of a brand far too seriously.

Gia pulled her thoughts away from make-up and towards coffee. She needed a coffee. Whenever she was in this mood, she would sit with her caffeine and phone to scroll through make-up looks, today she would have to settle for her laptop on the breakfast bar instead.

She was absorbed in the images she had pulled up, savouring the coffee she had made, when a slight noise behind her made her turn sharply. Rosa was surveying the ceiling, her glasses held up instead of on, she was lifting them away from her face and pulling them closer, as though she couldn't quite see properly.

'You OK, Nonna?' Gia asked as casually as she could.

'What did you do to him?'

'What did I do? Nothing. He's been coming after me for years. Wait, you know about him?' She failed to keep the surprise out of her voice.

'Of course. He's a mischievous ghost. Keys and other little bits go missing, but if you ask nicely they reappear in a different spot. He likes the house quiet and tidy. Sometimes I think it's your dad, he followed us here and he's just letting us know he's still around.'

'What if it's not, what if this thing was here before we came?' Gia challenged. She knew her father, or rather, she knew the memories she held of him, and quiet, or tidy, did not fit any of them. In her short bank of memories about him, he had been a rowdy troublemaker. Her grandmother stared at her for a minute, she blinked twice as she processed what Gia had thrown at her.

'Well, it is England, my dear. Every building comes with one. I'm going to take this coffee in my travel cup. If you two anger each other one of you needs to move.' Rosa searched the dishwasher for her stainless-steel mug. Gia was too stunned by the simplicity of her grandmother's assumptions to remember that she wanted to ask for a lift to the city to get a new phone. She went back to her pictures and her coffee. Then she got up and made another cup of coffee, still stunned.

A few hours later gentle knocking on the back door interrupted Gia's spiral into an ever more confusing search for phone contracts on her laptop. She opened the door to find Evie there. The day was grey, not yet drizzling or raining, but the pale grey sky cast a muted mellowed light on the ground. Gia made way for Evie to enter. It was just like old times. Evie had never used their front door, she had always slipped around to the back of the cottage, through the gardens, to use the back door. She told Gia once that she liked the walk around describing it as pretty at the sides, then an explosion of Italy once the back opened up. Her grandmother had planted a few herbs in a couple of raised beds for them to use in cooking. Beyond the raised beds was Rosa's cut flower garden, less Italian and more English, her grandmother had gone for a choice of year-round plants, the variety was small but the growing season long. She had finished off the garden with fruit trees; the old apple tree had come with the cottage, but the cherries, figs and plums were her choosing. Three times a year Rosa went out and actively tackled the growth in the blackberry hedgerow, cutting it back and down.

'Sorry, I did text you,' Evie apologised.

'I dropped my phone. I'm actually just looking up a UK contract and phone. Who do you use?'

In response Evie reeled off a name, and told Gia that if she went with certain other networks she would never get a signal in the village. Coverage was hit and miss in the village. Gia offered her a coffee. Evie nodded, her eyes widening in hope of caffeine.

'Isn't it still half term?' Gia asked her friend, noticing that Evie was alone.

'Yes. What are you doing tonight?'

'Nothing,' Gia shrugged.

'We're going to head to the community centre for the bonfire and fireworks that the scouts put on. Do you fancy coming? There will be a wine stand, their jacket potatoes have gotten good the last few years, there's a hog roast thing, the firework display is excellent, especially for the five-pound entry price. They've had to move it from the scout hut to bigger premises because so many people started turning up. And the more people they have, the more money they spend on fireworks so each year it just gets bigger and better.'

'You had me at wine and fireworks.' Gia nodded.

'Great, we'll stop by and pick you up around five and walk down. The bonfire is lit at half past six, the fireworks start at seven and everyone is heading home at eight. Then, next, what are you doing not this coming Friday but the one after?'

'Right now, all my days are the same. I stay here and either write or look for houses online.'

'You're looking for a house?'

'Yeah, not in the village though. As much as I'm in love with the idea of a flat above a shop on the high street that has a pretty balcony so I can people watch, there's no flats and I can't afford the cottages next to the high street in the village. When did it get so expensive for something so small?' The minimum price for a pretty village property like her grandmother's cottage was higher than she had estimated, the exquisite large houses on the outskirts of the village were the same price which seemed absurd.

Evie answered her, 'It was building up for a while, then it exploded after covid, when city people decided that they could work from home whilst living in the country. I can't complain, they spend a lot of money in the café and the farm shops.'

Gia gestured for them both to take their coffees and

sit down. Evie remarked that Atlas had mentioned Rosa had decorated the cottage. She said how nice it looked. Gia patiently took Evie back to the mention of the Friday, because she knew Evie would run away with the conversation and realise too late that she hadn't told her.

'I try and take Friday off from everything, the farm and work, so I was wondering if you either wanted a spa day or to go shopping in the city? But if you want to go house shopping, I can drive you around, and Robbie can give you an opinion from a builder's perspective.'

'I'm looking in Eastwood or the estates nearby. They have better public transport that side of town and lower house prices.'

The better public transport was only because it was a poorer area and people relied on the bus services more than they did in the village. Bus services in the village had been barely acceptable when she left; one bus an hour that had meandered slowly through the narrow village streets. Now it was one bus every two hours that stopped on the main road through the village only. Rosa had told her that much, and that if it wasn't for home delivery a few of the more elderly residents would have had to sell up and move elsewhere. Without a car Gia couldn't justify putting all her savings into a house in the village because she wanted to be there.

'Robbie grew up that side of town. He knows those houses. I really wanted to stop by and apologise for this week. I've wanted to catch up since Sunday, it's just, stuff sort of got in the way.' Evie was nervous in the same manner Atlas had been when trying to ask about magic.

'It's fine, Evie. You have two children and its half term.'

'Not that, it's, I, there was, um, you know how you were so open about magic on Sunday?'

'Yes. You shut down as soon as Robbie came back to the table in your café.' In that instant Gia knew both siblings had a secret.

'Something huge happened on Halloween and I've been dealing with the fall out since.'

'Is everyone OK?' Immediately her thoughts turned to Atlas and wondered if it concerned anything he had done following their conversation the night before Halloween over their pizza. She wanted to ask, but held back and waited for Evie to tell her. Evie would close down if she sensed Gia's enthusiasm to talk about the topic.

'Yes. Possibly a little scarred by it. Some of us have more to process than others. Maybe I should just show you, before I tell you anything. Are there any cameras in your garden?'

'No.'

Evie put her drink on the coffee table and hastened outside. Gia followed her. Evie crouched down and indicated for Gia to do the same. Gia bent down over the still green damp grass and looked at the water droplets. Evie stretched a hand low over the grass. Dark green ink jumped and danced around her hand and fingers. After five seconds Evie closed her hand and pulled it away. Gia looked at the still green grass, now without water droplets. She was about to ask Evie what was supposed to happen when she looked behind her friend. She stood up and turned around in a circle. A triple circle of ghostlike hare's foot inkcap mushrooms surrounded the pair of them, the mushrooms' mature frilly gilled surface upturned to the pale grey skies. Evie turned around, wonder on her face.

'OK, that's new, I'm still figuring out exactly what I can do. Mushrooms are easier to explain than flowers and fruit this time of year. Please don't tell me I'm a freak.'

'I— Evie— this is off the scale.'

'You said you had seen magic.' Her friend flicked her hair to the side, worry across her face.

'I have. But this is phenomenal.' Gia enthused. She turned around the full circle to look.

'Oh,' Evie's face fell, and to Gia, the gulf between them felt wider than ever.

'What?'

'It's nothing. Forget it.' Evie shut down the way she always had when people had talked about witches on the farm, she had a blank face, and her hands were pushed into her pockets.

'No, don't back out on me now. I'm honoured that you trusted me with this secret. Tell me.' Gia tried to encourage her friend to open up.

'I had an insane theory. I remembered the seven-pointed stars that Genevieve used to draw, and I sort of maybe thought perhaps we could all do something.' The words were soft and hesitant, as if expecting to be laughed at.

'Magic?'

'Yes.' When she looked into Evie's disappointed face Gia wanted to take her friend in a hug and tell her she might be right, at least about the two of them.

'What if I tell you that my magic is words and sigils? That I can summon entities?' Gia offered her own specialism up to Evie to keep her on the topic. Evie had always shut down any mention of witches or magic. The history of the farm was a taboo subject.

'How do you summon entities?' Evie was less cautious than she had been on Sunday with Robbie around. Her expression turned open and curious, not the mask Gia had previously seen.

'I'll show you, let's go inside and finish our coffee whilst I do it.'

'You make it sound so casual,' Evie's brow furrowed.

Gia shrugged. 'It is, I've been doing it since I was a child.'

'You never said anything.'

'It became second nature to hide it. Girls are especially cruel, they will instantly detect the slightest difference or hint of weirdness and be merciless. We saw what they did to Tess's stepsisters, and they weren't even too different.'

'They were different. I think they would have fitted in better if their mother hadn't tried so hard to make them stand out. Nina and her sisters came from the same background, but they slid into Oak Hall and fitted in because April didn't make them stand out. I wasn't worried about bullying, I was worried about the rumours being true about Witch Farm.'

'I was terrified that you'd all look at me like a freak and I wouldn't have friends anymore,' Gia admitted.

'Show me what you do.' It was a quiet request, spoken softly.

Once inside the cottage they became warm again. The fire spilled out heat with a fresh log on it and the back door was closed against the chill of late autumn. Gia drew a circle in chalk rescued from her suitcase, scribbled a few sigils around the edge whilst Evie asked the meaning of each one. Gia explained that her sigils were words drawn as a simplified shape. In the back of her mind each one had a purpose, she wanted revenge on the thing that had attacked her without provocation. She drew the spell to draw the house entity into the circle and visible. When she walked around the circle citing the words to call it forward a greige mist formed. Evie had the foresight to take her cup of coffee from the settee to the sitting room window and close the curtains. A precaution Gia almost always forgot.

As she had expected, the mist inside the circle turned murkier, a dirty shade that wasn't quite grey or brown but something else, then it formed itself into the oversized creature Gia had seen. Evie, mid sip with the coffee cup at her mouth, lowered the cup. Her eyes turned big and wide as she stared, but Gia didn't detect a hint of fear from her. Either she trusted Gia completely, or she had seen far worse. The hairy brown thing stooped downwards, its hunched back touching the ceiling, its concave chest and skeletal frame now contrasted with its thick hind legs. It tried to reach out with both arms to grab the women. Flashes of lightning hit it when it tried to extend its arms beyond the circle.

'What are you?' Gia asked.

'I am many things in your language,' it smirked, folding its arms and settling in.

'Name the many things we call you in our language that are true.' Gia watched the smirk go. An ancient intelligence danced in its eyes. It seemed to know how to play with words just like she did. That didn't faze her.

'You know more than I credited you with, child of the fae.' It failed to answer, but redirected the conversation, a tactic she had experienced before.

It had her interest now. She took a moment to dissect the information. It could be playing. It could be lying. It was a ploy to get out of telling her what she wanted, a distraction technique. Except the doubt in her head told her that lying whilst inside a circle had never been possible before. Redirection and word games certainly, but never a lie. Her brain raced. She tried to convince herself that it was simply a distraction that had worked, it had thrown her off balance. Nothing had ever said that to her before.

'Is my fae blood why you hate me?' As impulsive as ever she dived into the topic.

'Yes.' The answer was hissed, full of hatred. In that instant Gia could not doubt the truth of what had been said before.

'How do you know?' She put her emphasis on the word you. She didn't want it to see her unbalanced by that statement. She would process that in her own time.

'We always know one of our own, no matter how many pathetically short human life spans the lineage passes through.'

'Is my grandmother a child of the fae too?'

'No.'

That answer made sense to her. It had never attacked or terrorised her grandmother the way it had her. Rosa thought it nothing but a ghost. Since her childhood, Gia had been terrified of the thing in the dark that left scratch marks on her skin. It had probably watched her early attempts to call spirits in a circle.

'When did you know?'

'When you returned.'

Gia worked hard to keep a blank face at that answer, her confusion wanted to show itself. Her next question broke her own rules, she had never let the conversations get personal before, no matter how much the entities had thrown supposed revelations about her life at her. Gia folded her arms, 'So why hate me as a child?'

'You were an easy prey. No one believes the children when they talk of creatures in the house.'

She planned her next words carefully, they were nothing more than a wild guess, a shot in the dark, an attempt at answers after it had thrown her whole world upside down, 'I challenge you to tell me which fae. You couldn't possibly name one that goes so far back.'

The answer was a snort. Then silence. Then, in a less aggressive, more passive voice and compliant manner, it dipped its head, 'Your lineage goes back many centuries. Your blood belongs to an ancient resting king, a winter king. When we walked the earth alongside the humans, of us gods, they would sing.'

'Does his kin still live?' Even as she spoke the words, she scorned herself for the vulnerability, a hope thrown out into the open for some living family other than her grandmother.

'No. All danced to their deaths by the queen.'

'How do you determine that I'm from a winter king?'

'Ripening blood creates feuds and revelry. Resting blood ends all with hunts and fights. Spring Court blood smells of sunshine and daytime, light and flowery, Winter Court blood smells of the last blackberries, the first frosts and the richness of forest nights.'

'Did you forget the Summer and Autumn Courts?'

'You think your modern definitions are the only ones?' Its voice rose, it sneered. It didn't hide its dislike of her. This was the bully her younger self had feared was hidden amongst her peers. 'There was once the ripening, the harvesting and the resting seasons to your human kin in ancient times, you copied from us, you learnt the signs. Aeons ago the Harvest Royal Court were wiped out, the daughter taken to the Resting Court for a queen, the son raised in the Ripening Court.'

Gia was torn. On one hand, she needed to know what this thing was. On the other hand, she wanted to know about her fae blood. It sensed her indecision and sneered at her, its hostility returned.

'Fae don't hesitate. You'll never be one. You could be so much more yet even your words are used sparingly, instead of being a weapon you use them as a tool. Words are power. You have no idea of the magic that runs through your veins.'

'What are you?' she snapped.

The circle pulsed with iridescent light in response. 'You call me a brownie, a house spirit, a hearth sprite.' The reply was softer, still hateful but spat out barely above a whisper, some fear showing in its eyes. Gia didn't know what she had done, she would analyse it later. She shut down the circle and dismissed it, forbidding it to hurt her friend. She cleaned the chalk off the floor.

Only when she had finished, she heard Evie's voice, 'That was, Gia, I don't think I even have the words. You just, conjured up a brownie that looks nothing like what a brownie should look like. And you, he said you had fae blood.'

'I'm certain he was playing with words. Twisting the truth. It's what they do, Evie, you can't take any of it at face value. Words are different to them. It's a demon. I've dealt with them for years.'

'Consider, for a moment, when you got a little angry the effect that had on the circle, the light it created. You think what I can do is big? You're a whole other level. You have to explore what it's just told you.'

'I need to get a phone,' was all Gia could muster. She was still knocked sideways by the revelation. All she could think was that she needed a strong coffee or a full bottle of wine.

'I can't leave you after that. If it goes wrong you need a way to contact me, or Atlas. Robbie took Max and Rey to the park whilst I stopped by. Why don't I come back with them and the car and we can drive to the city, have some lunch, and get you a phone?'

'Sure. Only someone who's a witch would take that in their stride, Evie. You were so unfazed by it,' Gia smiled conspiratorially, a small smile, but she managed to dredge up a smile to reassure her friend that it was all fine.

Evie smiled back, 'As long as it remains someone else's problem and not mine I can be unfazed.'

Chapter 9

Gia queued for drinks in the wine tent, jostling with others wearing thicker winter coats and more suitable clothing. It seemed that the noise level inside the tent rose every few seconds. It might be a scout affair but there was nothing polite about queueing for drinks, it seemed to be a fight to get to the bar, unlike the very English queues at the food stalls.

The night was mild compared to recently and Gia was thankful for it. She had picked up a hat and fingerless gloves in the city with Evie earlier that day, both a lovely soft fawn shade. She was glad of the little bit of extra warmth. Gia grabbed the attention of a man with a slight tilt of her head and a deliberate curve of a suggestive smile as he headed towards her from behind the bar, she had his attention immediately, 'One lemonade, one fizzy orange, two proseccos, and a pint.' She told him what Robbie drank. It was their second round of drinks and she had insisted it was her turn.

'Make that two pints, I'll pay for these,' a deep, rich voice at her side added. She turned her head and a genuine smile crossed her face.

'I didn't think you'd come tonight.' It hadn't occurred to her that watching a scout bonfire surrounded by families would be on Atlas's list of things to do.

He gave her a wink, 'My favourite people are here.

Two little ones, my sister, and you. Robbie's OK as well.'

'Really? I'm still not sure. I know he adores Evie, and she deserves that.'

'I was suspicious of him at first. He's alright, Gia.'

'Does he know? About Evie?' she phrased it so that the question could mean anything, be about anything, if anyone overheard. The bartender placed their drinks in front of them.

Atlas's eyes darkened when he understood her meaning, their light dimmed, they narrowed. He kept a serious face as he paid and put the change into the poppy fundraiser box. 'Get our drinks, I'll take the rest over and say hello. Wait for me outside.' He was gone before she had a chance to even protest. His back stood out from the crowd. Even if she had shouted after him there were too many voices in the tent to make hers stand out. She carried their drinks outside.

Gia found a quiet corner, it wasn't too hard given the size of the outdoor space, or that everyone was as near to the bonfire as possible. She should have argued and taken the drinks over herself. It was the chance to be in close proximity to Atlas that failed her. She liked his new look. Realisation dawned that she had moved past liking Atlas, that whatever she was feeling was new to her, every time he was around she craved more time with him, normally by this point, she had begun to notice the little irritations which made her temper rise. It was messy too, separating Evie from Atlas, or Atlas from Evie was impossible. She couldn't have a fling with Atlas and think that Evie would never know, or that it wouldn't have an effect on their friendship.

They'd all had a crush on Evie's older brother at some

point in their teenage years. All six quietly knew time would cure it and it wasn't really mentioned, unless it was a slap on an arm when one of them was being overly flirty. This time around, she wasn't certain it could be attributed to a teenage crush. Gia liked his voice, the way he smiled, his sense of humour. Then she rolled her eyes at the cliché she had fallen into. Her best friend's older brother. She couldn't. She didn't do relationships and she ran away whenever anything looked like it was about to become serious. She was the problem that Atlas and Evie didn't need.

She picked Atlas out of the crowd easily when he walked back to her. He was taller than most people, the bun added to his height. His broadness from years of physical labour before they had machines to do the hard work turned most women's heads as he strode past. His eyes searched the shadows for her. He took his pint and downed half before speaking to her.

'How long have you known?'

'Today. She came by and told me. Showed me,' she corrected herself.

'Just like that? She trusted you?' The doubt in his voice hit her hard, a reminder that she had been gone for ten years and he knew his little sister better.

'There might have been a mutual exchange of secrets,' Gia arched an eyebrow at his tone.

'What would your secret be, Gia, you mentioned demons and circles?' The deep honeyed hues of his voice returned, seeking and teasing out her innermost secrets.

She countered back, 'What would yours be, Atlas? Do you want to share why your eyes change colour?'

He stared at her, she stared back. Behind his back, the

surrounding noise heightened with cheers from the crowd as the scout team prepared to light the first firework. Atlas finished his pint. He gave it to a nearby kid in a scout uniform with a five-pound note fished from his pocket, 'The money is for you if you can take my glass back for me.'

The child took the note and pocketed it, took the glass from Atlas and muttered a croaky, 'Thanks, mate.'

Atlas chuckled at that. He moved round to stand behind Gia to face the fireworks. One of his hands settled on her hip, the other on her waist. Blood rushed to her head. It was a moment that she wanted to extend into forever. She wondered if it was this easy. If other people stayed with someone because it was like this all the time.

He bent his head and murmured into her ear, 'Watch the fireworks whilst we talk. It's why we're here. Yes, Robbie knows about Evie. I wasn't sure about him either at first. Why aren't you?'

'There isn't anything that I can explain, just a feeling that there's more beneath the surface when it comes to him, it's like, he is kind, and he clearly loves her, but there's a ruthlessness underneath.' She didn't want to explain how uncomfortable she had been in the pub with Robbie's family. Gia didn't know how to transfer that from a feeling into words without giving away too much. She might fancy Atlas, but saying what she could do was dismissed easily, talking and revealing the depths of her ability was a different level, it was too intimate to share.

'There is more to him. He came through for her when he knew. His brother too. Don't judge them too quickly. I'm not saying you're wrong, I'm saying he will never hurt her.'

'You've always been there for her.'

'She's my sister. I also know you've answered her texts

no matter what time of the night.'

'There's a time difference to take into account,' Gia murmured, nestling her head back against Atlas, looking up at the first firework to shoot into the sky.

She felt his arms wrap around her and tighten. It was intimate, the type of squeeze someone would give a loved one, he relaxed his arms but didn't loosen them. It kept her as close to him as possible. She casually placed her free hand across one of his. His fingers interlinked with hers. They fell quiet whilst the fireworks exploded in the sky above them, conversation would have been irrelevant given the noise of the explosions. She took a breath and relaxed.

Gia loved to be outside, surrounded by the darkness of a night that was the end of autumn, not yet quite winter, a time that she adored with all her heart but would never admit to anyone because no one admitted they liked the darkness, especially not a darkness that was heading towards winter. To her, it provided a refuge, a place where she could be herself. Most of her books took place in the night because she was more comfortable with the dark than the daylight.

'I like your perfume,' he said, during a lull as the team scrambled to light more fireworks. It jolted her back to reality.

'My perfume?' Gia realised that she wasn't wearing any.

'I noticed it when I picked you up on Saturday. At first it reminded me of being in winter fields in the early hours when the air is sharp, clean, and there's a frost on the ground. Then I get ripe blackberries and that sexy earthiness of the woods in autumn and it smells authentic, you know, not synthetic sweetness. It's bloody sexy. What is it?'

'Winter Court.' She whispered the first words that came into her head. She took a drink to hide how uncomfortable she was that he had mentioned it. Murderous resentment rose inside her that she tried to quash. The brownie hadn't been lying. At least, not about the scent.

They stood there in silence, fireworks exploding over their heads, a sizzle of mixed emotions inside Gia which temporarily froze her ability to think, although if she was perfectly honest with herself that had more to do with Atlas's arms being around her than the fireworks. She finished her prosecco slowly. Neither of them spoke until the fireworks had finished. The display was too loud to have a discreet conversation. They could hear the argument of the couple next to them during lulls, petty digs at the fact he didn't want another slow cooker dinner and she argued back that they might have money to eat out like their friends if he stopped drinking so much after work with his colleagues. He countered that he drank to drown out the whining of the children at bedtime, she retorted that maybe if she had some help, their children wouldn't be accustomed to only being parented by one parent and they could share bedtimes. He said they should have stopped at two, but she had wanted more. Gia glanced to her side at this and noticed she had a baby strapped to her, a toddler in the pushchair she was holding, a child of about five or six hanging onto the pushchair with one hand and waving a glow stick in their other hand, and an older one passing a glow stick to the toddler in the pushchair. Having heard arguments like this repeatedly over the last ten years, Gia half listened, but watched the fireworks.

When the impressive finale was overhead, multiple fireworks exploding and lighting up the sky with false stars Gia relaxed enough to say, 'Those are my favourite, the ones that do that silver star cascade. You can take out the colours and just give me the silver sparkles.'

'This finishes pretty early. We could take a walk around the farm and watch other fireworks go off. Evie will probably put a children's film on and make a supper for Max and Rey before their bedtime.'

'OK.' Gia gave a nod. Her consent had less to do with being with Atlas, despite the fact that she did like him, and more that she didn't particularly want to be in the cottage. Atlas's comment about her perfume had raised a bitterness inside her towards the revelations the brownie had spat out. Gia noticed Max and Rey running in their direction. She pushed Atlas's arms off her.

Evie caught her arm on the walk back to the farm in a gentle tug to encourage her to fall back a couple of paces. Max and Rey were hanging off their uncle and pleading to go with him to watch the fireworks he was taking Gia to see. Evie stayed within eyesight of her children. She spoke quietly when she said, 'Genevieve sent me some books about our thing. She knew about my gift. Once Max and Rey are back at school, I'm a bit stricter on bedtime. Do you want to pop up one night and we'll see what we can find about the Resting Court? We can all sit and look.'

'Not with Robbie and Atlas,' Gia whispered back.

'They'll be OK with it, Gia.'

'I'm not.'

Nerves fluttered and banged against her stomach wall like bats. She couldn't explain why she didn't want Robbie to know. Even though she had told Atlas briefly about what she could do, the new development from the brownie had caused her to stumble and rethink. Gia had never had a reason to doubt who she was before. She had built an entire career on the fact she understood fully who she was and that she accepted her heritage of part human, part demon. Her skills and even her reckless behaviour were underpinned by the knowledge of her heritage. Now she had to rethink the concept. In her head fairies were dainty, delicate, magical beings. Demons were strong, powerful and fearless.

She changed the topic, 'How did Robbie find out about you?'

'I got backed into a corner and I had to show him or lose him by lying. I need to tell you the story, but Max and Rey don't know it and I don't want them to. I can't call you once they're asleep because you can hear everything in the caravan which is why I can't ask you up for a drink to talk about it either, I don't want to text it to you.'

'Because that's potentially evidence for someone,' Gia murmured, understanding.

'Actually, Atlas could tell you whilst you're up there tonight,' Evie's eyes flickered to her brother then back to Gia. Gia read the mischievous dance in her friend's face.

'It's not like that,' she shook her head. She didn't know what it was.

Evie winked, 'I hope it is. He likes you. We're friends. He's my brother. I'll stay out of it. But it's exciting to dream that it works out, and it's you that lives across the courtyard from me instead of some stuck up blonde.'

Gia laughed, the sound mixing with Evie's light laughter, she tightened her arm around Evie's. Robbie and Atlas glanced behind them at the pair before the children took their attention again, and Evie stepped forward to listen to Max. It was a lovely dream to listen to, living across the courtyard from Evie, being happy long term with Atlas. Gia waited until her friend was done with her son, a quiet but firm refusal to let him climb rocks in the dark, and pulled Evie out of hearing of the others.

'I—' Gia faltered. Evie looked at her, open and honest, waiting for her to finish. Gia grimaced then whispered in her friend's ear, 'I don't know how to have a relationship.'

'But you—' Evie kept her voice soft.

Gia shook her head, 'I know sex. I know dates. I don't know how to keep it together.'

'One day at a time. One conversation at a time. It isn't hard with the right person.'

Chapter 10

Atlas's voice was low and quiet as he told her the story of Halloween on the farm. Fireworks exploded in the sky over their heads in sporadic bursts from multiple directions. Gia suspected that Atlas was leaving parts out when he told her of the events of Halloween; he was factual and distant about it. Robbie and his brother Liam had been present, but Atlas couldn't say how or why they involved themselves. She remembered that Atlas had mentioned going to see someone to get answers when they had gone out for pizza. Gia brought it up, her hands were on a boulder as she used it to steady herself on the uneven climb upwards. The boulder was cold. The chill sank into her hands, the damp getting into her bones. This return to England was making her realise all the reasons she had left, the cold and damp had a way of getting under her skin. Atlas had described the incline as a gentle climb. Gia had never really thought of herself as a city girl, but she felt like one in that moment. She dreaded her hands going onto something on the boulder that wasn't rock, and the gentle incline Atlas had described was more of a steep hill to her.

'When we went for pizza, that was the night before Halloween. You talked about getting answers from someone. Did you?' she asked Atlas.

'That someone turned out to be the person that wanted to hurt Evie.'

'Nice deflection. Did you find the answers, Atlas?'

'Yes and no.'

'Are you going to tell me? Wow, this is beautiful.'

They had reached the top now. At the highest point Gia could see the village and in the distance the town, lights twinkling. Above them, fireworks flashed occasionally in the darkened sky underneath gathering grey clouds. Fields and barns spread out at their feet. Gia had come home, it sank into her quietly but comfortingly. Being surrounded not just by space, but the stillness of the night. To know this type of freedom in the darkness made her feel the most alive she ever had. Others wanted blankets, films and drinks, she wanted this – space, freedom, and the ability to merge with the dark hues of the night. She missed the shadows that ran down the hill, away from her, clinging to the rocks.

'I wish you could see your face right now.' Atlas smiled.

'I wish you could understand what I feel right now.' She took her eyes from him to look back at the freedom around her.

'That we're lucky to live here?'

'Not even close. I love being out at night. Being here right now is better than any bar or club.'

'Those places are just fun prisons.'

'That's a different take on it.'

'Think about it. You go from one to the next, so does everyone else. There's nothing else open at night so you have no choice unless you want to stay home. Everybody that feels like you do is forced to go to the same places.'

'Not everyone has somewhere like this though,' she breathed, barely above a whisper, scared if she said something too loud the feeling would break and run away from her.

Gia turned around to look in all directions. The fireworks faded and stopped. When she had turned in a slow, full circle, the shapes of the fields had changed. The locations of the barns were off, as though they had been moved just a few centimetres to the side. Atlas looked worried. Gia loved the strangeness of it. A sense of playful otherworldliness descended over her, this was an odd peculiarity yet comfortingly familiar, hitting a place inside her that screamed she belonged here. The sky grew lighter, emitting a plum hue instead of the normal darkness.

'Gia, we need to go back.'

'Just a few more minutes.' She wasn't cold anymore.

'Gia.'

She heard the urgency in Atlas's voice from a distance. It didn't sound like he was right next to her even though he was.

He grabbed her wrist and pointed over to a field. Shadows of riderless horses, not horses, deer, lit by an unseen source, galloped across the dark expanse, accompanied by smaller four-legged shadows running at their side.

'*The shadows will come for you*.' She repeated the brownie's words. Gia turned to Atlas. Despite his worry she was full of calmness, she had found serenity. She tilted her mouth in a half smile.

'What—' Atlas's words were cut off as Gia acted on impulse. She leaned up on tiptoes to kiss him. She had fully intended to brush his lips lightly in a goodbye, half believing that the brownie had been right.

Instead of the shadows taking her, Atlas pulled her in

close. He wrapped his arms around her, and kissed her back slowly, as though he was savouring every second that she gave him to kiss her. Gia didn't protest, she melted into the kiss, thoughts of the shadows below extinguished.

A firework exploded over their heads and made them break off and look up. The sky was normal again. He took a step back, looked at her again and lifted her red hood over her head with a smile, 'Red always was your colour. What was that about the shadows coming for you?'

'A kind of fortune teller thing. Except it wasn't a paid fortune teller. It was an entity I'd enclosed in a circle. It said I wasn't using my power correctly and that the shadows would come for me. That's what Evie saw today. I don't want her trapped between loyalty to me and the truth to you, so, yeah...'

'The shadows...' Atlas looked down.

Gia followed his glance. 'I guess they missed me this time.'

'I got to kiss you though.' He lifted her chin with his finger and kissed her again, lightly, as though testing her response. She kissed him back, then shivered. He broke the kiss off much to her disappointment, but asked, 'Do you want to warm up with a whisky in my caravan, or shall I walk you home?'

'I feel like I'm taking advantage of you if I say the whisky.'

'It might be the other way around. Since that morning the thing happened, I've wanted to see you naked in my bed with messed up hair and sleepy eyes. I've tried to dismiss it, thinking it would never happen.'

'Since that morning I've wanted to pull you on top of me and kiss you until you forget that you have to go and milk cows or whatever it is you do at that stupid time in a morning,' Gia responded.

Atlas let out a deep laugh at that, 'I do milk the cows at that time.'

'I'm trusting that you have a good whisky,' she teased.

'The best.' He gave a nod to confirm his statement.

'Why would you think it wouldn't happen?' Gia was curious. She had the same thoughts, but about her not being enough for Atlas. She could list her faults easily. Plenty of other people had thrown them in her face.

'You and Evie, and Tess, all of you, have gone onto such glamorous lives. I'm just a farmer. My sister walks down a street and people recognise her. You're a famous writer. Tess is well known for her art. Nina's a model. Kat's a huge social media influencer in her area.' He stumbled over the words.

Gia laughed, 'Gynaecology. She's a gynaecologist and posts about it. You won't die if you say it.'

'I deal with vets, Gia, not doctors. Talking of which, are you...' He trailed off but Gia understood his unspoken question.

'I have the copper coil in. It's over ninety per cent effective. I've used condoms with everyone. I do follow Kat online, plus it's guaranteed at the end of any group texts Kat will send the last message and it will be a reminder to use condoms.'

'You lot do group texts?' He sounded surprised.

'Yeah, why?'

'Evie mentions you all, but it's always singular. Kat's done this, Gia's in this State, I assumed it was her reaching out to everyone individually. I don't know why. That's on me.'

'There isn't much that's not said on the group chats. Because we're all over the world, there's almost always someone awake if you need them.'

'Kat always gets the last message in?' He was teasing now. His tone was light and playful.

Gia laughed, 'And I follow it. I'm not ready to be a mum.'

'No? Any particular reason why?' She couldn't guess any hidden meaning from his tone. They were already starting the climb down.

'Are you ready to be a father?' She pushed the question back at him. She knew her answer. She wanted to know his.

'Not at the moment. I'd like my house built first. I'd like to have some time having sex and getting to know someone before we're hit with the stress of sleepless nights. I've thought about it a lot. My parents didn't parent well, if at all. Evie's marriage broke up over the strain of having a baby. If I'm ever to be in that position, I want a solid relationship first. I want inside jokes, I want to know what she likes in and out of bed, I want to know her favourite foods, I want to know every expression she has so that I can walk into a room and know what to do straight away, whether she needs food or a break or sleep or a night out.'

'When do you get a break? Who takes care of you? Who knows your expressions?'

She was met with quietness. Gia realised that nobody had ever put Atlas first in his life. He'd started to clear the farm so he and his little sister could eat. She understood now that Evie must have played a more significant part in growing vegetables and fruit for them, and later the farmers market, than she had realised at the time.

'Did you ever want to leave the farm?' she asked. She knew his sister had.

'No. This place is home. I like watching the seasons change. I like being my own boss. Truthfully, I like the space more than anything. I can't imagine not owning acres of land. The thought of being cooped up inside a shared office answering to someone else makes me want to punch someone.'

They had reached the bottom of the incline now. It was flat smooth walking along footpaths from where they were to the caravan. Gia changed the subject to one she knew Evie loved, although she hadn't heard Atlas say anything about it, 'Evie loves the houses you're having built. Did you get much say in the design of yours?'

Her question generated a chuckle from Atlas, 'Yes. I'd have been happy with whatever. But Evie did insist I sat down with the architect. Even though both houses have the same footprint, they're different inside. The architect has everything sorted, even the paint colours. Robbie talks to her weekly. I don't think Evie and I need to do anything more.'

'Evie texted when she managed to get her on the project. Jean was on a TV programme when we were at university, one of those redesign your house things.'

'I know. She always said she was going to have Jean do our houses. She called it future proofing to have a female architect who was a few years ahead in terms of her own children's ages design a family home.'

'Tell me about your house?'

Atlas went on to give the briefest description, Gia had to prompt him for the details Evie readily offered. Evie had shared all the architect's ideas for her house, the plans and colours through messages. Likewise, Gia had posted the group pictures of her camper van, although she had shared them online too. Evie hadn't shared a single detail about her brother's house. Gia had no idea how his house differed from Evie's and she was having trouble picturing it from his blunt descriptions. He had been more descriptive when he had answered her questions about the farm over their pizza. When she asked if it would be white like Evie's he had laughed and said no, he liked dark colours.

His caravan interior didn't surprise her when she entered it. It was wood and leather, masculine and reassuring in the same way that being around Atlas was. She saw the new unlit scented candle, tools on the small dining table, a pale blue hat and gloves thrown on the television stand. It was cute that he was so involved with his nephew and niece.

He caught her looking, 'Max was looking a tool for his bike, Rey left her hat because she was too hot the other day. I didn't tidy up before I left to catch the fireworks.' He picked out two glasses and poured generous amounts of amber liquid into both. When Gia took the glass from him, she was surprised at how heavy it was. It was a whisky glass for real adults, not the type that was sold in a supermarket. The quiet luxury of it fitted this new version of Atlas, but it still brought conflict against the memories held of the boy she had once known. She was discovering depths to Atlas that she wouldn't have guessed at.

Chapter 11

'How long are you planning to stay with Rosa?' Atlas held her eyes as he kicked his boots off in the doorway, holding the heavy glass steady in his hand and then sank next to her on the settee with only a small gap between them. He nudged the footstool into the middle between them in an unspoken invitation for her to share it, then put his feet up.

Gia unzipped her own boots and put her legs on the footstool against his. She took a sip, appreciating the whisky, it was full bodied and rich. He hadn't lied when he said it was a good one.

'I was hoping a year, to get my head together, but it looks like it'll be less. I was talking to Evie about it today actually. She's offered to help me look at houses in Eastwood or that side of town anyway.'

'Eastwood? That's a forty-minute drive.'

'My other option is to look at another camper van with a log burner in for winter.'

'What's happening with Rosa? I thought she'd be glad to have you back.' Atlas frowned as though he couldn't understand. Out of everyone, she thought he'd understand not being wanted.

'I don't know. I feel like there's a distance between us, and not one that was caused by my running off to America as she puts it. It's always been there. It's like, she's pissed off that I'm not playing by the same rules she is. It's hard to describe because on the surface everything is fine, maybe it's just a generational thing.' To change the subject she hooked her leg over Atlas's shin and watched his face to gauge his response. His eyes left her face and trailed slowly along her, right down to her foot, then back up.

'How isn't it fine?' he asked.

'We didn't come here to talk about my grandma, Atlas.'

'No, you're right. I'm interested, that's all. I never had grandparents and the whole dynamic is new to me. She protected you a lot when you were growing up.'

'She did. Do you know I came up to the farmhouse to read all the books she never let me read. Evie had no restrictions on what she read. She'd give me the best horror books and all the open-door sex novels. Nonna would just say, *Wait until you're sixteen.*'

'Why?'

'She got pregnant at fifteen. Her parents threw her out. My dad got my mum pregnant when they were both fifteen. She feels like it was a family curse. She wanted me to sit my exams first. That fear of getting pregnant was instilled in me from an early age. I didn't come here to spill my life,' she downed her whisky.

'That's right, use me for my body then throw me away,' Atlas commented dryly.

Gia glanced at his serious face, until she saw the cheeky glimmer in his eyes, the smile he was trying to hide, and she laughed. He grinned with her. She let her free hand trail down his beard slowly, it was coarser than it looked, then she leaned forward and kissed him, much softer and more playfully than she had expected to. That surprised her, generally, she wasn't one of the soft girls like Tess and

Genevieve, or sometimes Evie when she wasn't being feral. Gia had no problem putting people in their place. She was tough, and it raised feelings of bewilderment inside her that she was different around Atlas. She had enough turmoil trying not to slip into being Rosa's *good* grand-daughter and hide her inner self, she didn't need an unknown, unrevealed added layer of herself that came out around Atlas.

She couldn't blame Atlas entirely for her confusion. It had started over a year ago around her thirtieth birthday. Slowly. She found herself drawn to softer make-up looks after having spent time making her signature look widely known and recognised throughout her twenties. The draw to a softer style of living, a slower pace had built gently, like a manuscript, one word at a time, until she noticed that there were paragraphs that formed a chapter; she was growing, changing, things were less black and white. She had started cooking for herself more and eating takeaway food less. She had thrown away friends and contacts who offered only superficial sustenance to her life; people who liked to say they were friends with her because of her name, not who she was. That had given her extra time alone, when she would have been with them, and she used her time to read more books. Now her book reviews had become something of a life in themselves on her social media pages.

Atlas broke off the kiss and extended a hand to pull her up. Still holding his hand, Gia followed him to the bedroom. Her leather jacket fell to the floor first. She pushed her hands under his jumper and shirt before dropping lower and letting a finger trace lazy circles on the fly of his jeans. She wasn't going to rush, she had nowhere to be and no one to consider.

They took their time. Slow and soft, it was the most sensual she had ever been. For the first time in the longest time, her brain slowed down enough for her body to be heard. She liked the way Atlas took his time to be in the moment, savouring every tiny extra bit of her skin revealed with calloused fingers and kisses. It made her head spin, it put her in a daze of isolation, there was nothing existing in the world but them and only them. Like it had been in the car, the outside world fell away, and they existed on a precipice.

Recently, even sex had been unable to quieten the narratives in her head. It had been quick and over, the more unsatisfactory it became, the more she indulged in risks until she was left as an observer to something that happened to her body, her brain unable to switch off. With Atlas, every muscle she had slowly relaxed. His touch was conscious, intimate, and possessive. They became a conscious meeting of both minds and bodies, so intention- ally slow she couldn't think about anything else except how she craved his touch on her skin. His hands, then just his fingers, his lips, then he'd whisper how beautiful she was until she reached out and pulled his head to hers to kiss him.

Afterwards, they laid together on the bed. Atlas was on his side. His leg was thrown over her, pinning her to the bed, one arm stretched over her torso, the other arm had slid underneath the pillow she was using. She had one hand lazily placed over his thigh, she could barely curve her hand around his heavily muscled legs. Gia had nestled her head into his shoulder where she could hear his heartbeat as it slowed down. She concluded, as she drifted off into a relaxed, contented sleep, sex with Atlas felt like being a goddess worshipped fully at an altar by a protective predator.

She was woken up as Atlas moved around the bedroom. Still full of sleep Gia sat up, she held the covers around her as protection from the cold inside the caravan.

Her movement attracted his attention, he turned around, 'I didn't mean to wake you.'

'It's OK.' Gia pushed the covers off. Her intention was to get up and walk back to her grandmother's cottage. Atlas pounced quickly and she found herself on her back and pinned to the bed before she could predict his movements.

'Stay there and go back to sleep, beautiful. I want you here when I get back, messy hair and sleepy eyes and everything. Then we'll go and get some breakfast.' Gia was about to argue, snap a retort when she noticed Atlas's expression. His eyes stared at her face, the expression told her that he'd never had anyone wait for him, and it cost him a lot to ask. He was uncertain about her answer. She relaxed her body into the bed, a place she would much rather be.

'Only for you, sexy,' she mumbled.

He smiled at her, 'I enjoyed last night.'

'I did too. I think you broke me,' she admitted, as her thoughts drifted back to how she had been able to switch off her brain and enjoy his touch.

'I broke you?' He had been backing himself off her. He stopped now, and stared at her, his face might have been expressionless, but the concern in his eyes spoke volumes.

'Yeah, no man is ever going to measure up to you,' she covered up that slip of her inner voice.

He chuckled at that. He leaned down and placed a kiss on her lips. 'You held your own, beautiful. I've never met someone who liked sex as much as you did last night.'

'That's probably because the Louises of this world are too hungry to have the stamina to keep up with you.' She wasn't wrong.

He laughed at that, long and loud, 'Get some rest. See you when I come back.' He pushed himself off the bed. Gia wanted to watch him finish getting ready, but her eyes were heavy.

He had broken her. Her head and body had always been two separate parts of a whole. Sometimes her body led, sometimes her head led, but they hadn't worked together in harmony since she was running around in the playground playing games like tig with Evie and the rest of their friendship group. For the first time since her childhood, they had joined last night. She had been whole, more complete than ever. Despite her analytical thoughts she was asleep before he left the bedroom.

She woke to loud knocking on the caravan door. The first thing Gia saw to wear in the bedroom was Atlas's dressing gown. She had barely finished fastening it when she opened the caravan door to Evie standing there, holding a takeaway coffee and a bag. She thrust both in Gia's direction.

'You might need these. Atlas normally comes back in about fifteen minutes. Just some extra PR gifts I had laying around, nothing big.' She shrugged.

Once Gia had taken both, before she could say thank you, Evie had already disappeared in the direction of her own caravan. Sipping the coffee Gia climbed back into the bed and opened the bag. The bag itself was branded, a brightly coloured skincare range. Inside sat mostly full-sized products, a face cleanser, a still wrapped promotional flannel, a moisturiser and separate spf. Evie had thrown in new make-up and hygiene products, all luxury labels Gia hadn't used in years. Each item was new and wrapped. Gia didn't need to check her reflection to guess that in all likelihood she had smudged eyeliner and mascara under her eyes.

She had barely finished the coffee when Atlas walked in. He came straight into the bedroom. He was clearly going to say something, he had a takeaway drink in each hand, but he stopped, his eyes looked at her empty takeaway container and the bag in her lap.

She reached out a hand for one of the drinks, 'Don't underestimate my ability to drink coffee,' Gia told him. He chuckled and passed her a drink. Gia told him Evie had brought her the previous drink and the bag.

Atlas narrowed his eyes, 'She had no right—' he started, but Gia cut him off.

'She came as my friend, not your sister. She's like a morning after fairy godmother. I need to up my game with PR packages compared to what she receives.' Her comment was met with a small laugh.

'Do you want me to give you five minutes to use that stuff then we'll go to the café to get breakfast? Or shall I run down and get you something to eat here? I can make toast?'

'What would you prefer, Atlas?' she asked.

He grinned, his eyes moved over her slowly. He didn't speak until they made their way back up to meet her own, 'You back in bed, but I'm a farmer and I can't skive off. The café does a decent fry up with toast and they always throw a bit extra in for me. I am hungry enough for that.'

'I'll get ready and have a breakfast pastry and a coffee, do you mind if I use your shower?' Her stomach flipped at the thought of a fry up.

Chapter 12

She left Atlas after breakfast. He had offered to walk with her to Rosa's cottage, or drive her, but she wanted time alone. Gia watched the branches of the trees thrash in the wind. The sky was blue dotted with thick white clouds whose middles held pale grey clusters. Not for the first time she marvelled at how wonderful it would be to live somewhere with so much land like Atlas and Evie had. Instead of turning and walking down the narrow lane towards the village, Gia chose to walk towards the public footpaths through the woods.

Her thoughts drifted to the previous night. She tried to analyse what had affected her so much that she had begun to feel a different person, a whole being instead of two separate parts. Even when she was walking there was a constant narrative in her head, a cacophony of voices. For years she had sat and talked to people who mentioned souls and enlightenment; she had laughed and shrugged it all off, dismissing it as metaphoric talk or religious rhetoric. Gia began to muse on whether she had been too focused on chasing stories for her books to really, truly, try and understand what the people she talked to in the magical community were speaking about. Her head still held all those conversations, she played them simultaneously, looking for the holes in her understanding.

The path she walked along took her to a small bank

before it curved. Gia looked down through the trees to see a house. It was surrounded by a high brick wall that opened only onto the road. A red car was parked in the paved yard but the house itself was blocked off with police tape. Yvonne's house.

Even she hadn't been able to miss the gossip on Yvonne. Her grandmother's friends told Rosa, and Rosa kept her up to date over their dinners. Gia stood and contemplated the house in her own way. She had so many questions about Yvonne. The gossip was unmissable, Yvonne had tried to set Evie up on their television show, telling other presenters not to turn up on Halloween and she had failed. Afterwards, Yvonne had disappeared, presumably having lost face. Even when Atlas had told her the truth last night, and despite all that she knew, Gia was still having trouble aligning Evie's blonde colleague with the image of a brown-haired vicious witch out to kill Evie.

Returning to her prior thoughts, Gia picked out several points that she had missed on achieving internal serenity. Learning how to control her racing thoughts had been one. Focus on breathing was another. Gia tried. She breathed in deeply and turned away from the house to follow the path. Already her thoughts had slipped back into the multitude of voices and ideas. She cleared her head again, and breathed deeply. This time she caught the deep scent of the earth, the richness of the woods. She focused on those and breathed in again. For a fleeting second, there was the same wholeness she had experienced with Atlas. Another step and character voices began to seep back, chattering at her about their stories. Gia pushed them out again. She let her hand trail along the bark of a tree. The feeling came easier this time, her head stayed clear, her breathing deep and steady, her body relaxed, her back went straighter, her shoulders lowered and pushed backwards to open up her lungs. Her eyes fluttered shut, just for a second.

She opened them to find the sky had changed colour, emitting a plum hue again. The path she was on in the woods had moved; the layout, the curve of it was unfamiliar. Gia retraced her steps. The house with the wall and police tape was now covered in neon graffiti that glowed in the low light levels. The graffiti signs and sigils were eerily similar to what she used in her circles. Gia turned and followed what should have been the path through the woods to the edge of the farm, although nothing looked familiar this time. Trees had changed places, they had lost their leaves and stood starkly bare compared to the autumn colours she had been in before. Everything around her in the woods had now changed to the shapes and colours of a harsh winter, all the bark the same shade of charcoal dark grey with intermittent patches of pale ash grey. Shadows darted between the trees, moving independently without a body. She followed a tiny footpath that used to lead to a clearing before she had moved away.

That particular clearing had always held a fascination for her. It was a wide circular area, the ground bare, oak branches arching overhead to protect it. Somewhere, in the back of her imagination, it had held old fashioned market stalls containing magical things and hidden knowledge. The clearing was still there. This time it held more darkness inside. Under the oak branches, rays of light lit the floor with the soft edge of winter sunlight, not quite stretching into the dark. Shadows danced and weaved. A light melody seemed to come from the ground. It faintly reached her ears and invoked images of frosted fields, white trees and shrubs, sumptuous feasts waiting to be eaten by the fireside on dark nights. A chittering voice spoke at her side, but Gia didn't catch the words, and when she turned there was no one there, just a running shadow, abruptly scuttling halfway up a tree, stopping, jumping across to another tree. Gia had the weirdest sensation that it was turning its head all the way around, a one-hundred-and-eighty degree turn, to look at her as it stayed still. Her heartbeat increased. Her feet were stuck to the floor. Then it went upwards, disappearing as it did so. Just like before on the hill with Atlas, she didn't feel either warm or cold, just perfectly comfortable. Above her head a bat fluttered, the first animal Gia had seen. She stepped away as it flew closer to her, its movements pushed her back onto the main path, back in the direction of where the village should be.

Her first instinct was to make notes on the experience. Her second was to call Atlas or Evie, but she remembered that they weren't teenagers anymore and both of the siblings had their own lives. When she finally cleared her thoughts, she noticed that it was already beginning to get dark, as though she had walked all day when it had only been half an hour at the most.

Gia let herself into her grandmother's cottage. A strong male aftershave hit her nose harshly after the natural scent of the woods. She closed the door behind her and saw her grandmother with another woman and man.

They stood up when they saw her, 'Gia, long time no see. How are you? Rosa caught me up on your life after church last week.' The man jumped into conversation immediately. He was dressed in a black suit, the tie double knotted, the shirt a weird off-white, as though it had gone through the washing machine with something it wasn't supposed to, he had brown hair and hard eyes, black lace-up shoes. The suit wasn't working for her. Gia stared at the man until he added, 'Oliver?'

Gia still wasn't sure who she was looking at, 'Oliver? Did your mum used to own the convenience store?'

'That's right.'

It fell into place. Oliver used to have brown hair that fell into his face when he looked down and a liking for Shakespeare and poetry. He had sung along to pop songs with her, they had talked about their English Literature books at sixth form, about their sociology course, he had told her what it was like living above a shop. He had played on the rugby team. She had considered him her friend.

'Coffee, Gia?' Rosa asked her.

'Yes please, Nonna. So, Oliver, you go to church now?' She tried to ignore the way Oliver was appraising her. She might get a rush when Atlas looked at her like he wanted her naked, but Oliver made her skin crawl. The other woman was wearing a priest's outfit. Gia began to wonder if she was being set up for something.

'Yes. I converted during university.'

'When?'

'Fresher's week actually.'

'They found you, they were really nice, they invited you for coffee a few times, then a study group, then to go to church with them after a month or so of them being your only friends?' Gia summarised one of the recruitment procedures. They were all so predictable.

'It wasn't like that. They were mentors. They're still my friends.'

'Of course they are. Until religion isn't central to your life.'

'But it always will be. I can't imagine not having the stability of the church to guide my soul through life's turbulent waters.'

'I'm happy to debate religion until our bones are dust. It's for control and nothing else. It controls men who then subject women to even further control and make decisions about their bodies in a deity's name. Normally one masculine deity despite the fact that there have been over twelve thousand deities since time began, and that's just the ones I'm aware of.'

'Gia, stop being argumentative, that's your mother's side there. I invited Oliver and Pearl here to see what he thought of the idea of identifying the ghost. After our conversation the other day I started to think that perhaps we should find out whether it's your father or not. I was saying to Oliver that you never came home last night. He was advising that you need to be missing for twenty-four hours before I could make a report.' Rosa passed Gia her coffee.

Gia stored that tiny slip of information about her mother away and added it to the rest of the little glimmers of her mum's personality that she held close to her, inside her heart. She was acutely aware that her memories of her mum were vague and influenced from a child's perspective. She would love to sit down with her now for a coffee without a child's idolatry. Rosa didn't talk about Gia's mother much. Comments here and there over the years had allowed Gia to build a mental image of her mother as a person. Out of the corner of her eye she could see Oliver looking up and down her body.

She stated the truth without shame, 'I'm fine. I went to watch the scout bonfire with Atlas and Evie and ended up staying the night on the farm.'

'With Evie?' Rosa asked.

'No, with Atlas.' She was distracted from her grandmother by the way Oliver was looking at her. She turned a defiant stare to him. He met her eyes with his own.

'His reputation hasn't changed over the years. He shows no sign of settling down. I'd be careful around that one,' Rosa said softly.

'Who says I want to settle down?' Gia asked.

'Don't most people?' Oliver asked.

Oliver had changed. The softly spoken boy with a sweet nature had hardened. His eyes were flat, his expression deliberately blank. She had experienced people like this. Life had changed him somehow, now he was dangerous because he saw some people in this world as less than him, and that made them unworthy of his empathy, pity, and preferably, his notice. His life was locked into a power play, designed by someone else, someone richer. Gia would guess someone who equated fear-based dominance with self-worth, essentially trapping him in a mind game he could never win. She changed tactics, Gia took a sip of coffee, and smiled at him, 'Nice to see our debates are still in place. We argued a lot in classics and sociology, didn't we?' She watched him lower his guard, relax his body, slowly a smile spread across his face.

He gave a nod, 'We did. You had me there.'

'What are you doing these days, Oliver?'

'I'm in the police.'

'He's a detective,' Rosa added.

Oliver allowed a self-satisfied smile of pride to cross

his face. 'I like the problem solving. Most people can't see the woods for the trees, but to me there's usually a way to cut through so the evidence gets boxed neatly together.'

She didn't like the way he said that either, the sinister undertone that he could frame people. 'I need to excuse myself. I bought a new phone and left it charging. I want to set it up.' Gia tried to find an excuse to leave.

'I should be going anyway. Rosa, I'd love to join your ghost hunt. Gia, I'm not sure what, if anything, is happening between you and Atlas but perhaps we could go for a drink together?'

'As old friends? Sure.'

'Maybe as the beginning of something new.'

Shivers went down Gia's back. Instead of shuddering she tilted her head, 'Let me see you out.' She wanted to make sure he walked down that path and away from her.

Oliver stopped at the door. His eyes flickered to Rosa and he asked Gia to step outside. Gia closed the door to the cottage behind her, her hand on the handle and waited for him to speak.

'I was looking through some footage and I saw you went to the food market with Atlas on Sunday night.'

'Yes.'

'Were you with him all night that night too?'

'Most of it. Until he went milking and I came back. Nonna was still asleep. Why?' she made a note to tell Atlas. She didn't know why she had lied, other than she didn't like Oliver and certainly didn't trust him.

'You spoke to one of his exes, Louise.'

'The thin one? Faux fur coat, blonde hair? She was with a man?'

'That's the one. Did you see her after?'

'No, we grabbed a table, ate our pizza, had a drink, and left. I don't know whether she was still there or not when we left. Why?'

'She was still there. She tried to employ the classic technique of attempting to make him jealous. Unfortunately, she was found dead in her flat the next day.'

'That's sad news. That was the first and only time I've seen her. Atlas wasn't bothered that he'd bumped into her.'

'No, his body language at the time said so. It's not even worth bringing it up really, I only asked in case he might have said something about her, anything.'

'He didn't.'

Back inside the warm cottage with the coffee warm in her hands, Gia turned to Rosa and Pearl. She was already bristling, defensive and on edge. She readied herself for the *talk*. Rosa wouldn't have invited a female minister unless it was intending to be a warning, an attempt to get Gia back on the pre-lit pre-marched levelled road that Rosa wanted her on with the masses.

'Will you be coming to the ghost hunt, Pearl?' she asked.

'I will. I'm interested. Rosa says you don't believe it's your father. What makes you say that?'

Gia looked at her grandmother before she answered, she chose her words carefully, 'I think Nonna remembers Dad being her cheeky little boy, he didn't really get a chance to grow up. I only ever saw him as an adult, as my dad. I found his body. It was empty. There was nothing, he had already gone.' She held back on saying more.

'You don't think it's a ghost.' Pearl picked up on the unspoken words.

Gia had to admit the other woman had intuition. 'No, I don't.'

'You think it's a demon?' Rosa looked at her alarmed.

Gia shook her head, 'No, Nonna. It's not a demon. Why is that always the first thing religious people think of?'

'What do you think it is?' Pearl asked.

Gia looked at her and knew. Rosa had told Pearl everything about Gia's past, about her mum. Pearl was assessing her, and her level of knowledge, 'Just a spirit. Not a ghost, a creature of the earth. Like an imp or a pixie.'

'Oh, like the Lincoln Imp?'

'Except, again, it's been twisted and the legend now says the imp was sent by the Devil. These things existed long before Christianity invented the eternal battle of control and free will.'

'That's an interesting turn of phrase,' Pearl remarked.

Gia nodded. 'I refuse to say good and evil. That phrase would indicate religious values are all good and non-religious lifestyles are evil. Many despicable things have been done in the name of religion. We can see that playing out across the world right now. Equally, many people who believe in helping their neighbours would be shunned by religion for their lifestyles.'

'Is that you, Gia?' Pearl asked. Gia gritted her teeth at the tone. It was the sickly sweetness she hated. The tone that overtly indicated that she was walking herself into a trap.

'No. I don't really do the Good Samaritan thing. I don't hide that I'm a bitch. I'd rather pay higher taxes and let a government department be the face of socialism.' She kept a straight face as she watched Pearl's reaction.

To her surprise, Pearl smiled, 'That's a breath of fresh

air. Do you know how many people moan about what their taxes support whilst saying they're a good person *but*?'

'Too many.'

'What's your ideal country, as it's run right now?' Pearl exchanged looks with Rosa.

Gia thought about it, it wasn't a question she had been asked before. 'I'm a little out of the loop, American news tends to be extremely isolationist, but any of the Scandinavian countries; Finland, Sweden, Denmark, they all seem to have intelligent well-informed adults that take social responsibility seriously.'

Rosa nodded approvingly and murmured about a good answer.

'I should go.' Pearl put her empty cup down. Gia caught the flash of disappointment on her grandmother's face.

Gia reassessed the relationship between her grandmother and Pearl within seconds. There was a closeness that Gia shared with her own friends. It had never occurred to her that Rosa had friends. Her straitlaced work-towards-the-next-goal-grandmother, her pregnant-at-fifteen-grandmother, her let's-emigrate-grandmother, had real-life friends. Twice now, she had seen Rosa with friends since coming home. The reality of her grandmother being a person, a child who had a child too young, a child who had taken on the burdens of financial responsibility for another child dawned on her. Perhaps Rosa hadn't been overprotective, perhaps she had experienced the worst and tried to give Gia a life beyond what she knew.

Gia took a breath before she said, 'Why don't I cook dinner for the three of us and you two open a bottle of wine and have a chat?'

When she ran upstairs to check her new phone, Gia already had messages waiting from Evie, who had put Gia's new number in her phone whilst they were still in the shop. There was a message from Atlas. A sweet one from Evie's son Max, asking if she had managed to set up her phone alright. Gia responded to Max first, then Evie, then she deleted her reply to Atlas and started again. Her finger deleted the second reply. She took the phone and went to sit on the bed. In her entire life she had never moved past casual. With the phone in her hand and every word in the world at her fingertips, she didn't know what to say to the man she had just slept with. The man she liked more than she had ever liked a man before.

Instead, Gia touched the internet tab and put her mother's name into the internet. As always, the article about her death was at the top of the search results. Even though she knew it off by heart, it was the first thing she had searched for when she had the privacy of her own phone, she read it again. The same words jumped out, once the article had finished being factual it descended into quotes from people who had known her. It delved into her mother's teenage pregnancy and ended with rumours from the medieval period of the family having demon blood, rumours that still persisted despite the modern age.

Then Gia did what she always did after reading about the rumours. She pricked her little finger with a needle, drew a three-centimetre circle and dropped the blood inside. She murmured a few words and watched the blood turn icy. Tiny patterns of frost formed before it melted as quickly as it started. She tried another spell. It did nothing. Gia paused, she tried a different assortment of words, part of a Latin exorcism, again the blood did nothing. She wiped the whole area clean with the skirt of her dress.

Gia was about to leave to go back downstairs to Rosa and Pearl, her hand already on the bedroom door handle when the idea hit. She turned and stared at the spot where she had drawn the circle, the conversation with the brownie on her mind. *The shadows will come for you*, it had said. She had seen the shadows with Atlas. None of the demon spells had worked on her blood. They never had. She never felt a single tug inside her when she said those words. There was the possibility that her blood wasn't demon blood, but fae, she had never tried fae spells. Gia shut the door and picked up her chalk.

Chapter 13

The tug inside the freshly drawn circle with new sigils was immediate. Gia felt it. It didn't hurt, but it pulled inside her. She watched the blood try to escape the circle. It dashed from side to side. She tried another spell, a collection of words, made up on the spot, hovering her hand over the blood, whispered secrets that were light and free, words that hurt her to say but whose truth could not be doubted.

Oak, ash, hazel, beech,
Or holly, berries and pine evergreen,
Show me what my blood does say,
Ripening, harvesting or resting fae.

The reaction was instant. There was no tug, no pull this time. Her own blood danced inside her, endorphins bubbled to the surface inexplicably, she was happy. The blood broke apart in tiny segments that resembled a holly leaf, then it frosted over. The message was clear enough. It matched the brownie's account, that caused a firepit of anger in her chest. Gia wanted to lash out and shout, but she had to be careful of Rosa. She had spent her life taking risks and living as close to the edge as she could, all because she thought that she had demon blood, only to discover, at the age of thirty-one that it wasn't demon blood at all. She struggled with the thought that she alone had kept herself safe, that she had done it all, it wasn't her demon powers that she called upon but her own witch strength.

Gia tried to distract herself by focusing on the bottom of the stairs as she descended to rejoin her grandmother, the new phone in her hand. She had always loved one particular spot. The first step, at the side of the door, was big and square. A low window allowed a view out, first to the ground, then the shrubs, then more of the garden as she descended the stairs until, on the final step, she could see the sky. Rosa's Christmas cactus sat in the window. It had a few opened flowers on it now.

Rosa and Pearl sat on the settee. They laughed about something that had happened at the university, Gia caught the end of the story as she descended. She looked at her grandmother and it was like they had never left Italy. Winter sun came through the window, the fire was on, she had the same spark in her eyes and the same smile. Gia saw where all her habits came from. She had subconsciously absorbed those of her grandmother. Hair tied back and out the way. Red lipstick. The way she emphasised her doe eyes in a liquid liner like her grandmother used a kohl pencil on hers. Her own stature was a version of Rosa's refusal to minimise who she was or what she was interested in. Their joint liking for quick to cook meals had come from a preference for reading, writing and studying, in different ways, but they still had the same pleasures, she preferred fiction whilst Rosa had developed a passion for non-fiction.

Gia made pizza for them all, sat with a glass of wine and chatted whilst the dough rose, and popped the leftover base into the freezer in individual portions for later in the week. Pearl was highly complimentary about her skills, Gia just shrugged, and said her grandmother had taught her to value her Italian heritage well. The conversation stayed around food, Gia learnt that Pearl and her grandmother didn't agree, Pearl said that cooking from scratch and producing healthy food was a luxury only those with time had, whilst Rosa argued back that pre-made pasta and a couple of handfuls of spinach barely took any time at all. Roasting vegetables wasn't effort inducing. Pearl argued that knowing all that required a level of skill that wasn't being taught in families or schools. Gia pointed out that the internet solved both arguments which only started another about the fact that most students couldn't even go an hour without a phone in their hands.

Once Pearl left, the absence of chat and laughter hung heavily in the now silent cottage. Gia busied herself with tidying away the pots into the dishwasher. Rosa took charge of cleaning the coffee and dining tables, they fell into their chores automatically. Gia knew that her grandmother liked to go to bed with a clean and tidy house, so that when she rose in the morning it was all ready for the day and she wasn't living in chaos. Gia asked her grandmother, in a careful, light tone, whether she had invited Pearl because they were friends or asked her to do an observational assessment on Gia. Rosa tied to insist that Pearl had dropped by but admitted that she was worried about Gia and the direction life was taking her.

It led to Gia telling her grandmother that she had known for years about the rumours surrounding her mother's family, that the internet was a search engine and all she had to do with her first phone was type in her father's name, location and date to get a new report about the double murder, made more sensational because a child and a parent were left behind. From that report, Gia had found her mother's name and had been able to search her online. It was the first time her grandmother had acknowledged the rumours Gia already knew about. Rosa admitted that she had told Pearl about the demons attached to Gia's mother. Pearl had been disappointed that Rosa believed medieval superstition.

'I asked her to come and meet you. I know that for the most part you're a good girl. The obsession you have with witchcraft, that comes from your mother too. But you're respectful, you've not brought it into my home. She practised in front of everyone,' Rosa said.

Gia was silent, the little she had done in the cottage wouldn't hurt Rosa. 'I don't recall you saying that before.'

'You didn't need to know. Perhaps I wouldn't have turned to the church as I did if I hadn't seen demons with my own eyes.'

'You saw what? Please?' Gia gestured to her grandmother to expand on that statement. She stopped what she was doing and leaned backwards against the kitchen worktop.

Rosa looked at her, hesitated, then said, 'It might have been a man, had he not been as black as night with wings that started at his shoulders and didn't stop until his ankles. His wings were the same colour as his skin. We talk about skin colour, but this wasn't a colour Gianna, this was darker than the remote control, it was—'

'I saw him too.' Gia stopped her grandmother.

Rosa looked at her in shock. 'She was a good mother. Better than I was. I would have thought she'd kept him away from you.'

'He wasn't a demon. He was another spirit. I can understand that he looked scary, but he wasn't a demon,

Nonna.'

'I would hesitate to declare that I know what demons look like, but I know what they're supposed to look like.' Rosa's face was set. Gia knew that look, even when she had pleaded for permission to do something as a child, to read a certain book as a teenager, the answer would never change.

'Because you're shown what they look like by religious texts. You're a politics professor. Look beyond the script. How can you be so brilliant at politics and not apply the same rules to religion?'

'Because when I saw him, I was frozen in fear.'

'That's perfectly normal around spirits of the earth, Nonna.'

'There's more of them?'

'There's more. Some look so different to us our first reaction is fear. After the fear comes the urge to eradicate them. That's why we can't move past wars no matter how advanced we seem to become, we have to eradicate what's different. You know that. Politics has shown you that.'

'You call them spirits of the earth?'

'I don't know what else to call them.'

'Demons. I think you've been working alongside them for too long if you can't see them for what they are. I always worried you'd turn out like your mother.'

'As opposed to a gang member like my dad and grandad?' Gia knew she shouldn't have said it the minute it came out. She tried to apologise but Rosa shook her head.

'I don't think Atlas is any good for you. He's too much like you. You both act first then think later. You need someone to keep the reins on your wilder side.'

'Really? Do not tell me that you think Oliver is better,' she struggled to keep her tone steady. If it had been anyone except her grandmother she would have lashed out.

'He has a steady job, a pension, he's respected, he's active in the church, everyone likes him.'

'That's surprising. I don't like him. He's changed.'

'We all change when we grow up. I suspect that his job has exposed him to the darker side of human nature.'

'Mine hasn't? Do you think I've been out there exploring love and lightness for ten years?'

'You—' Rosa started to speak then changed her mind.

'What? I what?' Gia tried not to demand an answer, but patience wasn't one of her strong points, or even a weak point. She had little patience, for anything.

'You were supposed to follow the same path.'

'You wanted me to go into the police?'

'No. I wanted you to walk the same path successful people follow. University, a career with an established company. A pension. But times have changed and are changing. Old names are collapsing. So many young people are choosing the risk of running their own self-employed schemes, they have little faith in established routes.'

'Those paths are rigid, the only people who profit from them are the ones already at the top, in which case we already fail by not being nepo babies with a network. My generation and the ones after see that, Nonna.'

'You were supposed to stay on the path though. So no one knew. Your blood would make sure you rose to the top. I had networks for you. I had a big publisher prepared to open their doors and let you trial there after graduation, reading their slush pile and seeing if you could pick out the good ones. I had a path set for you. All you had to do was follow it.'

'My blood? How would that affect my career? How would people even know?' Gia jumped on the comment. She couldn't hold back any longer. Her grandmother took a generous drink of wine. Rosa's body language was stiff and uncomfortable, Gia knew that she regretted being pulled into this conversation.

Her grandmother eventually spoke, 'Your mother's blood. Demon blood. It was how she was able to walk with them. I was told a long time ago it was stronger in you and you wouldn't fight the influence it had and that you would walk with them. It was why we had to leave Italy. I thought, somehow, being so far away from the demon blood would reduce its impact on you. I thought Yorkshire would be full of less temptations than London. They were right though, it's stronger in you than it was in her.'

'Who said this?'

'It was after the funerals. A homeless person grabbed my wrist. She said, *The little one runs with the darkness and glows with the moon, she will be the one to repay ancient debts*. I took it as meaning something terrible, that perhaps your mother's family had a debt with the demons. You were my baby's baby. A happy little girl. I vowed not to let them have you.'

'What about my mother's family? Didn't they say anything about you taking me?'

'They had their own problems; drugs, mental illness, alcohol. They're an old family. Really old Italian family, that's how the papers were able to trace her history. I don't know how your mother turned out so level-headed. She was sleeping rough in the forest on the edge of town when your father met her.'

'My mum was a runaway?'

'Yes.'

'How did they meet?'

'She stole from your dad. His phone and wallet. He chased her down. According to your father she had a mask on and her hood up, he hadn't realised it was a girl at that point.'

'You said she had curves though?' Gia was bewildered by the different descriptions. She had assumed that her parents had met in a more civilized manner.

'Not until well after you were born. She was a late bloomer, I only remember because she made a joke about it sometime just after you were born, saying that in her family all the babies were walking by nine months and hitting developmental milestones early but puberty didn't hit until after everyone else had been through it. I didn't think anything of it until I was here, with you, and worrying about how I was going to handle the teenage years with you. In the end, you made it so easy I wondered where all the horror stories came from. Then I remembered that I was the teenage horror story. That was the first time I really understood how like her you were. She made it easy to be around her too. They say that demons are seductive though.'

The way Rosa spoke of her mother and her mother's blood, her tone when she had said that Gia's mother had demonic blood inside her led Gia to conclude that she couldn't share any of the new things that were happening to her with Rosa. The insane shadows that had appeared on Atlas's farm, or that the sky had changed colour twice.

The whisper in her ear in the clearing when the woods looked different. That they had a brownie in the house. That she had fae blood not demon blood. In her own head it sounded enough to get her admitted for a psychiatric assessment, that was if her grandmother didn't call for an exorcism for the demon that was calling for its ancient debt.

Chapter 14

A week of performing new spells on her own blood, spells that formed intuitively and flowed easily, left Gia drained of energy and sleeping badly, her dreams full of vividly grotesque creatures like the brownie chasing her down in the forest, or of her falling down a tunnel at the base of tree roots in the woods into the fairy realm and staring into a sea of disappointed faces. Her research had consisted of tirelessly consuming all the texts and history around the fae that she could. In a week, she had discovered more old lore and history than she cared to recount. What had happened to her when the sky changed colour had different expressions but was a worldwide phenomenon, experienced all over, and every culture had a word for forest spirits too. She liked the Finnish word for it, metsänpeitto. Irish and Americans of Irish descent called it fairy-led. The more she learnt, the more spells came into her head to try out.

The side effects of the spell she had performed the previous afternoon had caused her to wake up with beads of sweat on her head and her body shaking. Gia had pushed the drops of her blood, separated from her by centimetres, to its limits, able to feel everything that she did to it inside her own body, she had pushed her blood to break past the magic circle and return to her body. It had taken every last ounce of strength she had to work her own blood past the magical circle, to break free and back into her palm. Her body had been wracked with pain. It was born of a desire to know her limits. The fae, fairies that lived a separate realm existing right alongside them on earth — she had never given them a thought beyond fairy tales. She still wasn't quite sure that she wholeheartedly believed. She had notes and notes of comparisons on fae to demons, wondering if the two could ever be mistakenly identified.

Rosa thought she had the flu. Gia made dinner at night and pushed it around her plate, already wondering when it would be polite to disappear to her room. By the time dinner was on the table, her head was already lost in thoughts about her book, her heart was trying to work out the puzzle of her ancestry, and her appetite was minimal. In between spells and research, Gia wrote more on Valentina's story, created an English heritage on her mother's side and sent her character off researching her ancestry to find a childless great-uncle with an obsessive library of eldritch horror and witchcraft, who told Valentina that she would not inherit any of his wealth or estate unless she earned a degree first. Gia realised towards the end of the week that the stuffy, eccentric but intelligent great uncle was simply her own grandmother packaged up for fiction. She ran with it.

When the bedroom began to spin around her in the darkness, she thought she had taken things too far. Gia lowered her face to her knees, and waited for the spinning to stop. She rested her face on her biceps and scrunched her hair with her hands, pulling softly to ease the headache threatening to take over her whole head. She only looked up when she heard that deep, melted chocolate over smooth whisky voice which belonged only to Atlas, 'Gia?'

Gia looked up. Her bed was in his caravan, her room was in his, her bedsheets fused with his. She fought and pushed back, covered her face with her hands and cleared her head. She wanted to be alone. Then Atlas was in her bedroom, half dressed. He sat on the bed. His hand ran comfortingly over her head, he twisted her hair around his hand and tugged it downwards gently so she had to lift her head. She looked at him. He traced under her eye with the pad of his thumb. She knew it was black. She was surviving on two or three hours of broken sleep every night.

'You look exhausted, are you ill?'

'No. Tired. I've been researching instead of sleeping. Too many stories led to bad dreams. This is what I'm like mid book. I live it so I can write it.'

'Come here.' He let go of her to get onto the bed and wrap himself around her. She snuggled into his chest. Her body relaxed. She heard pages being turned as he flipped through her notes whilst he held her, and she couldn't help but think that with anyone else she would have snapped about them looking at her personal things. Before she could ask him questions about what had happened or why, she was asleep again.

When she woke up there was a constant banging in the distance, her phone was ringing, and daylight poured through the open curtains, crisp coldness sneaked into every part of the room through the window that had been opened. It dawned on her, far too slowly, through a haze of sleep, that it was the middle of the day. The distant banging became a knocking on the door, the walls of her room started to blur. Her phone flashed with *Atlas*. In haste, she pulled on a red oversized sweatshirt to answer the door, pressing the green button to answer Atlas's call as she walked downstairs quickly to avoid the unconventional pull that she and Atlas seemed to have.

'Hey Atlas, I've just woken up, whatever magic you did, thank you. I actually slept,' she opened the door to see Atlas stood there, his car behind him on the lane.

He held a coffee balanced on a small hamper box stamped with the High Lēah farm logo, she knew from the size of the box it held the coffee blend that she had complimented in the café. A smirk spread across his face. He lowered his phone, 'You look better. You slept?' Gia nodded. She took the box and placed it on the large square stair. He wrapped his arms around her before she had even turned around and kissed the top of her head.

'That's good. I'm taking you to the farm café for lunch and out to dinner tonight.' He pushed his way into the cottage with a step and closed the door behind him, still keeping her tight to him with one arm.

'You don't need to,' Gia started. She turned around to face him. Her argument would have been fiercer if he hadn't slipped his hand from her covered waist to underneath her top and over her bum. It distracted her too much.

'I want to. I've messaged you daily and you said you were busy.'

'I was.'

'I've not been much of a gentleman. A midnight pizza and a climb to watch the fireworks hardly count as dates.'

'You never had a reputation as a gentleman, Atlas.' She arched an eyebrow in reference to where his hands were at that moment. One on her bum and another sliding up her stomach, over her ribs, a finger tracing the curve of her breast.

'Really?'

'What I'm trying to clumsily say is, I liked the man you were on bonfire night. I don't want to be taken out for fancy dinners. Midnight pizza suits me fine. I don't have a wardrobe for fancy dinners either. Do you?' she challenged.

He laughed at that, 'No. But I would get one. For you. Do you need waking up?' His eyes twinkled with mischief and darkness when he looked at her.

'You can't look at me like you want me naked and in bed,' Gia whispered.

'Why not?' Atlas challenged, desire openly showing in his eyes whilst his fingers continued a teasing trail to her nipple.

'Because it makes me want to do this,' she wrapped her arms around his neck and kissed him. He picked her up as though she weighed nothing. Gia wrapped her legs around him. He carried her to the kitchen counter kissing her back.

The cold worktop temporarily hit her legs and sank some sense into her through the shock of the coolness, but not enough to make her change her mind. When his hands left her body Gia slowly opened her eyes to see Atlas already half undressed. Anticipation shot down her stomach. His warm hands returned to cover her hips underneath her top as he kissed her and pulled her to the edge. Her arms slid around to his back and pulled him closer, her feet pushed his lower back towards her each time he pulled out. There was no outside world, no people, no brownie, just the two of them, he moved to kiss her neck, muttering how she tasted of blackberries. Her eyes fluttered and she thought she saw… she opened her eyes fully and focused, his shadow, it was a tiny bird at the edge of his shape, it grew into a sizable bird of prey, then it morphed into a large stag, a sleek cat, a fox, a wolf, before she couldn't think anymore.

Gia raised the subject over a cup of tea afterwards, when they sat on Rosa's green settee. The velvet was soft and yielding under her bare legs. Atlas had put the fire on whilst she made a pot of tea. Despite that they had just had sex, Atlas was at the other end of the settee. Gia wondered if she had imagined it, or if Atlas was— she pushed the thought aside, he wasn't different in any way. She was getting to know him still. She had no right to presume that she knew anything about him just because she'd been close to Evie growing up.

She chose to ignore her instincts that shouted he was different and dismissed them as her own weakness. She was the one who had never been in a relationship. Those feelings were nothing more than an alert to the fact that this was new and unusual, because she ran from anyone she started to get close to, usually to another state.

'Did anyone ever tell you you're a therianthrope?' was her direct, opening line. He looked surprised.

'A what?'

'An ancient tradition. It's the ability to change into animals. It's where all the werewolf stories and dog man legends come from. It's painted onto cave walls it's so old.'

'How did you come to that conclusion?' Atlas took a casual sip of his tea, as casual and relaxed as ever even if his eyes gave away that he was worried.

'Your shadows gave you away when I was on the kitchen counter a few minutes ago. They were shifting all over the place. I wanted to warn you, in case you decided to have sex with a normal person.'

'I'll remember the blindfold next time,' he drawled.

Gia smiled and shook her head, 'We can do all your kinks, Atlas, I guess we're not going to talk about you. How did you walk home barefoot and half-dressed this morning?'

'The few clothes I was wearing are under your bed. I used the window.' His self-satisfied smile aroused her curiosity.

'I'd say a robin or a wren but that doesn't seem quite what you'd choose, it's far too subtle.'

'A crow. Straight back to the caravan, then a cat because I hadn't left the window open wide enough for a crow.'

'It's not the first time?' Gia could imagine that happening, a proud, confident crow soaring on blue-black outstretched wings the distance from the cottage to the farm.

'Flying home from a woman's bedroom? It definitely was. It's only been about three weeks since I found out what I was, Gia. Why don't we talk about this morning and this pull to each other that we seem to have in the early hours?'

'I wasn't even thinking about you.'

'I was thinking about you in my bed with messed up hair and your—' he started. Then stopped.

Gia observed the expressions rolling across his face. The smirk at remembering what his thoughts had been, the realisation when he finally processed her words, a sense of shock, then his eyes widened in wonder, then a quietness that he mused on whilst she sipped her cup of tea.

'I did it? It was me?' His voice was low.

'What about the first time? What were you thinking?'

'I pictured you when I picked you up at the train station. You looked fucking incredible in that dark red leather jacket. You were, you are, so confident in yourself that nothing phased you. Like that offer to explore all my kinks just now. You always look so perfectly put together but leave no doubts that you're happy to tell someone to go and fuck themselves if they cross you.'

'Growing up I looked up to pair of siblings who were always perfectly turned out in their school uniforms and weren't shy to tell the whole world to go and fuck itself. They made their farm successful. I guess I learned a few things,' Gia leaned back.

He smiled at that. 'I try and care a little more about our reputation now.'

'Why?'

'Because none of us exists alone in a bubble. I fought Evie on her plan to take vegetables to the farmers market. But if she hadn't then we wouldn't have learnt the importance of the country shows, by doing the country shows we started learning what the judges wanted to see in animals, then we started to win, the farming community noticed us, the price of our animals shot up because of the awards. Now we have a really well-run business. One that's exceeded our childhood dreams, but without that community around us it wouldn't have happened. Everywhere I go, I have to remember that I'm representing the farm. Those wild days of playing rugby, getting drunk, fucking blondes, fighting, they're over.' He shrugged.

'Do you miss the blondes?' she teased.

'Not at all. They were fun for a few weeks. I'd get an inside glimpse into what a home looked like. I watched how the parents treated each other and the kids. I looked at what they ate, how free the kids were to get snacks, it taught me what I wanted when I grew up and more, what I didn't want. My reputation was something fun to have for a while, it made me feel like I belonged somewhere.'

'In case it missed your attention I'm neither blonde nor skinny.'

'You're beautiful and you have curves I know they'd kill for. I listened to them talk enough about each other to know that. But talking about lunch, I'm all the way over here so I'm not tempted to touch you again before you get dressed.'

'That doesn't come across as a threat, Atlas,' Gia smiled broadly even as she tried to keep a straight face.

He chuckled, 'Go and get dressed, Gia.'

Instead, she placed her hands on the hem and pulled her sweatshirt off and headed upstairs. She heard Atlas murmur, 'fuck lunch' before he followed her upstairs.

Gia laid in bed, sweat glistened on both bodies as their breathing slowed down. She was about to say something when Atlas shifted, he picked up his phone to look at the time. Silently, Gia readied herself for the goodbye, usually she looked forward to being left alone, but today, she didn't want him to leave. A warm hand cupped her face and lifted it so her eyes met his. He leaned down to place a kiss on her lips. Gia felt the difference immediately. His other kisses had been harder, her bruised lips barely registered the tenderness in that one.

'I'll pick you up for dinner tonight, beautiful. I have to leave you.' His rich husky voice made her sink further into the mattress.

'I know. The farm won't run itself,' she forced her eyes

open, and leaned up to give him a quick kiss before he moved away from her, taking what she could get from him in the last few seconds. She would love their bubble back, to lock the two of them away inside it for a few days. She stopped short of asking him to stay.

She rolled onto her side to watch Atlas dress and concluded that he dressed like a predator. He was unhurried, every movement careful, considered, and conscious. She could imagine him stalking potential prey. Gia realised he probably had to be conscious of every tiny movement he made given the size of the cows and bulls that he worked with daily. Cows scared her, any animal bigger than a domestic cat scared her, or any animal smaller than a domestic cat.

His next question surprised her though, 'Is it dangerous?' She knew immediately what he was referring to without him having to say it. His ability to change into animals.

'It depends on how you think. If you turn into a sparrow and sparrowhawk kills you, yes. If you forget your conscious self and merge fully into the animal, then you could stay that way forever. But a chance to see how the birds see blues where we see black, how an animal thinks, to understand communication noises, I wouldn't pass on that experience.'

Atlas was quiet for a moment. He redid his hair. He lifted his new work boots up to carry them before asking her in a quiet tone, 'Did you ever experience someone coming back from the dead? Not zombie dead or a ghost, like a demon or something?'

'That would be exceptionally rare. Demons are entities that, generally, are old. To become a new one means that a soul is beyond having any positive traits hidden away inside them. It's when the core of someone is so inextricably different that there's already nothing human left of them.'

'So, what? They go to hell and get rewarded with being a demon instead of torture?'

'That is a philosophical debate because I don't believe in heaven or hell. I'm not even sure I believe in demons anymore.'

'I'm confused. You don't believe in demons?'

'I believe in the darkness of entities people call demons. Hell seems to be very much an organised religion idea. The underworld was a thing before hell but it wasn't a bad place or a long-term place for a soul. Even in early Christian religion purgatory was a temporary place. I feel like we're having two different conversations here, one about whether someone can become a demon, and another about the popular concept sold to us of hell being a place of demons and eternal suffering.'

'OK.' Atlas drew out the word with a nod.

There was a long silence. Atlas kept meeting her eyes. He would look as though he was about to say something to her before shutting down.

After witnessing several attempts of him trying to raise a topic Gia asked, 'Do you want to go downstairs, get a coffee and talk about this?' She watched his eyes rove over her curves.

He sat on the bed and ran his hand over her hip before he answered, 'Honestly, I'd prefer to talk with you looking like that, but I do have work to do.'

'If you give me a name, I could cast a circle and ask.'

'Isn't it dangerous?' He looked at her alarmed.

Gia shrugged, 'I've been doing it for fun for years.'

Atlas removed his hand, picked up his boots and turned the handle on the door. Gia jumped up and threw a light, flimsy gown over herself to see him out. He turned his head to glance behind him at her movement, ever alert to his surroundings. Once she had moved from the bed her skin responded to the chill in the cottage with goosebumps and a shiver.

'Do you want me to start your fire?' Atlas looked at the fire in her bedroom.

Gia shook her head, 'I'm going to jump in the shower once you've gone.'

'Don't do anything stupid, I'd really like to see you again for dinner tonight.'

'It's a shower, Atlas,' she smiled. Acknowledging that he was going to leave she took a step nearer him, to follow him downstairs when he left. Tender fingertips, rough against her skin, held her jaw without any pressure.

He leaned in and whispered, 'You know what I mean. I want to see those beautiful eyes of yours again, Gia.'

'There I am thinking you just want my body,' she teased.

He allowed himself a smile, but returned with, 'That you're beautiful with a great body is just a bonus. I'll stand between you and the shadows any day.'

It was there, a flash. A hint. A glimmer of a difference in the person that she thought she knew from who he actually was. It wasn't what he had said, rather how it had been said, with knowledge in his eyes and a secret she didn't know. It was like reading a book where the prose was perfect but the plot was lacking and she read without taking anything in, then suddenly realised that she had no idea what was happening on the pages in front of her.

Chapter 15

The sun had dipped by the time Gia emerged from the shower. Slanted shafts of daylight pushed through the windows at angles. She dressed for a casual dinner, the same trousers she had worn to meet Evie that first Sunday and a crochet wraparound black top. She removed the brooch from the handknitted cardigan and pinned it on her top. When she had bought the cardigan at a house clearance, it still had the brooch attached to it, a black spider with ruby eyes. The seller, the owner's daughter, a bloated bottle blonde who dressed in clothes too small for her, declared it was grotesque and refused to let Gia hand it back even as Gia suggested that the red eyes might be rubies. She had been told that the elderly woman it had belonged to was too poor to have rubies. Gia had the brooch checked. The shop had cleaned off years of dirt, revealing not just the ruby eyes but the large, dark sapphires that made up the body and head. She liked to team it with her collection of ruby jewellery. Rubies were her favourite gems, but she was particular. Gia preferred them with rose gold and hated them paired with diamonds. For the last year and a bit she started to agree with Tess, both moonstone and pearl had a certain subtle understated attraction. Where Evie loved white décor, Tess loved white jewellery.

Dressed and downstairs, Gia measured out the gifted

coffee grains, prepared to open her laptop and pick up on continuing to write her new novel when she heard the light knock. It wasn't Evie's back door knock, or Atlas's heavy hammering. She opened the front door to see Oliver there in jeans and a fastened coat. He held a large bunch of sunflowers that he pushed towards her.

'Um. Thank you?' Gia took the flowers, unsure if they were meant for her.

'You said once that you liked yellow flowers.' She had. She remembered that moment. It had been late September, they were walking home from Oak Hall, their English class had been on a trip to see a touring play and they had arrived back at the school after the other students had left. The yellow flowers she had talked about were evening primrose. Evie had introduced her to them and their addictive, lemon honey scent.

'I thought I'd stop by to see if you fancied going for that drink? We could go into the city.'

'Actually, Oliver, I have dinner plans.'

'With Atlas?'

'With Atlas.'

'We could go to the hotel. It's quieter in there.'

'I'll get my coat.' Gia dashed upstairs for her leather jacket, yet another reminder that the English winter wasn't yet in full swing and she needed a warmer coat to see her through it.

A few minutes later they were in the bar at the old hotel. The subdued lighting mixed with the warmth of wood gave them a sense of enclosed privacy. The waiter carried their coffees over. Gia watched Oliver sugar his and stir it thoroughly. He looked up, and smiled, 'You're probably not a sugar in coffee person.'

'No,' Gia shook her head.

'It's the sweetness. It gives me something to hang onto when I'm stressed with a case.'

'Are you on a case at the moment?'

'Yvonne's disappearance. My boss really wants an answer to that. That and the locked room murder.' He shrugged.

'Lousie's?'

'I shouldn't have said that. Yes. Sorry.'

'Why are you calling it that?'

'Her door was bolted on the inside. Her window was open but she lives on the top floor in a block of flats. There's a camera opposite, no one but a pigeon went in and out all night.' Gia felt that Oliver had an ulterior motive for chatting. The way his eyes darted across her face and body put her on edge, he was assessing every expression, every move, every fidget.

'Was it messy?' she asked him.

'Louise? Yes. Unlike Yvonne who just vanished. She's not even logged into social media and she posted several times a day. Has done for years.' He was going to ask about Evie. Gia waited for it, 'I don't suppose Evie has said anything?' He looked hopeful.

'No.'

'I'm looking for anything that clears her name.' The lack of sincerity in his voice, mixed with his previous comments that implied he could set anyone up, made her conclude that it was the opposite.

'Evie was with me on Sunday, in the café and then the pub. She was in the city the day before, you know that because the papers got a picture of her leaving the theatre with her children. All I know is that Yvonne wasn't at work the following Monday. Didn't Yvonne contact the other presenters late on Sunday or early Monday and tell them they weren't required?'

'Evie didn't like Yvonne though?'

'Did we come here for a catch up or do you just want to talk about Evie?'

It dawned on her that he had always wanted to talk about Evie. Whenever they had walked home together after an English study session in sixth form, he had brought Evie up, those memories rushed back to her now. She had forgotten. She was discovering a new side to the village and its people. One that was pushing all the nostalgia away.

'I'm sorry. It's a habit. I did come here to catch up, you're right.'

'We always end up talking about Evie. I used to think it was because you had a secret crush on her. Looking at you now, you don't like her at all do you?'

'She used to steal from my mum. Did you know that? That spoilt brat would steal things like butter, salt, milk, like they didn't have all that up on the farm.' He spat the sentence out.

Gia wanted to defend her friend and tell Oliver the truth. But Evie would be deeply embarrassed if the truth was common knowledge, so she held it in and raised her chin, 'Your mum knew?'

'Yes. She said Evie wasn't stealing chocolate or sweets, and that by judging how skinny she and Atlas were they probably needed the milk and butter.'

'You resent Evie and your mum?'

'Mum should have done something. Neither of those ever went without.'

'Did you, Oliver?' she asked quietly. The question

resulted in a slew of words, about how it had been for him, not really fitting in, only attending the school because his father was the Head, and that he thought he and Gia were kindred spirits because she only had a place due to Rosa teaching languages and later, politics.

Although they chatted like old friends, it was an awkward, forced conversation on both sides. Gia pushed her extrovert chatty side to the limit. The more she talked to Oliver the less he said in return, and the more she felt compelled to maintain the air of civility, as though if she let the veneer between them slip, she would see the ugliness that existed inside him. It wasn't that she hadn't seen the ugliness before, or that she hadn't been alone with people like Oliver before. It was his attitude to her friend, it hurt that he didn't see Evie for who she really was. Underneath the self-preservation, her too casual act of being above everything the world had to offer, Evie was unassuming, sweet and caring. Evie had been hurt so much by life that she didn't give people a chance to hurt her first.

If Gia was testing a person out for her research, she would put them at ease with normal conversation before she launched into supernatural and paranormal talk. Here, she twisted her normal conversation around to religion and Oliver's life. She saw his eyes light up. He talked about how lonely he had been at university, how he hadn't measured up to play for the rugby team or fitted in with their personalities. He mentioned how he hadn't fitted with the public-educated pupils nor the state-educated pupils at university, drifting along in some sort of privately-educated but not rich middle ground. The church group had welcomed him with open arms, steered him from his chosen degree into one that they said promised him a future that matched his personality and helped to mould him into the type of man that would raise a family in the church.

'That's all they've asked of you?' Gia's suspicions were always raised after the first encounter with these types of people. Oliver had always been a bit of an outcast; he had played rugby, but he never joined in the inner circle shenanigans the way Atlas had. When she looked back, there had always been a hidden sneer on his face towards the siblings.

'Yes. They asked about the Yrsa legend. One of them had visited the village once, and they were intrigued. They asked a few years ago if I knew you. I think it was around the time your third book came out.'

'OK.'

'Don't you ever wonder what it is that makes you all so prominent? It's almost as if there's something special about you all. I remember that you rarely let any outsiders in. Liberty was the last, wasn't she? She turned up one day and you all took one look at her and that was it. We used to call you the seven sinners after that.'

'Us? There's nothing special about us.'

'There is. You with your books, Evie being on TV, Tess with her art, Kat with her women's issues channel, Nina's a model, Genevieve is always pictured at some millionaire society event. Liberty is quieter, but the financial pages talk about her if you look closely enough, like she has some Midas touch.' He shrugged as though reeling off a few things made them prominent.

Gia found it mildly concerning that he had kept tabs on them all, but in the days of instant access to people through social media it was hardly stalker level, he hadn't even remembered that the yellow flowers she liked were evening primrose, she shook her head, 'I think looking at it from the surface means you really don't see our normal everyday lives. Evie still works on the farm whilst doing her TV job. I spend most of my time alone in front of a laptop. Whilst you're busy feeling sorry for yourself because you didn't fit in with the private school kids, we're just busy forging our lives using the fact that we didn't fit in as a strength. I think anyone with half a brain feels like an alien in this world. Sometimes it feels that you can't have a different opinion from mainstream society, or they label you as weird, as if that's the worst thing anyone can ever be. What we've been through made us all left wing in terms of politics, that's the main reason we stuck together, because we were surrounded by rich idiots.'

'You all think the same? You talk about this?'

'Yes.'

She didn't say that most of the time when Nina joined the group chat her rambling messages were undeciphera-ble, or that no one had heard from Genevieve in ten years.

'Rosa hinted that your nomadic days living in a camper van were over. That will be a story your teenagers will love you for one day.' Oliver attempted to change the subject.

'Teenagers?' Gia blinked.

'Yeah, I'm laying my cards out Gia, I want a family. I think it would work out perfectly for us. You could still have a laptop and write when the kids are in school. It would enable you to be present for them when they're growing up. We'd have to talk about a few things. Maybe not politics. Perhaps change what you write. You've been so successful with witches but perhaps it's not quite the family image we would want to present.'

Gia picked her coffee cup up, realised that it was empty and cold, and put it back down. She wanted to answer but her brain was stuck trying to put together the rollercoaster loops Oliver had gone through, how he had gone from the pair of them going out for coffee as a friendly catch up, to being married and her becoming the default parent whilst he apparently got to continue his life.

She was saved from forming an answer by Atlas's rich, deep voice, 'Unless you've changed her mind in the space of one conversation Gia isn't planning on becoming a mother anytime soon.' Atlas put a glass of rum and coke in front of Gia, a pint down on the table, and made a point of pulling up a chair to the table loudly. He settled himself in, leaning back, stretching out his legs, and crossing him arms, 'Did he change your mind, Gia?'

'Absolutely fucking not. Why should I be the one that stays home?' Her anger had been temporarily misplaced by the shock of Oliver's unexpected conclusion of their relationship.

'Women feel different about working once they've had a baby.' Oliver shrugged.

'Men should feel different once they've had a baby too. It isn't about leaving it all up to her to deal with because you work,' Atlas offered, staring hard at Oliver.

'All I know is that its traditional. Men go out and work, women raise the children.'

'It's not traditional at all,' Gia rejoined the conversation, 'It's a very recent concept. If we're talking traditional, both parents worked because everyone was poor, or the family was rich enough to employ help with the house and the children through exploiting workers. Further back people lived in communities where women hunted alongside men and children were raised by everyone, a mum had leisure time and support. I'll tell my grandmother to pass you those studies, backed up by scientific research. I won't deny that research has shown it's beneficial for a child to have a parent at home.'

'You're turning my words against me. Don't make me a villain just because I want a wife who wants to be a good mum.'

'You're not giving her autonomy. You're making the choice for her. That's exactly why I don't do religion,' Gia pointed out

'The women at church tell me they felt different about things once they had a baby. I'm just trying to prepare for that eventuality.' Oliver shrugged.

'Maybe you should prepare for a hearing test first? Followed by a comprehension exercise,' Gia retorted.

Atlas chuckled, 'On that note, beautiful, shall we go for pre-dinner drinks somewhere else?'

'Sure,' Gia downed her drink. Atlas took her cue and drank his pint in five gulps.

'You'll drink with him?' Oliver looked at Atlas.

Gia sighed, she leaned forward slightly towards Oliver, 'Oliver, here's a secret, OK. Atlas listens to me and acts accordingly. I can have a couple of drinks around him and relax. Try that next time.'

'I thought you preferred blondes, Atlas,' the remark dripped with sarcasm.

Atlas grinned, 'You thought wrong. I like big brown eyes. Especially when they're full of trust.'

Chapter 16

Evie settled into the red chair opposite Gia with her hands wrapped around the spa's complimentary coffee. Gia held her own cup of coffee. Evie had warned her to wear comfortable baggy clothes. The closest Gia had to that description was the red sweatshirt she usually wore with leggings for extra casual days. Or the jumpsuit that she still had to buy trainers for. She had opted for the red sweatshirt with a red silk T-shirt underneath, black jeans and stilettos. The staff had taken one look at her shoes and provided waffle slippers. Evie looked extremely casual and adorable in a white tracksuit, a cute cropped hoody and matching bottoms. Her clean trainers had clearly never seen the farm or a workout.

'We need to get you spa clothes.' Evie smiled as she brought in the fresh air on her clothes and eyed up Gia's outfit.

Gia shook her head, 'I'm not wearing a tracksuit. They make me look like a sack of potatoes.'

Evie laughed at Gia's tone, not the words, and sipped her coffee. She changed the topic, 'What are your plans with my brother this weekend?'

'We haven't made any. What are your plans?'

'Robbie's leaving on a stag night after work tonight. Max and Ava both have stuff on all weekend with their friends.'

'How are things with you and Robbie?' Gia checked with her friend.

Evie beamed, happiness radiated from her. 'Good. I mean, it's still early, but good. I'm starting to relax. When he began to be around a lot after Halloween, I was waiting for the negative stuff to start, actively looking so that I didn't miss the red flags this time, but, he's genuine. He does a full day at work and still helps with dinner.'

Gia smiled at her friend's happiness. She hadn't forgotten how physically uncomfortable she had been in the pub around Robbie's family. One day she would find a way to bring it up and analyse it with Evie without it being an issue between them. For now, she had to keep quiet, so she phrased it differently, 'I need your perspective on something. If someone like us met a group of people and it felt like their blood was splitting into two, what would you think?' She watched Evie's reaction. Her friend showed her surprise on her face, then thoughtfulness. She took a few moments before she answered. Gia liked that Evie managed her reaction before responding. Reacting instantly on emotion was something she had to learn to stop doing.

She listened to Evie's response, 'I don't know without asking more questions. I've learnt more in the last few weeks than I ever thought was possible to be real. At the very base of the question, I'd hazard a guess that these were people she shouldn't be around and it's a warning that they mean her harm.'

Their attention was taken by four women walking in, talking. They looked at Evie and headed straight for her. Evie stiffened and plastered a smile across her face. The four greeted her. They were all dressed similarly, immaculate tracksuit bottoms, T-shirts which subtly matched their choice of tracksuit in colour tone, their glossy hair tied back in silk scrunchies or scarves. They descended on Evie like a horde of seagulls fighting over a piece of food. Evie matched their greetings with polite enquiries about their children, she introduced Gia who became their new target. The pair were battered with questions, half about Gia's work, half about Evie's work.

Gia understood Evie's tight smile and stiffened back half an hour later when one of the women, a person who claimed to have an English degree, decided to give Gia unsolicited advice on writing. The advice, that Gia's story weaving skills were on point, but that she needed to write a literary fiction novel that would be eligible for nomination to awards, barely masked blatant self-promotion, 'I could be your manager and contact agents for you.' The woman was saved from Gia's acidic response by Jae calling Evie and Gia out of the group and escorting them to a room set up for the both of them. When Jae disappeared to get them some water and the other beauty therapist, Evie sank into a chair and rolled her eyes at Gia.

'It's all status with most of them. Half of the parents are genuinely lovely, half are trying to outdo everyone.'

'They remind me of Tess's stepmum,' Gia said.

Evie suddenly sat up straight, 'That's so true! They do. How is your house hunting going?'

'Slow. There's too many distractions. I have a few saved on my phone. It's disappointing.'

'How?'

'I want to use my savings to buy the house. Another option is to only use what I need as a deposit and keep the rest, but I would need to secure a mortgage. If I buy without a mortgage in the village, I'll have to get a full-time job just to eat and pay bills. I kind of like being a full-time author. I don't mind having life happening around me, but at the same time, I'd quite like some space. I don't think I appreciated Nonna's cottage garden enough growing up, the way that it wraps around the house and insulates it.'

'What about renting?'

'I'm fine with that idea but Nonna talks about investments and getting a foot on the property ladder like I'm behind in developmental milestones.'

'What do you want though? It's your life.'

'I'm not so good at the level of commitment and official paperwork to sit through a mortgage process. I can write a book on a laptop from nothing. Ask me to fill in official documents and something switches in my head, I struggle with it.'

'I had noticed the three thousand unopened emails on your notification screen.' They both knew Evie was exaggerating, her tone was teasing, and Gia knew that she would never respond to those emails

'That's not... I have a secret one that my agent uses. No one else knows it. That means it's manageable and I get my work done. I have one for my website and a general one for purchases because you get spammed with emails.'

'Is that why you had a camper van in America? Because buying a home involves actual official paperwork?'

'Yes. I thought I'd drop the insecurity when I came home. It's still here.'

'What makes you insecure?'

'Making things official. Surprisingly. I remember the looks I got when my first book hit the bestseller lists overnight. I was twenty and unprepared. Here for a bit, there for a bit, write a book, move on, find the next exciting thing. I do miss waking up in a morning knowing that I'd see at least one of you that day.'

Gia hadn't realised it until she said it. She missed having real friends. Honest friends. Ones that supported her success but didn't treat her any different.

'I missed that too. I would rather have us all seventeen and together again, with the village hating me, than the loneliness of the last few years. I thought it was just me and the choices I had made.'

'No. I loved moving around but it was the group chats that really made me smile.'

'Was there a deciding factor in coming home?'

'There was one day in September. I had a feeling of wanting to come home. It was overwhelming. I couldn't shake it off like all the other times. Then, circumstances came together to make leaving America easier.' Their conversation stopped when Jae entered the room with the other therapist, their white uniforms straight and perfect.

'Evie, what are we starting with? The Indian head massage or facial?'

'Indian head massage. Gia too.' Evie didn't miss a beat when answering, as though this was something that she did all the time. Gia guessed that it was.

Gia's impression that an Indian head massage somehow focused on the scalp was incorrect. After finding herself wrapped in a towel and having experienced an upper back massage her therapist was pressing her occipital points, then her forehead and face. Evie had told her not to bother with make-up, or to only wear the lightest touch of mascara. Gia understood now, just as she understood Evie's silence. The almost permanent tension she felt across her shoulders from constantly being at a laptop trying to meet deadlines loosened. The sinus muscles at her eyebrows loosened with the massage. Like Evie, she closed her eyes and relaxed. This was why they had booked a day in the spa. In all her adventures, all the days she had shut herself away to write her books, she had never forgotten that she was a witch and author first. Life had become about the next book, research, writing, even reading new releases from other authors in her genre had become a sort of game for her social media. In the spa next to her friend, Gia realised that she had forgotten she was a person too, and that rest and relaxation were rejuvenating.

Chapter 17

Gia had twisted her hair back into its customary low bun, applied eyeliner and mascara to her bare face, along with a sheer red lip balm before she left the spa. Even now, at home in the village, habits were difficult to leave and she couldn't walk outside not looking like Gia Roselli, the author. Evie grabbed Gia's wrist in the car park outside and asked her if she would mind taking a look at a few photos Robbie had on his phone of a circle found in the old farmhouse. Gia, happy to help her friend out, told her to send her the pictures. Evie left then, in her big car that matched her brother's and headed towards Oak Hall to collect her children from school.

Gia ambled slowly along the high street. She missed the warmth of the spa, but in her relaxed state she couldn't be bothered to walk faster in her heels. When she had arrived back to the village in October, the trees had been a blaze of changing colours, now in November only a few handfuls of leaves clung onto their branches in rich autumnal jewelled colours. The sun was low but still vibrant in the cloudless blue sky, a halo of shimmering paleness around the yellow orb.

Gia walked past Harriet's café, just a few doors down from the spa. She had never been in. She had been waiting for the perfect moment. Impulsively, she opened the door to the gothic witchy café and walked in. It was quiet. A few tourists sat with drinks, a couple of elderly people sat with a pot of tea, one was reading a book. Behind the counter a pink-haired woman cleaned a coffee machine and another woman unloaded a tray of cups and saucers onto a shelf underneath the counter. Gia mused the board behind the counter that listed the drinks and eyed up the cake display.

The pink-haired woman turned around and smiled, the smiled dropped a little as a flash of recognition hit, then grew wider, 'You're Gia Roselli.'

'I am.'

'I love your books.'

'Do you have a favourite?'

'Abby. I know it's not the scariest one, but I love how she knew from an early age that she wanted her small-town community. When I was homesick at university on the wrong course, I reread it for the courage to come home and open my own café. I even debated calling this Abby's. Welcome to my dream, what can I get you?'

'A cortado please, and one of the caramelised apple tortes. I like your interior.'

'Thank you. Are you in the village for a while?'

'I'm back for a bit.'

'Back? I know you talk about growing up in Yorkshire,' Harriet trailed off, looking at Gia with uncertainty.

'I grew up here. I'm a friend of Evie's, I think you know her. We've just been in the spa together.'

'With Jae?'

'Yes, you know Jae?'

'We were at school together. We used to swap your books. Why don't you ever say you're from this village?'

'Mostly because it's hard enough to explain where Yorkshire is if people don't know.'

Gia had never talked about the tiny village she grew up in, she usually just said Yorkshire, or London then Yorkshire, or sometimes, when pressed, within travelling distance of Leeds/Sheffield/York/Harrogate. Not that the cities were interchangeable, just that she picked the ones people were likely to have heard of. Some of the Americans who had tried to pin her home location down appeared to get confused that there was an inhabited land mass between London ending and Scotland starting, or thought that Scotland started a few miles outside London which would have placed Yorkshire in Scotland. She didn't complain, America was big, driving across a state was sometimes the same length of time it took to drive the entire length of England, in the beginning of her time in America she wouldn't have been able to name all the states or find them on a map. She was back in England now, she ought to start saying where she came from.

They both turned as the door opened and the old entry bell above it rang. A woman stood there. She locked eyes with Gia. Gia held her breath, she could actually feel her eyes widening. The woman was her, in her normal version of herself. The same curly tendrils escaping, the same low bun, the same signature make-up, the all-black outfit, gold jewellery, the red leather jacket, except, she had the same cold maliciousness in her eyes as the man in the food hall. The other Gia stepped back out of the café and closed the door, still looking at Gia.

Harriet turned wide eyes to her, 'Was that a doppelganger?'

'Doppelgangers are talked of as being more like apparitions, I think.' The words tumbled from her mouth without thought of who she was talking to. Usually she was much more careful.

'A demon?'

'No. I don't think so. Maybe. I can't recall anything about demons taking on human images in folklore, in religion they tend to look for bodies to inhabit as a possession, if they could appear as human they wouldn't need to do that.'

'It still means bad luck?'

'It means something is definitely brewing in the village.' Yet her stomach jumped in excitement, she hid a smile at the thought that crazy was about to happen, and pushed the playfully psychotic part of her back down with a reminder that masking it under normal appearances was the only acceptable way to deal with that part of herself.

Gia was still in the café when Evie sent the photos to her phone after the school run, pictures of a forgotten chalk circle on a stone floor. Robbie and his team of workmen had found it underneath a wooden floor in the old farmhouse. Evie simply asked Gia if she knew any of the symbols and what it meant. At a first, casual glance, Gia had instantly identified loneliness, isolation and darkness. She had already responded to Evie, when her eye caught the picture again. She closed her phone and walked back to the cottage, her mind on the circle.

Once inside and alone, Gia screenshot the picture and turned the photo around using the tools on her screen. From the angle she was looking at now, the sigils worked to harness power towards a certain individual, the name was smudged. Intrigued, Gia turned the picture again. This time the carefully designed sigils changed again, they became boundary laws. From another angle, the boundary laws changed to punishments for those crossing into the territory.

Gia turned the picture backwards a turn to the boundary law. The boundary law was hidden and clever, wrapped into the loneliness, darkness and unease. The punishments on the turn after confused her until she realised that neither were targeted at humans of any kind. Not even witches. There were wild animals on the land, there had been as long as Gia remembered, Atlas had taught them the names of the birds, how to distinguish a hare from a rabbit, the difference between a grass snake and an adder. Evie had taught them how to identify different bird sounds, plants and trees. If the boundary sigils weren't for humans or animals, the challenging question was who would need such a boundary defined for them inside a circle. Or rather, what, would need a strong magical boundary to keep it out of the farm.

Her answer came when she was eating dinner; a quick pasta and salad. Rosa had gone out to dinner with university colleagues. Alone, Gia sat at the breakfast bar, her phone playing a film she was only listening to whilst she stared at the dark shrubs and hedges that served to mark out the boundary of their cottage when the memory of bonfire night resurfaced. The shadows of horses and dogs racing across the field without physical bodies were the answer. Atlas's cautious reaction that they should move away. His expression had suggested to Gia that the experience was as new to him as it was to her.

Gia shut the film down and read the text from Evie again, this time taking note that Evie said the circle origins could be older and it was possible that the floor above had been put down around the turn of the century to save it from being redrawn, that the origins of the actual floor were from the Stuart era. Gia's brain shifted. From taking in the sigils at every angle and understanding them to be more than they appeared, she began to look at the sigils as three-dimensional objects rather than flat hand-drawn chalk symbols. From there, she begun to see exactly how resourceful, original and cunning the creator of the circle had been. It was beautifully designed. Gia spent a good two hours marvelling over it. Then another hour criticising herself for not having even thought about that level of complexity and uniqueness in her own circles. She sent her friend a message that there was more to it than she thought and that they needed to get together.

Evie rang her almost immediately, 'Hi, Atlas is with me. You're on speakerphone. Should we be worried?'

'I don't know, I'm looking at it now, it's multi-layered, complex, and incredibly beautiful for a spell. The person who did this knew their craft well. Give me another day or two to study it further. It isolates the farm and the land, the people living on it, but beyond that there's border spells, something to do with darkness that I haven't quite understood yet, I think I know what it was supposed to keep out as well as keep the people in, but I want to understand the how and the why before I tell you. It's so pretty, I need to show you how it weaves together like a Celtic knot but also circles like a slow whirlwind. Each sigil forms connections with those next to it as it rises upwards and outwards and it creates another spell like a magical Fibonacci sequence.'

'Hey, beautiful, be safe, don't take unnecessary risks without me there.' Atlas's voice came over the phone, softly spoken in his husky, whisky voice.

At the same time he spoke, the door opened with a

soft rush and Rosa stepped over the threshold into the cottage. Gia said goodbye to Atlas and Evie, cautious to not let Rosa hear a word. Her grandmother's words had been troubling Gia. Rosa believed that Gia needed saving from herself, that her lineage made her a danger to herself, and she had reached that conclusion without talking to Gia, that wound Gia up. Not even a second later her phone pinged with a message. The message was from Atlas, a reminder that he could be there in seconds without Rosa knowing if she wanted to leave her window open. She couldn't help but smile, even so, her reply was firm, she needed time to herself. She was still learning to connect her head to her body and find a peace in the wholeness of being a united soul. Atlas and sex couldn't be her crutch for that. She wanted to master it herself, by herself, for herself, so she could access that sense of serenity and wholeness of being whenever she chose to.

Chapter 18

Gia let herself into the cottage, shopping bags in her hand. Behind her a light rain had started in the already dark winter evening, it came down sideways in the light from the door. Gia shut it out and turned into the room. Atlas was already chatting to Rosa over a cup of coffee on the settee, Rosa was smiling at him, whatever he had said must have been amusing. Gia took in the sight of Atlas on her grandmother's settee, his long brown hair in a bun, his beard was neater and a bit shorter; he must have been to the barbers, he was dressed casually in worn grey tracksuit bottoms and a mismatched black hoody.

Rosa glanced at her from over her shoulder, it was hard to glance backwards to the front door from the settee. She spoke before Gia had even closed the door, 'You didn't tell me you were thinking of purchasing a house in Eastwood. You could get a place in the city for the same price. Same style house but walkable to the city centre.'

'Telling tales on me, Atlas?' Gia looked at him.

'I was hoping your grandmother would persuade you out of moving so far away, but it seems she'd like you even further away from me.' His gentle tone was teasing.

'I want her safe, but she doesn't have a car. Buying outside of town, even in Eastwood, doesn't make sense. The city makes more sense.'

'I was also looking at camper vans and touring

England. Maybe even Europe on a digital nomad visa.'

She looked Atlas in the eye as she issued that statement and saw him flinch a little, but all he said was, 'I hope you've prepared for that better than you prepared for bonfire night.'

'I now own pyjamas and a warmer jumper,' Gia grinned, taking off her hat. Atlas laughed. Rosa looked between them, a ghost of a smile on her lips.

'I owe you a thank you for at least informing me this time that you're taking Gia out. And for the box you've brought.'

'Are you bribing my grandmother, Atlas?'

'Of course.'

'What's in the box?' Gia walked over to investigate. He had brought cheese, crackers, chutney, butter, and a wine to go with it all. She was mildly impressed, and half wanted to stay to eat it all with Rosa, 'What do I get?'

'Me.' The answer from Atlas came so fast Rosa laughed. Gia looked directly at him and raised her eyebrows. He met her look with a smirk and leaned back into the settee.

'My bag is upstairs. I won't be a minute.' She ran up the stairs. When she had arranged this night with Evie, an impromptu get together, Atlas had texted her to pack a bag and stay with him. Gia hadn't argued. She pushed the new jumper into the bag with the black thermals she had bought to wear as pyjamas, already knowing that she wouldn't be wearing them.

Evie's children had been invited to sleep at Robbie's parents. Gia didn't think an evening in the caravan talking about magic circles was what Robbie's parents had in mind when they had offered to take the children overnight.

Despite that, she had studied the circle, and the intricacy needed to be explained if the siblings were to really understand what they had removed. She carried her bag downstairs, Atlas stood up when he saw her, he took her bag from her and carried it straight to his car, leaving her to say goodbye to Rosa.

'I thought you preferred Oliver?' Gia was confused by her grandmother's warmth to Atlas.

'It's not my decision is it? You two look at each other the way your grandfather and I looked at each other. We had such a short time together. I can't refuse you that.'

'Oliver's not what you think he is,' Gia tried to warn Rosa.

Rosa gave a shake of her head, 'He doesn't have the same presence Atlas has, if Atlas was a wolf, Oliver would be a woodcutter. But the woodcutter builds a home from the wood, Gia, the wolf is a hunter that becomes hunted.'

'What happens when there's a stand-off? The wolf against the woodcutter? A predator's quickness against a human and an axe?' The play on words popped out before she even thought about them. Gia gave her grandmother a kiss on the cheek, picked up her laptop bag packed with essentials such as her charger, notepads and pens, and left the cottage.

She knew she was in Atlas's car immediately. Faint traces of juniper danced through the leather and fresh air. He turned to her as she shut the door. Gia gave him a nod, a sign to say she had everything, and he set off. She settled back and relaxed into the seat, 'A box? Really?' she teased.

Atlas didn't respond for a few seconds as he negotiated a sharp, narrow corner where someone had decided to park their car. Gia had begun to think she'd offended him, her brain rushed back to his childhood when he and his sister had been neglected and struggled to find food. His hand went to her thigh once they were past the corner, his voice was calm and full of smooth whisky charm when he said, 'That's nothing compared to what we've got for tonight. There's bottles of rum and coke for you and Evie. Beer and whisky. Water because Evie's not a big drinker these days. She likes to relax but not get drunk. Robbie and I took Evie's list to the farm shops and that box isn't even a quarter of what she wrote down for the charcuterie grazing board thing that's taken over my caravan.'

'Your caravan?'

'Yeah. I'm actually scared to mess up Evie's white perfection,' he joked. Gia hadn't seen Evie's caravan, but it didn't surprise her to hear that it was white inside. She would have predicted that about her friend.

'Evie always wanted a blank canvas to start from. It didn't matter how much we tried to tell her that families don't provide that. She never liked that she lived in the witch house up on witch farm. I understood in a way. I was the kid whose parents had been murdered. I never escaped that.'

'I'm sorry you had to go through that. Do you remember anything about Italy?' Atlas asked her.

'Bits. There's a memory of laughing with my mum. She wore a yellow dress that day and her ice cream was melting. I remember the heat of summer evenings and the chatter of conversation below me when I lay on the balcony. I remember wandering outside in winter to find out where the music was coming from which started endless stories of me sleepwalking. I wasn't. I was awake. I heard the music. I know it wasn't a dream.'

Atlas stopped the car outside his caravan. He didn't move to hurry out of the car, instead he turned to her. She felt the full focus of his grey and amber eyes when he asked, 'Tell me that the music was worth it at least?' his mouth curved in a smile.

She responded with a smile of her own, 'It was beautiful. Wild, free, haunting and beautiful. I can still hear it now when I really think about it. I've searched through classical music, but I haven't found which piece it was.' She looked up as movement outside caught her eye.

Evie and Robbie were walking out of her caravan. Evie put a clear dome-shaped umbrella up to cover her from the rain that was falling harder now. She looked stunning in a long length winter knitted dress and matching cardigan. She wore wellingtons but carried slippers. Her hair was wavy and her make-up was dewy but polished. Gia, in contrast, had a long red jersey skirt on, a black jumper, rose gold jewellery and her lace-up boots. She had forgotten slippers. Her hair was back in a low messy bun and she had her signature make-up on that never varied. She had tried to do a different look, but she looked too strange in the mirror once she had finished.

Gia tensed when she saw a taller version of Robbie with shorter hair. Liam locked the door of the caravan and passed the key to Evie.

She looked at Atlas, 'You didn't say Liam would be here.'

Atlas didn't answer. He shuffled around and reached into a pocket, at the same time he opened the car door and passed his key to Evie. 'Give us a minute.'

Even as the two brothers walked past her side of the

car to the caravan her whole body began to pull apart inside. The experience was a softer tug than in the pub but it still happened enough for her to feel it. Gia reasoned that she had sat through a whole afternoon in the pub, she could do one evening. She moved her hand to the door handle. A heavy hand pressed her in place, a car door closed with softness. Atlas's gruff voice wasn't soft, 'Talk.'

Gia hesitated. It was a struggle to begin to even try and put into words how she felt around Robbie and Liam. Her thoughts raced back to bonfire night when Atlas had reassured her that he had once had doubts about Robbie. It wasn't her nature to seek constant reassurance, she was practiced in self-reliance. She pushed a smile onto her face.

'It's nothing, I haven't seen much of Evie, I guess I just hoped we'd get more time to talk about what happened to her on Halloween. No offence to your version but it was a little short on actual details.'

'The facts were there.' He moved his arm from the door and out of her space.

'But no details.'

'Gia, talk to me, properly.'

'I already have, Atlas. Maybe I need to get to know Robbie and Liam better.'

'They make you uncomfortable, don't they? A little tug in your blood, it's a survival instinct.'

'How do—?' she didn't finish her sentence when she looked at him because he was smirking. He was turned towards her, his forearm casually resting across the top of the steering wheel, the other over the back of her seat.

'The same way as being around you feels like home.' There was something behind his eyes that reminded her of the man from the food hall. Both the words and the look, lead Gia to a realisation that she was missing inside information.

'We can turn the car around. Go to the city for pizza,' he offered, changing back into the Atlas she remembered, casual, confident, open.

Gia shook her head and answered softly, 'No. You said Evie's put effort into tonight. Plus, you both need to hear about the circle that was under the old farmhouse. Do Robbie and Liam have to know though?'

'At this point, they're probably more knowledgeable and involved than any of us. I didn't tell you their story, but they know more than you'd believe.' Atlas's explanation, short, precise and vague as it was, satisfied Gia little more. She shrugged off Atlas's hand and opened the car door. What had happened at the farm on Halloween had changed her friend's life. Now she was about to change it again. Gia had a lot of faults, but stepping up when she needed to was one of her strengths.

Atlas hadn't lied when he had said that Evie had sent him and Robbie to the farm shops with a list that was more than the box. The line of food would have been the first thing anyone noticed. Deep rich red shades of plums, pomegranates, figs, red grapes, blackberries, a wide selection of deli meats, cheese and crackers, dips, oranges, dried apricots, nuts, different breads sliced and some toasted. The rich, winter colour scheme complimented Atlas's caravan perfectly.

'Wow, Evie,' Gia took her eyes from the display of food to her friend.

'I copied it from a picture and the shop managers organised all the pretty stuff. I just had to take it out of the packaging.' Evie passed Gia a rum and coke. She already held one in her hand. Atlas came inside behind her, the caravan rocked from the movement of all the people in it. Evie pulled a phone from her pocket and looked at her messages, turning away from them all. A quick glance before she turned showed Gia that the message was from Atlas, that was why he had remained in the car a few seconds longer. Robbie and Liam sat on the corner settee.

'You should tell Gia your version of Halloween, and Robbie's family story.' Atlas said from behind Gia. Evie looked up from her message, a clear understanding across her face as she locked eyes with her brother. She started to pour him a drink whilst he put Gia's bag in his room. Gia sat at the edge of the dining booth, Atlas took the other dining booth seat across from her, Evie settled on the settee next to Robbie.

Over the next hour Gia heard of Harriet's involvement in switching the village tradition from Yrsa to Evie. She heard Robbie recount how the spell had worked from his point of view in Evie's caravan, she hadn't asked how he had gotten himself involved, but knowing that he had been present to witness the spell fitted with Evie's admission that she had been backed into a corner. Atlas provided a fuller picture, completing his absence from the events by telling the group that after he had dropped Gia off at the cottage, he had gotten half-ready for milking, then realising that he had some time, he had rushed off to an address he'd been given for answers. His plan to seek more knowledge had backfired. Once she had him down in the cellar, Yrsa had worked a spell that tapped into his biggest fear. The last thing he ever wanted was to abandon or pose a danger to his family. She used his gift against him to strike fear into him. It was only his sister whispering stories about the Faoladh that allowed the fear to dissipate.

Liam threw a cushion at Atlas, 'That was you the other day on site, the crow that pinched my bacon sandwich and flew off with it!'

Atlas laughed and threw the cushion back at him, 'I had to get you back for beating me at pool.'

'You need to play better then.' Liam shrugged.

Gia heard Robbie and Liam's story about constantly moving into houses that needed something removing from them, about how they had gotten rid of spirits, evil entities, and other things with a host of methods.

'How do you know what it is?' she asked them.

They looked at each other, 'We don't.' Liam said. 'You sort of get an instinct. Ghosts that haven't yet passed on are more common but not to be mistaken with visits from recently deceased that will cease of their own accord with time. Then the next level is angry restless spirits, then you move onto other options that are harder to erase. Demons have a darkness. There's some knowledge behind the guesswork. It helps that we can see things others can't.'

'How? Do I look different? Does Evie or Atlas?'

'The only time Evie is different is when she's using her gift fully, she has an assortment of different greens around her, like a full-length veil. Atlas gets a deep blue haze sometimes. You,' Robbie faltered. His glance at Liam confirmed Gia's suspicions.

'I what?'

'You sometimes get a white mist across you, but Mum and Paige also noticed that your eyes change to a reddish-purple, a non-human colour. You burst into a room with a scent of crisp, frozen air but up close you smell of—'

'Blackberries and the woods in autumn,' Atlas

finished, his eyes telling her that he realised she had lied about it being perfume.

'It smells like an entity. No offence Gia, it's a nice smell and you seem fun to be around,' Liam said.

'How do you know the difference between perfume and an entity smell?' Gia asked, not denying the unspoken, indirect statement.

'Again, just instinct. It hits your nervous system before it hits your brain. We respond to it instinctively. Perfume is the other way around, like, yeah that's a nice smell.' Robbie answered.

Gia gave a slow nod to show that she understood. Liam spoke next. He was thoughtful and quiet, which was unusual. Gia had only seen the fun-loving younger brother that riled Robbie up. Seeing Liam serious was something else, once he lost the fun edge, she saw how he was possibly more dangerous than her brain had allowed for, and that her instincts were right.

'We renovated a disgusting house before we moved to your old school house, when we first started throwing things into skips there was a smell, really faint; a mix of smoky November nights and sweet honey. It stayed there through the entire renovation until we realised what it was. That damn entity refused to leave no matter no what did. In the end we had to clean, cleanse the space by burning herbs, bleach, salt, and draw protection wards in every corner, under every window, across every threshold, and eventually it was trapped in the house and we killed it.'

'Did you see it?' Gia asked, she looked at both of them in turn.

'Only once we had it trapped. It was brown, huge, with

yellow eyes, hairy, it was so tall it stooped with a hunch-back where it hit the ceiling.,'

'With a chest that curved inwards and bony arms. Almost like a cross between a human nightmare and an overgrown hare that can talk,' Evie breathed, looking a Gia.

'A house brownie,' Gia looked back at Evie.

'A brownie? They're supposed to be little things about this high?' Liam held up his thumb and index finger with a small space between.

'The more important point to take from that is what have you two been up to together already? Trapping brownies?' Atlas looked between Gia and his sister.

It was there again, a hint of a knowledge that he shouldn't have. A hidden expression in his eyes that she couldn't fathom. She was definitely missing something. Atlas knew more than he let on. Unless Evie had told him something already.

Evie smiled mischievously and nestled closer into Robbie, 'We're both still here aren't we? Relax,' she told her brother.

'You said that you didn't believe or want to know about this stuff.' Robbie squeezed her shoulder when he spoke to her.

Evie looked at her glass, then at him, 'I was scared that night, more than I'd ever realised at the time. My anger overrode everything else after my instinct to survive. I don't think I can ignore it though, not anymore. Especially not if you see more in my friend than I do,' Evie answered.

'When did you see this brownie?' Gia heard how his voice changed when he spoke to Evie, how gentle it became. Robbie clearly adored her friend.

'With Gia.'

'Recently?'

'Mmmm, yes,' was the non-committal reply from Evie as she pretended to be busy finishing her drink. Evie stood and took Gia's glass from her without bothering to ask if she wanted another. She started to refill both their drinks.

'It's definitely a brownie? Liam looked at Gia and Evie. They both gave a nod. He looked at Robbie, 'We need to go in and kill it.'

'Not yet.' Gia shook her head. They looked at her and she couldn't explain why she was protecting the brownie. She changed the subject when Evie returned her glass to her, now full of rum and coke, 'Let me tell you about that circle you found.'

She passed her laptop around the group, showing the circle sigils from different angles and what she thought they meant, then brought up the three-dimensional version that she had created on her laptop. The image demonstrated exactly how the circle would work, reaching upwards and outwards, swirling anticlockwise constantly, rotating all the sigils in a never-ending loop, joined and reformed into new spells as it rose and circled in an ongoing pattern, until Evie had rubbed them out with her jacket. The group was silent for a while, all of them digesting what it meant. Liam was the first to stand up.

'I need some food and another beer before I ask what it was meant to keep out,' he announced.

'If this... if it sent some of our gift to Yrsa, why bind what we had?' Evie asked Gia.

'It worked as a magnifying glass. What little you accessed was sent to her multiplied. She couldn't use your gifts for herself, but the power inside you that gives you your gift helped to boost hers. My guess is by binding you,

you grew used to what little you had thereby not thinking that you were strong enough to face her.'

Atlas's eyes followed Liam's heaped plate as Liam strolled back to his seat. He stood up and picked up a plate in the kitchen. He didn't say anything, but it was clear he was using the plate and food as a distraction against saying whatever was on his mind. He was holding something back, Gia wanted to know what, and she wondered why he wasn't speaking up.

'I'm still curious as to when and where you both saw this brownie,' Robbie stood up and followed Atlas to the large selection of food laid out for them to graze on. Evie and Gia looked at each other but didn't answer him. Gia didn't trust Robbie enough to not kill the brownie or turn on her before she had a chance to fully discover what she was.

Chapter 19

Rain pattered on the roof in a soothing sound, Gia liked that she could hear each drop on the roof. Back in her grandmother's cottage, its thick walls blocked out most noise, it was no different from being in a library. Here the curtains remained open, the blackness outside was emphasised by the lack of light on the farm, wrapping the farm up as a distinct entity from the lit village below. It stood alone and secluded. Mostly quiet in the dark except for the noises of animals.

Gia liked being able to hear life happening when she was writing, cars, birds, rain, silence, conversations; it didn't matter as long as she had a connection to the outside. She could write in silence with the sound of birds in the trees, she could write in a café, but she had never managed to write in a library, in contrast to that, she had written in a museum before with people flowing around her looking at the artefacts on display.

Liam and Robbie asked questions about the circle, and as they all drank more, and nibbled on the selection of food, the chat turned more general, to how Gia worked with circles, to Liam and Robbie's experiences. They were all on common ground, until Atlas decided to throw in the shadows that he had seen with Gia on bonfire night. He described what he had seen, Liam leaned forward, his expression keen to hear something that was obviously new. Robbie echoed his brother's body language, but shifted so that even as he leaned forward, resting his forearms on his thighs, he was positioned in front of Evie, as though the danger was right there in the room with them all.

Gia saw Evie lean back and cast bored eyes at her brother as though she had heard this before. Given how close the siblings were, Gia had no doubts that Atlas had already told his sister about the shadows. It would make sense if Evie had already mentioned the brownie to him, after all, Gia had more or less said to Atlas on bonfire night that she had called it up. Evie finished her drink in one gulp and stared quizzically at her glass as though she was uncertain whether she wanted another or not.

Gia finished her own drink and answered Evie's inner question with a statement of her own, 'Another one, Evie?' Evie nodded. Gia's back was turned to the conversation, she wasn't paying much attention as she poured two drinks. Unlike Evie's generous measures of rum, Gia poured less rum in and more coke than Evie had. They'd both had a few already, her own head was already fuzzy and buzzing. When she sat back down the conversation was full of speculation about what they had seen. A glance at her fairy tale loving friend told her she had already correctly guessed. Evie moved from behind Robbie to the platter of food in the kitchen area. Gia set down her drink and followed her.

'You didn't tell Atlas what it was?' Evie asked quietly.

'I thought it was obvious. Not at the time, but afterwards. There's enough descriptions out there.'

'Since you're both so confident that you know what it is, why not tell us?' Robbie said loudly.

Evie ignored him. 'It said the shadows,' she started to say looking at Gia.

Gia cut her off, 'I know, and they didn't. Assume that part was wrong.'

'Hey, we're still here, do you mind telling us less well-versed peasants about your fairy tales? Specifically, the one with the shadow horse deer things?' Liam called. Both women helped themselves to plates before they went back to their seats.

Evie ate whilst Gia set her plate to one side before she told the group, 'The shadows were the Wild Hunt. That's what the borders were for. To keep out the fae.'

'That's—' Liam stopped himself from whatever he had been about to say.

'Insane?' she agreed.

He gave a nod, 'But why?' Liam furrowed his brows, in an effort to understand.

'I have a theory, if we saw the Wild Hunt, and we're in the twenty-first century, what if it was seen at other points in history on the land here? If the old farmhouse really went back to the Stuart era, then the reformation in England had only started a hundred years prior. The reformation took traditional fairies and made them demons. They weren't the tiny cute things until much later in history. Someone might have taken an older boundary spell and woven it into something else in the years between,' Gia explained.

'The circle wasn't originally intended for the house occupants?' Robbie asked her.

'No. It was originally intended as a warning to things like the Wild Hunt to stay off the property.'

'Because of the wars and the fighting like we were

told,' Evie added.

'Don't tell me there's Seelie and Unseelie Courts, and Shakespeare was right? That's all I remember of GCSE literature,' Robbie looked at Gia.

She shook her head, 'They call themselves the Ripening and Resting Courts. Similar to Spring and Winter. There used to be a Harvesting Court in the middle of the two but an internal war wiped them out. An estimate is that they used to last approximately four months each, but now they just split six months.'

'Which is how we get the Oak King and Holly King fighting myths,' Evie suddenly realised.

'What happens now that the circle has gone?' Robbie asked, a hand on Evie's leg. Gia saw his eyes hover between summer and winter, between warmth and ice, and suppressed a shiver as a cold trail inside her blood responded with a touch of fear.

'I don't know. We don't know if the circle was drawn because there was a war between the Courts and it spilled over onto the farm, or if the reformation had simply made people worried and paranoid, thinking that they had demons roaming. There's too many variables here.'

'Are we safe?' Robbie asked.

Gia's temper flared. He might as well have demanded *Is Evie safe from you?* Robbie moved forward to the edge of the seat.

'What happened there?' Liam asked, his finger flickered to his own eyes.

Gia looked at him and then Robbie, their own eyes were ice blue. They were tensed and ready to fight. Atlas had moved an arm to reach out across her body as soon as Robbie's body language changed. He was tensed too, ready to jump up if Robbie did.

'What happened?' she asked.

'Your eyes. They went full-on this weird purple shade. Like those red grapes,' Liam gave a nod to the half-eaten platter.

'I didn't see anything,' Evie said. Her eyes went to her brother, he shrugged and gave a slight incline of his head as a secret passed between the two of them. Evie's eyes widened a fraction, even as she tried to cover it.

'You really see things others don't?' Gia asked as she looked between the brothers, understanding why she felt uneasy around them. They didn't speak but nodded.

'She has a temper like all of us. Stop acting like she's going to attack any minute. Gia's here helping us. Don't forget that. She's my friend,' Evie spoke up.

She was looking directly at Robbie though, her words a quiet warning to him. Evie's hand curled around his bicep, her grey eyes a mix between being completely in love with the man next to her and a plea to back off. He settled back. Atlas moved his arm and rested it on the table.

Gia started to recount what she knew, what Evie knew as well, 'Before the reformation, the lore around fairies was more humanised. They were an old race, human-sized, human-looking, sometimes described as more beautiful than humans, but often mistaken for people. They had portals to their underground world or realm that they created during an ancient war with humans, which suggests, for all their supposed magic and power, that they were losing. They were feared at a later date, known for being clever and cunning.' She stopped there, memories resurfacing in her head.

Gia thought of the times she had talked teachers into

remarking her work, or giving her a better mark, the spells she had hidden in her exams for higher marks, and the spells hidden in her books to make them successful. Cunning. It wasn't a word she would have chosen. She had thought the spells more of a safety precaution, a ritualistic bit of fun to get her head to focus on what she was supposed to, a chance to make her books sell, not a guarantee that they would.

'Something we should know?' Robbie had picked up on her pause. There was still a hard edge to his voice. She wanted to react to it, but the situation called for control. Evie didn't need a fight between the pair of them.

'No, I was just thinking about that word. How it used to be used against how we use it now. A cunning person would be admired for their quickness, intelligence, and their ability to think on their feet. Now we used it as a derogatory insult, to mean deviant and criminal, sly and underhand.'

'I'm going to agree with Gia that the potential timings in the historical context could indicate that the farm owners were trying to keep fairies out. Now they're coming back. What is this Wild Hunt and how do we get rid of it?' Liam tried to wrangle space between Robbie and Gia with his words, bringing everyone's attention back to him.

Gia replied, 'From what I can put together, the Wild Hunt is exactly what it suggests, a hunt with no rules. They focus on a target or several and don't stop. They're the assassins of the fairy world. Whispered rumours that very few people have ever encountered. We could stop them by modifying the circle and putting it back on the land somewhere or creating a new one. Now I've seen this it's going to be easy to create a three-dimensional circle in the future.'

'Once winter is over, this Resting Court thing, they'll move on so the Spring Court can move in?' Robbie spoke.

'I think they'll follow the winter. But it's not to say that the Ripening Court doesn't have their own version of the Wild Hunt. I'd do protection wards in the corners of the houses even if you don't do it across the whole farm.'

'No.' Evie stood up.

She motioned to Gia to go outside and turned around. Looking between Robbie and her brother she told them to stay in the caravan.

It hadn't stopped raining. Water hung in the air around them, the type that got into clothes and below the skin and never left. Evie pressed a button on her umbrella and held it over both of them, sheltering them from the rain. She looked at Gia, she had brought her drink outside. Gia hadn't realised that they would need a drink, she hadn't thought to bring her own. Gia closed the door as Evie spoke in her quiet voice, her expression intense, 'If we put wards on the houses, how will that affect you? Will you still be able to come round and have drinks with me? Can you sleep in Atlas's house with protection wards against your kind?'

'I'm probably not even what it said I was.'

'Robbie and Liam told you that they see your eyes changing. I didn't see. Robbie's talked to me about the things he's encountered in houses and before all this, I wouldn't have believed him. Let's roll with it, theoretically, and believe the brownie.'

'I guess, then, we would have to choose. Do you keep your family safe or invite your friend in? I'm not a mum, Evie, but I'd tell you to always protect your children first.

True friends would understand.'

'Is there another option? Protection-only wards? So you can come into our houses but not hurt us.'

'Yes. But that won't get rid of the Wild Hunt like they want.'

At Gia's response Evie sighed. 'Nobody is getting what they want. Robbie wants his military friend to come in and install security cameras and alarms everywhere because he wants to keep me safe. Atlas just wants us all to be normal, he pretends he's having fun being able to change into animals but deep down he's still freaked out. Liam likes to make out that he's the annoying younger brother but he's probably more black and white than Robbie if he thinks his family is threatened. I'm still— then you're—'

'Figuring out who we are, why and for what purpose.'

'Yeah. That. It's alright to disbelieve, Gia. I did. I was blind to it all until Halloween. In hindsight I wish I had opened my eyes earlier. If you have the leisure to do that, I'd say do it.'

'You're telling me to drop almost twenty years of living recklessly because I thought having demon blood protected me, to accepting that I have fairy blood. I mean, it's not a big jump, but it's still a mindfuck when I had accepted the other version.'

'Demon blood?' Evie asked.

Gia smiled, her normal sense of humour returning to her, she heard the door behind them being opened. 'See, ten years ago I wouldn't have been able to share that with you.'

'Evie, come inside before you get pneumonia again, whatever it is you two need privacy for I'd rather it was the three of us stood outside,' Atlas appeared at the door with

Gia's drink.

'I've had enough to drink, I'm going to make a cup of tea. Do you want one, Gia?' Evie stepped inside, admitting that she was cold.

'No thanks.'

Inside the caravan Gia opened her phone at the article about her parents' death and searched through the associated items until she recognised the site that talked about her mother's lineage. She passed it to Evie to read while the kettle boiled. Evie read it and passed it back. Gia only had to look at her friend's expression to know the questions Evie had.

'I knew what I could do from an early age, I'd say six, maybe even before. I remember my mum teaching me something, I drew it on the back of her mirror then watched as the mirror turned pink. I thought making the mirror turn pink was fun. Without any other knowledge, I believed those rumours. I wanted to believe the rumours, it was a way of carrying mum's legacy with me.'

'Is that why Rosa doesn't like to talk about your mum?'

'I think that's more complicated. She told me the other night that my mum was a runaway, sleeping rough when she met my dad. She stole my dad's phone and wallet and he chased after her. I can't believe she kept that story from me. I swear she led me to believe that they met at school.'

'Although, being fair, you don't tell your grand-daughter that their mum was a homeless teenage runaway that didn't attend school. I mean, the way she pushed you to keep doing better in school.' Evie shrugged.

'I'm still not good enough. She's already told me she

prays for me. This latest revelation would have her packing me off somewhere in a straitjacket. I need to tread carefully around her. She thinks the brownie is my dad's ghost.'

'What revelation?' Robbie called out, dropping all pretence that the men weren't listening. Evie looked at Gia, Gia shrugged back.

She turned around and challenged them, 'Can you tell what I am? If I asked you to choose whether I was part demon or part other entity would you be able to determine that?'

'The red in your eyes would make me jump to demon and I'd do a Latin ritual on you.'

Gia knew which one he was talking about. It was one she had said herself. It was one she had listened to the priest doing. It wasn't the Latin that the so-called demons responded to, despite the church and television shows setting a precedent for that. It was intent. Intent could be done in any language, any ritual strong enough to signify it. She threw out the challenge.

'Do it.'

'No. We're not exorcising you,' Atlas had been quiet at the door of the caravan, but he made his way through the kitchen area to her now, 'No one's exorcising anyone. What we are, it's part of us. You can't get rid of it.'

'A mild possession could explain why your eyes change sometimes,' Robbie mused.

'Why do you want us to do it, Gia? What are you trying to prove here?' Liam walked over to Evie. He placed his beer bottle down and got a cup from the cupboard and proceeded to make himself a cup of tea with the leftover water in the kettle.

Gia was quiet, she didn't know what she wanted to prove, whether she hoped that she was still part demon as she had always believed, or whether the brownie had been right, a fact that infuriated her.

In the silence that hovered Evie spoke for her friend, 'We all had some processing to do after Halloween. Gia's processing now. We should have some patience and let her work through this. Gia had the answers to what was in the circle that I dusted away. Why don't we get the cards out and we can have a couple of games to take our mind off this stuff?'

'But we can redraw a circle to protect you from the Wild Hunt and get them off your land?' Robbie spoke to Evie.

'No. Gia and I will work on something new. I'm not drawing a protective circle around my land to stop the fae coming on it.'

Robbie's head whipped to Gia. So did Liam's. Nobody had to speak to understand. She had challenged them to exorcise her because she had known that it wouldn't work. They understood that after hearing Evie's words. Gia didn't want to admit what the brownie had told her, but she saw suspicion in their faces. They knew. Evie believed the brownie and so they believed Evie.

It was Atlas who shook his head, 'You came to the farm a lot as a kid. Why didn't the circle keep you away back then?'

'I don't know.' Gia looked at him when she answered.

Chapter 20

A plate of food was laid between them on the bed. Atlas slipped back under the warmth of the covers. Gia was amused by the fact that Atlas was becoming predictable to her, sex, food, work. Ideally in that order but not always. She was amused because she wasn't running away yet, for the first time. His predictability was endearing rather than annoying.

'Something funny?' He arched an eyebrow. She was still cooling off so didn't bother to hitch up the duvet when it fell down.

'You're getting predictable. Food and sex,' she smiled.

He laughed, 'What else is there? I have a beautiful woman who likes sex next to me, I have everything. You know what I noticed tonight?'

'What?'

'You didn't eat a single piece of meat.' It was her turn to give Atlas the arched eyebrow. He chuckled, 'Food, Gia. From the platter. The other night you picked the pasta off Rosa's lasagne and left the meat. You had a margherita pizza. You walked out of the butcher's when I took you in without buying anything. Is there something you haven't told me?'

Gia had noticed that change in herself. It had been gradual, a change that had crept up on her. The butcher's shop had turned her stomach and it had been all she could do to hide a retch from Atlas. Over the past sixteen months she had turned more and more to pasta, potatoes and vegetables rather than meat-based dishes.

'The smell of the butcher's shop made me feel sick, I needed more coffee to cope with that. I haven't enjoyed meat for the last year and a half. Not like I used to. I didn't eat any tonight because I didn't want to. I'm not intentionally a vegetarian, if that's what you're asking Atlas. I just don't like meat right now. It makes me feel heavy and like I'm—' she had been about to say it aloud, but even in her head it sounded stupid. Gia held back, she rethought her words.

'Like you're what?' he asked.

When she answered her voice was smaller, 'Like it lowers me. My mood, my energy, my magic, everything.'

'It started a year ago?' he asked.

'Yes. Why?'

'I feel that there's no coincidences these days. So I'm going to store that away until the day it makes sense. You brought your phone and laptop, right?'

'Yes?' She drew it out, looking at him.

'So, stay longer than a night. Maybe a couple of nights? There's a storm coming in tomorrow anyway, we'll be doing the bare minimum on the farm; milking, changing bedding, feeding the animals, then I'll be back. Evie and Robbie are going into the woods to do Evie's thing when the storm starts picking up. We could wander into the shops and get whatever you want to eat.'

'Why does Evie need to do her thing in the woods?'

'To stop the floods in the village. She thinks the woods were once a wetland and could hold water but someone drained them. She's going to unblock the old water paths.

It's not entirely altruistic. If the rainfall is bad the stream by the café will rise and it has the potential to flood the café and shops. It cost us a lot of money the last time it happened. We're closing the shops an hour early to let staff get home while it's still light. The worst of the storm is expected to hit during the evening and overnight. So, will you stay?'

'I'll stay tomorrow, as long as you have electricity to charge my laptop. The minute there's a power cut I'm going home.'

'There's other things to do in power cuts.' Atlas winked. She laughed at that. He paused, then spoke again, 'Would you mind if I brought my dogs into the caravan? Just whilst the storm is on? They usually sleep in comfort in a barn I converted to an oversized kennel. Evie's not big on them being around unsupervised and I'd never forgive myself if they nipped one of the kids trying to herd them like they do the sheep. I can put them in one of the bedrooms. They won't bother you. They don't like the wind.'

'What did you do with them bonfire night?'

'They have a tablet from the vet that knocks them out. That's why I didn't walk down with Evie. I stayed in the barn until they were asleep.'

'Bring them in if you're going to worry about them. I've never had a plant, never mind a pet, so don't assume I know how to do anything,' she warned him.

She stayed with Atlas the next day. Gia charged both their laptops when he was out on the farm, she downloaded a couple of films from his watchlist for them, daydreamed about Atlas, scoffed at herself, wrote, day-dreamed some more when she was supposed to be writing, then gave up trying. Gia could imagine that fantasy books were real when the weather was pure winter wildness, she could picture dragons raising great wings and playing with the strength of the air, soaring and flying in the wind which raged around the caravan. She wrote until her concentration ran out and she needed a break. She walked to the café to get herself a coffee.

Later in the evening, once the darkness had descended, the rain joined the wind to belt down so hard it sounded like stones instead of water. She and Atlas cooked dinner together in the tiny kitchen. They relished getting in each other's way, a chance to get their hands on each other when the other was occupied, teasing banter, laughter and innuendos flew around. Gia had pre-roasted leek, shallots, parsnip, carrots and swede, then added mushrooms and a rich creamy sauce into the pie case with the vegetables. They ate it with a potato gratin, accompanied by a glass of wine.

Predictably, the power cut came in the evening when they were already in bed. Her head was on Atlas's broad chest, listening to his heartbeat slow down and return to normal, her body stretched out diagonally on the bed. Gia had just picked up her book and read a few sentences when the caravan went black. Atlas reached out, stretching his body underneath her head. She heard a metallic clink under the bed. He shifted again, repositioning his body to how he had been. She looked around as the shadows danced, weaving closer to them. Gia stared hard, as though they were real and not figments of her overactive imagination. Light suddenly flowed from a small lantern and sent the shadows back to their normal places. He placed it next to her on the bed and picked up his own book.

'Thank you,' she murmured, reopening the book to the page she had been at.

'You're welcome, beautiful. You're not going anywhere, now that I've got you. We'll get through the storm.' His hand slid over her shoulder along to the base of her throat and rested there. He lifted his hand from her to turn the page occasionally, then replaced it in the same position each time. Gia suppressed a smile, there was more to Atlas underneath the surface than he let people see.

The weather was still rough but subsiding the next day. Atlas returned to the caravan to find her still in bed, updating her social media with reels of the wind blowing the trees about. Gia had filmed it the previous day when she had taken herself for a walk after chopping the vegetables.

He stood in the doorway of his bedroom, arms raised and leaning on the frame, 'I've arranged to meet Evie and the kids for brunch in the café. She says she has some news. Do you fancy coming along? It's not going to be urgent or private if she's telling me in the café when she lives next door.' He looked slightly self-conscious again at asking her to come along on what, to anyone else, was a family breakfast. Neither sibling would class it as a family breakfast, they would say that it was a casual brunch catch up if asked. Gia glanced up at him, her little nod was enough to have him diving onto the bed and taking the phone out of her hands.

An hour later Max and Rey burst into the café ahead of Evie and Robbie. They made their way with big smiles to Gia and Atlas who were nursing a coffee each. A waitress passed by, took a look at Max and Rey, looked outside, and asked Atlas if everyone was having their usual drinks. Atlas gave a nod.

'Mum's marrying Robbie, we're going to have a baby brother or sister,' Rey announced, sitting in a seat and telling her uncle everything that she wanted to eat.

Max sat across from his sister and added, 'I heard them talking last night and Robbie said he could book the registry office or they could go to Scotland but he'd like to start next year as a family.'

'Do we have to change our name?' Rey asked her brother.

Gia watched Atlas's face turn dark at the thought that Evie was already expecting. It would be the same pattern repeating itself all over again. He excused himself and walked outside to the pair. Gia saw him meet Evie and Robbie who were walking up slowly. He looked angry. To distract the children from the heated conversation that might be happening outside she talked to them about their walk in the woods during the storm. Halfway through their chat Gia asked if they thought anything was different about the farm since they had moved into the caravans. They glanced at each other.

Rey answered Max's silent question with a shrug. 'You mean the thing in the barn? The one nearest the woods?' Max asked.

'Tell me what you know.' Gia didn't say *What thing?* or even act surprised, although her intentions had been to ask about the appearance of fae on the land, she let them talk.

'We don't go in. Nothing that goes in ever comes out.' Rey looked at the table, dispirited.

'There's cobwebs and a big spider web. I don't mean big spider web like this big,' Max held up his hands, 'but the whole barn big. That's why nothing ever comes out. They get caught in the web.'

'Have you seen a spider that big on the farm?' Gia asked.

'No, it stays in the barn.'

'For now. While it has food.'

'But there's people bringing it food too,' Rey whispered.

'Go on.' Gia leaned towards her with her own whisper. She rested folded arms on the table and placed her chin on them so she could speak softly at their level.

Rey copied her posture, 'There's a girl at school called Charlotte, her mum used to date Uncle Atlas when they were in school. Charlotte said a man pretending to be Uncle Atlas came to the house and took her mum. She's got a pretend mum now who's going to leave soon. She says she'll feed Charlotte to the Spider Queen if she's naughty. That's where pretend Uncle Atlas took Charlotte's real mum,' Rey spoke in a low voice, her expression open and honest.

'How long ago did this happen?'

'This week. Monday.'

'Have you seen Charlotte's pretend mum?' Gia asked. Both nodded.

'Where?'

'She gets her from school like her real mum would.'

'What's your opinion? Is it Charlotte's real mum or is it a pretend mum?' Gia glanced up to see how much time she had left with the children before the other three walked in. Atlas was hugging Evie. Their faces were turned away from the glass and she couldn't judge their moods.

'It's her pretend mum,' Rey answered.

Gia brought her attention back to the conversation with the children. 'Can you tell me what the differences are?'

'She doesn't talk to the other mums anymore. She stands alone. Her skin is different. If anyone mentions it, she says she's having facials and drinking more water. It's like she has moonlight under her skin. Like yours. But you're nice. She makes me feel bad in my tummy.'

The sound of chairs being pulled out made the three of them break up their conversation and sit up. The waitress returned with a tray of six drinks which she began to place on the table.

'You three look as thick as thieves. What's happening?' Evie sat down.

'They were just telling me about school. Playground stuff amongst the older kids,' Gia said.

Evie shook her head, 'Alexander Stanley again? The school knows they have to keep an eye on him. He's such an arrogant little twat.' Her uncustomary outburst made the table look at her.

She shrugged, 'Vanessa is in his year. She stops for a chat once a week when she comes out the music room doors.' Evie explained that the music department was one of the few dedicated subject areas that all the years used, and the exit was near the doors Max and Rey came out of at the end of their day.

'Who's Vanessa?' Robbie asked. He paused in raising his coffee cup to look at Evie, as he found out something new about her life.

'My friend's little sister. Nina Cordoba?'

'The model?'

'Yes. Vanessa is still in school. She's in the sixth form.

The year Max started at Oak Hall was the last year that April did school runs with Vanessa. She used to bring Vanessa over to say hi and have a chat. There's been times when Vanessa has come over for a chat just to get away from him.'

'Sometimes mum drops her off at home,' Rey announced.

Evie shrugged, 'It's not really out of the way. Mostly she walks with her friends.'

'Look at mum's new ring, it's really sparkly,' Rey pulled Evie's hand to Gia and changed the conversation.

Evie walked back to the cottage with Gia that afternoon after a long congratulatory brunch in the café. Evie quietly told her that Atlas's assumptions had been wrong, and she was not expecting a baby, although that was in their future. Evie talked to Gia about how she wanted them all to be settled into the house when it was built for a few months before any plans were made for babies. She was so overwhelmed with everything, and worried about people letting her down because it wasn't in her nature to trust, that she was tense and on edge. She thought being able to move into the house would let her drop some of her worries, that allowing them all to get settled in would give them room to figure out how to be a family first, before a baby came into the picture. Her words were much an echo of Atlas's own, their desires to be in a safe space before a child came along were remarkably similar.

Max and Rey walked in front of Gia and Evie. Evie and Gia dropped Gia's belongings off at the cottage. Max and Rey stood in the doorway looking around for a few seconds before they continued to walk the children down to the big park in the dying winds of the end of the storm. The largest village park was located on the edge of the village, right next to the tennis club, bowling and cricket greens, it was one of the places they had all met up as teenagers, when they wanted to be away from the prying eyes of the village high street. With so few people around on the way there, only dog walkers intent on a quick walk and returning home, and no one at the park itself, Max and Rey ran and played. Evie told Gia in detail about what she had done in the woods as they walked around to keep warm, then about Robbie's proposal.

Gia asked, 'The woods were normal?'

'Completely. I think it's you that they change around.'

'Maybe it would be safer if you did just stop everything from entering the farm boundaries. We can still meet up in the village.'

Gia had been thinking about the circle since the conversation with Max and Rey in the café. She didn't understand why she was uneasy when she heard the children talk of something supernatural living on the farm, she just knew that it didn't quite sit right, not after everything Evie had been through to try and give the pair a normal childhood.

Evie answered her, 'I can't. I do understand why everyone wants to. Then I think of how I was supposed to go into Yrsa's basement where my brother was held, and I was supposed to die. I don't want anyone to go through something alone. I'd never forgive myself if you died on the border of our farm because you tried to get to us for help.'

'Why didn't you ask for help? How long were you getting the threats for?'

'Since I left Damian. At first, I thought it was perhaps one of his crazier football fans. Then a psycho. The longer they went on the more I ignored everything. So, with that knowledge, I'd confront everything if I had to live it all over again. Go after my brother and tell him how you feel. Go and chase those shadows, get them before they get you.'

'Solid advice. Get the shadows before they get you. How do you catch shadows?' Gia murmured, deliberately avoiding the subject of Atlas.

'You trap them,' Evie grinned mischievously at the reference.

'I'm trying to remember everything I can about fairy lore. Time moves differently in their realm. Don't eat or drink. Portals exist in natural areas.'

'Don't be rude, don't be kind, don't owe favours, don't return a gift with a gift, don't gift them anything lest it should offend them somehow. Words are not a tool they're a weapon,' Evie finished.

'Maybe you chose the wrong career. You should be a fantasy writer,' Gia laughed.

Evie laughed too, she shook her head slightly as a protest and added, 'Don't wear red. They don't like red. Only the queen of the fairies, also the queen of the witches is allowed to wear red. Humans wear red because the fairies leave them alone.'

'When Atlas used to tease you for loving fairy tales, I thought he meant actual fairy tales. Not all the lore in the entire world around the fae.'

'There's so much more than just that advice, but the rest depends on the type of beings you encounter. I loved fairy tales because of the magic in them.' She waved a hand to indicate exactly what magic she was referring to.

'So get my butt out there and confront the shadows.' Gia nodded.

'I'd say take Atlas, but he's more brute force unless animals are involved.' Evie's eyes widened as she remembered something, she looked at Gia. Gia saw her brain skip forwards a few beats until she let out a swear word.

'What?' Gia asked her.

'We had this obscure book of fairytales. I've never seen another one like it. It had notes in the margins in old handwriting, and booklice that walked across the page when you were reading it. It ended up on the fire. I'll try and remember what the annotations said, but I remember a story about children of the fairies. Every year they would return to the same spot and play with human children, but they got sad that the human children grew up faster than they did, even though they were physically the same, so they took their favourites into fairyland. It focused on how slowly the fairies came into their powers. Turning thirty was the fairy equivalent of being sixteen. That's when a fairy girl was old enough to be married. Fifty was considered the equivalent to twenty-one. Some point between thirty and fifty a fairy would start to have fairy powers. The human children were turned into the fairies' servants and lived miserable lives. I can't remember it all now, I wish we still had the book, but what if that was the answer. You could walk onto the farm as a child because you weren't fae back then, you were just Gia, a witch that could summon entities?'

'You're saying that my fae blood didn't really kick in until last year?' Atlas's words came back to her, I feel that there's no coincidences these days. So I'm going to store that away until the day it makes sense.

'I think we shouldn't have burnt that book. I wonder

what other books we burnt that might have had knowledge in them that we needed.'

'It's still weird that we're talking about this.'

'Do you want me to shut up?'

'No. I'm relieved. It just that we've both hidden who we are for so long. You never told me what you could do. I never told any of you that I was summoning entities for fun as a teenager, it makes me sort of sad to think of that wasted time.'

'I'm kind of glad,' Evie said, without any regret or judgement.

Gia looked at her, 'Glad that we kept it from each other?'

'Yes. I think we have some perspective on our gifts now and the danger that can come with them in a way that we didn't perceive as teenagers. We would have recklessly encouraged each other.'

Dinner that night in the cottage was Gia's choice of roasted Mediterranean vegetables with parmesan roasted potatoes. She listened to her grandmother tell her how disappointed Oliver had been about Atlas interrupting their date. It hadn't been a date and Gia had still forgotten to ask Atlas how he knew where she was that day. Her grandmother surprised her by saying that she had told Oliver exactly what she had told Gia, that her husband used to look at her like Atlas looked at Gia, and perhaps some things were just meant to be. Rosa asked about Gia's weekend. She shrugged and said she had spent time with both Evie and Atlas. She kept quiet about Evie's engagement. She would tell Rosa in a few days, after Robbie had told his family. Meanwhile she chatted to Rosa about Rosa's church friends and the service with all the manners she could pull up, whilst trying to find a way to wrangle the conversation around to what she really wanted to discuss.

At the end of the meal, Gia leaned back with a glass of wine, 'Nonna, can you remember why red was my favourite colour? When did it start?'

'Early. Your mum bought you a red winter coat, the first winter you were walking, and little red boots. You loved the coat. It was the only coat colour you wanted.'

Gia absorbed that news, it seemed to be building into a larger picture, one where her mother understood more about the fae than Gia did. Then she asked, 'You really believe it's Dad's ghost here?'

'I'd like to. You have a point. It might be something else. I have work to do, would you excuse me.'

'I have writing to do anyway.'

'How are you getting on with that?'

'Surprisingly well. Its two-thirds written. I'm editing what I have right now, dropping clues and hints in, building up the show of feelings and character development, then I'll write the end.'

'Is that how you work?'

'No. Sometimes I start with the end and work backwards. Sometimes I start in the middle and have months and months of research and struggles before the plot and characters emerge. It makes those like this, where it's easy, much more valued and fun. I was always scared to come back to Valentina, so many people loved her, even more hated her, I always wondered where I took that volatile nineteen-year-old but she's writing herself and its nothing like I thought she would be. She's evolved into someone I barely recognise.'

'How?'

'She's regal, she's ladylike, she commands a room when she walks in. The fights she used to have are child's play compared to the level she plays at now. She knows how to control herself. How to manipulate others.'

'I always wondered why you chose that name for a character.'

'Honestly?'

'Honestly.'

'I was supposed to do a find and replace on the finished document and change the name but I had a last-minute rethink and kept it, in honour of my mum, you told me she had wanted to call me Valentina, but you and dad argued for Giovanna because dad and grandad were both Giovanni, and that Gianna was a compromise.'

'It was. She said it was too religious a name. She wanted Valentina and a few other, non-Italian names, almost like she knew that you wouldn't be in Italy your whole life. In hindsight, it really wasn't such a big deal. You were beautiful and healthy. I do regret backing your father up on that. A child's name should be a parental decision. I had no right to have a say. Things were different back then and it didn't help that I saw them both as children.'

Once downstairs was cleaned up, Rosa settled on the settee with her laptop. Upstairs, Gia's head was ready to settle into her bed with own laptop, ideas already running through her thoughts, characters shouting inside her brain to be the first to come to the front and be written. Even as she got ready for bed, as she showered and put on new black pyjamas, she functioned as she always had, her head in one place and her body in another. It was only when she looked down, and realised that the long, ankle grazing cardigan she had bought to wear over the tight thermal top and bottoms wasn't the same shade of black as the pyjamas, more of a charcoal grey, that she had already forgotten her promise to herself to try and be whole, to not fall back into the habit of existing only inside her own head.

She combed through her wet hair, then started to finger curl strands into ringlets, an act that she did infrequently. Gia had always been conscious that the length of time it took to tame her thick brown hair into actual curls was too long, especially when she could be writing or scribbling notes. Evie always looked pretty, she never apologised about taking time for herself. Four more curls into the process her resolve to do her hair wavered. It would take up too much writing time. She needed a mirror to continue. Gia thought about picking up the comb and getting rid of the attempt at curls she had done so far. Determination won over the time battle. Gia took inspiration from her friend and allowed herself to spend time changing her everyday appearance, bringing her mind back into the real world by trying to focus on what she was doing, not daydreaming about her characters and their imaginary lives, or Atlas.

Since she had returned to her grandmother's cottage her small mirror had been sat on her writer's bureau face down. Gia had been using the larger one in the bathroom. Tonight, she propped it up on the fire mantlepiece so that she didn't have to venture into the steamy room with an open window to the cold air. She wanted to stay in her room where the radiators made it cosy and warm. She twisted her curls, soaked in conditioner, water and mousse, around a finger, turning to see in the tiny mirror. It was a lot like the mirror her mother had made her spell, the mirror that had turned pink. She hadn't thought about the pink effect for years before she had mentioned it in the caravan that night. It had gone to the back of her head, overtaken by her parents' murders, the trip to England and all the new experiences from London and then in the Yorkshire village where they had settled.

The mirror had just sat in her room on the top of her writer's bureau for years. She recalled that she had occasionally used it to apply make-up as a teenager, but otherwise, it was just there. When she had twisted the last strand, she wiped her hands on a towel, and flipped the mirror over. Her childish hand-drawn sigils were still there, very much faded, and she had to squint hard to see them. She traced over them with her finger. All her characters' persistent voices faded inside her head, her mother's patient voice was the only presence, telling her what each one meant. Gia traced the last, not noting the words, but focused on a voice that she had never recalled before. She flipped the mirror and put it back on the fireplace shelf.

She smiled as it turned pink, just as it had before when she was a child. She turned around, ready to get into bed and open up her laptop, except her bed was behind her, reflected in the mirror, not in front of her as it should be. Gia turned around, the mirror was there, on the fireplace. Then turned again, her back to the mirror except it was in front of her once again. That was her bed, over there in the reversed image, with her laptop, her hairbrush, crumpled towels on the floor that she had used. When she turned around again there was no mirror image. A black room, lit by a huge window that showed her a winter pink sunrise sky, stars on the ceiling, an ornately carved black wood bed in the centre of the room, no laptop, no hairbrush, no phone for her to call someone.

Chapter 21

The door to the room opened a fraction, then paused, allowing a murmur of voices to enter. Her heart beat faster, her body and feet frozen to the spot she stood in. Gia looked at the mirror again. The person was stood outside the door. Hiding flashed through her mind, quickly followed by Robbie's words about her entity scent. She picked up the mirror and turned it over. In a rush she traced the symbols. Gia's finger traced the last curve of the last sigil when the man from the food hall who had called her home came in. Her hands gripped the mirror, her eyes lifted to see him close the door and lean against it. He was unaware of her at the moment. He lifted his chin, his eyes closed as he stopped to take a breath, his calm cold smiling face dropped, stress and worry etched itself on his face instead. He was dressed in black, not the fine clothing she expected, but something thin with a leather-like sheen. It was his face that captured her. It changed so quickly from the mask he wore to his real face.

His expression changed to shock when he finally opened his eyes and noticed her. He reached out and took a step to her. A puddle of nerves swelled in her stomach at the thought of him reaching her. Gia put the mirror back. She looked into it at the reflection of the bed, then turned around, the mirror was in front of her again and she saw her own bedroom, complete with crumpled towels. She walked to it. When she turned to the mirror again a pink mist shrouded the edges, through it she saw his face clearly; beautiful, chiselled, ethereal, lit like moonlight was under his skin, inside his black eyes and short black hair. He put his finger to his lips and beckoned her back.

When she picked up the mirror to test the sigils a second time, a large part of her screamed at her not to do it. That she had barely escaped once, that she would be caught, and yet curiosity drove her hedonistic actions. Even as her head told her not to, excitement at the adventure flooded her body, her eyes twinkled with fun and she traced the shapes again, eager to see what happened.

Gia carefully placed the mirror back on the fireplace shelf. The edges softened and turned pink, just as it had before. She turned around and again, her bed was behind her in the mirror, not in front of her as it should be. Gia turned around. There was no mirror image. A black room, lit by a huge open window that showcased night frosted fields leading to frosted winter woods in the distance. The stars of the night sky merged into stars on the ceiling. An ornately carved black wooden bed took up the centre of the room, the same bed that she had seen before. This time he was asleep in the bed, the thin sheet pushed down. Even though there was no glass in the window and no obvious heat, she wasn't cold.

Gia took a moment to appreciate the muscles and contours of his body with strange blue tattoos resembling a strangely beautiful artistic mix of Celtic looking knots and shapes on his abdomen from which single threads emerged at intervals and stretched up over his torso to mix with other strands and disappeared over his shoulders, each knot different, as she studied the tattoo it merged seamlessly from Celtic knots to ancient Mediterranean symbols to eastern symbols, as though the tattoo followed the continents like a map. The blue tattoo glowed faintly, pulsing with light as though it were alive. His head was shaved now, when he turned over in his sleep, she saw tattoos across the side of his head. Gia picked up the mirror and traced the shapes again. When she looked into it and saw that he had woken up, her hands wobbled slightly, standing the mirror back where it belonged. He was looking at her. As quick as he was to move, she was quicker disappearing back into her own room. This time, his face in the mirror looked sad. He reached out but the mirror had returned to a solid state, his hand hit the surface. He mouthed a word to her, but he disappeared from her mirror before she could make out what he was trying to say.

Intrigued at the time difference in his world, which was just a few seconds apart in hers, Gia couldn't resist trying again. Playfully, with a ghost of a smile on her face at the excitement, she traced the symbols without fear. Again, the mirror misted pink, again she saw her room reverse. She stepped into what she thought was the black bedroom.

The curtains and windows must have been shut. It was extremely dark, the type of darkness that left no shadows and consumed everything. She turned around and felt a grip on her arm. Firm enough to bruise her. Hard enough that she couldn't break away. It pulled her up against a rock-hard body and a hand went over her mouth. A man's voice spoke in her ear, 'Don't scream.' With a huge effort Gia forced her body to relax. She had read somewhere that it made the attacker think that the victim wasn't going to fight so they relaxed too. The arms holding her slackened enough for her to shake the hands off.

Gia turned around, her eyes slowly adjusting to the dark and remarked, 'I'm not a screamer.' She crossed her arms.

He looked her up and down slowly, a smile started to form across his face. She stared back, his hair had grown, it covered the tattoos that she knew were there. He was dressed in the same black outfit, she wanted to reach out and find out what material looked so much like leather but thin enough and flexible enough to move like silk.

He had stubble and dark circles under his eyes this time as if times had become much harsher for him. He was still so beautiful, and exactly as Rey had described, *Like moonbeams under the skin*. Gia wondered if that was how she appeared to other people too. She didn't see it in herself when she looked in the mirror. She looked just like everyone else.

Despite how he looked, a fun glint appeared across his face, 'Want to test that theory?' he offered.

She smiled back at his fun open flirting. Then she pushed her hands into the low hung pockets of the cardigan, 'There's someone else, so no.' She shook her head.

'Is the farmer that deserving of your faithfulness? I wouldn't be leaving you alone to go through portals in that outfit.'

'It's different, a different time every time I come through.'

'How long between visits in your world?'

'Seconds. A minute at the most. What was the time difference here?'

'Four months since your first visit. One since your last impromptu appearance had me thrown out of the Night Palace. The threads of magic connecting our realms are becoming unstable.'

'I got you thrown out?' A brief visit didn't hold that much power.

'You carry the scent of the old royal daughters that she killed. She's a little on the anxious side about your sudden appearances and disappearances. She thinks I'm trying to commit treason. I've been waiting for you to come back. She senses you, whether you're here or in the human realm. She has the shadows following you. The question is, do I trust my instincts and side with someone who can get me killed, or do I beg her forgiveness when I hand you over?'

'Or do I just go back?' Gia picked up the mirror.

He chuckled, 'The Queen has already sent the new leader of the Wild Hunt to get you. She moves in your village freely since the farmers took the circle down. It's harder now for her to hide her true form here. The circle was a truce, a gift of our magic to your farmers in return for some of their magic to come here to her.'

Gia realised that she had guessed wrong. She had thought the circle took Atlas's and Evie's magic to Yrsa, not here, to a fae queen. Yet it made sense, the intricacy of the circle, the way it was a three-dimensional spell that came to life and swirled around. In hindsight she should have known that it hadn't been human in design.

'Why does she need the magic of human witches?'

'Because her true shape is hideous, the whole Harvesting Court were hideous, and more than anything she wants to be sexually desirable to her people. That's what she's reduced us to, appearances and desire, instant gratification, no thinking, no education, no depth. Other than in addition to absolutely wrecking the court and turning it into a prison. The farmers' human magic was enough for her to appear beautiful in the form she prefers.'

'The legend of the Fomhóraigh is true?' Gia breathed.

'I've not heard that word for centuries. Yes. They're true.'

'She comes on the farm now in her true form?'

'One of her true forms, she has several. Our queen is feeding on humans again, like the Harvesting Court used to.'

'And you're all helping her?' Gia remembered what Evie's children had told her.

'Only a few are allowed to pass to your side. Old Harvesting Court fae who remain faithful to her and her elite hunters. Everyone else is banned from setting a foot in the mortal realm.'

'But I saw you.'

'As I said, aside from a few elite hunters and those faithful to her, everyone else is banned from setting foot in the mortal realm.'

Thoughts ran through her head as his words and their meaning sank in. She had seen him in the food hall with Louise. Oliver had talked about Louise's murder. The door had been bolted. The window was open. Gia thought of the Wild Hunt and the brownie, and realised that seeing fae, really seeing them, was luck, or chance.

'Louise?' she asked, 'I saw you with her inside the food hall in the city, when Atlas and I popped out for a pizza.'

'Louise was unfortunate. Regretful. I had the situation in hand. My queen got greedy, eager for her prey.'

'Prey? She killed her to eat her?'

'Yes. In the old days humans were taught to offer up sacrifices in return for goodwill. Some of them eat humans, some like their blood, the Harvesting Court is not your human idea of a harvest. They took the ripeness season and introduced an exchange when humans first started farming.' He sighed and shook his head, 'there's centuries of complex history for you to learn if we pull this off and no books or anyone to teach you.'

'But the camera didn't pick anything up?' Gia took their conversation back to Louise.

'They wouldn't. Perhaps a shadow without a body.'

'How are you so detached?' They were having a conversation about a murder, and talking about it like they had ordered a takeaway.

'It's the only way to be. We're not human. Life here is long, it turns people cruel and somewhat twisted. We're only as good as our queen, and this one in particular excels at ruling an oppressive regime with an iron fist. I am getting rather weary of unwillingly enforcing her orders of slavery and murder. I miss parties. I miss laughing.'

'You don't have parties?'

'Not anymore. Not real ones. She has events where blood is spilt. Innocent fae sacrificed for her, humans when we can get them. Always for her gratification. She dislikes waiting.'

Gia let the enormity of those words sink in. This was half her world. It sounded like a dystopian nightmare. The man's words described a modern version of hell, he created a landscape more associated with demons than fae. She couldn't remember when humans had been fed to fae as sacrifices, that was something that existed in history books. Her mind jumped ahead and she wondered if it was possible that it was versions of the Fomhóraigh that had introduced the practice to ancient humans, and it had been misinterpreted as for the gods.

'Who are you?'

'Keld. What do I call you? Your bloodline is supposed to be dead, yet here you are, titles seem wrong when we have a queen. I cannot call you my queen even if you are of the lineage.'

'Gia.'

'Gia? Interesting to finally make the connection between her last words and your existence.'

'Her last words?' Her stomach turned. The black hair. It was so much like his. The way it fell, its shine. Her eyes dipped to his shoulders even as she assessed them and measured them against a memory of man she had promised herself to never forget. A man she had thought she would recognise the instant she saw him again.

'We killed the last of his human bloodline years ago.' He held her eyes as he said the words, if there was any emotion in him, then he hid it well.

'My parents died at the hands of a gang,' she protested. It sounded weak to her, more like a plea from a child yearning to be told a sugar-coated lie rather than the truth that rose from the pit of her stomach.

'You look like her, actually, she cried and begged us not to touch her *Gia*. I held her as the blood poured out just to see if she was as soft as she looked. She looked like a fae woman, she felt like a fae woman, I wonder if you would.' He put his head to one side and studied her.

Gia didn't reply. She traced a finger along the markings on the back of the mirror, markings that she couldn't see but knew after five passes through the portal. She placed the mirror back where it had been, and saw her room, then the brownie. It was reaching for the mirror, its hairy skeletal arm stretching out, it curled its claws around the back of the mirror and sent it crashing to the floor.

'You bastard,' Gia muttered, as it vanished from her room.

'I've been called that a few times. Why aren't you disappearing?' He walked next to her to look into the mirror. Her bedroom ceiling appeared in shattered shards, Rosa's face contorted across them, she looked confused, scared, then cross. Gia could only imagine the words she would get on her return for not cleaning up a smashed mirror before she left the house.

Chapter 22

Keld pointed to a corner of the room on the unbroken mirror that she held in her hands. Gia saw the same as he did. The brownie flickered, appearing and disappearing. Rosa didn't notice it at all. She left the room. They could hear her calling out for Gia. The brownie appeared with a self-satisfied expression, before disappearing from view completely. Rosa returned with a dustpan and brush, then she too disappeared and the mirror became a mirror again, reflecting their own eyes and the outlines of their faces against the dark surrounding them.

'It looks like you're here for some time at my mercy.'

She could feel his smirk. She didn't have to look at him to see it. Her eyes had adjusted to the darkness enough for her to make out that they were in a small room. She saw an unmade untidy bed, weapons, and nothing else. Wherever they were it was so dark outside that not even a slither of light let her know where a door might be, or a window.

'I can make it home on my own.' It was a feeble protest that she should have believed in.

'You probably could, but I'm prepared to make a deal.'

He opened a door when he spoke, showing her a way out. Gia hesitated to leave, her mind jumping several steps ahead. She assumed that it was a trick, that he wanted her to run away. She stayed still and watched him. All she needed to work on was how she would get home. She told herself it was no different from being lost in her camper van in America. She knew the sigils. It was merely a case of finding the right place to put them now. Evie's warnings about deals rang in her head.

'You might be, I'm not.' Gia put the mirror back from where she had picked it up. Fae deals were not deals, they were underhand tricks and she would come off worse. She looked at the weapons laid out.

He followed her eyes, and spoke again, 'I was angry when I came here. She gave me a week to find you and take you to her, but she also banned me from returning to the human world. I could take you to her now, or you could listen.' He stopped being friendly and playful.

Gia had her first glimpse of the terror he could inflict, the coldness of the murderer mask he wore. She wasn't scared of him. If he intended to harm her, he would have done it by now. He had brought the mirror here and waited for her return. She reasoned to herself that she was still standing and still whole, in spite of the weapons laid out. Caution rumbled through her. She sounded calmer than she felt when she said, 'Go on.'

'If I kill the Queen and have you crowned, you're mine for eternity, body and soul. Anything I want from you, you agree to. I rule from behind your crown. If you kill the Queen and accept the crown, I'll kneel at your feet and carry out your orders like the subject I am.'

'Both these situations seem to indicate that you want to replace the Queen.'

'The alternative is we are both killed by her for this particular encounter. The brownie will be sending word to her now. Vile creatures the lot of them. I'll be on her death list unless I present you in front of her in two seconds.'

'Yet you're still here.' She felt she had the upper hand at that moment in his hesitation.

He perused her slowly, assessing her, his appraisal less about her body and more about her character.

When he spoke again there was honesty in his voice, 'So it appears I have reached my own impasse because I do not wish the obvious route out of this. I can't help but think despite her best efforts to eradicate the old king's bloodline with his first wife the very fact that you still stand is a sign. My father used to tell me stories of the old king and how life had been different under him. Merry.'

'Old King Coel,' Gia shook her head in disbelief.

'You're a little young to know of King Coel. Even to fae he's just a legend from when times were better.'

'We have a nursery rhyme, told to children in England about Old King Coel being a merry old soul.'

'But will a merry old soul deign a return to the throne?'

'It rates slightly above being killed,' Gia concluded. A thrill ran through her unbidden and left her tingling in anticipation of the wildness ahead. It was the second she no longer doubted that she was fae. The thrill of wildness, chaos and being able to finally be free of restraints was enticing.

'So we are in agreement to commit treason.'

'No Keld, you're hot—'

'I'm a perfectly normal temperature.'

'You're fit,' she started again.

'I have to be but thank you.'

'They're words we use for attractive, you're attractive, but you killed my parents. I'm not making deals or working with you.'

The images inside her head fitted together and she spoke it aloud. She remembered a dark-haired man crying over her mother's body as he held her. The man in front of her merged and overlayed into the memory her fractured six-year-old self held. His proportions fitted. He wasn't a gang member after all, not in the way she had thought.

'I was following orders. This would be different. This would be acting in everyone's best interests, including my own. This would be doing something that I've wanted to do for years, for my own sanity.'

'Your sanity?' Gia was already questioning her own, and why she was even standing having a conversation with the man who had killed her parents.

'There's only so many fae I can kill or put in chains and tattoo her marks on before I stop feeling anything altogether. Any child born now is born a slave. At least I had the experience of tutors and parties. My father talked about vast institutions that taught fae knowledge and magic for free. He paid for the best tutors he could find, but there were years when I didn't have one.'

'She took education away?'

'She took away knowledge.'

'So, you weren't raised a killer?'

'I was. This role was my father's before mine. He trained me. Harshly, but as the only surviving child I had to be the best. What about you, Gia? What did you train to become?'

'A writer. I have access to all the books in the world. I read as much as I can to be good at what I do.'

Even in the darkness she saw his face light up in hope. Gia couldn't help but like that part of him, that he had kept his dreams and his optimism against an alleged oppressor that took away freedoms. It didn't change her heart, she would never forgive him.

'Out of our three options, which do you consider the best?'

'The fourth.'

'I don't recall a fourth.'

'You go your way and do your rebellion crusade, I find my own way home.'

'That's exactly the same as option three, it sees us both dead.' His tone was serious.

Gia believed him. She sighed, 'If things are so bad, why hasn't there already been a rebellion?'

'There were whispers of one, twenty-five or thirty years ago, the half fae, half-human woman I killed was supposed to lead us, we were waiting for her powers to emerge. She colluded with the Ripening Court to start the rebellion. The Queen got wind of it and ordered her death. I was ready to follow but I am bound to carry out the Queen's orders. Then afterwards, we had no one to take the Queen's place. No one to undo this that binds us to her will.' He lifted whatever he wore as a top to show the blue tattoo glowing faintly in the dark, pulsing. He rolled the collection of knives up, fastened it, slipped it into a bag and led the way out of the room.

Chapter 23

The corridor he led Gia into was the strangest corridor Gia had ever been in. Crystals hidden in the walls and the floor gave a soft glow here and there, just enough so she could see where she was placing her feet on the flat rug that appeared endless, decorated with images of fae of all shapes and sizes, dryads, centaurs; fae that looked like stone; fae that had wings emerging from behind their ears and another set on their backs; fae with feather wings of all sizes, small and large; fae with bat wings; fae with dragonfly wings; water sprites; moss covered fae; mythical creatures that she recognised, a lot that she didn't.

The walls themselves were carved into the selenite crystal rock face, jagged, diagonal and narrower at the top. They were rough and unfinished but hewn high enough to walk through. The walls met above them with just a scrape of a blade creating a hint of a ceiling headway, occasionally it had been arched out. At one point above her head she saw rough carvings of figures and trees, knotwork fading to hints of shapes that had been roughly etched and never polished.

'What is this place?'

'An ancient doorway, portals to various places in the world. King Coel had it planned to be a great palace full of lights and merriment even when the snow fell outside. He wanted it to be a place where fae were safe. After his death the Queen played with the idea of converting it, putting in traps and hidden rooms, eventually it fell out of favour and most forgot about its existence.'

'This carpet?'

'He intended the entire palace to be a visual of all the history of the Resting Court and the alliance with the Ripening Court.'

'There's an alliance?'

'No. There hasn't been for centuries now.'

'So, this, are, all these real fae?'

'Yes, or they were real and abundant at one time.'

'Tell me about the blue tattoo. You called it a marking?'

Keld explained that the marking was a type of magical tattoo that most of them had. Only a few had managed to avoid her mark, he told Gia. Those without it were considered outliers not worthy of her attention. The intricate tattoos, imbued with spells as they were, were painful to sit through and much akin to the human version of torture. It was considered a badge of honour if a fae stayed conscious for the entire period. They bound the wearer not only to the Queen, but to the seasonal court that they were in and were a declaration to everyone of to whom they belonged. Each thread in the knot was infused with a multitude of spells. Some of the spells would hurt them if they tried to cross to the Ripening Court, some gave them extraordinary strength, or agility, some spells gave boundaries that were wholly dependent upon the duties assigned or subset of fae.

'Were fae ever allowed to swap courts?' Gia interrupted

'Before her? Yes. My family comes from the Ripening

Court originally. Some fae might be better suited for other duties in other courts, or perhaps take a partner and defect peacefully. My father was trained by the top assassins and fighters in the Ripening Court. He came here to the palace under the old king to be a part of and to train the Wild Hunt. You have a word for it that we don't. Where you move? You humans do it all the time, move from one Kingdom to another.'

'Emigrate? You become an immigrant in another country and reside there.'

'You do read. One of the first changes my father noticed was the language changes. After we lost books and scrolls, our language became more basic over time. We stopped using the big words; the ones we kept were common usage ones. Rhyming and song became the way we kept traditions alive.'

'But you don't speak like that?'

'It's hard to adapt centuries of speaking into a new rhythm. But we needed to fit into your world, not stand out as strangers. We learnt your new cadence.'

'When did all this happen? When did she take away books?' They were still walking along the same endless corridor. Without windows or steps, corners or slopes Gia had no idea whether they were walking in a big circle or in a straight line.

'I think we're counting five centuries without books now. Seven since the very beginning when she killed the King in revenge for wiping out the Harvesting Court. Six centuries since we were banned from the Ripening Court, almost two centuries since she stopped us walking in the human world, until the farmers wiped that circle.'

'Wait, she's, she's the daughter that was taken?'

'What do you know of the Harvesting Court?'

'Only that it existed once.'

'They became called something else across the lands, your Fomhóraigh. Oral tradition tells us that they were greedy, and their greed showed in their shapes. They walked where and when they wanted. Humans became food for them, hence the Harvesting Court title, and the war between our races. The other royal families joined together. They thought that if they separated the children, raised them consciously, the Harvesting Court could start again, in tune with nature as we were supposed to be, as humans were meant to be. Then it all went wrong. The boy turned out OK. The girl however, well blood runs deep. I can't believe we didn't scent you when we killed your parents. How old are you?'

'Thirty-one. How old are you?' He stopped walking and turned around to look at her. He visibly shrank back from her.

'I pray to the goddess and she sends a baby? There's no way you can kill her. You won't even have your powers yet. You can't undo the markings. The Wild Hunt won't respect you. If you can't control them, you can't control the hordes. Every fae looks to the Wild Hunt. If they obey their queen then the entire court does.' He genuinely believed that she had to undo the spells that caused the markings, bring the Wild Hunt to heel, and kill the queen.

'I got myself here. Don't doubt my skills.'

He started walking again. Gia matched his pace. It clicked inside Gia why the fae had such a reputation around words and deals. If they couldn't disobey, they were nothing more than school children testing boundaries, and finding different ways to bend the rules.

'I was born around the time she banned books.' It came from nowhere. She wouldn't have believed that he was capable of offering as much information as he had. Gia thought that she would like to wake up. There was no way this could be anything but her falling asleep whilst doing those curls. She checked her hair. It was still damp but drying.

'How do I make the markings go away? What is it I'm supposed to do to them?'

'You'll know eventually, how to strip old markings and replace them.'

'You don't know, do you?' Gia squared her shoulders and looked at him.

'Nor do you, and there's books in your world.'

'The only thing we know about fae are what's left of your presence in folklore. There's not much of that left really.'

'Then you'll have to write it.'

He stopped so suddenly after walking so briskly that Gia almost ran into his back. She muttered about people needing brake lights, a favourite phrase of hers when someone stopped suddenly in front of her. He studied the wall and tapped twice. The wall opened exactly the same as a door would, with the exception that it was clearly a door for giants. He walked out into the night. Gia followed him. They were at the edge of Hightly Hall grounds. It was dark outside. A special type of glitter coated the ground. It had to be glitter, not frost, because she wasn't cold. It didn't crunch nor make her feet cold. The grass felt like velvet; soft, supporting, moving slightly under her feet.

Just like that night with Atlas up above the fields with the rocks, Gia would struggle to explain what was off about where they were. Neon graffiti on the road was the second physical difference she could find after the grass. Keld walked towards what she thought was the village. She followed him, taking everything in. The woods didn't exist, trees did from a distance, but up close they were rotten or dead. The farm was bare barren land with a ruined Hightly Hall visible when it should be hidden by the English landscape. Mist rolled around at ground level, a transparent whiteness that rose to fill the air. A dancing figure of soft light flickered, then started to move backwards, enticing her to follow it towards Hightly Hall. Keld grabbed her arm and shook his head. Gia turned away from the wisp, slightly ashamed at how easily she had been prepared to follow the light.

Yvonne's house was there, still covered in neon tags and sigils. They walked down towards the farm, towards what should have been tree-dotted landscapes with grass verges and mud. Even the trees drooped. Branches rotted on the ground. Icicles gathered in the place of leaves, glinting in the moonlight. There was no farm entrance, but a doorway of five sad looking, barely alive aspen trees arched over a path where the farm drive would have been. A wisp flickered in the centre. Gia looked away from the enticing light whose dance was a smooth snake-like writhing of sensuality.

Keld took her further down the lane, into the village. Shadowy figures shrank back into dismal, unlit alleyways. The only sounds were those of feet moving away from them in a hurry. The houses and cottages were all in ruins, all shades of burnt ash grey. There was no glass in the windows or doors in the doorways, as though the fae had built for things that ceased to exist. Overhanging each window was a singular stone gargoyle of varying designs. Roofs were in states of disrepair.

Here, everything seemed to present itself as a grotesque grey mimic of the human village. Window frames were distorted and wonky. Doorways too small. The walls gave the appearance of being thrown up in a hurry without much care or skill, as though someone had taken gothic structures, modelled a village, then altered it to film a horror. Keld led her in silence around to the high street. The brook that she loved was non-existent, the bridges that led over it ruined and fallen; a heap of bricks covered in mist and ash. There was light shining from the pub, the one building that resembled what it was meant to look like. It was also the place where the graffiti stopped being on the road and was all over the boundary wall and the building. A thin figure drifted onto the path a metre away brandishing an iron bar leading Gia to conclude that the rumours about iron repelling or hurting the fae were false. Underneath the hood Gia saw luminous white skin, painted black patterns on the face that matched some of the signs on the road, pale arms pulsing with blue tattoos, tattered black clothing and bare feet. Eyes so vibrantly turquoise blue they looked wrong amongst all the dull grey glared at them. The person started when they saw Keld's face, then backed away cowering.

'What's with the graffiti?' she asked, her eyes darting from the pink to the yellow to the green. The finish was more powdery, almost chalk-like rather than the spray paints she was used to seeing. From the expression on the fae's face that had backed away from Keld, his reputation went before him.

Keld let out a soft sigh, his shoulders slumped, his eyes

darted around and there was a long silence before he said, 'When people have nothing, they try to get something. When they're at the bottom of the pile, hungry, in rags, they've nothing to lose from lawlessness. They're trying to get what they need to survive. It's petty tribe symbols. They form alliances to try and make their lives better.'

'Gangs?'

'Gangs? I've read that in your newspapers. Yes. I suppose you could call it that.'

'They all seem scared of you?'

'Every so often some big tough fae thinks by taking me down they'll have the status they crave. I end them. They fight amongst themselves for scraps she allows them to have. These are Resting Court fae for the most part. True ones. They should be afforded more dignity.'

'The brownie in my cottage?' She already knew the answer.

'Old Harvesting Court fae. The half-fae half-human woman that I killed was going to change this. Do you have that same fire?'

Gia was silent. She didn't know if she had. She was hedonistic, impulsive and reckless. She wasn't her mother. Her mother had known about this world, had planned a rebellion. The most Gia had planned in her life was book outlines and a couple of impulsively purchased plane tickets. She turned around, looking, 'What did it use to look like? Before her?'

'Vibrant. Alive. We had communities, colour, music, feasts, culture was at the heart of everything. The lack of magic is making it grey.'

'Even if I take her down. I don't know how to bring the magic back.'

'Removing her magic would be enough, in the beginning. Greedy, divisive magic driven by hate caused this. Our world is but a reflection of our queen. The rest can be worked on.' The air felt heavy with expectation as he looked at her. He held out his hand to her, 'It's a onetime offer. I need an answer now. Say yes, remove my markings, I'll do whatever needs doing to assist you. Have I not shown you enough? Must we be reduced further, past degenerates? Our civilisation has already collapsed. She has taken everything, raped our realm of all its resources. Soon it won't even hold us, once the grey goes, in a few hundred years or less, we'll die too.'

'But if I refuse, you'll take me straight to her.' She didn't know why she was smiling.

The situation had surpassed strange, Gia wasn't scared now, just playful, as though it was all a joke and she would wake up from this dream at any moment. The grave expression on Keld's face, the level of seriousness in his eyes didn't stop her crazy smile. The box inside her had opened. The six-year-old crept out, desperately hungry to grab at a world this man said her mother had known about, her anger abundant and already planning revenge, her little hands clung to the threads Keld had thrown her, her heart filled with the thought of reclaiming part of a heritage and a mother she had grown up without knowing.

'Yes.' Keld looked serious.

'I'm probably going to die either way. I'm interested to see what happens. I'm in.'

She reached out to meet his hand. Instead of shaking it her fingers settled on his palm, a soft glow emitted from them that she hadn't noticed. Deep below them inside the ground a rumble started. A groan in the earth. Even as inexperienced in the fae as she was, Gia couldn't doubt the rise of old dormant forgotten magic. Keld groaned in pain and dropped to his knees. Her brow furrowed at his strange behaviour. Around them the mist froze, turning into intricate frozen patterns before it dissipated. The dark skies of night were swept away by fast moving clouds without a wind, first grey, then lighter, purple, plum, pink, tendrils of blue turning night to day, back to dusk, then night, returning to dawn again, three times.

Gia turned to look at Keld, sweat ran down his forehead. His jaw was clenched. The neon blue tattoo pulsed and moved around his body, visible on his neck, arms and hands now, writhing underneath his skin, disintegrating bit by bit but fighting back against erasure. From the houses, from the alleys, from the pub, screams and cries of pain filled the air. The light became brighter and more settled. Gia looked up to see the skies were clear, a low winter sun shone brightly in a pale blue sky. The sun held a wide halo around it, diamond dust creating a spectacular effect in the air. Yet, she remained the same. There was no magical moment of awakening or surge of special magic for her.

Keld rose slowly and painfully, he became taller than her again. He lifted his top. His pulsing blue tattoo had vanished. Around them came the sounds of movement. He reached his arm back and drew a sword from thin air, he nodded to a window, 'We have to get you out of here before the harvesting fae in the tavern come out to seek you. See if there's a mirror in there you can use to return to your world.'

'Can't you just show me how you do it?' She had seen him in her world, he could cross over.

'I did so with the magic given to me by her markings,

that she reversed and you just broke. It is impossible for me now.' Every now and then Keld said a phrase with an accent that was older than the ones which surrounded her every day.

Gia climbed in the nearest window. Keld followed, checking the room and the street with his eyes. Inside the room was just as grey as on the outside, faded colours, a settee that was chewed, broken, dirty stuffing hanging from it, the place looked like it was abandoned. The only hint that it wasn't unoccupied was a broom propped up in one corner, and that the room was clean and dust free. There was no mirror, there wasn't anything other than a broken piece of furniture. She ventured out of the room and up the stairs. The stairs held the brown remains of what had once been a carpet or runner, now broken down to the very same base threads which started the process.

The bathroom was empty, clean but bare, bereft of any personal items except a small old grey flannel, and a used thin strip of pale amber soap. There was no mirror to be seen. Noises started to emerge on the street below her. Gia went to look but Keld pulled her back roughly, not caring if he hurt her. She turned to look, again there was the cold expression on his face. He shook his head. When he spoke it was barely above a whisper, 'Remember the gangs. They're out there now. It wasn't just my markings that you removed, it was the entire village. Maybe further. I can't tell how far that magic stretched. The Harvesting Court creatures will be out for your blood. This isn't just treason, this is the rebellion we were promised years ago. The Queen won't kill us quietly, it will be a public spectacle that lasts for days. We will have to be made an example of, as a deterrent to any future rebellions. I am not scared of a fight, but I am wise enough to know that we are so vastly outnumbered right now that it would not be much of a fight.'

Now fear rippled through her in icy waves, stroking her skin and raising goosebumps. Bruises and cuts, she didn't mind. Death, that would be an adventure to see what was beyond life. But slow, excruciating, prolonged pain terrified her. Further exploration revealed no mirrors in the house, only one makeshift bed on the floor in a room. Gia crouched down to study the assembled objects that were next to it, a carved pregnant Venus figure that she recognised from archaeology pictures on the internet, a well-worn card that held a therianthropic figure in the style of a cave painting, another piece of card that had a hand drawn sigil on it and two worn candles.

'Keld, what's this?' Gia whispered.

Keld came over, 'We try to uphold the old ways. The statue is a celebration of fertility. Normally it's a post birth figure, because childbirth is dangerous, so we worship, and celebrate, the post birth body as the ultimate female form. But these have taken over since the birth rate fell low. It's what you would label-tacky, but popular. Louise taught me that phrase. The sigil is new. It looks like a wish for change, the therianthrope is the symbol of the Wild Hunt, its leader can change shapes at will, it's a normal popular altar. A household altar. Nothing of note. We'll go to the next house through the back door.'

The next imitation cottage building was the same. Clean inside, bare, no personal items, no furniture, numerous makeshift beds on the kitchen floor around a stove that was still warm, an altar with seven candles, a Venus figure that looked more postpartum than the previous one, a new card with the same therianthropic cave art style figure, an old worn dirty card showing a seven pointed star, and another two equally dirty cards, one showcasing a tree in full summer growth, an abundance of leaves, the second a faceless female. Keld walked past it, reminding her that they were looking for a mirror before the horde of the Harvesting Court found them.

They scrambled through the open windows into the next cottage. This was immediately different. Shelf upon shelf of pristine objects lined the walls of the kitchen, whose window they had just entered by. Dust accumulated on the items. Keld swore. He dragged Gia back to the window and told her to get out. Gia tried but couldn't. There was a barrier stopping her, a strong film of something transparent that she could touch but not move through, less like glass and more like a thick plastic film. Keld swore again and muttered something about the place having to have mirrors at least. They moved out of the kitchen into the entrance hall stacked with books in piles that rose from the ground to the ceiling. They manoeuvred around the piles and into the sitting room that yielded artworks on every wall, top to bottom, luxurious settees, a coffee table with a Turkish coffee set, draped golden curtains, thick rugs with intricate pictures of barely dressed humans wielding spears and arrows against delicate fae, but no mirrors.

Keld held back in the doorway of the dining room when Gia walked in, his sword in hand. He was looking at the doorway, 'Tell me that you see a mirror?' His back was to her, looking out for anyone approaching.

'I see a mirror.'

'Truly?' He sounded childishly hopeful.

'Six mirrors mounted across two walls and two china cabinets with mirrored backs.' The china cabinets were full of expensive looking plates and matching pieces.

'There's rules about a place like this. Firstly, you hope it's just a storage spot and not lived in. There's worse things than brownies here. Two, you do not touch anything. You get out as fast as possible.'

'OK,' Gia breathed. Her mind was still on the window and the way it had shimmered and bent but refused to let her out. The house overwhelmed her with its richness and sheer abundance of greed after the last two cottages. Her mind struggled with the contrast. The piles of goods constricted her senses, shrank her into a smaller space, caused her to tread carefully in a way that created a feeling of claustrophobia.

One of his hands left the sword and reached to his side. He passed her something, 'It'll write on any surface.'

'What am I missing? Where are the magic pens and swords coming from?'

'They're glamoured. It isn't an infinite bag of tricks. I carry less than I used to because I can't glamour it all anymore. Can you hurry?'

Compared to the previous cottages this was too much. There was something off about it. The dining room was sumptuous. The table filled the space. It was made from walnut with a shine high enough to almost see her reflection in. The eight chairs matched, their seats a damask pattern of dusky blues. All the mirrors were framed in elaborate displays of gold. Shadows moved inside the mirrors. Footsteps came towards them. Multiple footsteps on the polished wooden floor.

'Gia.' It was a warning to hurry.

Gia closed her eyes and ruffled her now dry curls, pushing them back. She concentrated on her breathing instead of the choice of what to draw on a mirror or where to go. Thoughts crowded her head, pushing for decisions she couldn't make, did she choose Evie or Atlas? The pub or the hotel? She took deep breaths and tried to focus on the way her lungs expanded. The outside edges of her inner kaleidoscope blurred. She held the pen up to the mirror, hesitated in a panic, then drew. When she wrote, she wasn't always conscious of the words that emerged from her fingers. It was the same with spells. This time she trusted the black space at the back of her mind. The spot people called intuition. A scrawled series of sigils began to appear.

It wasn't a pretty pink mist anymore, but a richer, deeper shade, she saw Atlas walking around his room in his farm overalls, unzipped to reveal the thermals underneath, putting down an empty cup. He put his hand on his bedroom door. She took a breath and turned round, she was in Atlas's bedroom. In his caravan. She let out a huge smile, and said, 'Hi.'

Atlas glowered back. She hadn't seen him angry at her before. He looked around the room, then down at her bare feet. Suddenly self-conscious of the tight thermal pyjamas Gia pushed her hands into the pockets of her cardigan and closed the open ends by pushing her pockets together.

'Where did you come from?'

'It's not easy to explain.'

'Explain.'

'What did I do?' Gia asked, her hands bunching into fists inside her cardigan.

'I thought we had something, Gia. I can accept that

maybe you didn't. But the way you disappeared, how do you walk out in the middle of the night and not take your phone or contact anyone for days?'

'One night.'

'It's been four days. I tried to find you. You were nowhere. Our thing wouldn't even happen.'

Gia watched Atlas struggle, his expressions gave her all the answers she needed. There was no trust left on his side anymore. The atmosphere between them cut her open. She looked away from him, she wasn't ready to see him look at her like she was a stranger, just another person. The words left her mouth before she had considered the implications, 'I'll leave.'

'Like that? With no shoes? No phone? No money?'

Gia looked down at herself. Bare feet, black thermal pyjamas, an oversized ankle length knit cardigan that didn't fasten because she hadn't been able to bear the unstylish dressing gowns in the shops. She shrugged and looked out the window when she said, 'Like I said a few days ago, I never asked you to be a gentleman, Atlas. That's the last thing I'd ever ask for from you. I like who you are.' The silence that met her words spoke more than he ever could. It lingered in the air and pressed down on her shoulders, she lowered her head.

'You did say that.' He folded his arms. She walked to him. Her intentions were to walk out and leave him alone. He didn't move.

'Excuse me please.' She already had her eyes on the door. He blocked her way in the bedroom doorway.

'You can't leave like that.'

'I can't stay.'

'At least let me drive you.' There wasn't any warmth

in his voice. It was a flat offer of assistance. Gia shrugged, it was better than walking.

'Hello Atlas.' A deep voice behind her drawled out the greeting. Atlas flicked his eyes to the other man.

'Keld,' he acknowledged.

Chapter 24

Keld stood in the exact spot Gia had stood in when she managed to make herself appear in the bedroom. He held out the pen she had used and left behind.

'Block it with haste.' She took in his dishevelled appearance and accepted the pen without question; her role without thinking, she blocked their side of the mirror with a simple circle. Gia looked at Atlas. He was staring at Keld. Gia recalled that in the past, Evie had said her brother was indomitable when he was angry. She was inclined to agree with Evie now when she looked at Atlas. Even so, as she looked between the two men, darkly dangerous, icy cold Keld with hidden depths, and warm, humorous, protective Atlas, she wanted to watch the fall out.

'Enjoy the reunion.' She slipped out past Atlas.

Her hand was on the door handle, about to open it and leave the caravan when Keld called out after her, his voice low but playful. It touched a part of her that felt at home with him, 'Aren't you going to ask how we know each other?' He was talking to her.

'No.' She opened the door. Internally her curiosity was tearing her up, but she didn't want to be around Atlas. She needed some time to recover from his hostility.

'Gia, look. You deserve to know who you're dealing with.' Before anyone could speak Keld had yanked Atlas's thermal top up. Gia saw as she turned. A hint of a pulsing, neon blue tattoo on his skin, before Atlas pushed Keld off so hard the dark-haired man ended up at the other side of the caravan.

The cards. The Wild Hunt. Gia turned wide eyes on Atlas. She looked him up and down, much like the first time they had met. This time she didn't smile. Her head told her they could never go back, yet her heart leapt in mischievous, manipulative liveliness at a chance to play games on a level she loved. Even as the half-smile curved onto her face, she already knew which had been chosen. She was nobody's good little girl in the red coat. She was Gia.

'Is there something you want to tell me, Atlas?'

'Have you been with him for four days?'

'One night,' she corrected at the same time Keld said *Yes*.

'We'll invite you to join us next time,' he finished, his eyes fixed on Atlas, purposefully provoking him, his smile was wide.

'Next time? You're making it into much more than it was, Keld.' Gia retorted, her spirit dancing and jumping, revelling in the banter and word play. She knew that she shouldn't, that it wasn't right to tease Atlas.

'I don't know, your first night in your homeland was pretty eventful.' His smirk and direct eye contact with her made her laugh.

She was pushed against the door she had just opened. The caravan door was flimsy and light. It slammed shut with a force that rocked the caravan. Atlas kept her there. He clenched his jaw. Anger and calmness, jealousy and tenderness fought in his eyes and his face. She heard Keld say something about the leader of the Wild Hunt, mockingly, but she couldn't take her eyes from Atlas.

'Everything I've done was to keep you safe. She told me to hunt you. If you were here with me then I didn't need to hunt you down. I ignored the implication that I was to take you to her once I had you. She found out and she put that tattoo on me, whilst you were with him.'

'I wasn't with him, Atlas. Not that way. He's the one that killed my parents. Do you really think I'd go there?'

She cupped Atlas's face and brought it down to her level. She kissed him.

One hand went into her hair and scrunched tight, tilting her head up to him, the other around her waist, pulling her against him.

'When did it happen?' she whispered. Not the tattoo, but him. He understood the question.

'The morning I left your bedroom window. They were circling the cottage. I didn't think, I just—' he broke off.

Gia could piece together the rest of the story. 'Are you going to take me to her?' she asked. She saw his thoughts move quickly, and the fight in his eyes.

He smiled and whispered into her ear, 'She's scared you'll break whatever spell she put into the tattoo. I can't take you if you attempt to break it. She's more obsessed with power and control than destroying you, that includes control over her Wild Hunt. Don't trust me right now, Gia. I can't make promises to keep you safe.'

'Through the storm, right?' She curled her hand around to his neck. There was a pause.

Then she heard the faintest whisper back, 'Through the storms.' His hand tightened in her hair and his fingers sank into the skin on her waist for a fraction of a second.

She chuckled, 'At least I don't have to explain this fae thing to you,' she said, her tone low and soft, meant for only him to hear.

He laughed softly into her neck, 'I can see why people call us demons.'

'Talking of demons. I should go and see Nonna.'

'I don't advise that.' Keld's voice came from behind them. He was leaning against the wall, gleefully watching, his whole demeanour suggesting that he found the scene titillating and amusing.

Gia met his eyes, 'Why?'

'You've been replaced. It tends not to go well when simple humans are confronted with two versions of one person.'

'He's right, as much as I hate to say it.' Atlas muttered.

Gia was adamant that she wanted to return to the cottage. It was the only move she had. She needed shoes, at least, and some clothes, and she wanted to make certain Rosa was alive. Atlas insisted that he drove her. Keld disappeared quickly when the caravan door was opened a second time. She was too lost in her own struggles on the way to the car to care. She didn't notice the unnatural dip in the sun. She did notice, and cast her eyes upwards as the light around her turned to dusk, to see a pinkish sky. Her first thought was that it was Keld. Until she saw the shadows of racing deer. They approached with speed. She braced herself to see the actual solid bodies running towards her, but the shadows passed. There was nothing except a blast of cold air, the snorting of an out of breath animal, and a smell of frost. The shadows circled around her, again the cold air hit her. This time, a rich comforting warmth rose up inside her. She raised her hand to the shadow. The deer changed. The shadow became covered in frost, it turned pale with a moonlit glow.

Antlers came towards her. It was then that Gia finally understood what the blasts of cold air were. The first time it had run at her it had tried to take her up into the air on those antlers. It would have run away with her had its plan succeeded. The shadows were after her, like the brownie had said. It would seem that they couldn't quite grasp how to get her, because she was neither human nor fae but something in between, some hybrid mix of both.

Instantly her brain jumped to genetics. If fae and humans could mix and produce children, potentially the number of people around the world with fae genes could be either a minority or a majority. She didn't know how far back it had happened in her mother's lineage. She wondered if it was like red hair that appeared strongly every few generations, she thought about DNA ancestry companies and whether they had worked out this unspoken secret. That would be huge.

Just like that, she had a new plot, genetics, magic, a scientist working on DNA, and an agency that quickly saw numerous ways to profit from a discovery at the expense of ethics. Then the shadow of a wolf tore down the stag in front of her, joined by Keld.

Chapter 25

She was four. Haunting melodies filtered through her bedroom window like a longed-for breeze in the summer night. Gia was hot and sticky. She heard the main door open and click half shut when her grandmother came home, and listened to tired footsteps as her exhausted, thin body went to bed. In her mind's eye she saw her grandmother in the worn-out blue dress, then her mother in the sitting room, surrounded by books, glowingly beautiful. Gia got off the bed and walked to the door. Her mum was curled up on the settee by the window, a book in her hand, waiting for Gia's dad to return. Sometimes the door didn't catch properly, it was old. Gia prised it open and walked out. Behind them narrow streets led through the old city. In front of them were a few goats, fields and trees.

A parade of people danced to the faintest stream of music coming from behind the trees. Their clothes were light. Their bodies glowed faintly, even the dark ones had a glow. They were far back. The music was too far away. Gia started to walk towards it. She hadn't gotten far with her small legs and feet when something was thrown over her, she caught a glimpse of red, she was scooped up and nestled in a pair of arms.

'You cannot, *tesoruccia*, do not be exceptional, they cannot know about you yet.'

She was five, sitting in the garden, the concrete beneath her radiated heat from the day's sun. Her garden chair was comfy. A soft burning filled the air from the setting sun, and she was fighting to keep her eyes open. The visitors were her mum's friends and funny looking. A man had made butterflies appear from his hands for her. They sat around with a drink. She didn't like two of them. They scared her. They had funny faces, hollow and scary, their clothes were in rags and they needed a wash. The other two were strange, beautiful, but different. The woman glowed from the inside, her skin was radiant. The man, he was dark, he sat on a stool rather than a chair, so his big wings didn't get in the way, but he glowed too. Her mum had asked him to make the wings go away and complete the transformation. He had laughed, kissed her mum on the cheek and said something Gia couldn't hear. The group talked about never being together after this point, setting the stage, starting whispered rumours, so when the time came, her mum would lead a rebellion and send someone to prison. Gia had heard most of the words they used before, usually from her dad. She wasn't supposed to know where her dad got his money, but she did. The man told her to try and make a butterfly herself. Gia tried and tried the entire time the grownups sat and talked. Nothing happened, she picked up an olive and ate it, complaining to the man that she couldn't do it. Her mother chastised the man and told him to stop filling Gia's head with ideas, she wasn't the exception. Gia decided there and then to prove her wrong and opened her palm to release a black butterfly. It rose from her hand, frosted over, and melted. A delighted cheer went around the table and everyone smiled at her.

She was six. Her mum worked at the big office in town where important town things happened. Everyone thought her mum was beautiful.

She was six. Dark blood coated her hands and clothes. Her parent's bodies were blue and stiff. Someone was screaming. Then she was exceptional, then people looked at her. The teachers didn't raise their voices or mind if she came in late. Even Nonna had gotten tired of it and took them both off to the UK to start again. To be normal, not exceptional.

She was twenty and published, in her second year at university. Evie was pregnant. Tess had secured a painting apprenticeship with a portrait artist in Italy after graduation the following year. Genevieve had quit her English university the previous year to move to Paris and blog about beauty, books, coffee, and clothes. Nina was working with big names in the fashion industry after failing her A Levels. Liberty had set up a finance business side gig to pay for university.

Yet Gia couldn't remember what she had written in her last essay because editing with publishers had taken every part of her brain for longer than she could ever have imagined. She was walking around in an end of academic year-tired daze. Half the students on her course stared at her in contempt because her work hadn't been literary enough. Others stared in jealousy, wishing it had been them. Gia dreamt of escaping the exceptional situation of being the twenty-year-old with a publishing deal, and the exceptionally disappointing student that was probably going to have to re-sit the year. She quit the course with an official email on the way to the airport, aiming to go somewhere she could be just Gia Roselli, the author.

She was six again. The memory she lied about to everyone was still there. A man crying as he held her mother's body. Her father was laying still, covered in blood that had clotted, turning from bright red to dark. She couldn't see the man, only the back of him. He had long black hair. She heard his sobs, she watched his shoulders and his back move with each one. She watched as he leaned down and placed a gentle kiss on her mum's head. She didn't hear what he whispered. Rage filled her tiny body at the unfairness that he got to cry about killing her mum. The anger took a piece of her that might otherwise have been calm, soft and gentle like her mum. It started the seeds of detachment; the separation of her head and her body. Her mum had told her to hide, that she had to grow up. Gia wanted to be there right between her mum and dad, even if it meant being dead.

Now she was exceptional again. The woman that the Wild Hunt couldn't take. They would be back to try again. Right at that moment she fully understood Evie's desire for spa days. Gia would love to be back in the spa having an Indian head massage, drinking the spa prosecco with Evie and chatting, no worries at all. She picked up the keys Atlas had dropped, pushed up her cardigan sleeves and prepared to wade her way into the fight.

Keld pushed her out, 'Go. Get away. They need to sort this out themselves.'

'I can't let them kill Atlas.'

'He'll get no respect if he can't hold his own fights and challenges. He needs to quash this on his own. I'll fight by his side.'

'As will I.'

'You fail to understand our ways, Gia. If you were

ordinary fae I'd say fine, stay and fight, have a chance to join the Wild Hunt. His reputation cannot be because royal blood fights for him.' Keld stared at her, his arms crossed, his chest heaving from the exertion of fighting.

Chapter 26

She wasn't planning to remain in the cottage long. Practically, she needed some shoes and perhaps her purse with her bank cards, then at least she could pay for a coffee somewhere. She walked into the front garden through the green gate and looked at the door framed by holly trees as she approached. The holly trees that were supposed to prevent her from entering. She remembered the version of her back in October that had once been so scared of the brownie that she had paused to enter. Not only had she thought it was a demon, she had also thought that it was stronger and more powerful than her. Demons and fae were supposed to be different beings. Except her reality told her that both were interchangeable in the eyes of most humans. She thought of Shakespeare's portrayal of the fae, and realised that they too could be demons in another human's mind, playing tricks on mortals the way they did.

Gia had already spent too many years wondering why the demon rituals failed to elicit any response in her. Not even in her wildest imaginings had she thought of the race of faeries being real. In spite of the stories about them going back to the beginning of time and existing on every continent, she had thought, if she thought at all, that they were remnants of human history from a period when they didn't have explanations for events, from a time when superstitions preceded science.

The cottage door was unlocked. Being careful to tread gently, Gia entered and closed the door in the hope she could get upstairs without being seen or heard. Once she looked around, she stopped and stared. It was the smell that hit her first. It wasn't the faint smokiness of autumn nights that she was used to. It was beautiful fresh rain on the ground, petrichor. She could be around it all day. Shock grounded her feet to the floor. Gia shook her head in disbelief. It was her. The version of herself from Harriet's café, sat at the breakfast bar flicking through a magazine and drinking a glass of white wine as though she belonged in the cottage. She wore Gia's black jumpsuit and her hand-knitted cardigan with the spider brooch. Gia's favourite stilettos rested on the bottom of the bar stool, casually loose, her foot slipping out of one. There was nothing to note her as different except when she turned around. Her cold eyes and stony expression were not quite an exact copy of Gia's. They were her doe eyes, big and brown, outlined in black in an attempt to get the sleek vixen eye Gia liked and wanted, but they lacked warmth.

She recognised Gia. It fluttered briefly across her cold face. Shock, surprise, and a glimmer of hesitation. She recovered quickly, throwing down the glass of wine in her hand and jumping unnaturally from the bar stool to reach Gia. Gia ran up the stairs and slammed her bedroom door, muttering an old incantation to keep the door closed and secure. It was one she had written and practised since her early days in America, when she had parked up in places and her camper van door had been tried persistently from someone on the outside. She reached for the cabin bag, pushed under the bed and grabbed a mix of clothes from her wardrobe and drawers to shove hastily in a bag; jeans and a skirt, jumpers, some underwear and socks, to the rattle of the door. Gia concentrated on how she chanted the spell, one slip and the fake-Gia could burst in with the upper hand. She couldn't afford to mess up the spell.

Hastily she pulled socks and then her boots on, a long black skirt over her pyjama bottoms, a soft cashmere jumper over her top, and pushed her toiletries and make-up into the top of the cabin bag. Her handbag, her phone, her purse, they were all lying in her room, as though the fae impersonating her had no need of those things. She pushed them into the half-filled bag too, and then she picked up the car keys from the bed where she had thrown them down in her rush.

Gia changed her incantation, opened the door and held out a stretched hand, her palm faced outwards. Her fae impersonator flew into the wall then tumbled down the stairs. Gia followed her, still speaking the spell. She watched her fake self fly across the room to the fireplace. Gia took a couple of steps into the room. She had left her key on the kitchen counter and intended to retrieve it. The fae impersonator put her head to one side and a slow, malicious grin spread across the exact copy of Gia's own face, a sparkle in her eyes.

'Aren't you just full of delicious surprises, witch,' she drawled. Her eyes diverted to the front door of the cottage, just inches away from Gia. Gia heard the noises outside too. The door opened and Rosa walked in with her arms full, holding a tray of pastries. She was followed by a flushed Harriet juggling two trays. They stopped and stared, large, shocked eyes on her.

Gia released her fae self, but not early enough. Rosa

and Harriet saw fake her pinned back against the wall, her feet above the floor. To their eyes, the real Gia was being attacked.

Gia saw herself as others saw her; tall, straight back, hair back in a messy low bun, curly tendrils around her face, winged eyeliner, red lips, enough make-up to look like she wore make-up. It was a contrast to how she looked now, no make-up, not even mascara on her lashes, her hair was down and curled properly for the first time. She wasn't wearing anything red, not even lipstick.

Rosa went pale, 'Lucia?' she whispered.

Stunned and disturbed that Rosa didn't recognise her at all, Gia stared back. Lucia. Her mother's name. The name Gia would have chosen for a daughter, just as Atlas had said he liked Valentina. Lucia. Laughter on the wind, a yellow dress, magic, a body bathed in blood. Sounds of shouts belonging to people rolled around the cottage and brought her back to the present, the image of her mother's body faded as the cottage's furnishings entered her view.

Gia wanted to respond to her grandmother, but she found her brain frozen. She didn't know what to say to refute the suggestion that she was somehow Lucia returned. Harriet was glancing between fake-Gia with loved up eyes, then confusion at seeing the real Gia. The fake-Gia took a step forward.

Rosa's face turned pale, then hateful, Gia's presence provoked an intense reaction in her, 'I cast you out demon, in the name of the Lord. You are a child of the devil and an enemy of everything that is right, you are full of all kinds of deceit and trickery.' Rosa seemed to search for what to say next. Gia could imagine her brain whizzing through bible verses.

'I'm not a demon,' Gia protested.

Rosa's hand went to the cross necklace at her throat and the tray she was holding started to slide. The fake-Gia darted across the room to gallantly rescue it. Rosa edged forward, still holding her necklace and recited words Gia knew would have no effect on her. It didn't stop her heart from beating faster and her breath catching in her throat, 'It's me, Nonna. Why don't you recognise your granddaughter?'

Stood behind Rosa but in front of Harriet, the fake-Gia smirked. Rosa refused to falter even a step. Gia responded to her grandmother's advance by taking a step backwards with every forward step Rosa made. She tried desperately to think of something only Rosa and she knew. As words and thoughts swirled around inside her brain, no matter what she wanted to say, it would sound as though it came from a demon. The more Gia tried to find something, the more she thought that anything she said would sound like something that a real demon would say.

'Submit yourself to God, Lucia. Resist the devil, and he will flee from you.'

'Nonna, it's Gia.'

'Come out of this woman, you impure spirit! I have been preparing for you for fifteen years. I command you to come out of her and never enter her again.'

'I quit university because I didn't enjoy the snobbery about perceived literature against popular reads. Every book is valid in that it tells us of a subculture or a point in history that people would prefer to overlook because it makes them too uncomfortable to address the reasons behind why it was written, subverting against the prevailing social constructs,' she blurted. It had been the planned outline of her dissertation, the one she had never written.

Rosa stopped. She hesitated. Doubt registered in her eyes.

She turned to the other Gia who smiled sweetly and didn't miss a beat to pull out Gia's official line of ten years, 'I quit university because my publishers offered me a once in a lifetime chance to sign a series deal if I could produce a successful second book. I could always return to education.' Her eyes glittered as they drifted to Gia. Rosa gave a nod.

'Social constructs. What does a demon know of social constructs. You might have been human once, Lucia, but not anymore,' she scoffed. Gia's head refused to give her anything else to work with, no conversations, no revelations, nothing she had inside her was private given the amount that she had put on social media over the last ten years.

Except just one thing, she looked at the fake-Gia, 'Name my six best friends.'

Fake-Gia laughed. 'I don't have friends. Not anymore. I have flings.'

Rosa gave a nod of agreement. Her expression told Gia that she thought the childhood friendships had long been left behind. Gia cursed at not mentioning her friends more to her grandmother over the years. On the surface that was exactly how her life looked. Independent, free, no ties nor friends, she sought out people who were interesting to her for a time, she slept with who she wanted, and didn't stay around to say goodbye to anyone. Gia walked further back into the kitchen. The first step she had taken away from Rosa already made her guilty, she was a demon, her hand reached behind her for the door handle as Rosa resumed her prayer. Gia turned the handle.

The door was locked. The key sat in the lock taunting her. She turned her back to the room to unlock the door and open it, then sprinted down the back garden path to the gate they rarely used, her cabin bag jostled against her as she steadied it with a hand. The rarely used wrought iron gate squeaked as it opened and closed. Gia stood on a narrow grit alleyway stretching either side, brambles, holly, and bare trees in front of her. On the other side of the trees and brambles a row of green iron railings denoted the boundary of the churchyard.

Grateful for the early darkness of English wintertime, Gia walked slowly along the dimly lit back lane, round the corner and warily back to Atlas's car. She locked the doors as soon as she was in, and drove off, not quite sure where she was going.

Chapter 27

Gia swerved off the country road, bumped over the verge and parked the car across a field gate on one of the lanes that ran through the farm. It meant that the car was set back from the road so that it wasn't a danger, a dark unlit car on a dark night, parked off an unlit road, but she was out of the way of people. She leaned her head against the headrest and regretted her decision to leave Rosa with the fake-Gia.

If she was honest with herself, she could have attempted to take on the fae. Her brain fought herself for a few minutes until she realised the truth. She had run because she was scared of what might happen if caught. Religion scared her. Rosa wouldn't be alone, it was her ghost hunt night tonight. She had members of the university faculty arriving, hence the trays of pastries from Harriet's café. Gia closed her eyes, she was unable to predict how they would react if they saw a Gia that looked like Gia and a Gia that looked like a dead person, one that Rosa declared a demon. She hadn't realised that without make-up she looked so like her mother.

Rosa saw Gia, or the granddaughter she thought she had, as a person in need of being guided back to the main path. Gia was fine stepping over tree roots and treading softly on an unmarked trail in her own darkness. The path she walked had always been a dark one. Rosa's version of who Gia should be held her in a small prison. She sighed into the quiet coldness, her breath forming a slight mist. In the silence and the stillness of the evening words popped into her head. Words had been her solace and her best friend for years.

She whispered aloud with closed eyes,

The whisper within,
Rises above my skin,
No longer bound,
My voice not drowned.
I am all, all is me,
Strength, power and magic mine be.

Nothing much happened. The air and fields around her failed to offer a grand announcement that they had acknowledged her whisper. Yet Gia knew from experience that sometimes it was the quietest spells which had the biggest impact.

A dark motorbike pulled over. Gia sighed. Liam was the last person she wanted to deal with, despite the stalker helmet cover. She recognised the painted skeleton that it was supposed to be. It was exactly how she had described it in a book, Abby's book actually, when military psychic experiments on her high school sweetheart created a being that left him only partly human. Jack rode a motorbike with that exact helmet, half skeletal, half floral. He had a crack in the skull running from his forehead down past the corner of his eye to the cheekbone, which mirrored the scar on his real face. A glowing, ghostly white peace lily painted onto the other side of the helmet showcased Abby's favourite flower.

Her thoughts came back to the present and focused

on the person pulling off their helmet. The full extent of her fandom sometimes terrified Gia, how much they could fight and argue over what was a fictional work. She had never done a deep dive through fan comments after her fifth book, shocked and horrified at the gatekeeping, the possessiveness and again, the self-righteousness of wrong opinions that people seemed to spew with little regard for others. Instead, she had written it into Abby's story, a tale of small-town America and big politics, where those who understood its subtlety had gathered in huge numbers to fight the fans who caused the crushing waves of entitlement online. A knock on Gia's window made her lower it. Jae stood there. When the window was lowered Gia felt the full force of the frost that was spreading. The temperature had dropped. Everything would be white soon.

'You OK?' Jae asked Gia. Gia gave a nod.

'You cosplay?' Gia referred to the helmet Jae had taken off.

Suddenly they looked slightly embarrassed, they shifted their weight from one foot to the other. 'Yeah. It's not fan crazy stalker stupid despite the mask. I have a social media account doing cosplay. I've done it since I was sixteen, I was just filming some content now on my bike.'

'Are you going to be doing your ASMR as a cosplay character?'

'The cosplay I do tends to be either bike stuff or situations from books and comics, or gaming. Spa based ASMR is geared for people who want that experience. I wouldn't even know where to start to design a studio that fits both. I have different user names and accounts. Then there's screen expectations. Cosplay tends to focus on the character you're being, you fill the screen. ASMR focuses on sounds and the other person.'

'But you've thought about it?' Gia's intuition was usually correct.

'If I did it would be a series on American magic. There's so many quotes and spells you've written that people love. It'd be perfect. Your characters lean towards that. You write in hair appointments, and nails, massages. People have done AI images of your characters so there's a generally accepted look about them which I can create with make-up. Why do you do that? Put the salon breaks in?'

'When Evie and I were at school there was a group of us who were really close. Genevieve's mum would treat us to a spa day for Genevieve's birthday. Tess's stepmum started doing it too. I'd love to see what you can do with my books. I think you're perfect to bring them to an ASMR audience.'

Tess's stepmum had done it to show that they could afford to, and to get rid of Tess for the day. V.V's mum had done it with love, and the intention to treat the young women she saw them growing into. The seven of them had vowed that they would have regular spa days together as adults. They had all gone their separate ways, so Gia had written it into her books to show that she still remembered their teenage promises, despite never setting a foot in a spa in America.

'I don't get you. You seem nice. But your behaviour the last few days has been, unhinged?' it was there, the lilt at the end of the voice, the uncertainty of not wanting to set her off.

'Jae, I don't know what I'm supposed to have done this

week. I'm out here because one of those crazy stalker people has somehow convinced Rosa that they're me. She looks like me, she's wearing my clothes. I went off on a research trip four days ago. I came back tonight, and things are crazy,' Gia lied about her disappearance.

'She's been awful to Evie, yet I saw you two together in the spa. You were friends.'

'I kept some of the details of my life secret from fans. Especially who my friends are.'

'If it were anyone else, I'd say you're being crazy. But it kind of makes sense. The way she blanked me when I said hello and tried to ask if she wanted to be in one of my videos, and she denied knowing who I was, yet you're here talking to me. The way she's snubbed Atlas for Oliver even though the whole village knew you two were trying to keep your relationship low key. She's a bitch.'

That was news for Gia to digest. Another bombshell. Keld knew about Gia and Atlas, he had said so. She couldn't put her finger on why the fake her would encourage Oliver over Atlas. Perhaps it was a personal preference, which would indicate that they were nothing alike. She answered Jae, 'I can be a huge bitch. I'm nice to people most of the time. But I don't forgive and forget. I remember and seek revenge.'

Jae laughed at that, 'I like that.'

'How do you get to be so comfortable with telling people who you are?'

'I'm not comfortable at all. I was one of those *normal* mainstream people who scoffed at this stuff and thought it cringe. But it's better to be happy. I'd rather be cosplaying, ASMR, hairdresser Jae than fake Jade who fitted in with the popular crowd because she was blonde and girly. I see some of the old crowd in the gym. They're on the treadmills and I'm lifting weights and I'm so glad being strong is my goal as opposed to being thin because you're never thin enough in that mindset. So, listen, instead of sitting out in the cold why don't I ask you again if you want to do a video with me like Evie did? I don't understand why you're not calling the police, but I can offer you somewhere warm to think.'

'Where would you go to do it? You filmed in the salon with Evie, didn't you?' Gia asked.

Jae laughed a little and leaned on the open window of the car, 'My mum owns the spa. I have a set of keys. I just need to text her that I'm using it.'

'Is it what you wanted to do?'

'Sort of. It wasn't the dream. I said I wanted a job where I could just go and do it. Mum said I was too creative to work in a supermarket and colouring hair might suit me. So here I am, for lack of any other ideas on what to do with my life, I'm just enjoying the ride.'

Gia followed Jae a short while later, having agreed to an ASMR video. She had no plan on how to fix the situation and nowhere else to be. The salon had been her warmest option. Gia made cups of tea in the tiny cupboard of a kitchen, whilst Jae gathered a bowl, tubes of hair dye and brushes in a slightly larger cupboard room off the kitchen whose other door at the far end led through to the main spa. She put them in a box that had her name on it. At a glance Gia recognised the jade combs, the chopsticks, things she had used on Evie's hair in the video. Gia gave Jae permission to do whatever with her hair, so long as they didn't cut it too short. She wanted to still be able to put it back in a bun or a claw clip.

'I was thinking, we'll do your nails whilst your colour sits. You described Abby as having brown curls and I have Jack's costume here, we can throw your idea of a cosplay into the massage. See if it works.'

'Sure, do you take sugar?'

'One, please.'

'Do you mind if I lock the door to keep us safe? I wouldn't be able to relax if I knew anyone could walk in.' She didn't state who anyone was, but Jae gave a nod of agreement.

Sat in the chair Gia kept her eyes closed, it was surprising how quickly her body started to fall asleep. Jae did a twenty-minute hair play video, their touch was light and gentle. Gia found it much more relaxing than she expected, it was a fight to keep her head up. The sensations were taken away and Gia felt the metal tail of a comb creating sections in her hair, the sections quickly twisted and clipped, a coldness on her scalp of a brush loaded with product before it softly glided downwards. Then she had to wake up and they swapped her short red nails for far longer ones that had a subtle gold shimmer with black ombre pointed tips, the type she had always wanted but never tried because they looked impractical. They rinsed her hair colour out and toned the hair. Gia heard the crisp snips of sharp scissors with her eyes closed, not even tempted to look. Styling products were put on her new hair, and Jae dried it with a diffuser.

'Keep your eyes closed. I've just had an idea for a fantastic make-up look to match. Kind of Abby-ish, you'll see.' Gia was ready to fall asleep. She kept her eyes closed.

When she was finally allowed to look after various brushes had gone over her skin, from sumptuously soft, to ticklish to bristly and scratchy, then back to soft, Gia tried not to focus on the fact that the mirror was slightly misty. Jae didn't appear to see it. Gia was convinced someone was watching them through it. She wondered if humans were like a reality TV show to the fae, then remembered the Resting Court were banned from walking in the human world. Jae fluffed Gia's curls. Her hair had been given a good trim, the dark rich brown suited her much better than the ombre she had hidden in a bun. Jae had been right about the make-up too. The layered, loose curls had a bohemian feel, as did the natural but dark make-up. Her customary sharp liquid eyeliner was replaced with a softer line of eyeshadow, smoky brown shades on her eyes, a hint of peach on her cheeks, and her red gloss lipstick substituted for a matte lipstick in a coffee shade. It seemed appropriate that, when she was in the middle of an identity crisis and in the biggest personal mess she had ever created, Jae had magicked up a new being from it, a much more darkly feminine version of herself than Gia had ever tried out before, more than she had imagined girl next door Abby to be when writing her, but reader interpretation really was different. The Gia in the mirror stared back, challenging her, mocking her inaction. She saw the resemblance to her mother in the moment, she looked almost exactly like her with the shorter, browner, curlier hair and darker make-up.

Jae had to plug her phone in to record the massage, their battery was low after filming content on their motorbike. They arranged everything that they needed for the aesthetic set up around the plug socket they wanted to use whilst Gia changed to fit Jae's vision of how they wanted her to look for this. Jae brought their motorbike helmet into the room and Gia let a chuckle escape.

It was unexpected, and slightly uncomfortable so she took a moment to sit with it, 'This is the first time I've ever done a cosplay, weird how it's one of my own characters,' she said.

Jae grinned, 'The first time is always the most self-conscious, especially if you've been so used to trying to maintain one face for the world to see, like you have with your signature style. I was the same at school. Cutting off my hair felt like losing part of me, but I felt freer afterwards, like I wasn't defined by how other people saw me anymore. You can have your eyes closed, it's just a neck and shoulder massage.'

'Would that be OK?'

'Sure. It's what Evie did. Here's my plan, shout out about anything you're not alright with,' Jae talked Gia through their planned vision for the video and how the massage would play out.

Gia stepped outside after the massage, her shoulders had dropped several inches and the stress she hadn't realised that she was carrying in her neck gone. Even her jaw was less tight. It occurred to her how dark the rear car park was. A single streetlight lit a corner of the building, the only entry and exit to the car park, dark glittering frost swathed the rest of the tarmac covered area. She crossed to the car. She had a sense that she was being watched. Her eyes darted around, trying to find the source.

From the darkest corner a hooded figure emerged. Tall. Broad. Well built. Gia barely had a second to notice him before he had crossed the car park at an unnatural speed and crushed her against the car, one hand ready to squeeze her throat, ghostly, glowing white antlers emerging through his hood. Dragging her gaze down from the antlers she caught the grey eyes with flecks of gold. They were as cold as Keld's eyes.

He whispered in her ear, 'Act as though you hate you me. I'm trying really hard to balance out her demands for us to take you to her against keeping you alive. The only way to prolong the inevitable is you fighting against us until we figure out a plan.'

Reacting to his words with absolute trust, Gia reached out and wrapped her fingers around his wrist, touching skin. Out of the corner of her eye she saw the vaguest sparkle of frost on his skin. Atlas let go and took a step back. He looked her up and down several times.

The menacing presence hadn't gone from him, but he slowly took her in, 'I like the new look. It suits you.'

'How do you always seem to know where I am?' She had changed her clothes in the spa, but right at that moment she wished she still had the thermals on as well as the skirt and jumper.

'Instinct. Scent.' Atlas shrugged.

'What do you want?'

'To help you.'

'I said last month I can handle my own shit and if I wanted help I'd ask.'

'Did you know?'

'That you'd replace him? Yes. Anyone who knows fairy tales knows that.'

'Thank you for saving me would have been nice.'

'And yet you're stood here in his place, doing his job.'

'Unforeseen setback, it means you're still alive right now.' He shrugged it off, as though it meant nothing. He leaned in to kiss her. Gia forgot everything, she wrapped her arms around him and pulled him closer, sinking into the moment, the dark, the kiss, Atlas.

The sound of a door being slammed behind him made Gia look up. Jae had their key in the door, turning it. They turned and looked at Atlas. Then they looked at Gia and asked if she was alright. Gia promised that she was in a voice more confident than she felt. Jae's motorbike filled the silence, then left the pair alone.

'What was it like, after you killed him?'

'Strange. Like being on a field when thick fog descends rapidly. All his memories, his knowledge, his skills became mine. I know the history back to the beginning of the Wild Hunt. I know the continents like my own farm. I have memories of places I've never been to, chasing prey along the Ganges, standing in the snow in St Petersburg on the verge of the First World War looking for my prey. It felt fucking fantastic. I can move faster. Human perception is so wrong about solid matter and time, it's all flexible.'

Just off the high street the unfamiliar sounds of sirens passing by startled her. She had forgotten how little action the village saw aside from middle class tourists. Sounds of a car crashing into another made her jump.

Atlas looked serious, 'She's changed the rules. Her court favourites can walk in the village and cause as much harm as they like until you're caught. Are you going to run and hide? Protect my sister? Or maybe you'll choose your grandmother?'

'Why are you here choosing me? Are you going to let her get Evie? I told you I can look after myself,' she spat. Even as the words left her mouth, she knew her anger wasn't at the messenger. Keld had told her that the leader of the Wild Hunt had been sent after her. She saw a flash in his eyes, the way the inside corners narrowed as he registered what she had said. Then he was gone.

An alliance, that was what she needed, Gia thought. Not with Atlas, with Evie. If the siblings had told their story right, they didn't understand the implications. Evie wasn't just a nature witch any longer. She was on par with the women who had been revered and turned into nature goddesses of old lore, and more powerful than she thought.

Chapter 28

Harriet had been the one to do the spell on Evie. If anyone was likely to remember what the circle had looked like that night, it would be her. Then Gia remembered that Harriet was with her grandmother, in the cottage; tonight was the night her grandmother had wanted to do the ghost hunt. Harriet's café was two shops down the street, and she lived above it. Gia wondered if she'd kept a copy of the spell or the circle. After some deliberation, she chose to leave the car parked behind the spa, took her handbag out and left the cabin bag, then walked to Harriet's café amidst the alarms and sirens that seemed to be everywhere.

The pretty high street seemed to be deserted. Shouts and noises came from either end, the hotel and the pub, but more noise came from the pub than the hotel. Gia paused when she reached Harriet's pink café and stopped to think that Harriet wouldn't keep something so special in the café where a drink could be spilt on it. A small side door said 22a in painted purple numbers. The café door said 22 in polished brass. Gia hoped she had the right flat. She studied the door. It was old, a couple of decades old, at least, and plastic. She remembered the technique for this, hold the handle, lift it up, pull it slightly towards her gently, not a yank and don't pull hard, then still pulling it towards her body, slam it down fast.

At the time, she had filed knowing how to break an old

door under useless information collected during research. A criminal had told her how to do it, on a date where Gia had been fishing for names for a story she had heard about. Despite that there hadn't been a second date, the information had proved useful on occasions. Holding the door handle down, she pushed. It opened. Gia stepped inside and closed it behind her. A set of stairs led upwards to the flat, the black painted walls rising either side, blocking her in. Harriet had hung large pictures of tarot cards all the way up, alternating the major and minor arcana. It was an interesting choice.

Inside the colourful flat Gia looked around. The mismatch of second-hand furniture was something she was used to, it reminded her of her childhood. Bright throws and colourful cushions matched the colour on the walls. Turquoise and coral seemed to be the main colours Harriet used. After the café Gia had expected more pink in the flat, it seemed to be Harriet's favourite colour. The spell she was searching for wouldn't have been left sitting about. It would have been placed somewhere meaningful to Harriet. She flicked the light on and made her way to the bookshelf. Harriet wouldn't hide it in a novel unless it was a special copy, not in a witchcraft book, that was clearly too obvious. It was the first handwritten, real spell Harriet had been given. Gia brought up what she knew about Harriet in her head and sorted through it logically.

Harriet loved Gia's character Abby from *American Magic*. Abby would have hidden it in the bedroom, in a box of treasured papers like letters from her father, from Jack. Gia marched into the bedroom. As soon as she saw the antique dressing table with its tiny drawers and cubby holes she knew it would be in there. The second drawer she opened had a folded piece of material in. Gia pulled it out, the spell and a candle stub fell from the material.

It was her writing, the way she drew sigils. The level of complexity in the circle was something she had only recently discovered, although it was her hand, it wasn't something that she had drawn. Gia saved that problem for another day. She studied it quickly, it was exactly what she had suspected from the descriptions of the spell. Evie was much more than she had told her. Gia folded the fabric up and put it back, the paper with the spell on it was pushed in her handbag, she turned off the lights and left Harriet's flat. That had been surprisingly easy. She hadn't even had time to be worried about Harriet coming home and finding her.

Gia didn't know where to go next. Atlas would be back to try and retrieve her for the Queen, she didn't have too long. Her heart wanted to make peace with Rosa, to check in with her, and she pictured a particular knife in Rosa's cutlery drawer which could come in useful. Her thoughts were still in her head when her feet started to walk towards the cottage, around her she could hear sirens and alarms. She jumped off the road onto the pavement as a police car raced past her and changed her mind about going to her grandmother's cottage. Rosa's ghost hunt would be in full swing. Gia felt uncomfortable about appearing as her mother and being called a demon in front of everyone when her mind played out the worst possible outcomes. Even her playful reckless side deserted her when she counted the number of people in the room who could work together to overpower her and do whatever religious people did to demons. Keld had been right, there was a time to fight and a time to realise that she was outnumbered.

She looked up, a chance to take a moment and gather her thoughts, the stars were overhead now that the clouds were beginning to clear in the wind, and she breathed in deeply, the crispness of the cold air hit her lungs. Thoughts jumped into the back of her head that hinted the key to joining her body and head back together could be as easy as simply allowing the six-year-old girl to feel rage and avenge her parents. It was useless just peeking in and taking bits from the cage she kept her fury in, it regenerated and burned brighter inside her every time she closed the lid. The separated part of herself had become a secluded, fractured, psychotic caricature that she seemed to be losing control of whenever she came out, and she was starting to come out more and more.

Gia set off up the lane to the farm. The further away she walked from the chaotic noise in the village, the more she saw slips of figures in the darkness, ghostly figures, there then not there, so slight as to be imagined, but real. Fae. They could adapt their forms and change to suit the environment around them. That much was in the books. The way Atlas had moved so quickly wasn't in the books. By letting a few fae slip in, no doubt the worst of all them if the chaos and the murders were indicative of their nature, Gia was being given a warning; that much worse could happen if she didn't yield and die. Gia wondered if the Queen even knew that witnessing her parents' murders had irrevocably changed Gia's brain, that it had created a darkness most decent people didn't have.

The farm came into view. Frosted fields and hills as far as the horizon, underneath a dark sky filled with stars. Gia walked slowly up to the caravans. She stopped, took a breath, cranked her neck from side to side hearing the clicks in it that Jae had loosened up. She took a deep breath, 'Remember when I used to ask *Why* and you told me to just conform and accept the rules, Nonna? The rules don't exist. They're made up. We stay civilised as long as we collectively agree to abide by unwritten manners and behaviour, that's what you said, or it's anarchy. Tonight is the anarchy. I'm sorry that this is how we said goodbye. We deserved something more dignified than you attempting to exorcise a demon from your home.' Gia didn't know if they would ever move past that night, whether her grandmother would ever see her as Gia again, or if she would always look at her with suspicion that the demon Lucia resided in the body she called a granddaughter. Gia walked to Evie's caravan and knocked. She had no idea what she was going to say. An owl watched from a tree.

The door opened a fraction. A little face peeked out, followed by another above it. Two identical pairs of blue eyes in similar faces, only their character determined the difference. Rey had a mischievous cheekiness like Evie, unlike Evie, hers wasn't hidden. Max was more serious.

'Is your mum in?'

'No, she went to meet the police at Yvonne's house about something.'

'Robbie?'

'No. He went out with his brothers.'

'Atlas?'

They shook their heads. Gia bit back the urge to shout. They were children. This wasn't the night for them to be left alone. She didn't want to go back into the village to take them to Robbie's parents who might not even be in.

'Where did Robbie go with his brothers?' If it was the

pub she'd make it her job to break him and Evie up, even though she could have predicted the words that Max was going to say.

'To the barn. He said he wouldn't be long, and mum would be back in a minute.'

'It's been three hours. There's things out there tonight that aren't even there on Halloween. It's supposed to be nearly Christmas,' Rey whispered.

Gia suppressed a smile, 'Get your mum to tell you about Krampus.'

'You're the real one. Not the one that made mum upset.'

'Yeah.' They surprised her then by holding the door open. The level of trust tugged at her. She stepped into the caravan and closed the door behind her.

Gia hadn't seen Evie's caravan before. It was white and pristine. Christmas cushions and red blankets adorned the settee. Natural garlands hung from pine and ivy-wrapped tension poles on the ceiling. A green Christmas tree was decorated in red and gold ornaments. It was a perfect Christmas scene.

'Have you eaten?' She sounded like Rosa in that moment.

'I'm kind of getting hungry again,' Max said.

'I'll take a look in the cupboards. I need you both to find me a pen, a permanent marker or a felt tip pen. The colour doesn't matter. I'm going to draw something to keep you safe tonight, and it won't hurt your mum or Robbie when they come home.' Gia was already opening the cupboards to see what Evie had to cook. The cupboards were fully stocked, and more. The fridge was bursting.

'Would you prefer toasties or vegetable quesadilla?'

Gia asked. She found two table trays, one navy, one pale blue and matching drink cups with a straw.

'Toasties.'

Gia assembled the toasties and filled the trays with sliced bell peppers, cucumber, crisps, carrot batons and a couple of packs of snack biscuits. Max and Rey gave their drink preferences and she filled their cups. Max came back with a permanent marker. Gia pulled Evie's quilt from her bed and prayed her friend would forgive her as she drew a rectangle along the edges and filled the protective sigils in on its perfectly white, unsullied cover.

'I thought magic circles had to be a circle?' Rey watched her.

'They're any shape that you want them to be,' Gia replied, doing the same with the children's blankets. She threw the quilt on the floor, so the rectangle with the sigils was face down, added cushions from the sofa, for comfort, fetched pillows and quilts from their bedrooms, and put the blankets down over the individual quilts. She laid their trays down and passed them the remote control. They chose a channel whilst Gia drew the same rectangle in the kitchen area, one by the door, and one on the loo seat. Coming out of the bathroom, she realised her mistake, she would have to cross the circles, designed to protect the children against any fae, in order to leave. She stood where she was. Max and Rey looked at her.

'Right, if you need to move, you wrap those blankets around yourselves. If you want to fall asleep, you stay together on that quilt. If you hear anything that isn't your mum or Robbie, you turn the TV up and ignore it. Those circles—'

'Rectangles,' Max pointed out.

'Rectangles, protect you from what's out there but not people.'

'And you're stuck,' Rey noticed.

'Yeah.'

'I can do this, you're going to walk to the door and I'll fix it,' Rey stood up and rubbed a tiny bit of the rectangle with hand sanitiser, it smeared the tiniest bit. Gia hopped along to the door. Gia had never had a child tell her to do something, not someone with a gift like Rey's. She found her feet obeying Rey. That child was going to be dangerous in a few years when she fully understood how special she was, especially if she started testing her boundaries like Gia had.

Even as Gia reached over to pull open the door, the rectangle kept her trapped. She managed to open door. She took a step, her legs wobbled, her eyes threatened to roll back in her head. Rey was behind her, smudging part of it with a drop of hand sanitiser on her finger, holding the pen over the tiniest fraction of a break. Gia met the little girl's eyes and nodded her thanks. Rey responded with a nod of her own that meant good luck, even though she didn't say it.

Gia closed the door behind her, then opened it a fraction, 'Hey, Rey?'

'Yes?' She looked up from fixing the mark. Max stood over her, he held his arms outstretched with corners of the blanket in his hands, protecting his sister.

'Can you tell me which barn I'm supposed to be going to?'

Gia sped up as she followed the directions Rey had given her. She didn't see any point in going slowly and delaying the inevitable. Her rage had dimmed out in the caravan. It had been put back, quietly, normally, blandly, her six-year-old self had gone back to the prison unwanted and alone like she always had, much like a child who had become accustomed to being ignored.

She concentrated on her feet, looking down at one foot being placed in front of the other. One laced-up black boot, she paused, and stopped, then bent down to double knot the laces. She had seen the films where an undone shoelace caused a trip that lost the fight. When she stood up again, she was knocked to the frozen ground and something landed on top of her. Instead of hitting the cold, hard ground she was tucked into a person, landing on top of them before they rolled so she was underneath. She looked up to two grey eyes with gold flecks, a furrowed brow and cold hatred. Even as she tensed, she took a deep breath and forced her muscles to relax. Just like she had with the possessions with the priest, just like she had with the brownie, like she had every time she felt threatened because she thought her demon blood afforded her some protection. She had survived so far in life. Atlas might be bigger and stronger, but she was Gia. Last time she had found his skin and touched him, he had backed off. Gia kept her eyes on Atlas. For the leader of the Wild Hunt, he seemed to be considering his next move. The Wild Hunt circled her, a pack of wolves looking at their prey, clearly trusting their leader to catch her.

'What did she do to you, Atlas?'

'She fixed me, you're all out my system, Gia.'

Gia smirked at that answer. Their connection had been too real and too deep for shallow magic to remove it.

'If you can find me, I'm still in your system, she just put a plaster over it. Where is she?'

'It's not time yet.'

'When?' Gia asked.

Atlas paused. He didn't answer.

Gia sighed. 'Robbie and Liam didn't do well in the barn, did they?'

'They didn't do anything,' Atlas chuckled but it rang hollow, it wasn't amusement, it was for show.

Gia read the unspoken worry and stress. She saw the fight in his eyes that shouted without words. He was struggling against whatever had happened to him, against who he was supposed to be now. If he let the pretence fall, he risked one of the Wild Hunt killing him for his place thus losing everything he was trying to fight for. He was testing her. Not just her magic but her willingness to fight, scoping out what her strengths were so he could play them. His relaxed stance provoked her irritation as easily as it had meant to do. They both knew how fast he could move now. She wasn't going to escape unless she could disappear into the air. It wasn't a spell she had ever tried, and even if it were possible, she doubted it was so easily mastered as to work the first time.

'I'm on my way to her anyway.'

'You don't stand a chance.'

'No, Atlas, I do. You however, I'm disappointed in. Fae spells or not I thought you were better than being a twat. Why are you even here?'

'I can't get to Evie. The same circle that was on the farmhouse floor is carved into the foundation concrete of Yvonne's house. I'll make a pact, you get her out, I'll do whatever you request. The farm is an easy entry portal for the fae, the village will become feeding grounds once you die. It's you against the entire Harvesting Court tonight.'

For a second or two she saw Atlas again, the one she knew cared about people.

'Liam was able to help you when you were in Yvonne's house.' Gia pointed out an alternate plan.

'Liam is otherwise occupied. It'll take longer to help him than to get to my sister.'

'If you can't get into that place, I can't either.'

Atlas changed before her eyes. 'You'll find a way. Or Evie dies, Robbie dies, Liam dies, then you die.'

She was swept up into his arms, a strong wind rustled through her hair and past her. They were moving. He whispered something but the wind took whatever his words were. It might have been *I'm sorry*, it might have been *Don't worry*, she couldn't hear, then they were on solid ground again. Gia looked around. They were on a country lane, the one that led to Hightly Hall, the woods that belonged to the farm came right up to the boundary lines. She turned her head, knowing what she would see, a brick wall, decorated with neon graffiti, unseen to human eyes, all the intended sigils and slurs were against the previous owner. She took a breath. Atlas told her exactly where she was expected to go, to the outside storage building that looked like a wine cellar where she would find a door that opened to a descending staircase.

'Don't touch the bars on the cage, they're like a taser to us,' was his warning.

'So this pact—'

'Evie is inside—'

'What do I get?'

'I want my sister out of that cage.'

'Then I'll state my price when I get her out.'

'I'll wait.' He sat down, oblivious to the cold. Around

him the Wild Hunt drifted off into the shadows and laid down in various animal guises.

'You don't think I can do it.' She grinned. She might have her own doubts, but her playful side relished the challenge after she failed to break past the circle she had drawn in the caravan, it danced and held hands with anger and darkness inside her.

'I don't. I don't think you'll be able to cross the court-yard before you turn around.' He folded his arms.

'The difference between you and me, Atlas, is that you're new to the whole witch thing.'

'I barely had a chance to be a witch before I became fae.'

'You're still you, Atlas. I'm still me. Fae aren't as strong magically as the stories make out. If they were, they wouldn't have needed to create a realm for themselves to live in during the war with humans. Look at your fae team, they're stuck in animal form whilst you can switch.'

'They'll change once they're back home.' He waved his hand, then realised his words were an echo of her own. That he was stronger than the Wild Hunt members. She winked, then turned around.

Chapter 29

Gia ducked under the police tape and saw the door that she was supposed to enter. It was across from the main house. It wasn't that far. She took a few steps towards it, aware that Atlas could see her from where he sat. She stopped halfway across the bricked courtyard. Each footstep nearer to the door felt the effects of the spell in the foundation. She hadn't fully realised Atlas's words when he had told her. It started with every bone in her foot, she had broken bones in her feet before, she knew the feeling, it hadn't stopped her walking then, and it wouldn't now. The pain travelled up to her ankles and legs. She didn't stop walking again, she wouldn't give Atlas the satisfaction of knowing that he had been right, that the spell did affect her.

Gia pulled open the door to the wine cellar, exactly across the yard from the back door to the house. She wanted to turn back. Doubts were telling her that she wouldn't get out alive. She focused on the fact that her friend was down there in the darkness. She was doing this for Evie, who had seen the brownie and trusted her to handle it. Having the leader of the Wild Hunt owe her a debt could only be advantageous for the future.

Oliver's voice floated up the stairs. Gia stopped a second to listen to the outrageous, or perhaps not so outrageous, accusations of witchcraft that he was levelling at Evie. She reached into her bag, her fingers ran through the contents until she found the rectangular shape she was searching for. Gia pulled out her phone to start recording, it took a couple of attempts to get her hands to cooperate. The pain inside them wasn't real, but they were responding to the spell as though it was, the pulsing ache inside every bone slowed her down. She leaned against the wall and slid down, her back against the wall that took most of her weight, holding her phone steady and treading lightly in the darkness on the unlit stone stairs. Gia made certain, in her slowness, that she captured his voice and his threats to kill Evie. The threats were veiled behind bible quotes, selected ones that he thought gave him the right to kill a witch. In her experience of fanatics, video evidence came in useful. His voice floated up the stairs and fuelled her determination to beat the pain until Evie was safe.

'It says so, Evie, it says in Exodus, *You shall not allow a sorceress to live*. That means I would be forgiven for killing you.' He went rambling on, talking about Kings and Revelations. If Gia hadn't been in so much pain, she would have rolled her eyes at the situation. The one thing she feared above all, a religious fanatic. Never in her wildest fears had she imagined that she would have to face one on ground built over a magic circle that made her weak.

Gia entered the room quietly, holding up her phone, capturing Oliver looking at Evie. A small lamp stood on the table that took up the middle of the room, it illuminated his face from below, giving it a creepy mad look. Her friend displayed defiance with crossed arms in her hooded winter coat, staring straight at Oliver and not reacting. Gia got a quick shot before they both realised that she was in the room.

Gia focused the camera on Oliver, she spoke calmly, 'For evidence. We all know how much the police need evidence. If you stay calm, I'll put the phone away. I might even delete the evidence if you're right.' She had no intention of doing that, but it was a sweetener to bring him onside. Gia realised she was in the same position as Atlas, inside enemy territory, on unfamiliar grounds, and playing to stay alive.

'You're the one who told me to do this. You told me she was a witch!'

That answered all her questions about why the fake-Gia had chosen Oliver over Atlas. It had been leading up to this point. Everyone had been masterfully manipulated. Fake-Gia had talked an already impressionable, unstable Oliver into taking Evie. It was impressive though. Oliver had taken Evie to the one place they couldn't rescue her from.

Gia turned off the recording. Her hand had a slight tremor from the pain. She wished she could wipe the spell away. Etched in concrete, it would be hard to erase. She lowered her phone and carefully put it away in her bag, her expression was purposefully and deliberately calm. She already knew her plan.

'Evie isn't the witch here, Oliver,' Gia deflected him from Evie.

'Jackson McGregor told me what she did to his brother.'

'She didn't do anything to the McGregor brothers.'

'She did! She pinned them down with ivy and beat them up.'

'I pinned them down with ivy and watched Evie hit them for all the times they'd hurt her.'

'You?' Oliver looked shocked, 'I liked you, Gia, we

were going to have a future together. We laid in bed last night and discussed this and you never once said you did it. Why would you set me up like this?'

From the corner of her eye she saw Evie react for the first time. She turned narrowed eyes on Gia, her accusation of Gia cheating on her brother written clearly across her face.

Gia shook her head slightly, 'That wasn't me last night. It was someone else.'

'It was you. You told me Evie was a witch. You said to bring her here because Yvonne knew about the witches and had the house blessed in a way that hurts them.'

'It's hurting me right now, not Evie. Let her out.'

'No. You gave me this!'

Oliver pulled a piece of paper out and started reading the words on it. Evie and Gia both stumbled on the fifth word. Gia caught herself on the wall and leaned against it. Evie fell to a sitting position on the floor. Gia shot a practiced spell out with an outstretched hand, the same one she had used on the fae version of herself. Oliver flew backwards into the wall, a visible red handprint appearing on his neck that started blistering. Unlike in the cottage, Gia didn't hold back with her fury, her pent up emotion towards religion was unleashed on Oliver. The paper dropped from his hand. Evie stood back up.

She stopped the incantation long enough to let Oliver fall to his knees. She was starting to fall apart. All her testing on herself and magic circles had underestimated how impactful being in one could hurt. She struggled to control herself and stop herself from crawling out on her hands and knees. She couldn't give up.

'Undo the cage, Oliver.'

'No.' His hands scrambled to pick up the piece of paper.

Gia raised her hand and started the incantation again. She held him several seconds longer this time, until she was fighting herself to let him go against her anger that demanded more, to make him atone for his disrespect to her friend. The blisters turned to burns. She forced herself to let go. When she did, she deflated, all she wanted was to close her eyes and let the pain wash over her until she passed out. Forcing her voice to sound stronger than she felt, she said it again, 'Undo. The cage. Oliver.'

He started to cry. Tears rolled down his face. Gia thought it was shock. In her limited experience, shock tended to hit people first when they realised that magic was real. He crawled towards the door and pulled out a key from his pocket. The door unlocked with surprising quietness, an unsatisfactory undramatic ending to the situation. Oliver swung it open. Gia told him to back up against the far wall. He didn't move fast enough for her, but the situation was resolved when Evie launched herself at him, winding him in a single punch. Oliver raised his fist to punch Evie, but Gia cleared her throat and raised her hand. He whimpered and backed off. Evie picked up the paper he had been reading from and slipped it into her coat pocket, every move she made was measured, careful, as though she knew there were things in there that would hurt her if she touched them. Gia recalled Atlas's warning about the bars on the cage and wondered if he had told his sister, or whether she had discovered the pain herself.

Evie joined her on the stairs and ran up to the exit. Gia backed herself up the steps the same way she had gone down, with her back and her weight against the wall, one step at a time. Evie returned to Gia struggling upwards. She felt Evie's arm loop around her waist in a smooth movement, and her friend pulled her up each step not asking what was wrong, just whispering encouragement to keep going. She helped Gia across the courtyard. Each step seemed to take minutes, although Gia knew that they were normal steps, taken at a normal pace. Her head was pounding as though she had the worst hangover possible, she felt sick from the pain, even her fingers pulsed with the ache of broken bones. She concentrated on the pain in her fingers, because if she thought about the rest of her body, she would either stop walking or stop breathing. As they crossed the yard the pain had progressed from her spine and was now starting to crack open her skull. She heard noises behind them. Shouting. Oliver was coming.

She pushed Evie off her, 'Run. Atlas is waiting outside. He'll look after you. Get to him.'

At the police tape she watched Evie duck underneath. Gia's body wouldn't respond anymore. Her eyes rolled up and back, her legs buckled, her knees couldn't manage the weight of her body. Her head cleared as relief hit, a thick blackness took over the inside of her thoughts. She hit the bricks on the ground harder than she intended, but the pain was far away, even as ivy from the roadside snaked its way around her arm and started pulling her towards it.

Gia saw the stars first, twinkling silver specks in the night sky. Strange looking men moved through the woods. Not strange, but resembling those from a television show. A girl similar to a younger Evie, in a spider's web dress, put a finger on her lips. With her was someone who looked like her mother. She had a bruised face, pointed ears, a proud stance, and bound wrists that the girl was undoing whilst whispering, over and over, in a different language each time, 'This connection is your bond. It will carry into the future until needed, prisoner of Eric and beloved daughter of Coel. You are our distinguished wielder of the chaos and the night, Nótt. When this time repeats itself from the other side, your debt is paid.'

Gia's breath changed as she breathed out. Then she became aware of the cold air that entered her lungs, fresh night air that held the crispness of a frost. Whilst her back was cold, it wasn't damp. She was hovering mid-air. In a pair of arms. Atlas, she realised. She asked to have her feet on the ground, he put her down. Gia looked behind her. Evie followed her eyes.

'I pulled you out. Atlas already told me this week's version of you wasn't you. It's not nice being on the wrong side of you. You really can be a bitch.'

'Oliver?'

'He retreated when he saw Atlas waiting. Not before he saw me manipulate the ivy to pull you away from him. He knows what we can both do now.'

'He won't let it go.' Gia said it to herself rather than anyone else. She flexed her fingers and her toes, everything was normal again.

Evie looked at Gia but didn't reply. Instead, she turned to punch her brother, 'You, you stupid idiot. Why did you send Gia in?' She stared at her brother. He looked at her in silence.

Gia answered, 'Because he can't step into the house.'

'Why?'

'Because he's an idiot who killed the leader of the Wild Hunt.'

She watched Evie cast her eyes upwards, roll them

and still explode. 'I knew that. Why did he send you? Why couldn't he come in there and beat Oliver up?'

'You knew?'

'The day it happened.' Evie gave a nod.

'And?'

'I was thinking of telling you. Or getting him to tell you. Then you dropped the whole *I might have fae blood* thing, and I just thought that it made you both perfect to be together and I should stay out of your relationship. So why couldn't he come in there himself? Why did you collapse?'

'There's a spell. The same one as was on your farm.'

'The boundary spell?' Evie whispered.

Gia's brain clicked and undid the locks, it replayed the conversation with Evie in the caravan on the night Robbie and Liam had been present. 'You didn't want to redraw it for Atlas,' she stared at her friend.

'For you both,' asserted Evie, tilting her chin up defiantly.

Gia turned to Atlas, 'We had a pact if I got Evie out.'

'I owe you.' It was a mock, a slight arch of his eyebrow, a glitter of fun in his eyes.

Once upon a time she would have met that fun with a smirk of her own and claimed the return in the bedroom. Not anymore. Favours were collected and stored until she needed them. She was stopped from having to say anything about his debt by Evie.

'Who owns you right now?' Evie crossed her arms and stared at her brother.

'The Queen,' Gia answered.

'Of the Resting Court?' Evie asked. Atlas gave a nod. Evie turned angry eyes on Gia and demanded, 'What do we need to do for you to take her place?'

'You already know.'

'Will you?'

'Can you handle it if I do?'

'It's no different from what I've done. How can I help?'

'How do you both know this stuff intuitively?' Atlas asked. They ignored him.

'I'd love to team up with you and watch you rescue your brother from her. I think we might need your ability to pin people down with ivy, but Max and Rey need you. I've got it.' Gia gave a soft shake of her head.

'Who's with them?'

'No one, which is why they need you. I've drawn protection sigils on a few things in the caravan. You'll be safe tonight. They're safe. I've got this.'

Evie started walking along the lane that led them back to the farm. Gia and Atlas followed.

'I can't let you do this alone. If she knows, she'll send Atlas after you.' Evie turned her head as she talked and threw the words behind her, her pace an indicator that she wanted to return to her children as fast as possible.

Gia caught up with her, 'She's already done that twice tonight, Evie. He's found ways around it. I'd love nothing more than to have you with me when I confront her, but your childhood was messed up, I have an insane recklessness about risks from my own childhood trauma, let's not give your two babies more issues than they need to have.'

'He hasn't...' Evie trailed off. Gia knew what she meant to say. She was asking if Atlas had hurt her.

'Not yet.'

'For what it's worth, under normal circumstances, he's smiled a lot more lately.'

'I'm still here,' Atlas spoke from behind them.

'I don't know, Evie. I bring extra craziness into your lives, maybe it's better if it didn't work out.' At Gia's words, her friend glanced behind her, and turned with a sly grin to Gia. Gia saw the mischief dance on her friend's face.

'Again, I'm still here,' he said. Gia found herself smiling at the dryness in his tone.

'I appreciate what you just did for me. Thank you,' Evie said.

They were nearing the farm entrance now, although it was still a couple of metres away. The caravans and half-built houses were darker than the rest of the area. Light spilled from closed curtains in one caravan. It would seem that every time she got one step nearer to the Resting Court Queen, she was taken back to somewhere else.

Chapter 30

Atlas didn't give either of them time to say goodbye to Evie. Once Evie's hand was on the door of the caravan Atlas wrapped an arm around her waist and they were off so fast the scenery blurred. He stopped in the woods.

Gia pushed him away from her, 'Stop doing that.'

He acknowledged her words with a tiny tilt of his head and a flick of his eyebrow upwards. He didn't change his expression. 'I wouldn't have attacked the Wild Hunt if you hadn't come into my life like some version of a dark red riding hood. I'm trying everything that I can think of to stop her getting you, and you seem determined to waltz in there like you know what you're confronting. It destroyed me watching you stop halfway across that courtyard yet carry on. I want to buy us some time. There's talk about you. Even I can hear the whispers of how you wiped all the tattoo bonds from the fae. And what you did to me earlier, with the frost, the spell... how did you do that?'

Gia didn't know. She couldn't give him an answer. It was wrong to say that the words came into her head when she needed them. It seemed too simple an explanation, too convenient.

'Are you going to keep me from the barn?' Gia looked at Atlas.

'Until you have a plan. This is for you, not her.'

'We could have gone into your caravan for a whisky

and be civilised about it.'

'I wanted to keep the fae away from the children.'

Gia started to walk away from him in the direction of the barn. Atlas followed behind, a reminder that the hunter had caught its prey and was taunting it now. She trod carefully through the woods, hesitant steps reflected her state of mind, Atlas was right, she had no plan and the evening had taught her the Queen was one of the conniving, never resting, always prepared for the next point of play people, not people, fae. Gia hadn't just met her match, she'd stepped up to a level that she had never played at before.

Her pace faltered when she reached the barn. It was the only place around them that the frost hadn't touched. A wet, damp barn. She had no idea what was waiting for her inside, she expected some dark fae with a crown and a knowledge of magic far beyond her own. Gia pushed the wooden door open slowly and entered the barn on unsteady feet. Her inner six-year-old self had retreated now she had gotten Gia this far. Gia needed her to battle the fear away and bring out the craziness, in a way that she had never asked her to before. Atlas stood a few paces away outside in the cold, away from the door. He didn't try and stop her. Gia turned around to look at him. He stood like a soldier, watching her. It struck her that perhaps his orders were to ensure that she actually entered the trap, and to keep others out. The barn was old and the wooden door threatened to disintegrate in her hand. She wafted away the cobwebs as she entered.

It was almost too dark inside to see. At the far end of the barn silver threads glistened in the moonlight and across the ceiling. Gia took a few seconds to piece together the puzzle in front of her. A giant web stretched across the back wall. On the floor around her lay scattered carcasses of cocooned, hollowed out humans, already consumed. Stuck to the web were three men partially covered in spider silk whose furious icy blue eyes shone out in the darkness. The brothers. The barn smelt of white spirit. Gia immediately knew that their plan was to burn the place down.

'How did you get caught?' She looked at Robbie when she spoke, but it was Liam who answered.

'Bodhi touched the web. It's stickier than it looks. Don't touch it. I went to help him, Robbie came to help us both.'

A scurrying sound overhead made her look up. The largest spider in the world hung above her. Her heart raced so loudly it was all she could hear. The spider's body was the same size as she was. She could see the hairs covering it, coarse and thick, the same type as the brownie had. Two antenna came out of its head which closely resembled scorpion tails. It had legs longer than her own. The protruding fangs were small. The speckle of white dots across its back resembled the first scattering of fallen snow on the ground.

Confusion escalated the panic in her body, her heart beat faster and her palms became clammy. Gia didn't know if this was another fae, a sort of guard, a protector she had to get past, a fairy tale type curse on someone she shouldn't kill, or, her brain refused to think that this could be the Queen. She glanced over to the brothers strung up in the web. Her worst fears were confirmed when she met their eyes. This was the Queen, a predatory being full of enough venom that turned a human to liquid for meals. Gia walked out into the night.

She ignored Atlas as he stood there, that he took a step forward ready to go after her if she ran. She needed a minute or two. Gia walked backwards and forwards, pacing in front of the open door. A soft chitter emerged that sounded a lot like laughter. She stopped and closed her eyes. Her heart still beat too loudly for her to hear her own thoughts. Gia took out the sharpie and the knife that she had slipped into her bag from Evie's caravan. She stopped and focused on a piece of stone in the barn wall. Her breathing was ragged when she talked to herself.

'OK. We've got this. Time to play. Come on. I've never needed you to join together as much as this before, I need to feel this strength more, come out of the cage and play.' She drew on each palm, an upside down arch that started at the bottom of her little finger down to the bottom of her palm, it balanced on a smaller semi-circle half the size but the right way around. Then she drew three straight lines to resemble rays from each arch. The arches made up half of the triple goddess sign, they focused on the child, the maiden, the one she kept locked away inside because crazy anger couldn't be let loose in civilisation. The rays of the moon herself, the brain, the body, the soul. She dropped the pen back into her bag. With the knife in her hand, she re-entered the barn.

The change happened as soon as her foot went over the threshold. The fear dissolved, it bubbled away, and recklessness replaced it along with an impish glee. If she was going to die, there was little point in stressing over it. The worries in her head eased, now replaced with a dangerous glint of playful insanity. Her eyes sought out the spider again, it had retreated towards its web. She kept her eyes on it as her fingers twisted the knife handle through them until the blade point downwards, then she wrapped her palm tight around the handle, a smile emerged on her face.

'You want to fight in your true form, you get my true form too. The one you created.'

There wasn't an answer, not that Gia expected one. A chittering answered her. She shook her head and answered, 'I don't want to be that tourist who asks everyone to speak in English. I know Italian, French and Spanish. I can pass in basic Portuguese thanks to a coastal town in America, but spider? I never got the chance to learn.' The chittering started again, it sounded angry. Gia shrugged and muttered, 'That's a no.' She walked to the web and started cutting it down, thread by thread, starting at the floor. It was tough like old bread. She was careful not to touch it, sawing the knife through the strands. Each cut thread pinged upwards slightly and swung. The chittering lasted a second this time, the spider edged nearer to her. She put the knife in her mouth, holding it in place with her teeth, and pulled out a lighter. Gia put her thumb on the spark wheel, rolled it down and the flame danced before her. She held it to the web.

A small flame trailed along each thread and politely melted it away. It headed towards Robbie and his brothers. She hoped they'd be alright. A tendril of heat wouldn't be more than running a burning candle over bare skin. They would survive. A small clattering on the floor showed what she thought were dew drops on the web, or water droplets, to be mirrored orbs instead, every reflection a view into her life or the lives of various fae. Gia watched as the orbs showed fae going about their daily activities, ragged fae spraying graffiti signs, soldier fae, camps of starving fae, Atlas stood outside, a brownie in a blood-smeared cottage with a green sofa.

The chittering was more of a hiss now. Gia thought she glanced a shadowed figure in the doorway, but barely recognised it was Atlas. She was focused on the fun of destruction. Gia took the knife out of her mouth and looked between the lighter and the knife, then at the spider, 'So, what next? Flames or knife? You're tempted to throw some silk around me and see if it sticks, but you've just watched your web melt away.' The spider edged nearer, scuttling round, keeping close to the walls. Gia kept her eyes on it and turned. Robbie joined her side.

'We're going to torch the place with her in it. Get ready to run. Liam and Bodhi are finishing what they started with the lighter fuel.'

'You go,' Gia wasn't walking out of the barn. She already knew that. She'd die stopping that thing leaving too. One of his brothers shouted to him. Gia pushed him. He tried to pull her out. Gia wrestled her arm free. Liam shouted at Robbie to leave before the flames got too high. Flames shot around the perimeter of the barn faster than she expected them to, their heat intense and immediate. The light inside the barn changed as orange flames encircled her, forcing the spider queen to drop and edge closer to her.

It was bigger than she thought when it was close. Hate emanated from it, rolling off in waves Gia could feel. It was the type of hate that she feared, that she had run away from. The desire to crush others, the narcissistic view that only one's own self mattered, that this queen would rather rule over a destroyed Resting Court if it meant she had complete control over every emotion, every piece of dirt, every step someone took. She craved that ultimate deadly power of crushed opposition.

She should have anticipated the next move, both of them testing the floor before they moved. Gia couldn't look down at the orbs, she didn't take her eyes from the spider. Someone else was inside the barn with them. She pushed her shoulders back, her neck clicked again.

That one fraction of a second was what the spider had waited for. The one click of her neck and Gia landed on her back on the floor, arms out, the knife falling from her hand and clattering on top of the fallen orbs. The fangs moved, flaring outwards whilst its head came downwards. Gia put up her hands and held the head, keeping those fangs well away from any part of her own body.

'Maybe today, but not right now. I am all, all is me,' she grinned. To her side a shadow figure moved in front of the flames, too quick for her to see anything. Gia refocused, her hands moved to grab the fangs and a moonlit shimmering frost began to spread across them from her own fingers. White frost spread out over the face from the fangs in slow, creeping tendrils of sharp frozen daggers. The spider started to struggle against her.

Gia gripped tighter. Its strength was a force she hadn't fought before. It took everything she had to continue to hold on. The spider shook its head violently. Gia's grip was welded on with the frost itself, the skin on her hands were stuck as much as the spider's fangs were, her back scraped against the floor as the spider fought against her grip. Something blue trickled down its head and onto her hand. It was warm. It felt like blood, her brow furrowed as she realised it was blood. Blue blood. The spider sagged on top of her, she was pinned underneath it. Atlas jumped down, his arms and clothes stained blue. The spider twitched. From the twisted angle of her head she saw Atlas begin to cut off the legs, one at a time, throwing them to the flames. Gia glanced between the spreading frost and Atlas's actions. The spider's full weight was on her now. She couldn't move.

The fire was too close to them, one last drop of blue blood froze, then unfroze and dripped onto the floor. Atlas pulled her out from underneath the legless spider even as the flames began to lick at the hairs on the body, the heat diminished her frost and her hands slipped from the fangs. He wrapped his arms around her. He might have said something, but the roar of flames was all she could hear, the heat was unbearable, even to someone who liked to be cosy and warm. Gia closed her eyes and wished for winter again, her lips mouthed silent words.

She was cold. Wind swirled around them, lifting her hair. Gia looked up to the fiercest snowstorm, a blizzard that surrounded the pair of them. Atlas took her hand and led her out of the barn, the flames consumed the body of the spider queen and melted the mirrored orbs. Once out of the barn, the snowstorm hit the waiting brothers. The three of them braced themselves against the wind and the cold, then it died down. Atlas's hand left her own. Gia stood alone.

Silence covered the five of them like a thick blanket of snow that was falling slower and slower over the patch where they stood. Flames in the barn contrasted against the blanket of white, natural frost outside. No one quite knew what to say. A single white snowflake fluttered down and the weather around them became the same as that all over the fields within seconds. The eerie silence interrupted her thoughts and sat heavily, she felt awkward, Gia had too many questions for herself. She turned away, back towards the flames, human instinct making her find the warmth against a cold night. Robbie's phone rang.

Chapter 31

They raced towards the caravans. Gia tried to shout to Atlas to hold back, but he bypassed rational thinking to get to his sister. By the time the rest of them had reached the caravans, Atlas had already beaten Oliver, the trespasser lay on the floor, an eye already swollen shut, bloodied and curled up against Atlas's rage. Evie stood at the caravan door, pale, her arms wrapped around her thin frame, Max and Rey were looking through a window. Robbie raced over to her. Liam and his younger brother Bodhi pulled Atlas off Oliver. Gia stepped between Atlas and the man on the ground.

She looked at Evie, 'I could finish him, he'll never bother us again. Magically or physically. Take your pick.' Gia offered. All six faces turned to look at her. She stared back, her soul cold and calm.

'We leave him alive,' Evie said.

Gia looked at her, 'If we do there'll be a next time. He's not going to walk away from us,' she warned.

'Leave him for now, taking a life is a big thing, Gia,' Liam put his hand on her shoulder.

'So is kidnap. You didn't hear him tell Evie that the bible gives him the right to kill witches.'

'He threatened to kill you?' Robbie looked even angrier than before. He strode over to where Oliver was raising himself and yanked him up. 'You even look in Evie's direction again and I'll kill you before you have a chance to look away.' He let Oliver out of his grip and the man collapsed.

Inwardly Gia rolled her eyes. A threat was fine. A curse from a witch was scarier. She walked over to Oliver and let the darkness that lived inside her become the loose cannon once again, she crouched down even as the bloodied mess of a man in front of her tried to scoot backwards.

'It's Evie's decision to keep you alive not mine. I'm going to hex you to choke on your own blood if you go near her or her family again. Blood will fill your mouth and your lungs, and you'll drown as your eyes take in the constant stream of fresh redness coming from inside you. If I find you threatening another so-called witch, I'll cut your intestines from your body and torture you until you die. You know I know how to.' She reached out and ripped a small selection of hair from his scalp. She needed that for the hex, not that he should know.

'You're fucking crazy,' he gasped.

Gia laughed, 'I'm dangerous, not crazy. I've also got a nice little video of you holding Evie hostage and threatening her with biblical righteousness. I'm going to distribute that to several people. Any misdemeanour will see it sent to all the police commissioners in the country. Be a good little boy from now on and stop messing with the grown-ups.' She turned the demeaning infantile attitude he had given her over coffee back on him. Oliver picked himself up and hobbled off the farm, clearly outnumbered. Gia didn't miss the backward hate-filled look he gave them. Her instinct told her he would be making trouble for them all if he could.

Atlas and Gia sat with a drink each in the warm

caravan. Atlas had whisky. She held a rum and coke. Evie opened the door and came inside. She carried her cup of tea in her hand and a plain book in the other, they went down on the kitchen counter. Evie took off her thick winter coat and sheepskin boots before carrying a book and her cup of tea over to Gia.

'I want to learn how,' she said to Gia.

'How to hex someone?' Gia checked. Evie gave a nod.

'I found some ways in this book.'

'It's as simple as you want to make it. I work with their DNA, I needed his hair.'

'Where's Max and Rey?' Atlas looked at his sister.

'Watching TV still snuggled up on the floor where Gia left them. Robbie, Liam and Bodhi are using hand sanitiser to clean the marker up. It's a bit cramped in there.' Her tone and expression indicated she had ensured that her children were safe before crossing the short distance to her brother's caravan.

'I'm sorry—' Gia started.

Evie waved her apology away, 'You kept them safe. Tonight could have gone in an entirely different way. Which is why I need to learn more. If there's a way to learn what you do, then I want to.'

'Let's start with the hex. We'll need foil or wire wool, pepper, blood, tissue paper,' Gia thought aloud.

Atlas had kitchen foil. Gia gave the foil to Evie, with instructions to roll it into thin worms to make a human stick man whilst picturing Oliver. A nod from Gia towards the door made Atlas return a small nod of agreement back, they carried their drinks outside and left Evie to concentrate. Outside the temperature had dropped further.

Atlas stretched, 'What did you draw on your hands?'

'Just a moon symbol, one that's personal to me. My recklessness deserted me for a while. I needed it in there.'

'I'm glad it returned.'

'I thought you were standing guard to make sure I didn't walk away.' She wanted to ask him why he'd chosen to help at the last minute. Both of them had stained clothing where the blue blood had dried. They had washed their hands. Atlas took a few seconds to answer.

'I was figuring something out.'

It was the hesitation and his tone that made Gia look at him. He kept his eyes on the horizon. He was tense. Gia followed his eyes but couldn't see anything. She looked at him again and downed her drink, a foolish move given the hex she was about to do but she really needed to get drunk. There was too much on her mind. She could still hear sirens and alarms shrieking at them from down in the village.

'What are you hiding from me, Atlas?'

'That wasn't the Queen. She had another fae take her place. The real one smells like fresh rain on dry ground.'

Immediately Gia swore. She took herself back inside the caravan and poured herself a soft fizzy drink. She needed the sweetness. She looked at Evie. Evie was muttering 'Oliver' over and over as she twisted the thin roll of foil into a stick man. Gia walked through the caravan and sat opposite her in the dining booth. She picked up the piece of Oliver's hair, 'Do you want me to do this part?' she asked. Some witches were queasy. Evie nodded.

'Only because I want to know what to do and why. Explain it to me.'

'I'm weaving Oliver's hair around the figure you made to add his DNA into the spell. Way back before we knew about DNA we called it part of a person, or their essence. Then we're going to wrap a layer of tissue over Oliver's entire body. Between the first and second layers of tissue we'll add the pepper for burning his insides. After that we'll take little stick man Oliver outside and add blood, yours and mine, it's important that you put your drops of blood on the tissue to make his eyes, OK.'

'OK.'

'I'll add mine, do the spell, then you do what only you can do, make the earth swallow him down so he's not found, so the spell can sit.'

'Just like that? The book says you need to put it in a glass jar with nails, a match, some vinegar and other bits.'

'The problem with doing things that way is that you end up with lots of jars containing lots of DNA and effigies. Caravans and camper vans aren't the largest. It messes with the whole aesthetic thing we have to do,' Gia half joked.

Evie laughed softly, 'Your van looked so cute on your pictures. I thought we could pull off caravans whilst we got the houses built. How did you cope? I'm already getting annoyed and frustrated at us tripping over each other. Yours was the same size as my kitchen. No offence.'

'No offence taken. It was small. I did get lazy and I kept the bed down even though it converted to a sitting area. I bought a proper double mattress rather than the thin fold up one that it came with. I ate, slept, and worked on the bed. It helped me focus actually. I mean, I did get cabin fever, but there wasn't another room, so I was able to go into my head and write.' She kept a picture of Oliver in her head as they talked, and picked up a tissue. Gia wrapped it around the figure, her fingers doing it quickly, giving away how many times she had done similar work. She laid the next tissue down flat and let Evie sprinkle a generous dose of pepper over it before the stick man Oliver was laid on it and it was wrapped around the figure.

Gia carried the delicate effigy made entirely of quick to grab household materials outside. Evie led her to the side of a footpath which she said would be perfect and undisturbed. Gia saw Evie pushed the tip of a knife into her finger and dropped her blood onto the space where Oliver's eyes would be. Two small red droplets gave him crimson buttonlike eyes. Gia took the knife from Evie and made a deep incision on her own arm. For the amount of blood she had promised, she needed to give a lot.

> *Blood and fire, winds of change,*
> *From my storm inside, to the cold night air,*
> *I cast this spell, my words your cage.*
> *Divert your eyes, your hate enclosed,*
> *Else on this blood, you die and choke.*

She bled all over the figure until it was drowned in blood, then nodded at Evie. Evie put her hand to the ground and the figure was immediately swallowed up by the dirt and frosted grass, Gia kept bleeding over the area until Evie lifted up her hand when the area had returned to grass and mud.

Evie took Gia's arm and inspected the deep cut with concern, 'You never said you needed to do that.'

'It should have been your blood, but Robbie would probably be planning ways to kill me if I let you go back with a cut this deep.'

'Let's get that bandaged. Tell me next time. I'll do it. Whatever I need to do.' Evie didn't deny that Robbie was on the protective side. Gia knew Evie meant every word, just as Evie's tone told her that she would deal with Robbie if that situation occurred.

'Do you want to have a bit of fun?' Gia asked, a smile playing on her face. Evie responded immediately, her mischievous nature coming out in an instant.

'How?'

'Can you grow an evening primrose plant?'

'I can see if there's any seeds.' Evie put her hand to the ground. Within a second, five fully grown evening primrose plants were upright in the grass. Gia walked over to the nearest one. She breathed in the scent, and broke two flowers off with her unbloodied hand. She passed one to Evie and held one herself. Gia wiped her blood on it. Evie watched, then copied her. Gia pressed the bloodied sides of the two flowers together.

She left the flowers in Evie's hand, and held her own, clean hand over Evie's. 'In silence and shadows, we share this dark path of strength and intuition, of feminine tradition.' It was a spell, but this time a simpler one, a reunification of their friendship, a realisation that they shared the same secrets, no matter how different they were to each other.

'In silence and shadows, we share this dark path, of strength and intuition, of feminine tradition,' Evie repeated back. She sparkled when she said it, then she buried the two flowers in the earth with her gift.

Evie took her into Atlas's caravan and pulled out a first aid kit from underneath the dining booth seats, Gia didn't even know Atlas had a first aid kit in the caravan. Atlas took a glance at the cut, told Gia she should stop playing with knives and asked whether she wanted a rum and coke or a coffee. Evie turned down the offer of a drink. Gia opted for the warmth of fresh ginger and hot water whilst Evie bandaged her arm. Even as she heard her own voice ask Atlas for the drink, and watched as he sliced ginger root for her, she wondered where that came from. She had never had ginger tea in her life before. It had risen up, just like the snowstorm, from some knowledge inside her that she held but couldn't consciously reach.

Chapter 32

The fallen glass orb from the burnt-out web with its glimpse into her grandmother's cottage had played on Gia's mind as Evie wrapped the bandage around her arm with gentle fingers. Gia wanted to go and see Rosa, check on her. Atlas murmured that it wasn't a good decision, but that only urged Gia to go more in the worry that fake-Gia could have hurt her grandmother. Atlas pointed out that walking into Rosa's cottage, at midnight, when another Gia was already in her place, with her newly changed physical appearance, would make her look like the demon Rosa had accused her of being. Gia put her ginger tea down and stared intently at Atlas.

'How did you know that's what she said to me.'

'You must have told me.'

'I didn't.'

Atlas didn't answer. He finished his whisky and stared into the empty glass, his face was unreadable but serious. Gia prompted him again. Not for the first time with Atlas, she was left with an instinctive feeling that he knew more than she did.

He met her eyes and sighed, 'When you were missing, I learnt that she and the Queen were swapping places in imitating you. When she spoke, the chitter you heard, she was begging you not to kill her. She was trying to tell you she wasn't going to hurt Robbie and his brothers, that she had seen you with the Queen through the orbs.'

'Why would I have believed that?'

'You wouldn't have. She was only making sure they stayed there as food.'

'So why did you come in and kill her.'

'It was quicker than the way you were killing her. If we had let her go, she would have run and told tales anyway.'

'I should have known. Of course the tattoo markings mean you can't hurt the Queen, that's why the Wild Hunt couldn't get me when they tried, they're spelled against harming—' Gia kept the rest of her thoughts to herself, she didn't want to say *harming royalty*. Keld had told her that the markings, the tattoos, were spells, and that they couldn't act against the Queen. Atlas wouldn't have been able to kill the Queen if she had been the spider. Keld on the other hand, didn't have the tattoo markings any longer. She had removed them, and their pact was still in place.

Atlas wouldn't, or couldn't let her go to the cottage because the Queen was there with Rosa. It was possible that Keld was there too, if he knew. She had entered so lightly into that pact, thinking it was a game in another dream world, but now it had spilled over into the real world. This mess, that was older than she was, had gotten her mother killed, and was about to get Rosa killed too. She stood up and picked up her bag, 'I'm going.'

'Gia.'

'I don't care what you do, Atlas. Stay or come with me. I have to see if my grandmother is alright.'

'Phone her?'

'I don't want to. Any fae could answer it and pretend.'

'I'll be behind you. But I can't promise help.'

'Do you want me to remove her tattoos from you?'

'Can you?'

'I can try. It hurt Keld though, maybe be prepared for that.'

'It hurt when she put them on. It couldn't hurt much more to take them off.'

Gia adjusted her bag and put her boots back on. She had taken them off when she'd gone into Atlas's caravan. Evie left them for own caravan to see how the cleaning up was going, murmuring that they knew where she was if they needed her, but she couldn't watch her brother in pain. Atlas held out his wrist. Gia touched him. Nothing happened. she closed her eyes. Still nothing happened. Not even a spell came to mind.

'Where were you? When you removed Keld's?'

'Outside, in the village. Not our village. Their version of our village. It's...' she stopped when she saw recognition in Atlas's eyes. Gia sighed, 'You've already seen it haven't you?'

'She sent me after Keld when she learnt he'd let you go. We uprooted the village to find him. It was the first time I had seen it.'

'What did you think?'

'It's horrible. I'd rather be here. It's dark, disintegrating, they're experiencing a slow genocide at the hands of their own queen.'

'Keld seems to think I can take over.'

'Not just Keld. A lot of them.' It was the way his eyes met hers that told her he truly believed that she should. Her stomach sank through the floor.

'I don't believe in monarchies. I don't even feel qualified for a coup.'

'Did you feel qualified to publish your first book?'

There was a hint of an Atlas smile on his face when he asked. Gia shook her head and a small smile appeared on her own face.

'No. I ran off to America to avoid that feeling.'

'You don't feel qualified enough to settle down to buy a house either, you're still running.' His words hit a nerve. He was right. She was still running. Still hiding. Still facing the world with her Gia-Roselli-The-Author face and attitude when she wasn't that person anymore, because nobody was that one-dimensional. He took a step forward and asked, 'Could you really be any worse than her?'

'Did you find Keld?' Gia changed the subject.

'Yes.'

'Is he dead?'

'I don't think so. Not yet. She's keeping him alive.'

'For me. Because of our pact. She's working on a way to use it to her advantage. If I were her, I'd make it look like Keld killed her, so I would have to uphold my side of the pact. She continues to live here, with human prey, whilst the fae realm becomes my problem to fix, with her instructing Keld to sabotage me behind my back so I'm constantly failing.' Gia pushed past him to leave the caravan. She stepped down onto the grass.

'There are some big jumps.' Atlas followed her.

'At this point I'm just assuming everyone knows everything.'

'What was your pact with Keld?'

'His bargaining chip to stay alive. Why didn't I see what he was doing? I'm such an idiot,' Gia raised the palms of her hands to her eyes.

'OK, talk to me. What was the pact?' Atlas gently pulled her hands down. He stood in front of her looking like the old Atlas again, not the leader of the Wild Hunt, just a human man. His eyes held hers in a gentle steady gaze. His hands were warm around her own. Gia resisted the urge to kiss him.

'Before I tell you I want to remind you that you once told me you liked my character, Valentina.'

'What did you do, Gia?' it was amazing how his voice could change when he realised how serious the situation was. It sank lower, the words were asked with a quiet calmness that encouraged trust.

'I agreed he could have me and the crown if he killed the Queen before I did. I didn't want to believe it was real, he was real, that the fae thing was real. I treated it like he was joking.'

'You entered an agreement with another man, that he could have you if he killed the Queen?' Atlas broke eye contact with her. His hands turned into fists. His jaw clenched. He took a couple of deep breaths, his fists unclenched.

'I'll deal with Keld later. You're going to have to work harder to get these markings off me.'

'It's my mess, Atlas.'

'Not anymore.'

'It's my mess. I'll fix it,' she repeated firmly.

She had never felt more like Valentina in that moment. She had walked into this mess with assumptions that she knew enough. That might have been true in America, she might have picked up enough knowledge about being a witch. Since she had encountered the brownie, she had acted like a bull in a china shop. Evie had tried to advise her about the fae, but Gia had taken it with a pinch of salt. It had led her from one disastrous situation to another. She hadn't stopped to think about her words, her actions, or any consequences. She would finish what she started, perhaps she could do so with some more grace and thought. Gia stood on her tiptoes and kissed Atlas, sliding her hand around his neck, the tip of her middle finger moved three times in a circle in an unconscious movement as he kissed her back.

From the ground came a rumbling, it shook beneath their feet, just as Atlas groaned and staggered away. The rumble turned into a roar, the sounds of earth splitting open, splintering and thundering as mature trees fell, the sounds of animals crying out and scurrying away. High pitched shrieks came from the village of the likes Gia had never heard before, sounds that would have sent even the most seasoned Appalachians into their homes for the night. Unearthly, the screams moved on the air around them. They both covered their ears as the door to Evie's caravan opened and Robbie stood there silhouetted by the light spilling from the interior. He held up his hands in the universal questioning gesture. Gia responded with a single raised hand, indicating that they didn't know what was happening either.

When the screaming stopped, the silence around them was too much. Atlas stood up. Their eyes roved that still expectant darkness with a sense of foreboding. Her eyes met his and he gave a single nod and lifted his top in a silent reply. His blue tattoos had vanished. They waited. Soon, shadows, too dark for the night, danced and weaved around the peripheral edges on the horizon. From the woods came the haunting, eerie sounds of music played on fiddles. Screams and battle cries hit out from the other direction, heading up the hill from the village, crossing the same path that Gia used to take to the old farmhouse when Evie had lived in it as a child. Atlas and Gia turned their faces, from the direction of the woods, to the café, and back again before they looked at each other.

'Shit.'

Gia should know how fae magic worked. She should know how her own magic worked. Up to this point everything had been spells, collections of words, nothing had prepared her for an explosion like this.

Evie came to stand next to her, 'When was the last time you didn't wear something red?'

'Tonight. I've had red nails, red lipstick, that red jacket or reddish toned clothes for years.'

'It was your signature colour. I think it's either helpful to you to direct your magic or it holds you back from your chaos,' her friend murmured.

'You're saying, my magic is this?'

'Chaotic. Spilling in all directions. I think when you said your strength is spells and words it's because it channels your chaos.'

'Red is the colour that helps that?'

'Red is everything; strength, power, wisdom, danger, luck, prosperity, love, blood, sacrifice, confidence, energy, fearlessness...'

'Why does your theory sound so right about me?' Gia sighed.

'Let's get through the chaos. I don't think throwing something red on will help right now.'

'I'm going to step back and watch these two sides battle it out.'

'You'll have to choose a side.'

'Our side. The third side. The *Perhaps I'll kill the Queen and stay alive* side.' Although she realised that she had said almost the same thing to Keld, and that hadn't worked out.

'If one side is the Queen, what's the other?'

'King Coel and his fiddlers three. From the nursery rhyme. But I was told that he's dead.'

'Not dead. Buried. Bound and chained and buried deep in the earth by the Queen and her lover, the first leader of the Wild Hunt,' Atlas joined the conversation.

'That's why the circle was in place on the farm? It wasn't just keeping the fae out and stopping them from finding him, it was keeping him enclosed inside the earth too,' Gia breathed, picturing the circle again and realising what she had missed. Loneliness, isolation, darkness, it had been right in front of her eyes.

'Why, Atlas? Why did the Queen do it?' Evie looked fiercely at her brother.

Atlas blinked, then the inside of his eyes narrowed slightly before he answered, 'He's mad. Whatever he smoked in his pipe sent him mad. The modern translation would be unstable and unpredictable wild behaviour caused by continuous drug use. Gradually his worst stories merged with those of the devil we know about today, he took fae souls and corrupted humans. He really became that vile she had no alternative. The only way to take his magic and reduce his power is for him to pass the crown on. He would never give it to her, so she bound and buried him deep in the soil of the farm.'

'We're dealing with an addict?' Evie and Gia looked at each other, both clearly thinking the same thing.

'What did I miss?' Atlas asked.

'We can't deal with Nina, never mind someone that's been taking drugs since the dawn of the earth,' Gia said.

'We're going to have to,' he stated, as the shadows drew nearer and took their forms.

Over the hill, coming over the half-built roofless, windowless skeleton of the siblings' future homes were the Fomhóraigh. Hideous and monstrous, Gia didn't know which form to look at first, or who was leading. She spied several brownies, she couldn't tell the difference between them or if one was the one from her cottage. Equally grotesque and tall were the ones that had grossly distorted swollen bellies and small heads with moulded rubber facial features, long thick arms and oversized hands, stick thin legs with long narrow feet. Others scurried around on the ground, primordial fishlike beings with arms and legs in the shape of fins, scales over their bodies and eyes on the sides of their protruding flattened faces. Trolls with multiple horns, pointed ears, large ugly wartlike coverings that gave the impression they were molehills over their otherwise smooth muscled bodies strode towards them. Gia stared at the obvious disconnect, their lower jaws stretched out further than they should, two rows of razor-sharp teeth on show. Other beings flitted from shadow to solid forms and back again, too quickly to get a full glimpse. Some had green skin, some blue, initially some looked beautiful but out of proportion, until a more detailed glimpse caught veins on the outside of their skin, horns, scales. Gia thought some of the smaller ones with white beards and grumpy, angry faces could be goblins. A flutter of leaf-headed beings caught her attention, the jewel colours of autumn leaves cascaded from their heads instead of hair. They were beautiful. Yet their expressions were pure hatred, and they screamed battle cries as they walked. It was strange how a facial expression could alter a concept of beauty.

In the centre of them all were owl eyes that morphed into humanlike beings. Their hair turned into short feathers over their necks, gradually getting longer and longer until Gia realised that she was looking at wings, huge expansive owl wings. Behind them walked the largest wolf she had ever seen. The head reached the shoulders of the human-looking owls. It was covered in brown fur. The wolf struggled as they walked, trying and failing to appear human, each time going back into a wolf, sometimes briefly, the large spider Gia had seen in the barn. Between transitions Gia caught a glimpse of a woman with long brown hair.

'She wants to be beautiful. Even in the middle of a fight she wants your sensuality and sexiness,' Atlas whispered to Gia. She didn't answer. Trailing behind the wolf, chains around him that pinned his arms to his body was Keld. A mask was over his mouth and nose, only his eyes showing. She bit down a chuckle at the thought that someone else found his words annoying.

Gia turned her head in the other direction. A much smaller crowd came across the fields. Three fiddlers, slim and dressed in overly pointed shoes, two in rags, one in a ballgown, lead a procession of beautiful winter fae. Behind them was a stout man dressed in white, wearing the remains of what once would have been a red cape, carrying a staff of hollow wooden tubes wound with holly pieces that banged together in his own war cry. In his other hand he was smoking a pipe. Dark brown curly hair and a brown beard framed his face. His expression however was what scared her. It was crazy. Crazy like her own natural inclinations. It was social convention that had held her back from the craziness. The need to be normal. He had no such constraints.

Atlas turned to look behind him. Gia turned too. Shyly but steadily a crowd was forming behind her and Atlas. Animal shapes of the Wild Hunt, fae, either with white skin or dark skin but all shades were beautifully luminous. They were human-looking, some wore the black or white painted marks on their faces that resembled both runes and Celtic shapes. They were male and female, wearing mostly black hooded cloak type coverings.

A braver one met her eyes and bowed her head, dark head to toe with black wings from her shoulders to her ankles, 'The leader of the Wild Hunt stands by you. We also recognise you and stand by you.'

Keld's words came back to her at that point. That getting the leader of the Wild Hunt on her side was key to getting the fae to follow. Gia nodded, suddenly overwhelmed by the uncalled-for faith in herself when she didn't even have a plan.

Atlas looked at her, as though he had read her mind. 'What do you want us to do?'

'Stay back. It's my fight. If I can't do this then I shouldn't be stood here.' Still, she had no plan.

'Gia—' he started.

Gia cupped his face in her hands and gave him a quick kiss, 'I started this chaos. If it weren't for me, you'd still be Atlas. You'll know what to do, when to attack, when to watch my back. This is my storm.' She brought her hands down and looked at her palms.

Gia took a breath. She closed her eyes. The answer to why she had always felt separated flashed before her. She had been raised in order and normality when her heart beat fiercely for chaos. This was how she thrived. It was why she loved travelling around. When she opened her eyes the pen marks in her hands glowed with a muted white brightness.

Atlas stared at her, 'Your eyes…' he didn't finish.

Gia didn't need him to. The shadows became much more than shadows. She saw solid figures shrouded by ancient magic. She saw more fae beings than she had seen with her human eyes. She saw figures hesitating, hovering at the back, wondering who would win and what it meant for their own lives. Their hesitation pushed her forward. She read the desperation to survive in their eyes. Determination to fight for them made her feet move.

When the two sides were about to meet and clash, she rushed towards them to join in.

Chapter 33

Gia had no plan as she moved forward into the middle of the ground where the two sides would meet. Her stomach danced to the chaotic nature of the battle and the urge to make her own stand against these beings who had turned her life upside down from the minute she had returned to Yorkshire. The glowing symbols on her hands extended as she pushed forward, they extended into glimmers of a slim beam emitting from each finger. She played with her fingers, a beam sliced through a Fomhóraigh as a sharp sword would. Gia took in the sight. She tried again. The beam sliced through one of the goblin creatures.

Knowing what she could bring to the battle, Gia picked up her pace to run into the darkness and into the middle of the two sides, reckless and hedonistic, humming a song, then singing it out loudly in abandoned wildness, a song of true colours, to herself, about herself, to the little six-year-old inside her and to the teenager forced into red coats who had felt trapped and restricted, to their newfound freedom, and to the chaos that surrounded her on acres of land which allowed her to be her true self in the night.

In the middle of a fae battle, among the ferocious screams and battle cries, the fiddlers picked up the tune she was singing and played along. The harsh clash of metal on metal reminded her of all the scrapes she'd had in the camper van. The rhythmic thumping of King Coel's staff grew closer as he thumped the ground with it, wielding it as a weapon and warning. Heads were broken with one expert swing, smashed and splintered, the bone, blood and brain smattered across the nearest fae or the ground. Gia heard growls and hooves behind her and assumed the Wild Hunt had stepped in. She turned to watch as they tore through the Fomhóraigh. She protected as much of her Wild Hunt as she could, she cut through the monstrous beasts. This time she remembered Keld's words to let them fight. Then King Coel went down, pounced on by the ginormous wolf whilst he was swinging his staff towards one of the brownies. She carried on singing.

He emerged again, struggling to stand, bloodied and torn. Red stained his clothes, it spread as the blood soaked in. The large wolf was close enough so Gia could see red glowing spots in its eyes, it circled him and changed temporarily, into a beautiful woman; the glamour didn't last. The pair eyed each other before the wolf leapt towards him in a second attack. Gia followed the line of its stomach with a beam from her finger. A human figure fell out from it and hit the ground, then the wolf's insides fell in a bloodied trail, followed by the wolf. Gia stopped singing and watched the body.

Everyone stopped. Time seemed to stand still. A shout of success went out. The old King Coel's eyes met hers. Even the air electrified and stood still, frost thickening and cracking between them as he closed the distance. Gia readied herself for a fight. Except he smiled. He had no teeth left. Just stubs and gaps. He put his pipe back into his mouth.

'Which one are you? Morrigan? Walburga? Hel? Diana?'

'I'm Gianna.'

'Who was your mother, child?'

'Lucia.'

'I don't know of her.'

'You've been underground a long time.'

'Aye. Too long, lass.' His breathing was ragged and hoarse. She could hear his chest rattling. He held out his staff, 'You look like them. My daughters. You carry their scent. Take it, see if you are from them. If not, well, it's a shame to lose a good fighter.'

Nótt. Even though he hadn't meant to say her name, it popped into her head, 'Who was Nótt?'

'Nótt was my eldest daughter, born at the beginning of time, the personification of night and chaos in a woman if I ever saw it. Are you hers?'

'Give or take several generations,' Gia murmured.

When the beams from her fingers passed through him there was nothing. No slicing or ill effect. They were already fading. She curled her fingers around the wood that was still warm from his hand. It was ancient, old, wise, and almost alive. The magic inside it flowed through into her, calming and grounding her. It changed beneath her grip, moulding itself to the contours of her hand, slimming down, transforming into a silver birch staff, unpredictable waves of green light began to flow from the hollow tubes. Gia watched them change into tiny lanterns fashioned from the same silver birch the staff had mutated into. The old King Coel unfastened his ragged red cloak and indicated for her to step forward so that he could throw it over her shoulders.

Wary, ready for an attack, her eyes looking at his every movement, she stepped forward, as tall as the man in front of her. Atlas appeared at her side with the Wild Hunt pawing restlessly behind him. The old King Coel's eyes roamed approvingly over them before he threw the red rag over her.

As it landed on her it evolved and grew into a warm woollen ankle-length lined red cloak, beautifully embroidered around the edges in bronze, silver and gold skeletal leaves. A hood appeared over her face. When he pushed it down, he smiled with fatherly approval. He coughed again, blood coming from his mouth. Winter fae rushed to his side. He laid down on the floor, fighting for breath, slipping out of consciousness. The fae who had spoken to her took the crown of dead branches from his head and carried it tentatively to Gia, as carefully as if it were a bomb, 'He gave you two of the three symbols, this should have been next.'

Once near her, it changed and blossomed, a crown of evergreen fir, rosehips, hawthorn berries, with occasional holly leaves. It looked prickly and uncomfortable. Gia accepted it anyway. It slid onto her head as though it had been made to fit. Fae magic. A sea of expectant faces looked at her. She saw a tiredness that was etched into their souls. A fatigue of hopelessness after centuries of living with bare scraps for survival. They didn't dare hope that she would be any different from the ones before her, they showed respect to her only because Atlas did.

'Rest up. Eat. Tomorrow we'll make plans to rebuild your world.' Aware that she hadn't slept, Gia had no idea how long it had been since she had been in her bed, she wanted to take her own advice.

'We will clean up here. Take our dead back. What would you have us do with that?' the fae nodded over to the dead body that had fallen from the wolf.

The moment Gia looked, she wished she hadn't. Bile rose up and coated her mouth. She pushed it down. Her grandmother's body lay still, lifeless eyes seemingly looking directly at her, the skin showed signs of beginning to be broken down by the lining of the wolf's stomach.

'Take her back and give her the respect we give our dead. That's the woman who raised me.' Gia spoke softly.

Gia turned around looking for the Fomhóraigh. The survivors looked at her warily. Unlike the Resting Court fae with their fatigued hopelessness, she saw resentment and rebellion dance in their eyes. She met it with her own fire, the challenge inside rose unbidden, the ground trembled and snow clouds gathered. The wind rose. A chilling northern wind. They backed away, scurrying, bowing slightly, and left a bound Keld helpless on the ground. He struggled into a standing position. She read the humiliation in his eyes.

Atlas walked up to her, bags under his eyes, sweat and dirt on him from the fight, he murmured in her ear, low and private so no one else heard. 'He had a chance to kill you. It might be wise to return the favour he showed.'

'OK. But I swear, if he steps out of line,' Gia started.

'I know.' Atlas nodded. He looked over at some fae. They ran over to Keld and took the chains from his body. She was tired. Physically tired enough to sleep for hours, but she knew that she'd never sleep in the cottage. She didn't know if she could walk into it again without Rosa.

Chapter 34

Once free, Keld walked towards them. Atlas took a step forward, putting himself between the pair. Keld bowed, deep and low, and spoke about keeping his word. Gia realised that she had kept their pact. In the moment she had killed the Queen she hadn't been thinking about it, or her actions, or the consequences. As usual, she had recklessly strode in and acted however she wanted.

She turned wide eyes to Atlas, 'Evie! The children.'

'We're fine. They saw some of it, it was a bit blurred, mostly just shadows and you singing.' Evie spoke from a distance away. Gia was relieved they had been spared the sight of the battle. She looked at the three brothers. They were pale beneath their tans. They had seen it all.

'Can I borrow you? To try something?' Gia asked her friend.

'Sure.'

Gia took Evie's hand and led her down the old driveway to the farm, the same way they had used to keep hold of each other weaving their way through crowded pubs once upon a time. Robbie, Atlas and Keld walked behind. When they reached the gate Gia gently bounced the staff on the ground. The gate faded in a hazy mist and the rotten trees came into view, along with the neon graffiti-covered grey road. It was a dismal sight. Nature dying before their eyes.

'Can you do anything to fix this?' she asked Evie.

'No. You tried that field of poison once, after the McGregors dumped those chemicals on it. You were ill for a year.' Atlas shook his head.

'I still cured the field.' Evie pointed out.

Robbie caught her arm, 'Don't hurt yourself.' It was said gently, but the intent was clear. Evie responded with an understanding nod. She walked forward and touched a tree.

Nothing seemed to happen. Everything stayed as lifeless and as dull as before. Green ink danced from Evie's fingers around the tree. It jumped from the tree to the next, then along the ground. Faces appeared from the shadows, faces with luminous skin and sigils, shapes and signs painted on to make them look fierce. Their hardened expressions changed to wonder as they watched Evie work. The mud grew grass, the fields turned bare brown rather than grey, the trees seemed to stand straighter. Evie pulled away after a few minutes, the bags underneath her eyes much darker than before, 'It's not going to be an instant fix. I'll come back.' She turned to walk back towards the caravan. As she walked, tiny green shoots followed in her steps. They all noticed.

Evie offered to let her crash on the settee if Gia could wait long enough for them to finish cleaning the circles up. Gia shook her head and told her friend it was alright, Evie needed to get some sleep, not clean. Atlas put his hand on her shoulder and indicated his caravan, as though he understood her reluctance to go back to the cottage. Gia nodded her agreement to stay, her fight drained. She took the crown off as she walked up the steps, her eyes already closing.

'Do you need another to keep you warm?' a voice shouted out. Gia turned to see Keld. Atlas was ready to respond when Keld shrugged, 'You'll stay alive long enough, it's an open offer. We don't have the same boundaries as you.'

'You bitch!' a shout came from behind them. It was definitely human. Gia put the staff and crown just inside the caravan. She was too tired and drained to explain them away. Harriet came into view.

'This one I probably do deserve,' Gia muttered to Atlas. He didn't say anything, but he moved the crown and the staff further into the caravan and returned to stand behind her. Keld leaned against the caravan and folded his arms. His face danced in amusement.

'I know it was you,' Harriet shouted.

'Hello, Harriet.'

'Give it back.'

'Give what back?' Atlas asked from behind Gia, his hands moving to her shoulders and massaging them. It felt nice, but it was a warning. He was telling her not to say anything.

Harriet stared at Atlas, then Keld, whose grin could be entirely misinterpreted Gia suddenly realised, then back at Gia. Gia struggled to keep her eyes open.

'What, Harriet?'

'You stole my spell and killed Rosa. I've just come from the cottage. The police are there. There's blood everywhere.'

'Harriet, wasn't I in the cottage with you tonight for the ghost hunt?' Gia asked. Harriet stopped suddenly. She looked Gia up and down, 'That was, what did you call it? Ka? Karin? the doppelganger? Rosa kicked you out. She called you Lucia and kicked you out.'

'Where was the spell?'

'In my flat. You know that. You might as well admit it.'

'I couldn't be in two places at once.'

'What did you want it for anyway?'

'Information. Do you fully understand what you've done to Evie?'

'We made Yrsa weaker when we swapped the blood ritual from her to Evie.'

'You made Evie almost immortal. Just like Yrsa was. She'll watch her children, her grandchildren and great grandchildren grow up, grow old, fade and die whilst she stays thirty-one. Do you think she can just live here forever without hiding her youth?'

'We, I, that's not what we intended.'

'It's what happened. That's why you don't get to keep the spell, Harriet.'

'A woman came. She wore a veil. She insisted that we did the circle. She gave me the drawing and the ritual.'

'Who?'

'I was sworn to secrecy. She didn't give me her name anyway.'

'Why do you need the spell now it's done?'

'Why do you need it?' Harriet challenged back. Gia held up her palm, pale light filtered with a soft glow from the lines she had drawn. Harriet gasped.

'Go home, Harriet. It might be returned with more spells as a thank you one day.'

'You're a real witch too?'

'What do you think?' Gia was too tired to fight now

'And tonight, in the village, what was all that, all the demons?'

'You think it was demons?'

'Let's see, shadows, death, disaster, car crashes, fake versions of you,' Harriet ticked the list off her fingers.

'It was a night of otherworldly madness that won't happen again in your lifetime, hopefully.'

'You and Evie just managed to deal with it all from here?' Harriet's tone was sarcastic.

Keld laughed, 'Yes. They did. Do you want anything else? There's children asleep.' He nodded over to Evie's caravan.

'I'm leaving because I like Evie. You…' she stared at Gia.

'I write good books. I don't win personality competitions.'

'I don't know about that,' Atlas murmured. Gia tilted her head upwards to look at him. His hand moved from her shoulder to her throat, his index finger kept her chin raised whilst he planted a quick kiss on her lips.

Harriet pointed a finger at Gia, 'I want it back.'

'Like I said, perhaps one day with a thank you.'

Chapter 35

Gia was already half asleep when she heard Atlas come into the bedroom, she had pulled her pillow down in the centre of the bed where she was curled up. She heard him whisper if she minded him sleeping on the bed too. She felt the bed dip as he got in. He had showered, she could smell the synthetic scent of the shower cream he washed with. Robbie was right, there was a difference between the beautiful, rich, nature scents of the fae and the human manufactured ones. He didn't put his arm around her and pull her close. He whispered good night and left a gap between them. Gia wanted to sit up and challenge him, but her tired brain told her that forcing an argument with Atlas over whether he was being respectful or still carrying some resentment, just because she was still wound up, would not be in her best interests, so she concentrated on her breathing and tried to block the images of Rosa falling from the wolf's stomach and lying on the ground.

Five minutes later and still wide awake but tired at the same time, frustration got the better of her. She wanted to sleep but it bothered her that Atlas had left a gap, that he was turned away from her. She pushed her pillow upwards, next to his.

He rolled over, he wasn't asleep either, 'You OK, beautiful?'

'No.'

'Come here. I wasn't sure if you'd want a hug or to be left alone.' He wrapped his arms around her.

Gia sighed and admitted, 'I wasn't sure if you were still mad at me about the pact with Keld.'

'A little. But I've been in the village too. It's easy to lose sight of reality in there. I think it's another thing that happens with the fae, the distortion of our boundaries. Things that we wouldn't do, or agree to, somehow become normal around them.'

'It doesn't feel real does it? Distorted sums it up.'

'It's like you're waiting to wake up from a bad dream.'

'I promise not to make that pact again.'

'You'd better not, beautiful. Once is forgivable, twice is careless.' His voice was already heavy with sleep. Gia closed her eyes too.

Loud banging on the caravan woke Gia. Atlas started and sat up bedside her. He reached for his phone. He shook his head and muttered that it wasn't even milking time. The sound of someone walking around the caravan banging on it continued. A male voice called out her name. Atlas threw her his thick winter robe to put on from the back of the bedroom door, he pulled on tracksuit bottoms and a hoody before he opened the caravan door.

It was the old King Coel. His eyes held that crazy look that only an addict could have. When he saw Gia step out the caravan behind Atlas he lurched forward, coughing blood and spluttering before launching into a tirade, 'That's right, you took it didn't you. You stole it. You're a thief. Where's my magic? Where's my guards? I order them to take you away. To the dungeon with you. It's treason. A rebellion is treason. Why did I have daughters that think they know better than I? Where is my army? Where are my people? You've killed them all haven't you? You murderer! You want to murder me too? Is that why you stole my crown, my cloak and my staff? You think that you can rule, lass? You think it's easy? Forever winter, forever cold, forever bleak frozen landscapes. You took it all didn't you? You made the winter. You are winter. Where's my army? Where's my guards? I order them to take you away. To the dungeon with you. No more winter!' The old King Coel waved his arms as though to try and summon his magic. His outburst brought on another bout of coughing. More blood dribbled from his mouth. He tried to take a swing at her. His fist met Atlas's outstretched hand. He shook his head at the old man, a warning not to try and strike her again.

'You know you're not the king anymore, you can retire. Go somewhere nice and sunny. Sit and soak up the sun's warmth.' Her words gave him pause. He looked at her.

'Go to the sun?'

'Go to the sun,' Gia confirmed with a nod. He wandered away, muttering those same four words over and over until a white mist formed around him and he was all but out of sight.

'You know that's not the last time we're going to see crazy grandpa,' Atlas spoke softly.

'Unless he dies. He's not exactly in the best of health. I can't keep killing people. I mean, I can, I will if I have to, but right now I'd rather go back to bed. He has no magic to speak of anymore. He passed it to me. Maybe I'll be able to control or understand mine better from now on.' Gia knew who she was now, where she was from, and the psychopathic traits she tried to bury seemed natural in her new world.

Gia felt sick when blue lights began to follow their retreat inside the caravan almost immediately, her eyelids drooped and refused to open fully. Atlas watched them get closer and asked what story they were agreeing on. Gia remembered to finally tell him the lie she had told Oliver, about her being with him after their pizza date. His smile and his nod told her he would go along with it. When the uniformed police arrived at the caravan, there were only simple questions about where she had been, when she had left the cottage and how long she had been out. She told the police her grandmother had invited people to conduct a ghost hunt, subtly dropping the information that Oliver had been invited. There was a quiet satisfaction at the thought of his being questioned even if it was just for a few hours. With a shrug she told the police that they normally only discussed Rosa's day over dinner, then Gia's progress with her book, their normal everyday family conversations. The officer's eyes widened when she finally linked Gia's name to her books.

'I've read them.'

'Do you have a favourite?' It was her default, polite enquiry.

'Merryn. I always thought if you gave Valentina a few more years to grow up instead of being nineteen that she would mature into Merryn. It would be interesting to see how she did turn out. Whether she was an absolute fruit loop, seasoned criminal, or if she had some mentor to mature into a responsible person.'

'I was nineteen myself when I wrote Valentina. Don't judge her too harshly,' Gia said, thinking that the last two comments summoned up Valentina's character in her new book.

The officer laughed, the lines on her face when she laughed told Gia that she was slightly older than herself, 'I arrest people three times her age for the same behaviours, hurt children in adult bodies that probably need a lifetime of counselling to become decent. Were you with your grandmother tonight?'

'No. I filmed some social media content in the spa with Jae. They changed my hair. Nonna hired a lookalike to be there in my place. I don't know where from or who organised it all.' When the police were finally leaving. Gia said quietly to the officer, 'You'll contact me if you find my grandmother?' The expression on the woman's face told Gia that she had already been in the cottage and seen the blood inside it. It was hidden quickly, and confident reassurances offered that Gia would be the first to know if they found her grandmother.

The following day was tough for Gia. Her body ached, her energy was low, she was still drained physically from the previous day and faced an emotionally draining day filled with tough, honest conversations, although Liam had made her laugh a few times. The hardest conversation had been alone with Atlas, she'd opted for a hot chocolate over coffee. They talked about their feelings for each other, about how he had felt hearing that she had so casually promised Keld more than she should ever promise someone. Gia looked out across frozen fields as they leaned on a fence to talk, escaping the confines of the caravan and avoiding people in the café. The daytime temperature hadn't risen above zero despite the sun in the sky. Tucked comfortably into a padded coat that reached almost to her ankles, one of Atlas's scarves around her neck, Gia was happy to have the conversation outside.

'I say and do reckless things, I'll try, but I can't promise I won't slip up occasionally.'

'I'm not here for games, Gia. I'd like this to work between us. I'm sorry it's been an absolute clusterfuck so far.'

'I wouldn't say that. You being able to see and understand the mess I'm in makes it easier. I don't have to lie to you, or walk away because I could never explain being fae.'

'If I can't find you, I know where to look now.'

'How do you do that?'

'I still don't understand it. I tried when she put those tattoos on me and it wouldn't work. That first time I asked you to stay and wait for me to return from milking was when I knew that you meant more to me than I realised. Actually, that's a lie, it was when you were asking me about my house the night before. You said something about the shadows coming to take you away then wandered off into a conversation about my house because Evie was so excited about hers, and I realised that I had this big house that was future-proofed, but no future. I saw us in there, in the house, together, happy, and you smiling at me the way you did when I saw you at the crossing with your suitcases. I realised that I'd never seen that far into the future with anyone else. I didn't want to lose you to the shadows.'

'That's why you went after them that day? For what it's worth, I'm glad you're the leader of my Wild Hunt.'

'I'm equally glad you became my queen. What are you going to do with the cottage?'

'I can't bear the thought of even entering. I guess I'll have to go inside and clean it up.'

'Stay with me?' he blurted out before she had a

chance to say what she was going to say next.

Gia looked at him, 'Stay with you?' She wanted him to ask again, she wasn't entirely certain she had heard right. Gia didn't know whether he meant move in, or simply stay a bit longer until she was ready to face the cottage.

'Would it be that bad?'

'No. I'm confused. Are you offering to have me to stay until I can face the cottage or—?'

'Bloody hell, Gia. For someone intelligent you're not good at picking up on this stuff. Move in. Will you move in with me?'

'Yes. But Atlas, don't be cryptic when you ask me stuff like that. It's like my brain goes off and does a mind map of all the possible reasons for you to ask and interpretations of the question. I'm not good at relationships.'

'In what way? So I'm prepared.'

'In the way that I've never taken one seriously. Except this one.' She looked at him, thinking that it would scare him off.

He laughed, 'That's good. Because I'm serious, beautiful.'

He had gone to Rosa's cottage with Evie to retrieve her belongings which now sat in their bedroom waiting to be put away. Evie passed Gia a cup of ginger tea, carried her own and Liam's cups of tea through from the kitchen to the sitting area. She left her brother's mug, and Robbie's, on the side for them to pick up and started the interrogation she had been holding inside since they had left Yvonne's house. Gia wrapped her hands around the cup and readied herself. She remembered the look Evie had given her from inside the cage.

'When did you go on a date with Oliver?' That was the

first question.

'It wasn't a date. It was supposed to be a catch up between two old school friends.'

They all felt Atlas walk into the caravan, followed by Robbie. The pair carried a takeaway from the café. Max and Rey jumped up, eager for theirs. The caravan rocked slightly.

'I was there when he surprised Gia with his plan for them to get married and have a family, for her to be a stay-at-home mum and put her writing to one side as a hobby.' Atlas spoke up from the kitchen area, dishing out the children's orders to them.

'He said that to Gia and you let him?' Evie narrowed her eyes at her brother.

He shrugged, 'Gia is a grown woman who chooses who she's with, Evie. Those stupid insecure days when I punched other boys for flirting are gone. She handled it herself. It taught me a lesson too. I realised that a self-assured woman is sexier than a daddy's princess who gets off on creating jealousy for attention.'

He looked at Gia as he said the last sentence. She met his eyes, read the message, and gave him a smile. Gia thought, in that moment, that it was the most beautiful and sexiest, she had seen Atlas at. Stood in the kitchen, one hand on the counter, another holding his cup of tea, confident, relaxed, assured, and certain of where her loyalty lay when it came to him. She broke her eyes away when she heard her friend speak again.

'OK, so next. Where did you learn the whoosh,' Evie pushed her hand out the way Gia hand when she started the incantation, 'and the urgh,' Evie circled her neck with a finger to indicate the burning and blistering Gia had caused on Oliver.

'My strength is words. I told you that. I'm not a nature goddess like you.'

'Can you teach me?'

'I can try.'

'Let's eat first,' Robbie passed Evie a plate that held a box with her name on it, he stretched out his other hand with a plate to Bodhi, the box carried his name on it.

'Changing the subject,' Evie glanced up shyly, her eyes met Robbie's. He broke out in a wide grin. She looked at her brother then Gia, 'We set a date.'

Chapter 36

Evie's wedding day was the coldest day of the year, with a forecast of snow that was nothing to do with Gia. Phoebe had organised most of the day, breakfast in the farm café with all of Robbie's siblings before a walk to the spa for hair and make-up which included Rey. Then they went their own separate ways for an hour, much to Evie's relief. Gia could tell she loved being around the family, but she was still a person who had grown up alone and very much liked her own space.

Inside Evie's caravan they watched Rey twirl around in her bridesmaid's dress surrounded by flowers from fans and industry colleagues who had somehow found out about the quiet low-key wedding through word of mouth. Evie was completely unflustered when Rey dropped jam onto the red dress, and mentioned casually that she had bought her daughter two dresses because she knew it would happen.

Gia excused herself to get ready thirty minutes before the cars were due to arrive, 'I should go and get my dress on. Give me a shout, or text if you need me. Do you want me to send Keld over to stand outside the caravan?' Gia stood up. She had something that she wanted to do before the wedding. She had been hoping to get back to her caravan ages ago, but Evie seemed a little nervous. Whether it was about the wedding or something else she wouldn't say. There were only so many times Gia could ask.

'We'll be fine.' Evie said. Her phone pinged, she showed Gia the message, 'Look, Robbie's on his way back with Max and Atlas.'

'I just feel like—'

'It's not over with Oliver, I know. Me too. I'm just hoping he doesn't show up with a plan to ruin today. How are things going with the fae?'

'Slow but positive. You're helping so much. You know you'll be welcomed there when the time comes for you to retreat from here.'

A shadow went over Evie's bright face, 'When you said it was a mindfuck, I didn't understand. But now I do. I wish I'd known the full implications of stepping into Yrsa's shadow. I agree that it feels like we're walking further and further down a dark path without light, but I know there's an end. Eventually. At least we have each other now.' Evie's bright face held hope. Gia smiled back.

The idea of living with Atlas in his house and having Evie just across the courtyard was comforting and reassuring. Even the fact that Robbie and his brothers knew everything was comforting. She understood his protectiveness towards Evie now. Evie might have been semi-feral but Gia had seen her in that cage, and Evie had no way to protect herself. Even thinking about it made Gia shudder, she wondered if she would ever have the strength to do that again, to walk in there and get her friend out. She was still wiped out after the fight, it was taking time to get back to normal.

'I'll put my dress on and come back.'

'You could put your dress on here,' Evie offered.

'I know. I just need five minutes. Go to the loo, put my

dress on, then I'll be back.' Gia faltered, having run out of excuses. She needed about three minutes alone.

She wouldn't tell Evie but she had been having vivid dreams and weekly nightmares about finding herself in that cage, in pain and alone. She woke up as her grandmother's body fell from the ceiling, followed by the wolf, and a grinning Oliver appeared, standing over it all. She could only sleep when someone was in the caravan with her. It wasn't right, she felt it inside her, something was different. The dreams of fear were different from her normal dreams. Gia scanned the landscape as she crossed from Evie's caravan to her own. Robbie and his brothers, their security friend Shane, along with Atlas, and Keld, had installed a raised walkway bridge between the two caravans, along with perimeter security cameras and alarms. It was Oliver who had been the final straw for Atlas and Evie. Evie was flippant about the fae. Oliver had scared her as much as he had scared Gia. Neither of them spoke about it, but they thought about him more than they would like, and they both had a feeling deep in their gut that it wasn't over. Hatred like his didn't die.

Gia was putting the final touches to her outfit when Atlas walked into the caravan, she heard the door opening and his hello. Her hair and make-up had been done in the spa, all she had needed to do was to put her dress on, a beautiful cinnamon silk dress, apply another coat of lipstick and add simple rose gold jewellery. Her shoes matched her dress. She returned his *hello* to him dand was putting the lipstick into her small clutch when she heard a noise that made her stop in her tracks. Running water from the cistern.

Panic ran through her. It was too late. He walked into

the bedroom in his suit. Gia had never seen him in a suit before. She couldn't resist looking him up and down with a smile, 'You look good.'

'You look incredible. But that thing in the bathroom.' He folded his arms. She grimaced.

'I haven't even checked it yet.'

'I'm the only one that knows?' He seemed to grow taller, happy in that knowledge.

'Atlas don't. Please. I'll play and banter about most things but not now,' her stomach was turning around on itself in fear of her own reaction, then his.

'It's positive. You're pregnant.'

'Fuck. We messed up.' Gia couldn't look at Atlas. She turned to the window. She wasn't even able to decipher her own reaction to the news. She needed time. The cars would be outside soon. Her hands shook. She could use something to eat, a biscuit, anything.

'Is it mine? Not that it matters.'

Gia's head whipped round to stare Atlas down. 'I was on my period when I flew back. I've skipped November and now December. We didn't use a condom that one time on Nonna's kitchen counter. You—' she cut herself off.

'Say it.'

'Nothing, I was lashing out. I was going to say you must have fucking super sperm to get past the coil.' Her comment was met with laughter.

'What do you want to do?' he asked.

'What do you want to do?' she challenged. He kept an impressive blank face. His eyes scanned her expression searching for the right answer. Purposefully, she kept her face as blank as his own.

Eventually he said, 'Keep little Valentina. Give her a

nursery in the new house. Persuade her mum to move in with me when the houses are built and go to bed with me every night. Then we'll have another little girl and call her Lucia.'

Gia didn't speak. Those words sank deep into her, they reached a place, a level, that she didn't know she had. This wasn't the chaos that she loved. This wasn't recklessness, or playfulness. She had actively tried to avoid this situation and had taken every precaution aside from being celibate. Even with an unexpected pregnancy, celibacy still seemed something other people chose. She couldn't imagine a night without Atlas.

'Gia?' Atlas held her eyes. Gia came back to the present. She softened, she always did around him. One day he'd figure out the effect he had on her. She gave him a nod of agreement. He swept her up in strong arms, lifted her off the ground and kissed her.

Her fears slowed down and calmed. Excitement raced into her. It was reckless, it was playful. It was quitting university and running away to America all over again. It was exceptional. She would work to make it alright. She reasoned that becoming a mother was just another unknown path to walk.

'Are you ready to go?' he asked. Again, Gia nodded. She wasn't, she needed space to think and time to get her head around the news. But at least she could walk into the wedding with an answer instead of the question twisting itself around her mind every few seconds, the way it had been persistently plaguing her since the day after her grandmother's death.

The whole wedding was a beautiful relaxed intimate affair, almost entirely centred around Evie's love of old blues, soul and jazz music. Evie and Robbie had opted for a short private service in a nearby country house. Her friend wore an understated elegantly simple ivory dress with beading, that swept the floor and oozed old Hollywood glamour. Gia sat and watched Evie as she glided around the hotel room holding a glass of champagne and talking to people between the early afternoon ceremony and the formal afternoon tea, accompanied by a blues band. Later that evening, the country house chefs set up a grilled meat buffet with a rainbow spread of vegetables and sides in a room that was set up to look like an old jazz club. The singer was exceptional. She did a few greatest songs from different singers, changing her look and costume between sets, even changing her voice to sound like each star. Evie came and sat next to her when Atlas had gone back to the buffet.

'You're very quiet and chilled today.' Evie flopped into Atlas's vacant chair.

'I'm enjoying watching you be the centre of attention for a change.' Gia smiled.

'You and Atlas keep looking at each other. He's stayed really close to you all day. You're either secretly engaged, planning to run off and elope, or there's another secret.'

'Can't you just enjoy one day without worrying about other people?'

'I don't like secrets anymore. Here's mine. Robbie wants to try for a baby.'

'What do you want?'

'I love the idea of a big family. Especially having you and Atlas so close. Its everything that I didn't have growing up. It would be gorgeous for little cousins to be running around together, to have the courtyard filled with family dinners during summer.'

'Were you going to consult us on this plan?' Atlas put his plate down on the table. Gia avoided his eyes. She didn't know how to look at him and not let her body language tell Evie.

'Eventually. I might also be a little drunker than I thought I was.' Evie looked at her glass of champagne. Atlas laughed and offered her another. She gave a nod. She had clearly thrown caution to the wind and was much more like teenage Evie again than the shadow of a person she had been when Gia had returned to the village in October.

Robbie carried four glasses over, 'I'm on it,' he told Atlas, handing out the glasses. Gia accepted hers with a smile that told Evie's penetrating stare nothing.

'Are you trying to get my sister drunk?'

'I'm helping my wife enjoy her wedding day,' Robbie bantered back.

'To Atlas and Gia. Before last month I would never have dreamt that the pair of you would end up together, I thought you'd be a fling, but you work really well, and you look good together.'

'I think you've had enough to drink.' Atlas laughed at his sister.

She pulled a face. 'I know. It's nice though, seeing you both happy.'

'Did you get their secret?' Robbie looked at Evie. Evie shook her head.

'Who says we have a secret?' Gia asked.

Robbie looked at her, 'The entire room knows you have a secret. Mum's guess is that you're pregnant. Evie thinks we'll wake up tomorrow and discover you've eloped, although I've told her Gretna Green is probably closed on New Year's Eve.'

'Enough drunken guesses, go and speak to other people and enjoy your wedding day. Bloody village mentality. We'll still be here tomorrow.' Atlas swore. Robbie and Evie laughed and floated away to talk to their other guests.

Chapter 37

Atlas and Gia walked through the dark village together after the wedding had finished. Atlas was still in his suit, Gia still wore her dress. The neon sigils on the road had faded, although gangs were still rife, there were glimmers of hope emerging even this quickly, and fae were starting to work together instead of against each other. Keld walked in front of them. The rest of the Wild Hunt walked behind in their normal fae forms. Gia was getting used to them being with her every time she came into the realm. The Fomhóraigh were still a real threat, having successfully repressed the Resting Court fae for so many years, and built hordes of artwork, books and gold that even dragons would approve of. They weren't scared enough to stay away yet. She saw them in the alleyways, always more than five of them, always hoping that she would be alone. Previously, they had tried to launch an attack on her, Keld and Atlas had told the Wild Hunt not to leave her to walk through their lands alone.

The village had improved. Small changes were noticeable. The brook had a trickle of water now. Fae had cleared it out. The cottages stood a little straighter.

Gia nodded to the cottage that had the mirrors in, through which she had escaped, 'Have you found out who stored everything in there?' she asked Keld.

'The fae named to be residing in the cottage was killed

a hundred years ago. No one has been seen to go in or out since. I've got people watching it.'

'Do we know how many Resting Court fae survived her rule?'

'Our numbers are low. We're still counting people. A few hundred rather than a few hundred thousand. The Fomhóraigh number low thousands. I'm hoping some Resting Court fae slipped through the portals and live unnoticed in your forests and woods as we did once, before the war with humans.'

'The breeding camps are closed?'

'We followed your instructions and escorted everyone home.'

'Keld, what age had been normal to have a first child before all this horror?'

'It was looked down upon for a fae to have a child before they reached a hundred when times were affluent and gentle. Nobody would wish to bring a child into this.' Gia looked at Atlas. He met her eyes with a wink. She smiled, she couldn't help it. A broad smile appeared on her face with no effort from herself.

'Which castle should I prepare for your residence?' Keld asked as he always did. Gia had avoided an answer so far.

'We'll talk about it later. I do like the windows in the one you call the Night Palace. The other one didn't have windows.'

'It does. We were under the ground. I'd be happy to show you.'

Atlas wrapped his hand around hers. He stepped closer and matched her pace. Gia felt her palm rub against his shirt cuff. He looked serious, deep in thought, when she lifted her eyes from the village to him, he gave a little concerned shrug, 'Are you going to come and live here?'

'Eventually. With Evie too. She'll need somewhere to hide when Max and Rey are grandparents and she's still thirty-one. You will too.'

'But not now. We can't disappear. Do you understand what that will look like? First Yvonne, then Rosa, then us. Evie will bear the suspicion. The police will never leave her alone.'

'I understand what you're saying. There's so much to do here first. We have generations here that haven't been taught literacy. I have to make this the best it can be, somewhere I would want my family to live. Then we'll come here.'

The group left the village behind and continued the walk along the lane up to the entrance to the farm. Recklessness spread inside Gia at the sight of the vast expanse of space. She squeezed Atlas's hand quickly, 'Want to run, my leader of the Wild Hunt?' she asked.

He grinned and raised her hand to his lips and placed a kiss on her knuckles, 'Always, my Queen.'

It had become part of their night routine. The Resting Court territory fell north of the tropic of cancer. They ran free in the night with the Wild Hunt. Keld often joined them. There was much laughter and wildness. Recklessness was as natural to the Wild Hunt as it was to her. Their feet barely touched the ground, they left no imprint on soil, sand, or snow when running. The first time she had crossed the sea with the Wild Hunt Gia had hesitated on the banks, stood on the sand. Atlas had told her she would be fine as long as she ran. He held out his hand to her and told her that they would run together. Gia took a breath and gave him her trust. He had been right. Waves had joined them the third time they ran across the North Sea, waves which turned into water fae.

As long as they ran, they were the breeze in the night, a delicious stroke of cool air, shadows without bodies, through forests, waterfalls, over mountains and volcanoes, across crisp snow-filled lands under the northern lights, through deliciously scented lemon groves, and then they played on the Giants Causeway before heading back home across the Irish Sea, to Yorkshire, to the farm, laughing, marvelling at the freedom to run across the land at will.

Bonus chapter: Evie

Evie opened the door to her brother's caravan and stepped inside. The beautiful scent of ripe blackberries and the woods hung in the air. She stepped over Atlas's overalls that lay in a storm blue heap near the door. Her brother was in the kitchen watching the kettle boil, one of their farm mugs in front of it. He gave her a nod and picked up another cup out of the cupboard for her. She shrugged her farm overalls off and placed them next to those her brother had thrown on the floor at the same time the kettle boiled.

'Where's Gia?'

'London. She's back tonight. I'm picking her up from the station.' Atlas made her a cup of tea in the mug and handed it to her. Evie took it over to the settee and picked up his chess set. She began to set up her pieces.

'It's sort of weird, seeing you two together.'

'I have to watch Robbie put his hands on you.'

'I didn't mean that. Gia lights up when you touch her. I know you're not really into hugs and little touches in public but if you saw her smile when you squeezed her shoulder last night as you sat down in the restaurant, you'd know what it means to her. What I meant was that you two are polar opposites, it's weird seeing you fit together so well.'

'How?'

'You're all about staying in one place and routines on the farm. She's the free spirit that travels where she wants, I don't think she'd know what a routine looks like.'

'I am not all about routines.' Atlas sat down and followed her lead, putting his chess pieces in their home places.

'Atlas, I bet you have an app downloaded onto your phone right now that tracks the train she's coming home on and will tell you if its delayed or not.'

'Did you come here just to insult me or was there a purpose? If you're in a mood you have a husband to take it out on now.' His tone was dry as he moved his piece. Evie laughed. He was right.

She met his move with her own, 'Yeah, I did come to talk to you about something,' a small sigh escaped when she thought about it.

She didn't want to burst her brother's bubble. He looked good with Gia. The skinny blondes that used to hang off his arm, the same ones he had never brought back to the farm after she had returned, looked wrong with his frame. Gia matched his energy, her vivaciousness sparkled. In return, Atlas had dropped a lot of his walls and let her in. He really did smile and laugh more. Evie looked down at the pieces and took a sip of tea.

Atlas took her silence to mean something else, 'If you're having a baby it's OK. I won't yell. Ours was a happy accident. Gia almost yelled at me. Then I thought she was going to cry.' He had been waiting for her to take her turn. Evie moved a piece. He moved almost immediately after she did, as if he had predicted her move and was only waiting for it.

'I bet you really knew what to do with yourself at that point,' Evie murmured, torn between sarcasm to rile her brother and amusement at the picture he painted. She couldn't wait to see how flustered he became when Gia's waters broke in seven months. She had a feeling that this baby would be another one with an August birthday in the family. Her brother was carrying on the tradition.

'Again, you have a husband if you're in a mood.'

'I am but I need to tell you.' She pondered which piece to move and settled on her rook.

'Tell me what?'

'I've received a letter. Two actually. They came yesterday. The first one was from our parents.' She tried hard to keep her voice steady.

Evie told her brother the contents of the letter over the game of chess. That they had congratulated her on overcoming Yrsa, warned her that there was something called a Circle of Leif, named after one of Yrsa's sons, a council of sorts, tasked not only with monitoring Yrsa's descendants, but storing magical knowledge in archives. They told her to obey the council, and that she was subject to it. She finished with, 'V.V sent me a letter. A note really. Again, she said she was coming as fast as she could get here. It literally said, fuck the council, do not go through the initiations with the Circle of Leif, do not let them control you. They didn't control Yrsa and now they're scared of you because you had the strength to beat her. She also said our parents are part of it and they'll manipulate both of us any way they can to get control over us.'

Their phones pinged. They both opened the same picture, Gia had sent them a picture of her and Tess, whom she had arranged to meet in London. A second later Evie's phone pinged again.

She looked at it and smiled, flipping it around to show Atlas, 'An invite to Tess's latest gallery opening next month.'

'You should go.'

'I never said I wasn't.'

'It's the hesitation on your face. Take Robbie and the children. Make a weekend of it. She was in New York for another gallery thing when you got married, wasn't she?'

'Yes.' Evie bit her cheek to avoid saying more. Tess had been breaking up with the man she had been engaged to for six years.

'Say it?' Her brother's raised eyebrow meant he had picked up on her short answer.

'I sort of feel bad. She said that if Robbie was that committed to getting married that he'd do a small wedding with minimal arrangements, she had second thoughts about the big wedding Tom wants but isn't willing to set a date for. The size of it intimidated her from the beginning. I mean, who really needs, what was it?' Evie checked her phone, she scrolled back a few days' worth of messages to find the number Tess had sent, *Two thousand guests, half of which come from his parents' network.* Liberty knows him through work circles, and she told Tess to get rid of him immediately.'

'It's been six years since she got engaged to the Oxford guy? That's gone fast. I'm sorry your other friends couldn't make it.'

'I didn't expect them to be able to make it with just a

few days' notice. We were booking the registry office until Phoebe and Gia encouraged us to go a teeny bit bigger. We didn't want a fuss. Robbie really wanted to start the new year married.'

She looked at her brother. He was happy, for the first time in the longest time he had a smile on his face at a secret she knew about, and he wasn't full of warnings about not using their gifts. She hesitated on her next words. Evie wanted to make sure they came out right. She moved a few pieces in turn, each a better move than she had played before Halloween, the challenger to her brother was back.

When Atlas took a turn with his knight, taking her pawn, she said, 'Jean sort of got Robbie and Liam a new job.'

'The architect?'

'She's designed a house for someone, they signed up to a DIY build show, the producers approached Jean to do some more work and she put Robbie forward because they wanted a personable and knowledgeable builder to talk to people, and she likes him. He went for a meeting. Then he and Liam went for another meeting. It's a pilot. There's no guarantee of anything right now. They're not even sure if they want Robbie or Robbie and Liam.'

'How do you feel about Robbie stepping on your toes?'

'It's a house programme. I don't know how to build houses or remodel them. It's not as though he's telling me how to garden.' Evie shrugged. She had been happy for Robbie and the new opportunity. He had said that physically building houses was starting to tell on his body. If he had the chance to do something with his knowledge and his skills that required less labouring from him, she thought he should take it.

'It's also a good excuse for them to find out how many houses have things in them,' Atlas arched an eyebrow, 'What if those things follow him back here though? Have you discussed that?'

'Between you, Robbie, Gia, and myself, I think we're starting to get a grip on the uncanny.' Evie leaned back and looked at the board. She thought about her next move before she made it.

'If your theory about the seven-pointed star stuff is right, how are you going to ask your friends?'

'I guess we just wait until the right time. I said to Gia that I'm glad it didn't come out when we were teenagers because we would have been a nightmare to society and a danger to ourselves. I have to trust that there is a right time.'

'Are you ready for tonight?'

'No. Are you?'

'I still don't understand why Gia wouldn't just let the Wild Hunt go after it.'

'Robbie kills fae. She's part fae. He sees that side of her. She sees that side of him. It's a step towards some sort of middle ground trust.'

Evie was leaning against the windowsill of the cottage, next to the settee when the door opened and Gia walked in with Atlas. Her friend looked tired, her eyes had the beginning of black under them, as though she'd had a long day. No one had wanted to sit on the blood-stained settee. Gia's eyes went to it. She murmured something to Atlas; Evie caught the mention of a skip rather than a clean. He gave a small nod.

Evie explained the open windows, 'I brought bin bags. I've cleared out the fridge and cupboards of everything that had gone off or was going off.'

'No, she didn't. She made us do it.' Bodhi winked.

Evie laughed, 'He's right. Thank them. Are you OK?'

'Just a long day, travelling never wiped me out like this before.' Her friend's smile wasn't as big as normal, she looked a little pale. She joined Evie at the window.

'We were waiting for you. We're ready when you are,' Robbie said.

Evie smiled at him, he looked good stood there with his brothers. Their eyes locked and for a second it was the two of them, her leaning in to kiss him for the first time outside the farmhouse door. He winked at her. Liam cleared his throat.

'So, we're ready then.'

Atlas closed the door. Robbie and his brothers started their work. Evie watched them draw the circles on the floor. It wasn't as fluid as Gia's had been, not as intuitive, they had argued over the sigils, pulled up pictures, Liam stomped silently, leaving the argument to Robbie and Bodhi whilst he prepared the rosemary and lavender bunches to burn. They had daggers and knives, an electromagnetic field reader.

Gia spoke at her side, 'It would be easier if you stop thinking so much about it and use the gift of sight that you've been given.'

'We can see. That doesn't help us get rid of it.' Liam pointed out. Evie stayed silent. She glanced at Gia, then at

Atlas before returning to watching Robbie and his brothers. Liam lit the homemade smudge sticks. It made sense to use locally grown herbs, Evie didn't have to ask why they had chosen that. Rosemary and lavender were a good mix. Maybe not what she would chose, or at least, she would have added nettles and cedar, but nettles were out of season.

The brothers started upstairs, one in each room, before they followed each other down the stairs. Bodhi stayed on the stairs, on the big square, guarding the path back upstairs.

Liam went into the downstairs bathroom, Robbie stayed by the back door. As they stepped closer and closer to the circle drawn on the floor, a shadow began to form, it had undiscernible muted edges, but it was a noticeable shadow that turned into a dark shape, then, only when pushed into the circle by the brothers, did its true monstrous shape emerge. The brothers looked up at it. It stared at Gia. The clock ticked faster and seemingly louder to Evie. Instinctively she glanced at her brother to see if he had noticed the clock too. He met her eyes and understood. She received a slight nod from him.

'You will disallow us our homes?' It stared at Gia.

She shrugged, 'It isn't your choice of home that's the problem. It's your attitude.'

'I didn't eat you, kidnap you, nor feast on your blood, for that you should be grateful.'

'You took delight in terrorising me.'

'All fae grow up terrified. It keeps us alert and alive.'

'See, if you had really taken note, you'd know that humans are trying hard to move past the mentality of trauma denial in generational upbringing.'

'So many big words now you've taken King Coel's cape and crown, and killed our queen.'

'Which makes me your queen, for the next few seconds.'

Evie jumped as it emitted an unexpected deep, ferocious growl. At her side Gia started too although Evie jumped higher and reacted more. Gia recovered herself quickly. It made Evie wonder what she had seen in America, and she resolved to wander over to Atlas's caravan one Friday to find out. She didn't miss that Robbie noticed her reaction and plunged a knife into the brownie. The brownie didn't take its eyes off Gia. Evie turned to look at her friend. Gia held its gaze with her own steady eyes until its last breath, almost not breathing herself. Evie saw, for the first time, her friend's eye colour the way Robbie saw it. They were the colour of ripe red grapes as Liam had said, and yet, they were more, the colour and depth were not human, they had a deep intensity, yet they sparkled, they held dark depths whilst they managed to glow like the moon. Gia blinked as they watched the brownie burn up from the inside and crumble onto the floor in the way that demons did in films. Gia's eyes returned to their normal brown. Regret passed over her face.

Evie squeezed her hand, 'Are you OK?'

'Yes. I just wish... I know there wasn't another way, I know it had to be done if we're going to let someone else live here, but I don't want to be killing fae.'

'You'd kill Oliver though,' Robbie said.

Gia met his eyes. 'Yes. For locking Evie in that cage. For kidnapping her. For luring her to that house under false pretences. The hate he carries inside him won't die. The people around him won't help him change for the better.

He's a miserable man who hates himself and his life and he isn't wise enough to realise his hatred for Evie, and probably myself now, comes from his own mind games. You don't hurt my friends and not expect revenge.'

'Gia,' Evie spoke up.

She directed her friend's attention to the beams of light extending from her fingers. Soft moonbeams. Evie had only seen the moonlight coming from Gia's fingers as she waved it around like lights in a club that night the shadows had turned up on the farm. Atlas and Robbie had filled her in on how it sliced though the fae. Gia shook her hands and the light dimmed a little.

Atlas moved over to her, 'Do you want to run it off?'

'Yes.'

'Gia, I'm glad you're angry at Oliver. It kills me to think of Evie in that cage,' Robbie said. It was his way of making peace. Evie was their common ground.

Gia gave him a nod, 'You only had a minor problem with me until you saw me kill that spider.'

'I'd like to say it's complicated but it's not. You brought the fae to Evie's door and put her in danger.'

'I brought the fae to my own door. I wiped away that chalk circle remember, with no idea what it meant or what would happen,' Evie interjected. Wisely, neither replied to her admission.

'Are you OK to lock up or do you want me to stay?' Gia asked Evie. Evie saw the raw pain of being in the cottage in her friend's face. She told Gia to go.

Evie locked the cottage door. Robbie was behind her, loading the knives into a hidden part of Bodhi's car boot. She heard the lock click into place and took her hand from the cold metal handle, pocketing the key. Her use of the front cottage door had only started after Rosa's death and she still missed skipping round to the side, it really was the end of an era. The herb beds had been one of her first introductions to Mediterranean gardens. Rosa had given her cuttings for the farm after she had asked what they were for. She had nurtured those cuttings into full plants by the end of the day, and planted them.

'Hey, Evie.' She heard the Australian drawl. Evie pocketed the key and turned around. He held out a glass to her, with a smile.

'Prosecco?' she asked. He gave a nod. Evie walked down the path, closed the gate behind her, and took the glass from Robbie. She took a sip and closed her eyes as the bubbles went down, 'I needed this.'

'You forget I can read you now. You've been overthinking for days. Ever since Halloween, we'd barely had time to deal with that before everything got turned upside down a second time. Why are we treating Gia with kid gloves? She's a warrior. She stood up and fought twice in one night with more than a hint of crazy.'

'Remember how carefully you treated me just three months ago? Gia's a runner. She's pregnant, scared, hurt and navigating something new. She needs a bit of patience. Even you didn't realise these things were fae.'

'True.'

He caught her free hand and they started to walk slowly up to the farm. Evie sipped her drink again. She resisted the urge to bite back and defend her friend. There would be a time and a place, when she was calmer, when everyone was a little calmer. She didn't hold Gia responsible for the recent chaos in their lives.

'I don't understand something. That King...'

'King Coel?'

'If the chalk circle you wiped away was responsible for keeping him enclosed, why didn't he spring up from the earth immediately?'

'Residual magic. It's like when you throw a stone into a calm lake and it disappears, but the ripples take a while to vanish. I removed an incredibly strong spell, but it took Gia's new magical abilities, along with some time for all the magic holding him to evaporate. What was on the knife? Why did the brownie burn up like that?'

'It's a family recipe for those things. It's rowan and hawthorn twigs, dehydrated and ground to a powder. Then we add rose water to it and coat the knives. It works on some but not others, now we know it's a fae recipe not a demon one. I was thinking you should know about it and we should keep some in the caravan or the house. Just in case.'

'Promise me you won't use it on Gia or Atlas?'

She was met with silence. Robbie struggled to answer. He knew how much she loved and valued her brother because he felt the same about his family. He offered her the best he could, 'I can't promise never, but as long as things stay as they are, it's all fine.'

'Are you going to trust that Gia might be able to help you with the curse?' Evie took another drink. She felt her shoulders relax. Robbie held out the bottle and topped her glass up. She looked at him.

'Maybe.' His jaw set at an angle that told her he didn't want to talk about it.

'Filming might involve more than forty-eight hours away from me. I don't want you to suffer,' she took a sip of her drink.

His hand tightened on hers when he said, 'I will find a way. I promised you that I wasn't walking away. I don't see it as a curse. It's a blessing. It means time with you, with Max and Rey, with our babies.'

'Do you remember when we did this walk the first time. We talked about monsters and fairytales?'

'Yes. I thought that if you already believed in monsters I was already halfway to being able to tell you who I was. I never thought I'd have to tell you that your best friend is one, or that she'd be responsible for turning your brother into one.' He took a drink from the bottle.

'You told me about your house on Sevenoaks Close,' she smiled at the memory and changed the subject. Her friend and her brother were not monsters, but that was a conversation for a calmer time.

'It's still not finished. I've lost the heart to do it now. I'd rather spend my time with you. Liam and Bodhi are in there finishing it off for me. I didn't ask them to. Although they said a bit of painting and flooring isn't really work. Liam said he quite likes the house and might buy it off me. Bodhi is talking about buying on that street.'

Ahead of them, the last streetlight cast a glow downwards. Behind it, there was only a dark lane leading up to the farm and the woods. The woods were shadowed with secrets and fae. Evie finished her drink. Robbie refilled the glass for her. Evie wanted to get home to the caravan, it was a few degrees colder than it had been when they had first made this walk at night. Max and Rey were with Robbie's parents. Robbie seemed to want to drag out the walk home.

'Aren't you cold?' she asked.

He smiled at her, 'Yes. I just want to remember that

first night I walked you home. You kissed me at your door and said to meet you in the café the next day.'

'I thought you were ready to walk away. I realised that I didn't want you to.'

'This time I get to walk you back and stay with you. I still can't believe how lucky I am.'

'I was worried for a bit. I know the stuff with Gia stressed you out. I was wondering, waiting, thinking that perhaps it was all too much to ask someone to handle, especially so quickly after what happened to us at Halloween,' she confessed why she had been so tense lately. She had been waiting for him to walk away. Evie had fallen into the trap her parents and her ex-husband had set up for her, the trap of everyone walking out of her life.

'Is that why you've been overthinking? Evie! It's never too much. So long as I have you, I promise everything is OK. Don't ever think like that. I'm not going anywhere.'

'Then can we go home?'

'Yes sweetheart. Let's go home.'

'I can't wait until I can say that and we're walking back to an actual house.' They passed the last streetlight, hand in hand, their wedding bands glittered under the light for a second, and they walked up the dark lane, drinking and chatting as they headed to the caravan with Robbie's promises trailing in the air that the houses would be ready on schedule.

Acknowledgements

Thanks to Pat and Iain for believing in me.

Georgie St-Claire writes the books she wanted to read but struggled to find. She's creating a contemporary urban fantasy series weaving dark cottagecore aesthetic with folkloric themes. She loves turning mundane moments into a potential setting for a dark fantasy scene.

Georgie lives in the Yorkshire that she writes about. She has her own continuing romance with her husband which included a moonlit midnight proposal by a lake as swans glided past. Georgie has been an avid reader since childhood when she couldn't hear the TV due to deafness and found her relaxation inside books instead. She remembers reading scary books on local folklore in her auntie's house which first sparked her interest in the subject as an early reader, and her interest has only grown since. Forever a romantic, Georgie values soft mornings, intentional choices, quiet evenings and meaningful connections.

You can find out more about Georgie's White Rose Witches world on georgiest-claire.com. She posts on Threads daily, Instagram two to three times a week and occasionally on Facebook & TikTok.

BAD PRESS iNK,

publishers of niche, alternative and cult fiction

Visit

www.BADPRESS.iNK

for details of all our books, and sign up to
be notified of future releases and offers

How well do we really know the ones we love?

Especially once they are dead?

My Husband's Child by Allison Lee

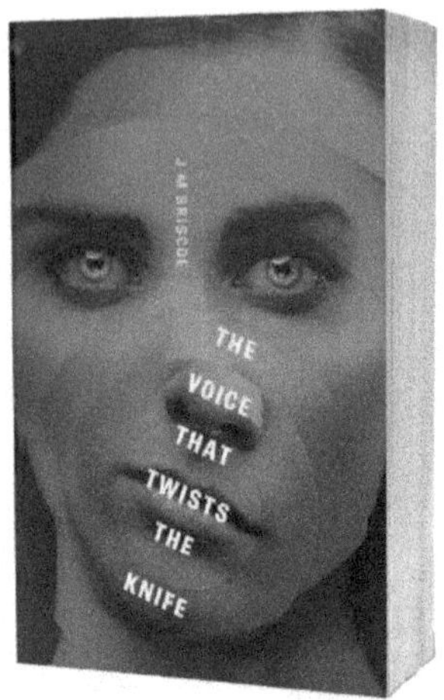

Bella is defective. You need to take her back.
Everyone tells her she is normal. Everyone is lying.
Eugenics, chimeras and the fierceness of a mother's
love in a terrifying near future.
All three books in the Take Her Back Trilogy
by J M Briscoe

Two love affairs and two summers, 75 years apart.

Cantankerous Tilly is determined to grow old disgracefully.

Shy Ava is finding out looking after the elderly was never meant to be like this!

The Blue Hour by M J Greenwood

Welcome to The King George.

You know it. Your old local. Back in the day.

The stink of beer and piss, sticky carpets, nicotine stains on the ceiling, soggy bar towels, and the chance of a punch-up on a Saturday night – or anytime for that matter.

And in amongst it all an awkward 20-year-old, trapped behind the bar, with nothing to do but pull pints and wait for the next fag break.

Until he finds Amy. And life. And an escape – if he dares.

The Sadness of The King George by Shaun Hand

Get Carter meets Sons of Anarchy in this gritty British crime thriller series.

From being in a gang to becoming a gangster, the Heavy Duty trilogy invented Biker Noir.

Damage's club has had an offer it can't refuse, to patch over to join The Brethren MC. But as the bikes rumble and roar across the wild Northern fells, what does this mean for Damage and his brothers? What choices will they have to make as they ride through the wind? What bloody oil-stained history might it reawaken? And why are The Brethren making this offer? Loyalty to his club and his brothers has been Damage's life and route to wealth, but what happens when business becomes serious and brother starts killing brother?

The Heavy Duty trilogy by Iain Parke

Important Notice – Please Read

BAD PRESS iNK Limited as the publisher of this book does not give permission for it to be used for the training of Large Language Models, Artificial Intelligence or any similar systems other than by prior written agreement of the publisher, or on the contractual terms below.

Default training usage contract

By obtaining and using the contents of this book for the training of Large Language Models, Artificial Intelligence or any similar systems without the prior written agreement of BAD PRESS iNK Limited (the 'Publisher') you (the 'User') are deemed to accept these contractual terms and agree to pay the publisher a licence fee of £10,000.

This fee is deemed due and payable on the date the User acquires the book text.

The publisher gives notice of our right to add interest and collection costs for late payment under The Late Payment of Commercial Debts (Interest) Act 1998 Act as amended and supplemented by The Late Payment of Commercial Debts Regulations 2002 and Statutory interest will be charged at a rate of 8% over the Bank of England base rate.

The User agrees that the use of this book for the above training purposes is at the User's risk and the publisher offers no warranties and accepts no liability to the User for the use of the text of this book for the above purposes or any consequential losses that may arise.

This contract is governed by and to be construed in accordance with English law and the parties irrevocably submit to the non-exclusive jurisdiction of the Courts of England and Wales in respect of any claim, dispute or difference arising out of or in connection with this contract.

www.ingramcontent.com/pod-product-compliance
Lightning Source LLC
Chambersburg PA
CBHW061053100726
47911CB00012B/211